Readers love
the Haven Prime series
by ALBERT NOTHLIT

Earthshatter

"...if you're looking for a wonderful story to immerse yourself in that leaves you on the edge of your seat gasping for breath at times then this is for you."

—MM Good Book Reviews

"If you are a science fiction lover looking for a novel into which you can sink your teeth (and mind), look no further."

—Prism Book Alliance

"Whoo boy! This book was pretty much one non-stop ride from the first page to the last."

—Love Bytes Reviews

Light Shaper

"…fantastic world-building, great characters, and fast-paced plots. It also has elements of a mystery... definitely read this series. Definitely."

—The Novel Approach

"I loved it. The MCs were new and original; their struggle interesting and built upon what book 1 already gave us, while leaving room for more."

—Eclectic Me

By ALBERT NOTHLIT

HAVEN PRIME
Earthshatter
Light Shaper

WURL
Life Seed

Published by DSP PUBLICATIONS
www.dsppublications.com

life seed

albert nothlit

DSP PUBLICATIONS

Published by

DSP PUBLICATIONS

5032 Capital Circle SW, Suite 2, PMB# 279, Tallahassee, FL 32305-7886 USA
www.dsppublications.com

Life Seed
© 2021 Albert Nothlit

Cover Art
© 2021 Stef Masciandaro
http://www.stefmasc.com/
Cover content is for illustrative purposes only and any person depicted on the cover is a model.

Mass Market Paperback ISBN: 978-1-64108-251-8
Trade Paperback ISBN: 978-1-64405-920-3
Digital ISBN: 978-1-64405-919-7
Trade Paperback published October 2021
First Edition
v. 1.0

Printed in the United States of America
∞
This paper meets the requirements of
ANSI/NISO Z39.48-1992 (Permanence of Paper).

For Chris and Graham, who helped me more than they will ever know.

life seed

albert nothlit

Chapter 1
The Wurl

ELIAS TROST was on his way to the old lab when the wurl attacked.

The harsh electronic siren boomed throughout the entire colony, a terrible sound with which everyone was all too familiar. Elias knew he should get indoors, preferably at his parents' house, but he was already close to the laboratory. Maybe he could sneak past—

"Citizen!" a youthful, booming voice called. "You cannot be outdoors. Not unless you actually want to help."

That last sentence had been spoken with open scorn, and Elias was forced to stop in his tracks. The youngest member of the Colony Patrol approached him, clutching his shock spear in both hands. His helmet's visor was open, and his intense brown eyes stared daggers at Elias from beneath bushy eyebrows.

"Leave me alone, Tristan," Elias said. "Go poke some wurl with your giant stick."

Tristan's frown deepened. His mouth was set in a thin straight line, and in spite of himself, Elias had to admit that Tristan MacLeod was attractive. He was sixteen, just like Elias, but he looked far older wearing the uniform of the Colony Patrol. More dangerous.

"You could come with me, get some hands-on experience," Tristan told Elias, dropping the formal speech altogether and stopping a couple paces away. Elias refused to back down from the unspoken threat. He was tired of being bullied by Tristan at every corner.

"No thanks, soldier boy. I'm a scientist, not a knucklehead."

Tristan twirled the shock spear casually in both hands, almost hitting Elias. "You wouldn't even be alive if it weren't for us *knuckleheads*. What would you do if the Patrol wasn't here, huh? Wet your pants in a corner of your abandoned laboratory, waiting for the wurl to pepper you with spines?"

"Violence is the resort of a weak mind," Elias retorted.

"Tell that to the wurl who attack us all the time. Oh, that's right. You've never stood your ground in front of one of them. You're a man now, of an age to contribute to the colony, and instead of helping us you waste your time reading old records. You're a coward."

"Says the guy holding the weapon," Elias said, biting down his anger. As much as he would have liked to punch Tristan in the nose, he knew Tristan was a far better fighter—stronger, quicker, and taller.

The alarm changed tone to a repetitive keening.

"They're inside the perimeter," a tinny female voice said from Tristan's helmet. "All units, converge next to the generator array. We have three juveniles, very aggressive."

"Sounds like fun," Tristan said into his mike, grinning at Elias. Then he muted the channel. "Go hide in your laboratory, scientist. I'm off to save your life."

He left before Elias could think of anything cutting enough to say. Now alone, Elias ran the rest of the way to the abandoned laboratory. He hated to admit it, but Tristan was right. He had to go hide unless he wanted to be impaled by one of the wurl's spines.

But I'm not a coward. I'm working to save the colony, just like Tristan. Only in my own way.

The entrance to the dilapidated compound that had once been a laboratory was well hidden. The entire building had been built against the slope of one of the hills closest to the colony, about three kilometers away from the main cluster of prefabricated homes. Elias had uncovered it three summers ago, almost by accident. He had been gathering interesting bits of scrap metal to use for his latest project when his terrain surveyor had told him that the ground beneath him was hollow. Getting in that first time had been hazardous, but since then he had improved and reinforced the structure of the narrow chute that served as his main entryway. Now he barely thought about navigating the intricate way down, deeper into the hillside, and into the buried laboratory.

The familiar, comforting smells of wet earth and burnt circuitry greeted him as he stumbled upright at the end of the chute. He walked precisely four steps forward and two to the right, felt around briefly, and hit the switch that started up the generator he had installed two years ago. Light flooded the space, flickering down from several retrofitted neon tubes that Elias had hung from the ceiling, connected directly to the generator's output lead. The harsh white light revealed a single large room partitioned into smaller spaces by weak drywall divisions. Many of them had long since crumbled into dust, the fragments joining the piles of broken machinery, desiccated plant life, dust, and garbage that littered the floor.

He sat down at the one workstation that had been thoroughly cleaned. He kept most of his notes there, as well as one barely-functional computer terminal, which served as his data repository. He picked up where he had left off the day before, trying to puzzle out the location of a hidden room in the lab that Dr. Wright's notes seemed to hint at. At first he couldn't concentrate, however. The incessant whine of the alarm siren echoed even in the lab, and Elias felt a momentary pang of guilt.

Should he really be out there, fighting against the overgrown reptiles of this unforgiving winter world? Or should he be poring over notes that had to be at least a hundred years old, trying to find a way to save the colony?

The alarm died away. Grabbing a thermoisolating blanket he had brought from home, Elias tried to ignore the cold and set to work.

It was not long before he was fully engrossed in what he was doing. The laboratory had belonged to Dr. Thomas Wright, one of the founding members of the colony. That meant that Dr. Wright had been one of the original crew members on board the generation ship *Ionas*, which had made planetfall 113 years ago on the world they had named New Skye. As always, Elias couldn't suppress a faint but pervasive feeling of awe as he navigated the intricate virtual labyrinth of the doctor's files. He was reading reports, log entries, and experimental data written by someone who had traveled through the stars, someone who had probably grown up surrounded by technological marvels Elias could only imagine. It was fascinating reading, all the more so because Elias had seen no mention of him anywhere else in the colony's archives.

It was strange, in a way. All the original colonists were larger-than-life figures in the history books. There was Captain MacLeod, who had founded the first and only settlement in New Skye: Portree. An obelisk dedicated to him had been erected in the center of the colony plaza, which Elias saw every day. There was the chief engineer, Ileana Jones, whom the Colony Patrol had elevated to near-goddess status because it was she who first designed the shock spears they used to fight off wurl. Prayers were still said thanking virologist Ai Hino, the gifted medical officer who created the engineered virus with which she infected the entire fledgling colony, allowing the human immune system to adapt to the alien environment and all its microorganisms. And so on and so forth.

It was odd that Elias had never heard of Dr. Wright, even more so since Elias was certain that the doctor had been an important scientist for the colony of Portree. He appeared to have been a biologist, since most of the notes Elias has found were detailed accounts of the flora and fauna of New Skye, each one carefully labeled in the terminal mainframe and linked to a series of incomprehensible spreadsheets that presumably listed all the properties of each new life form. Elias had spent nearly the entire summer reading those notes, fascinated by the wealth of knowledge of the early colonists. Nowadays, people barely left Portree for any reason, but it appeared that in the past there had been expeditions to the far reaches of the continent, and the creatures they had found were marvelous. The doctor appeared to have been an agronomist as well, given the thorough stacks of files which covered things such as food output, average plot yield, chemical composition of fertilizers used, and many other things Elias found fascinating. He would have suspected the data to be fabricated if not for the obvious professionalism of each report. It was hard to believe, though. Portree as a thriving colony with a surplus of food each year destined for long-term storage? It sounded like a fairy tale.

Elias spent nearly an hour reading about the suspected medicinal properties of a flower endemic to the high mountain passes of the west before he remembered that he was supposed to be looking for a blueprint of the laboratory or something that could tell him where the secret room was located. He immediately switched focus, plugging one of the auxiliary drives he had found in the lab into the mainframe.

The computer drive was full of errors and unreadable code, a far cry from the perfectly preserved files in the mainframe, but Elias had developed a parsing algorithm that allowed him to at least extract simple text blocks to analyze. It was boring, repetitive work, but his curiosity had been piqued. He discarded irrelevant data files, his fingers dancing on the tactile interface, until he found something promising. It looked like an efficiency report of a heat generator located in the lab, and Elias quickly extracted all the useful bits of information. As he had hoped, the report had been broken down into two separate areas, one for the main laboratory building and the other for the secret room. The document even listed the room's location: the northern wall.

Elias looked around the frigid laboratory with mounting excitement. The northern wall was half-buried in debris from a landslide that had happened sometime in the past, so he had left it alone. Now that he knew a hidden room was there, though, things were different.

He stood up and walked to a spot near the entrance where he had stashed a shovel. Time to get to work.

Clearing out the debris was a brutal endeavor. Before an hour had gone by, Elias had taken off his jacket and shirt, sweating even in the chill of winter. Most of the debris was hard-packed, some of it even frozen solid, and if it hadn't been for the monomolecular edge of the shovel's autodeploy function, he wouldn't have been able to clear even a tiny segment of the blockage. Elias didn't give up, though, and little by little his progress grew. His stomach rumbled with hunger, but he was used to that. He came across a pile of broken concrete and spent another hour dislodging each fragment from the mess and piling it against a nearby wall. After that was done, there was more dirt and ice to go through. He kept going. He was in the lab for so long that the generator began to whine, protesting its extended work period. Elias's arms were trembling with exhaustion and his lower back was hurting by the time his shovel finally clanged against something metallic, big, and solid.

On all fours, Elias cleared out that section of the wall and sighed in exhausted relief at seeing the unmistakable outline of a metal door. He continued working with renewed effort and soon was rewarded with the sudden collapse of the remaining layer of dirt and debris, which fell off the door like a discarded skin.

Panting and leaning on his shovel, Elias regarded the secret door of the lab.

It looked heavy, imposing, and mildly threatening. There was no sign of rust or corrosion on its frame, which told Elias that it was of pioneer build, flawless and efficient. The handle on it held in one piece when Elias tugged, but the door did not budge. Above it, an input panel waited patiently for the right code. Elias tapped some of the number keys experimentally. The panel lit up, startling him. Anything that was still working after a hundred years had to have its own power source somewhere. That was incredible. It also meant that whatever was in the room was really important.

There were ten number keys to try, and the display panel above had space for four integers. Doing some quick math, Elias realized that meant ten thousand different codes to try if he wanted to gain access. Too many. Elias stepped back from the door, tired and disappointed. He wiped the sweat from his brow and got dressed again. A quick glance at his wrist link, a flat computer interface with a holographic projector, showed him that it was almost time for dinner anyway. And he was starving.

He shut down the terminal and covered everything in case of any unexpected water leaks. He put the shovel aside, tried to wipe some grime from his hands, and walked back to his entry chute. Getting out was a little more complicated because there were no stairs or ladders to use to climb up. Instead, Elias had hung a rope from a sturdy metal latch at ground level. He grabbed his rope, tested it with a couple of yanks, and started up.

Even though his arms were tired, he was able to pull himself up the three or so meters that separated him from the surface easily if he helped himself along with his feet against the walls of the chute. As soon as his head cleared the hole in the ground, a frigid blast of wind greeted him, making his teeth chatter. Elias climbed awkwardly out, wincing at a faint ache in his left shoulder, and rolled away from the hole until he was lying on his back on the gentle slope of the hillside, looking up at a dark, cloudy sky. The light of the moons struggled to shine through, bathing everything in a dull silver twilight. It was even colder now that the sun had set, and Elias knew he had to get home quick if he didn't want to get into trouble yet again.

Grunting, he sat up—and saw the wurl.

The beast was standing less than ten meters away, and it appeared to be as startled by Elias's sudden appearance as Elias was at seeing it. There was a brief, brittle moment of mutual regard as both of them looked at each other, breathless, immobile.

Then the wurl roared.

It was a terrible, earsplitting sound, a screech like two sharp metal plates grinding together, amplified and overlaid in a guttural, threatening boom. Elias jumped to his feet and tried to run in the direction of the colony, but the wurl was much faster. It jumped up in the air, tucking its six legs into its underbelly, and rolled like a needle-spiked donut downhill, cutting off Elias's retreat.

Elias was forced to stop, terrified, as the wurl halted and uncoiled into a graceful, predatory crouch. The silver moonlight glinted off the obsidian plates that covered a slender, sinuous body almost five meters long and nearly as tall as Elias. Its arrow-shaped head stayed low to the ground, its jaws half open, showing row after row of jagged white teeth. On the top of its skull, the wurl had three eyes, red, luminescing faintly and locked on Elias, watching him with a disturbingly intelligent look.

Elias was very close to panicking. He wasn't prepared for this. He tried running to the right, but the wurl slithered on the ground, faster than thought, to cut him off, its tail hissing through the air from the speed of its motion. The moonlight threw sharp reflections off the spines that covered the creature's back. Each of those spines was as long as Elias's forearm and nearly as thick. Elias knew the wurl could launch them from distances of nearly ten meters with enough force to punch through anything not armored. Including human flesh.

"Help!" Elias shouted, abruptly remembering he had a voice. "Somebody, help!"

The wurl growled low at the sound. It was only a juvenile from the looks of it, but that made it even more dangerous. The older wurl were big and lumbering. This one looked quick. Deadly.

The lab! Elias could hide in the lab. He turned around without a second thought and dashed uphill. He could see the entry chute now. It was just—

Schwook.

An obsidian spine hissed through the air and punched into the ground right in front of Elias. He stopped in horrified shock and jumped out of the way as a volley of three more spines impaled the dirt exactly where he had been standing. He rolled down the slope, out of control, for nearly three seconds before he was able to stop himself. Then he stumbled upright, chest heaving, and looked back.

The wurl was standing between him and the laboratory entrance now. The hard-packed ground in front of its hulking frame had cracked where the spines had hit.

No way out. I'm going to die here.

The wurl charged.

It opened its maw, and its three eyes appeared to blaze with malevolence as it tucked its legs into its body, folded its head in, and started rolling downhill at Elias.

Elias ran for it. He pumped every inch of strength he had into his desperate flight, stumbling over rocks, wishing he could get inside the perimeter of the colony that was so near and yet impossibly far. Behind him he heard the wurl gaining speed, and a fleeting glance back showed him that it was almost upon him.

Elias was forced to jump to the left. The wurl surged by, trailing a sharp reptile scent, and rolled to a stop a few meters away. Then it uncoiled, settling on its three pairs of legs. It looked at Elias, tilting its head to the right.

It's playing with me, Elias realized. *It could have killed me three times over. It's just dragging it out before ending this.*

Like all the colonists, Elias knew about wurl. They were supposed to be borderline intelligent and were certainly very dangerous. They were also meant to be a threat for others to deal with. But now….

"Help!" Elias shouted again, this time remembering to hit his link with his other hand. He activated the communication function and sent out a distress signal.

Please. Please, someone….

The wurl walked closer, tilting its head left and then right as it advanced. It was terrifying because the red eyes never wavered, never blinked. Elias tried backing away, but he tripped on a boulder and fell hard on the frozen ground.

The wurl strode up to him, close enough to touch. Its alien stench was overpowering, and as it opened its maw, Elias saw clearly the second row of teeth hidden behind the first.

Elias's bladder simply let go. The wurl closed its jaws and sniffed the air once, as if curious.

"Kee-yah!"

The war cry startled both Elias and the wurl. The creature looked downhill, and Elias saw someone running straight at them, holding a blazing shock spear in one hand. The weapon's two ends shone blindingly bright in the dim twilight—blue and white, surging with arcs of pure electricity.

The wurl twisted its body around, crouched low to the ground, and fired.

Elias had never seen a wurl attack with spines from up close. A ripple made its obsidian plates tremble, and what must have been a powerful muscle contraction gathered explosive strength beneath the nearest spine. The projectile discharged with a wet squelch, almost as fast as a gun firing.

The spine found its mark now that the wurl wasn't playing. The running figure took a hit square in the chest and stumbled backward.

The spine fell away from the dented armor. The warrior kept coming.

"Kee-yah!"

Elias recognized the voice now. It was Tristan, charging fearlessly at a wurl twice his size. The creature seemed to sense the threat, because it slithered away, farther up the hillside, firing spines as it went. Speechless, Elias watched Tristan dodge them. The wurl screeched at the top of its voice, rolled up into a ball, and attacked.

Tristan never stopped running. He faced the rolling, spine-covered armored beast head-on, shock spear in hand, and at the last possible moment jumped out of the way, slicing the air with his weapon.

The spear found its mark. Searing electricity surged through its tip when it made contact with the alien creature's plating and shredded through its entire body.

The wurl stopped rolling, roared, and fell on its side. Tristan followed the momentum of his own motion, rolled on the ground, and jumped up without missing a beat. He assumed a fighting stance, facing the beast.

The creature crouched on the ground and fired another spine. It bounced off Tristan's armor. The wurl opened its jaws in a threatening display, the luminescence in its eyes flaring, and approached Tristan, twisting its head left and right.

Tristan stood motionless with the spear in his right hand, and Elias was about to cry out in warning when the wurl gathered speed, rushing up at the armored fighter to crush him under its bulk.

The impact never came. Elias's cry died in his throat when he saw the wurl stop mere centimeters away from Tristan. He couldn't see Tristan's face because of the helmet, but he could see the wurl. After it stopped, it growled at Tristan once, earsplittingly loud. In response, Tristan lowered his electrified spear.

The wurl turned away immediately and slithered downhill. It quickly tucked its body into a ball again and rolled away, out of sight.

Elias's heart was hammering in his chest. He watched, spellbound, as Tristan approached with apparent calm. Tristan took off his helmet and revealed a confident, perfect smile.

"No need to thank me," he said smugly. "I'm sure something in your lab would have saved you if I hadn't come. Right?"

Elias could think of nothing to say.

Tristan got close enough that Elias could see the moonlight reflected in his dark eyes. "Maybe next time, before calling me a knucklehead, remember I saved your life. *Scientist.*"

By the time a comeback came to Elias, Tristan was almost out of earshot. Elias did not shout it out, though. The anger simmering inside him was fueled by deep shame. Tristan had saved him. Elias had been powerless, helpless. Even the wurl had known. It had played with him when it could have killed him several times over. Not like when Tristan had come. Tristan had been a threat, dangerous enough to make that powerful creature retreat.

Elias bunched his hands into fists as he walked home in the deepening twilight. A small part of him wished Tristan hadn't saved him. Because now Elias's life would be a living hell.

Chapter 2
A Heartfelt Whisper

ELIAS WAS still fuming by the time he made it all the way to his home, a medium-sized prefabricated house in the eastern quarter of the colony. One of the moons had set, deepening the shadows of the waxing night. He was one of the last people to be walking out in the open, aside from the ever-present Colony Patrol officers who kept watch at night. Even though Portree didn't have an official curfew, everyone knew it was much safer to be indoors after dark in case of any unexpected incidents with marauding wurl.

Just like what had happened to Elias.

He grabbed the door handle to his house but paused for a moment, trying to calm down. He should be thankful he was alive, that his blunder of staying outside for too long had not ended up catastrophically. He was usually much more careful, but the prospect of discovering what was hidden in that secret room in the laboratory had driven all other thoughts from his mind.

"Elias, is that you?" a feminine voice called out.

"It's me, Mom," Elias replied. He pushed open the door and stepped inside.

The blast of warm air was very welcome. The savory smell filling the house told Elias that it was curry night, and his stomach rumbled in anticipation as he took off his soiled clothes in the laundry room. He grabbed a new pair of shorts from the clean pile and tossed the rest of the clothing into the washing machine on his way to the dining room.

"Eli!" an excited voice called. Elias's younger brother, Oscar, was sitting at the table and beamed when Elias walked into the room.

"Hey, Oscar," Elias said, smiling.

"So glad you could finally join us," a deeper voice said from the other side of the table. Elias's father put down a tablet he had been reading and looked at his oldest son with a frown.

Elias sat down on his usual chair. "Hi, Dad."

"Were you at the laboratory again?" Oscar asked eagerly.

"Yeah," Elias answered defiantly, not missing how his father's frown deepened. "I think there's a secret room of some kind. I found the door today. I'm thinking it could lead to—"

"Just what do you think you are playing at, Elias?" his father interrupted in a stern tone.

"What do you mean?"

"Dinner's almost ready!" Elias's mom called from the kitchen.

His father leaned forward and spoke low enough that his mother wouldn't hear. "My link went off twenty minutes ago with your distress signal. As did nearly everyone else's. Your mother was taking a bath, thankfully, so she didn't hear. Care to explain why you were careless enough to run into a *wurl*?"

Elias looked at Oscar, whose half-guilty, half-scared expression betrayed the fact that he also knew.

"I'm here, aren't I?" Elias answered. "That's all there is to it."

"That's *not* all there is to it," his father retorted angrily. "You could have been killed! If it weren't for Tristan...."

"How do you know Tristan was there?"

His father pinched the bridge of his nose. "He was the one who told us you were okay after the crisis was averted. Since you apparently forgot to update your status on your link after you were safe."

Elias's face burned. His father was right; he had completely forgotten about updating his status. Which meant that Tristan's update had gone out to everyone. So by now everyone knew that Tristan had saved his life after a stupid blunder.

"I'm sorry," he said between gritted teeth. "Okay? Won't happen again."

"Damn right it won't happen again," his father told him. "This is it, Elias. I think I've been too lenient with you. Starting tomorrow, you go to the Colony Patrol and tell them you want to apply."

"What?" Elias asked, aghast.

"Unless you have another idea? An apprenticeship with someone, like your aunt Laura?"

"But I'm doing something important!" Elias protested. "Those records have been lost for ages. The colony used to be different, Dad. Crops used to be viable—I've seen the spreadsheets! If I can figure out how they did it, maybe I can find a solution. Maybe then the colony won't starve to death slowly like it's doing now."

Elias's father slammed his fist on the table, making both of his children jump. "Enough! I won't have you talking like that in front of your brother, do you hear me?"

"Dinner's here," Elias's mother said, coming into the room with a large tray. Elias had been about to reply with something scathing, but he kept his mouth shut. The colony's physician, Armand Ferry, had told them that his mother's condition would only worsen if she became distressed in any way. With a huge effort, Elias settled on his chair as if they hadn't been arguing a second ago. He saw his father do the same, while Oscar looked at both of them with wide eyes.

"Curry with rice," Elias's father said, smiling. "My favorite."

His wife leaned forward for a quick kiss on the lips. "I know. Eat up, everyone. Before it gets cold."

It was hard to be silent while his mother did the evening ritual of giving everyone his or her carefully measured portion of food for the day. His father acted like it was a lot for him, just like every night, and insisted on giving some to both of his growing children. His mother tried to do the same with her much smaller portion, but they quickly told her that she needed to eat to keep up her strength. The words they said had become a litany by now, and Elias wanted to scream. He was ravenous after all his work, but even with a bit of his father's portion, the food on his plate wasn't nearly enough. Couldn't they see it? Couldn't they see that it was pathetic, that every year their portions were smaller and smaller? How could they smile when they knew very well it was only going to get worse?

He was hungry, though. So he ate.

Their food was gone very fast, but as usual the family lingered at the table to drink tea and share the news of what they had done during the day. Now that he had eaten, Elias felt marginally better. Enough to smile and pretend nothing was wrong while his mother was there.

"How did it go today, dear?" Elias's mother asked his dad. "Did you catch any transmissions from Out There?"

Another ritual question, which she had asked every night for as long as Elias could remember. His father's answer was always the same.

"Not today, no. But I'm sure they're out there, listening and transmitting. One day we'll hear them, and they'll hear us."

"Yeah, right," Elias muttered sarcastically. He was saved from his father's angry retort by Oscar.

"We learned about relativity and the constant speed of light today at school," he said. "Hey, Dad, is that why it takes so long to get a message Out There?"

"Right on, Oscar," his father replied, smiling. "New Skye is our home, but it's very far away from other star systems where people live. Even the nearest one is ten light-years away. That means that the messages I send them take ten years to travel, and then it takes another ten years for their reply to reach us."

"But why haven't we heard from them—ever?" Oscar asked innocently.

"There are lots of reasons," Elias's mother replied. "There's a nebula that shelters this system from others. It may be that something in the nebula is interfering with electromagnetic radiation leaving New Skye. Or it could be a number of other things. Maybe our message was received, but we don't have the proper listening equipment to hear the answer. Maybe something happened to the people living on the planets closest to us. The best we can do for now is listen and transmit every day. This is why your daddy's job is so important."

"I also want to be a telecommunications specialist when I am of age," Oscar announced.

His father smiled broadly, his look softening like it rarely ever did anymore. Elias tried to tell himself that the sharp stab of envy he felt was due to something else, but he couldn't really deny it. Oscar was speaking the words his father had hoped Elias would say one day. And which he never had.

"You really mean that?" his mother asked.

Oscar nodded. "I'm going to turn eleven this summer. All the kids are getting apprenticeships, and I want to learn with Dad."

"I'll have to talk with Director O'Rourke," his father said. "Get the paperwork sorted out. She is sure to authorize it; she's been bothering me to take on an apprentice for years now. I only held her off because...."

Because you were hoping it would be me, Elias finished for him silently. His father said nothing, though. He just let the silence stretch awkwardly.

"Well, I think that's great news," Elias's mother said. "I've always thought telecommunications to be such a fascinating subject. And it's not all about listening for whatever is Out There. You'll learn all about how the links work, how our network operates."

"And about sensors," Elias's father continued, his tone enthusiastic again. "Air, water, pollution, even proximity sensors in case any wurl come close. There's also all sorts of automatization going on in the gene labs, and all of it depends on me to keep running. Well, on us."

"That sounds really cool," Oscar said with a smile. "Hey, Eli, you should totally come with us."

Oscar seemed to realize that he had said the wrong thing when Elias didn't reply, looking at his father with a defiant stare. "I have the lab" was all Elias said.

"That reminds me," Elias's mother quickly said into the silence, "Sarah's mother called a while ago. She says Sarah is having some trouble at the gene plant with one of the automated systems regulating new crop strains. She said she could use some help, and I told her you'd be happy to come by, Eli. Since you have so much experience with pioneer computer systems from working at the lab, maybe you could give her a tip or two."

The comment had been innocent enough, but Elias heard the unspoken recrimination.

"Right. Because Sarah is about my age, and I have to start thinking about getting married. Have children, yeah? To keep the colony from dying out?"

"That's… not what I meant."

"Elias, apologize to your mother right now," his father said sternly.

"Why?" Elias asked, a bit more loudly than he had intended. All his frustrations from the day piled up, and he couldn't take it anymore. "For saying the truth? You guys are ashamed of me. Admit it. I'm the disappointment, the guy with no apprenticeship even though he's almost of age. The one who wastes his time in an abandoned lab instead of working for the good of Portree."

"Elias...," his father warned him.

"No!" Elias protested. "I'm not keeping quiet this time, pretending like nothing's happening because of Mom's condition. She's not a fragile housewife, Dad. She used to be our senior astrophysicist before she got sick, and she knows what I'm talking about. Hell, everyone knows. This colony is dying out. We're *starving*. I can go and get an apprenticeship at some useless job like the Patrol, or I could actually try and fix this, which is what I'm doing in the lab. And you're not stopping me, unless you want to keep me chained to my bed!"

Then Elias stormed out and went upstairs, into the bedroom he shared with Oscar. He slammed the door shut, sat down on the floor with his back against it, and told himself that he wasn't going to cry.

It was a long time before he heard a timid knock on the door.

"Eli?" Oscar asked quietly. "Can I come in?"

Elias considered shouting at him to leave. Then he remembered that this was Oscar's room too. "Sure," he grumbled, moving out of the way. "Knock yourself out."

Elias plopped down on his bed and refused to look up as he heard Oscar enter. Oscar moved around the room, arranging things on his bed, closing the blinds, and finally clicking the lights off. Only then did Elias turn around to lie on his back and look at the dark ceiling overhead. Silence enveloped him as angry thoughts chased themselves in circles in his head.

"Are you asleep?" Oscar asked timidly.

Grudgingly, Elias turned to the right so he would be looking at his brother's bed. Oscar was sitting on it, facing his way. "Obviously not."

"I'm sorry about today," Oscar said. "I shouldn't have said anything about you coming to the telecommunications studio with us."

"Yeah, you shouldn't have," Elias replied scathingly. Then he caught himself. "No, wait. It's not your fault, Oscar. It's just.... Things are complicated, okay?"

"I'm not a little kid anymore, Eli," he replied in a tone Elias had seldom heard him use. It was dead serious. "I've wanted to work with Dad for a long time, but what decided me today was that you almost got killed by a wurl. I was terrified. I realized that living here really is dangerous, and I want to help. I'm not very good at fighting like Shinji or Marion, but I'm good at this, and I'm going to do it."

"Good for you," Elias replied. He couldn't decide if he was being sarcastic or sincere.

"Yeah. Hey, Eli. Is it really true, what you say? That we're starving?"

"Do you really want to know?"

"I'm not a little—"

"—kid anymore, I know. Fine, here's what I know for sure." Elias sat up on the bed, looking at his brother in the faint light that filtered in through the window. As he did, he had a sudden shift in perception. As he'd said, Oscar wasn't so little anymore. Just because he was soft-spoken and kind it didn't mean that he wasn't growing. Elias put his simmering anger aside and considered his brother's question earnestly. "Fact number one: the food rations that each family receives are getting smaller every year. Maybe you don't remember, but it used to be we would have lots of food in the fridge, sitting there in case anybody wanted to have some. It wasn't like now when Dad has to go get the rations from the director's office every day. I mean, sure, we can replicate stuff like spices because they're essentially raw chemicals, but actual food...? We need to grow it, and now it's not working out anymore. Before, it used to be much better, according to the records I've read."

"Much better how?"

Elias shook his head. How to summarize three years' worth of discoveries? He tried anyway. "As far as I can tell, way back when the colony started, this planet was a paradise. It was *chosen* because it was such a good place for people to live. Good weather, breathable atmosphere, decent gravity... it had everything. There were a few hard years, sure, like what they tell you about in school. The Great Sickness and all that. But at the end of the day, we adapted. The colony began to thrive. If the records are right, there used to be at least two thousand people living here at the height of the colony's success."

"Two *thousand?*"

"I know. Sounds crazy, right? How many live here now? Less than a hundred, give or take. There's a reason why so many prefab houses in the southern sector are empty. There aren't enough people living here anymore."

"Were there really ever so many? How did it even work?"

"I'm not sure," Elias conceded, "but I do know that they explored the continent a lot. Maybe they even wanted to found a second colony somewhere."

"But we can't go anywhere. Not with wurl attacking us all the time. Besides, the Life Seed is here. How would the second colony survive without it?"

"Like I said, no clue. It's taken me a while, but I've learned a lot from Dr. Wright's notes about the way people were back then. They used to be explorers—fearless. Hopeful. Not the way we are now, with everyone too scared to do anything. I think if the pioneers who came here on the *Ionas* visited us right now, they would be disappointed. All anyone ever expects of you today is to settle down, find a job, marry as quickly as possible, and breed."

"Is that why you got angry at Mom?" Oscar asked.

"What?"

"She keeps trying to set you up with girls. You always say no."

"Yeah, well, it's not like there's a lot of them to choose from. Only Sarah is my age, and she's insufferable. There's a couple of girls who are older or younger, but…." Elias's voice trailed off, betraying his sudden awkwardness.

"But you don't like girls," Oscar finished for him in a soft voice.

"What did you say?" Elias snapped.

"It's okay, Eli. It's who you are."

"You're making things up," Elias said quickly, hoping the deep shadows would mask his sudden discomfort. His voice betrayed him, though. It wavered, uncertain.

He had been so careful, always, about keeping up appearances. Nobody knew. Nobody even suspected. Except for his brother, it seemed.

"It's not a bad thing," Oscar continued. "I've read the history files. Out There, on the other settled planets of the Core Systems, it was considered normal for some people to be gay."

"Don't use that word!" Elias all but shouted.

Oscar looked at him, a hurt expression in his eyes. "Why not?"

"You don't understand. You're still a kid, even if you say you aren't. There's expectations to meet, things people want you to do. Want you to be. Maybe way back it was okay to be different, but now it's not. There's simply too few of us left. Everybody counts. Everybody's expected to do something for the colony, and that includes having kids."

"But Director O'Rourke isn't married. And she didn't have kids."

"Yeah, but it's different."

"Why is it different?"

"Because she's the director!" Elias exploded. "And besides.... No. You know what? I don't have time for this. You're making things up, and I *really* don't need this right now. Okay? Good night."

Elias settled back down on his bed and turned away from his brother. He covered himself with a comforter and pretended to be asleep. He kept up the charade for long enough that he thought Oscar had gone to sleep too.

"I still love you, no matter what," Oscar whispered into the darkness.

Startled, Elias almost answered him. He was still angry, though. At the world, at his brother, and at himself. So instead he let the silence drag on into the quiet night, broken only by the mournful howl of a wurl in the distance.

Chapter 3
Hanging Up Banners

"I MEANT what I told you yesterday," Elias's father said after breakfast. "No more going to the lab for you. It's time you did some useful work."

"I *already* do some useful work," Elias retorted. He had been about to go to his room to pick up some spare supplies and head to the lab to try and break the code of the secret room. His father had ambushed him on the staircase, though. "I work Monday through Friday at the recycling center."

"You know what I mean," his father said, not moving an inch. "This is not about fulfilling your work quota for the colony. It's about starting an apprenticeship for a useful profession."

"Like what? Telecommunications specialist?"

Elias could tell that his father was getting angry when he next spoke in a curt, measured tone. "No. You've made it abundantly clear that you don't want to follow in my footsteps. Today you'll start by helping out with the Midwinter Feast preparations. Head on over to the Main Hall and do whatever they tell you to do."

"But I had plans, and it's Midwinter Day! And Sunday. I have stuff to do."

"Well, now you have more stuff to do. Come on, get going. I already told Harold you'd be helping out today."

"Harold MacLeod? From the director's office? Why him?"

"Because he will tell me whether you worked your fair share or not."

"But...."

"That's enough. *Go.*"

Elias thought about disobeying, but old habits were hard to break. It was one thing to go to the laboratory in his free time, when he could technically do whatever he wanted. It was another thing entirely to disobey his father to his face, especially now that Elias was expected to help over at the Main Hall.

Grumbling, he postponed his plans and left to go help.

In the dim winter light of early morning, the colony looked very different from the way it did at night. Many people were out and about—working, running errands, or simply chatting. Elias knew everyone by name, and he exchanged polite greetings with several of them as he walked. He ran into Aiko, the lively twenty-four-year-old who single-handedly ran the colony preschool. She appeared to be taking her students on a little field trip, and the young children all greeted Elias in a chorus when he stopped to say hi. Elias answered back, smiling, trying not to think about the fact that every year it seemed Aiko's class got smaller.

Near the edge of the eastern quarter, Elias passed by the fields. They covered the entire northern sector of the colony, a breathtaking array of high-tech greenhouses with carefully controlled environments in which food was grown. Many of the colony's senior citizens were employed there, and Elias spotted his grandmother tending to something that looked a lot like a tomato plant. He waved, but she didn't see him. Shrugging, he kept on his way until he reached the main plaza, a big square space right in the middle of the colony. There were no paved streets in Portree since they had no working vehicles anymore, so the plaza had been transformed into a garden, a beautiful expanse of carefully trimmed wild grass and several of the short, stunted conifers with dark red needles that were endemic to the region, called red pines. The obelisk to Captain MacLeod stood in the center. There were supposed to be flowers there too, planted in complex patterns, but it had been many years since a flower had bloomed out in the wild. If it weren't for old video records of public events held in the main plaza from decades ago, when the terrain had been vibrant with a shocking array of red, blue, and orange flowers, Elias probably wouldn't even believe that such a thing was possible.

His boots crunched on the brittle, dry winter grass as he approached Portree's Main Hall. Aside from the greenhouses, it was the only building that was not a drab gray box made out of self-replicating polymer, as most of the colony's structures were. Elias had always liked the hall's graceful, slanting architecture, with its white walls made from a mixture of marble and concrete. Three spires crowned the three-story complex, glinting in the morning sunlight. Its many windows were set at sharp angles to one another, allowing glimpses of the beautiful artworks on display inside. Elias looked around wistfully. A couple of kids played nearby, and he wished to be able to enjoy his Sunday like them, doing whatever he really wanted to do. Instead he was stuck doing civic duty.

Well, maybe he could get it over with quickly. The secrets of the laboratory, beckoning tantalizingly though they were, would have to wait.

Elias pushed open the doors and stepped into the hall. The temperature changed immediately from chilly to pleasantly warm, and he was greeted by the holiday scent of cinnamon and nutmeg. It was a smell he associated strongly with being very small and feeling excited about the Midwinter Feast. It had always been a magical time of discovery and excitement, with plenty of food to go around and even some presents for the kids. There would be a roaring fire in the Main Hall, and they would turn off central heating to emphasize the feeling of it being the longest night of the year. People would tell stories, and of course there was the ceremonial gift-giving. He supposed things were still the same, but now his perception of the feast had changed. Walking into the huge, echoing chamber that was big enough for every person in a colony ten times as large to gather, Elias couldn't suppress a mild shiver. They were running out of time, no matter how much everybody liked to pretend they weren't. Every year the feast was a little less grand. Every year, less food. Every generation, fewer people.

"Elias!" a raspy, deep voice called from the right. "Glad you made it."

"Hello, Harold," Elias replied. He clasped forearms with Harold briefly. It might have been Elias's imagination, but Harold looked even more harassed than usual. His salt-and-pepper hair already made him look much older than his thirty years, and he'd had bags under his eyes for as long as Elias had known him.

"Can't stop to talk, I'm afraid. Just head on over to the fireplace and ask Sarah if there's anything she needs you to do, okay? We have a lot to prepare and very little time. I can't believe we're only doing preparations now! And the feast is *tonight*. I petitioned the director for people to do it last week, but no, there are always other projects, all of them more important! Nobody cares about this celebration anymore, I tell you. But at the same time, everyone expects it to be perfect. Every year. Every year! Who's going to take care of the logistics?"

Elias cracked a smile. "You will?"

The question stopped Harold's rant in its tracks. He made as if to say something, then actually focused on Elias for a moment. "Always a smartass, eh?"

"You know it."

"Fine," Harold conceded, chuckling. "Off with you, then. I have a lot to do!"

Elias watched Harold leave, clutching at least four different tablets in his arms. Out of all the people in the colony, Elias suspected Harold worked the hardest to keep everything running along. He looked gaunt, slightly past the threshold of being thin, but healthy.

The thought made Elias blink. He had never really thought about it, but there wasn't a single overweight person in all of Portree.

"Elias, good morning!" someone else called from farther down the hall, shaking him out of his thoughts. A girl's voice, haughty with authority.

Elias turned, noticing Sarah Parker standing with a group of young people near the fireplace. All at once, he wished he were anywhere but there.

"Hi," he said noncommittally. She had already seen him, so he resigned himself to approach the group.

"Nice of you to join us, if a little bit late," Sarah commented as soon as he was close enough. She was a pretty girl, Elias supposed. Her milky pale skin contrasted with her deep black hair and the vibrant red of her lips. At the moment, she had her hair tucked into a practical ponytail and was wearing work overalls while simultaneously managing to still look feminine and stylish.

A quick glance at the group told Elias he wasn't the only one noticing her beauty. Standing nearby were five other youths. Two of them were the McGregor brothers, Tim and Jim, one year older than Elias and the future doctors of the colony if the rumors were true. They were ogling Sarah with impunity, even chuckling to each other when Sarah dropped her stylus and had to bend over to pick it up. Elias rolled his eyes. Those two made him glad sometimes that he wasn't another hormone-driven straight male.

Next to them were two girls, Yuki and Evelyn. They were a year younger, and they both wanted to study applied psychology, but the similarities ended there. Yuki was petite and demure, seldom saying a word. Out of all of them, she was the closest Elias had to a friend, although she was more of a passively neutral acquaintance. Evelyn, on the other hand, was taller than Elias and very sociable. She was best friends with Sarah, and Elias was sure that their little clique would have included more beautiful, outgoing girls of their age if there had been any in the colony. As it was, it was just the two of them, but most of the time that was more than enough.

The last person in the group, casually leaning against the wall in the back, was Tristan.

Elias aimed a quick, defiant glance at him. Tristan answered it with a smug grin, raising an eyebrow. Elias would have bet anything that Tristan had already shared every last embarrassing detail of Elias's encounter with the wurl yesterday, while making sure to paint himself in the most heroic light.

"Hey, Elias," Tristan said. "Nice to see you're still alive."

The McGregor brothers chuckled, and all the girls followed suit. Elias's pulse quickened with anger. It didn't help at all that Tristan looked even better when not in his uniform. Younger. He wore his brown hair buzzed short, and the black tank top he was wearing left no doubt as to the fitness of his physique. Every muscle in his arms was clearly defined against his smooth, flawless skin. His shoulders were wide, and his waist was narrow. It wasn't a coincidence that nearly every girl of marrying age had tagged him as a future husband.

Too bad he's an insufferable prick. Out loud, he only said, "Morning, Tristan. Thanks for the save yesterday. You really came through when I needed it."

His reply appeared to catch the rest of the group by surprise, because Elias heard no more chuckles.

Figures.

After three years of dedicating himself to a project most people thought was a waste of time and enduring endless taunts by his peers, Elias had discovered that sometimes the easiest way to stop people from making fun of you was to own up to whatever you were doing. Like now.

"Right," Tristan answered in an uncertain tone. He was probably deciding whether Elias was being sarcastic or not.

Sarah clapped her hands once. "Anyway, enough chitchat, people. We have a lot to do before the feast tonight. I created a spreadsheet you can download to your links that lists all the tasks that need doing. Pick one, write your name, and notify me when you're done. If everything's all right, I'll update the status of the task and attribute it to you online. There's seventeen tasks in total and seven of us, so I expect each person to do at least two. Some of the tasks need more than one person, like bringing in all the firewood for tonight's fire. On those, tag your percentage contribution. Everything clear?" The youths looked at each other. Tim whispered something that sounded a lot like "bossy," but he shut up when Sarah glared at him. "Very well, let's begin! Tristan, I want you to help me on the first task."

Grumbling to himself, Elias downloaded the spreadsheet to his link along with everyone else. He saw that most of the tasks were easy enough—setting up decorations, arranging tables, and the like. If they all pitched in, they could probably be done in a couple of hours.

He clicked on Hang Season Banners from Hall, task number three, and typed his name under it.

"Ooh, I wouldn't do that one, Elias," Jim said right away in response to the automatic update on the file. "You could fall and die! I mean, we almost lost you last night. If it happens again, I think it's going to be too much for my heart to handle."

"Yeah," Tim pitched in eagerly. "If you're gone, who will be left to do…. What is it you do for the colony again?"

"Shut the hell up," Elias said to both of them.

"Or what?" Jim asked, cracking his knuckles.

"Guys, cut it out!" Sarah protested, although she was very obviously trying not to laugh along with Evelyn. "But seriously, Elias. Try to help out this time instead of just heading off to do whatever in your mystery lab. Do your part for the colony."

"Whatever," Elias replied, pushing roughly past the brothers on his way to the stack of banners. He couldn't help but exchange another look with Tristan as he passed him by. Tristan hadn't laughed, but the look he gave Elias was full of silent reproach.

Decorating the Main Hall took much longer than Elias had expected. He spent a miserable four and a half hours trying not to talk to people, deliberately choosing the tasks that required no help to perform. Unfortunately, that included a lot of trips to the kitchens to assist Chef Matsuo in carrying refrigeration equipment to the hall and listening to unending boring minutiae of how every dish was going to be served and when. On the positive side, he got to sample many of the delicious things the Chef was cooking, but every time Elias walked back into the hall, his spirits sank a little bit more.

The McGregors did their best to tease him at every opportunity, and although they weren't very inventive, they were insistent. To Elias's dismay, Yuki had gravitated toward Jim, and she would often laugh at his crude attempts at making fun of Elias. Nearby was also the nonstop, seemingly lighthearted arguing of Evelyn and Sarah over who got to spend more time with Tristan, and for some reason that made Elias far angrier than the jibes at his expense.

That's pathetic, he thought, looking up from setting a particularly large refrigeration unit on a table to see Evelyn pretending not to know how to tie a bow so Tristan could show her. Then Sarah noticed, and she loudly proclaimed she wasn't strong enough to lift one of the stacks of firewood, asking Tristan for help even though Jim and Tim were much closer. Elias couldn't understand why Tristan didn't tell them how annoying they were being. On the contrary, he seemed to be enjoying the attention, particularly when doing something that required physical strength.

When it was time to set up the poles around the big circular space that was traditionally left empty in the middle of the Hall for the gift-giving speeches, Tristan refused Jim and Tim's help and did everything alone. The girls watched, apparently enraptured, as he grunted and struggled to place the heavy poles in their slots. Each one was twice as tall as Tristan and quite thick. In spite of himself, Elias found he was watching too. It was fascinating to see the ripple of muscle translated into strength. And when Tristan took off his tank top, complaining he was too hot, the sight of Tristan's big, powerful chest muscles and ripped abs made the stirring of arousal all too evident in Elias's pants.

Mortified, he hid behind the refrigeration unit to be out of sight and pretended to fine-tune its specs for much longer than was necessary.

When the last of his tasks was done and Sarah had grudgingly verified their completion on her link, Elias left as fast as he could. He calculated he had at least seven hours before nightfall, and he planned to make good use of them. Besides, he was glad to be out of that place. Tristan was a narcissistic showoff, and everyone else was all too happy to play along. Not Elias, though. He had actual work to do. Something that was important, even if nobody else believed it.

Chapter 4
A Safe in a Safe Room

THE QUICKEST route to the lab from the main plaza went right through the genetics complex, a very familiar path to Elias. His aunt Laura worked in the Life Seed chamber as a senior technician, and whenever Elias ran across a particularly important piece of information from Doctor Wright's notes, he made sure to share it with her. He had never confided this to anyone, but Elias supposed that if he had to be an apprentice for anything, it would be as a xenobiologist in the gene labs.

His link granted him access to the seemingly unremarkable building with its drab façade, but once inside, it was an entirely different story. The sharp smell of antiseptic assaulted Elias's nostrils at the same time as another more pervasive smell—the fragrance of wet earth and growing things. The temperature inside the genetics complex was cold enough to make Elias's breath steam in front of his face, but he didn't mind. He knew it was necessary to keep it this way so the delicate machinery in the laboratories could work at optimal efficiency. As he made his way past the reception area, he skirted a large inner courtyard and headed down an immaculate hallway until he came to a heavy set of double doors, which were automated. He stopped in front of them while they scanned him to verify his identity, and then they opened with a soft hiss of escaping air.

Elias walked into the inner sanctum of the compound, a single open floor space enclosed by a ceiling twice as tall as normal. It occupied an entire block, and although Elias knew his way around already, the frantic, chaotic-seeming buzz of activity never ceased to amaze him.

Workstations of every shape and size were scattered at regular intervals around the room. Each of them was manned by at least one citizen, which made this space the single most crowded place in all of Portree. Nearly a third of the colony's inhabitants were employed here, all of them working toward the critical goal of improving crop yield and securing a food supply for the coming years. The entire left wall was lined with glass cylinders three meters tall and one meter thick. They were full of bluish liquid, a nutrient mixture that was needed for the different plant strains that grew inside. Bright lights illuminated several workstations near the cylinders, raised platforms that had been modified to simulate the different layers of the soil of New Skye. Carefully labeled strains of plants grew in each of them, grains for the most part, since they were what the colony needed the most. Elias had watched the process long enough to know that experimental strains of useful plants would first be developed inside the large test tubes, and those that seemed the most promising would be transplanted into the controlled soil reproductions to verify how they grew. Any plants that survived would then be sent to the greenhouses to be tested for real.

The main work of the gene complex, though, happened on the other side of the room. There the workstations were full of computer monitors, laboratory equipment, and gene-splicing machines. Making his way through the busy walkways, Elias greeted some of the technicians with friendly waves. He spotted his aunt at the very center of the splicing section, as usual. She was working at a standup desk, busily typing into her terminal. Behind her, isolated from the rest of the lab by an intricately constructed magnetic cradle, was the Life Seed.

Elias stopped a couple of paces away from his aunt, waiting for her to finish whatever she was typing. He gazed at the Life Seed, marveling at its beauty as he always did. It resembled a basketball-sized flower bud, dark red in color, its three petals still closed tight. It hovered noiselessly in the magnetic field that kept it safe, twirling ever so slowly like a diamond on display. Intricate patterns of veins traversed the outside of the flower petals, looking to Elias almost like the circuitry of a motherboard, where each connecting wire throbbed with life. It was amazing to think that the Life Seed had existed for as long as the colony had, and probably far longer, still alive although it required no nourishment whatsoever. In all the history of Portree, it had never wilted. It had also never opened, and the consensus among the scientists was that it never would because it wasn't necessarily a flower.

It looked like one, but its internal genetic structure was so complex that it was likely this was its final stable form.

"Mesmerizing, isn't it?" Laura Matsuo said.

"Hi, Aunt Laura," Elias answered. "Yeah. It's pretty cool to look at."

"That it is," Laura conceded. She wore her hair in a utilitarian crewcut, and her lab coat looked wrinkled, almost as if she had slept in it. Knowing her, Elias decided that it was a strong possibility. His aunt loved her work and had dedicated her life to studying the Life Seed.

"Is any extraction planned for today?" Elias asked her.

"As a matter of fact, it is," Laura answered. "It's scheduled for…. Oh heavens. Right now. Excuse me for a moment, will you?"

Elias nodded as she rushed away to talk to a couple of technicians. The three of them headed to one of the largest robotic stations that had been erected next to the Life Seed. Elias watched them key in a series of commands, and a few minutes later, a slender robotic arm whirred into motion. It approached the Life Seed with perfect precision until it was a few centimeters away. Then it deployed a syringe from the end of its arm, prepped it, and sunk it into the Seed.

At that instant, the lights dimmed in the entire room. Elias witnessed the extraction along with many of the scientists and technicians who looked up from their workstations.

The Seed did not change in any way as the robotic arm retracted the end of the syringe, creating a vacuum that filled the plastic tube with a dark red liquid from the core of the alien plant. When the syringe was full, the robotic arm moved back gently. Elias found that he could not look away from the Seed as the puncture wound the syringe had left behind closed over, healing at an incredible speed. It was almost like watching a sped-up recording of human tissue healing, except that when it was done, not even a scar remained. The Life Seed resumed its gentle spinning as if nothing had happened.

The light level returned to normal. Elias watched the robotic arm pump the contents of the syringe into a reinforced container with mechanical precision. The container was then transported via a vacuum tube to the genetic splicing mainframe, a fast computer terminal whose monitors covered a good portion of the far wall. Xenobiologists at the station resumed their work in a flurry of activity.

"Now the fun begins," Laura told Elias, walking over to him again.

"What are you using the genetic material on this time?" Elias asked.

"Oh, Rodriguez thinks he can use the Life Seed's regenerative properties to come up with a strain of rice that won't react so strongly with the symbiotic bacteria that live in the soil around here. So far it's just a guess, but his is the only new idea, so we are going with it."

Elias nodded grimly. Extracting genetic material from the Life Seed to boost Terran plant genes was originally supposed to be a last-resort attempt, something to do when everything else failed. The fact that they were doing it more and more often lately only underscored the severity of the food situation.

"It's bad, isn't it?" Elias asked.

Laura sighed. "Perhaps. It's hard to say. I thought we had come up with a robust strain of wheat this year, but you saw the harvest. Only a tenth of what we planted survived, and the grains they produced…. I don't know. Sometimes I get the feeling that plants don't *want* to grow on this planet. We are forcing them to, because we need them to survive, but we can only push so hard. Thankfully, we have the Life Seed. Without it the colony wouldn't have survived as long as it has. It's such a complex organism, self-contained, evident in its adaptability, yet mysterious. I wonder if we'll ever unlock all of its secrets."

"Maybe I'll find something about it in Dr. Wright's notes. I'm going to the lab right now, see what I can find. I think he had a secret room." He considered mentioning the door he had found but decided against it. He wanted to be sure there was something there worth sharing.

"Well, don't let me keep you," his aunt replied. "I doubt you'll find anything useful there, though. I never read any mention of this Dr. Wright's research in the journals we have."

"But I've shown you his records of the flora and fauna! I've never seen anything like that before."

"Yes, but which portion of them is true? He claims to have explored the continent far and wide, but you know how dangerous it is to go out into the wilds. We simply don't do it anymore. There are too many wurl. It's hard to think Wright was able to go on long field trips with no protection only to study the local wildlife."

"I think it's the real thing," Elias insisted stubbornly.

Laura smiled in faint condescension. "Have you reconsidered my offer, Eli?"

"About becoming your apprentice?"

"Precisely. You turn seventeen next year. You'll be of age, and you need to have a steady position."

"Yeah. Maybe. I mean, I want to see what I can find in the lab first. Besides, I have my recycling job during the week."

"Very well. Just keep it in mind, okay?"

"Sure. Thanks, Aunt Laura. See you around."

She nodded absently, already distracted by an urgent message on her link from the looks of it. Elias walked past busy scientists until he reached the exit. The automated doors let him out with quiet efficiency, and he hurried to Dr. Wright's lab.

Elias ran the entire three kilometers and arrived, panting, at the hidden spot on the hillside. This time, though, he was much more careful and made sure to scan the area for any marauding wurl. He did a quick check with his link for anything unusual, finding nothing. That was good. He felt much safer as he went down the entry chute and into the forsaken lab.

It was cold down there, cold enough that the generator sputtered to a halt twice before starting up properly to heat the space and provide illumination. Elias's notes were where he had left them, his computer terminal waiting patiently for any input commands. Elias settled down on his chair, ignoring the faint rumbling of his stomach demanding food. He rubbed his hands together for warmth, and then he set to work.

He needed to crack the code on the secret door. There were 10,000 possibilities to choose from, though. Testing manually was out of the question. Instead, he needed something automated.

He connected his link wirelessly to the computer terminal, opened a simple text processor, and began to code a brute-force iteration program to test all the possibilities, one after the other, until they were exhausted. He was done in a few lines. All he needed was to establish a counter, increase it by one each cycle, and divert the four-digit output to his link. Once that was done, he grabbed a universal connector from his stash and walked over to the heavy secret door. The security panel was not active, but it started up at a touch of Elias's finger. He then looked for an input port of some kind, found it, and plugged his link directly into the door. He brought up the iteration program on the link, compiled it for compatibility with external hardware, and started it up.

Testing took nearly twenty minutes, because there was a brief fraction of a second delay between each failed attempt when the door's input panel wouldn't accept new data. It was also bad luck that the actual code turned out to be 9742, one of the last to be tested. To Elias, however, it didn't matter. His heart leapt in his chest when the door panel flashed green, clicked, and unlocked the hidden door.

Elias yanked the connector cable out of the way and pushed. He was met with some resistance, so he pushed the door harder. There was a sharp crack in response, and the door swung open all the way, smashing against the opposite wall. Elias winced, hoping he hadn't broken anything critical. Then he stepped into the room.

The damp smell of mildew was nearly overpowering, and at first glance the room was a complete disappointment. It was small, maybe three by three meters at most, with a very low ceiling, cracked walls, and an ankle-high layer of debris on the floor. Aside from the debris, there was nothing of interest to be seen, not even when Elias clicked the LED on his link and used its light to scan every inch of the walls for something noteworthy. Refusing to give up, Elias turned his attention to the debris at his feet. It was an untidy mixture of frozen mud, pieces of wall, and…

Elias spotted the glint of metal and rushed toward it. It was a corner of something, poking out through the dirt. Unfortunately, the dirt around it was frozen solid, so Elias grabbed his shovel from the other room and resigned himself to another long digging session.

His efforts were rewarded very soon, however. The metal corner turned out to belong to a box, a safe of some kind, which he was able to pull out after a few minutes of frantic digging. His prize was heavy, and he could barely carry it in both arms as he made his way back to the workstation to see what it was he had found. He plopped it down on the table with relief, stepped back, and looked at it.

It was definitely a safe. One of the corners was dented, the metal surface was scored, and it was filthy, but it still appeared to be in one piece. Hopefully, whatever had been valuable enough to place inside would still be in good condition. The safe appeared to be airtight. Approaching, Elias grabbed a rag and wiped it, looking for an input panel of some kind. He soon found it, but initially he was completely puzzled by the panel. It wasn't electronic. It was a mechanical dial, circular, with a white mark on one end. The dial could be moved 360 degrees in either direction, but after a few test turns, the safe stayed resolutely shut.

Confused, Elias brought up his link's wiki. He searched for ancient safekeeping devices and was thrilled to see that the second entry matched the description of his safe perfectly. It was a mechanical model made of interlocking gears. The dial, which could be turned, had to match a certain number of digits etched into the safe itself in order for it to swing open. Supposedly it was possible to hear when the correct number had been entered because the mechanism would click.

Elias turned his attention back to the dusty safe on his tabletop. He was now faced with a new problem. He had no idea how many numbers were required for the combination, and the scoring on the surface made most of the numerals around the dial unreadable.

Then again, the safe had to be made of stainless steel or an equivalent alloy.

Nothing that could really stand up to a monomolecular blade.

Elias set the safe on the floor, grabbed his shovel again, and looked around for the best place to strike. He found a faint wedge, encrusted with dirt, which ostensibly corresponded to the safe's door. He wedged the tip of the shovel in, set a foot on top of it, and pushed.

He spent a miserable ten minutes trying to get the thing open, poking and kicking it, hacking at it with the shovel. He tried not to think of what his father would do to him when he realized Elias had ruined the shovel beyond repair. The colony didn't have the technology to make monomolecular blades anymore, so this was a permanent loss.

Whatever, he thought to himself, sweat streaming from his brow with the exertion. *This is more important. Has to be.*

He tried to ignore the faint but persistent doubt that the safe would be empty, or worse, that it would be full of something that had once held value but was now worthless, like gold or gems or money. It couldn't be, though. Dr. Wright had been a brilliant scientist, of that Elias was sure.

Anything important enough to be stored in a safe *inside* a safe room had to be proportionally meaningful. Something too valuable to leave out in the open.

He nearly cried out in relief when he finally managed to wedge the tip of the shovel into an opening on the safe's door. He slammed the shovel a couple of times against the lock mechanism, hearing the telltale wrenches and groans of metal being twisted, scored, and hopefully broken. The shovel gave way after another forceful try, but by then the safe's door was already partially open. Elias grabbed it, hoping there wasn't anything breakable inside, and smashed the entire thing against the nearest wall with all his strength.

The safe broke open, spilling its contents on the floor. Panting, with trembling hands and barely concealed excitement, Elias knelt down on the dirt to examine the reward for his effort.

The safe had contained only one thing. At first he thought it was a tablet, broken beyond repair. He picked it up, and it was heavy in his hands. Its surface was dull, featureless, dark blue, and strangely rough to his fingertips. He turned it over, feeling around the side for an On button or something similar. The tablet opened up around the middle, though, making Elias yelp and drop it. He thought he had broken it, but then he realized he had opened it. There were words written on the inside.

That's paper. This thing is a book!

Elias picked it up again, flipping pages experimentally. Yes, it was an actual book, a notebook, each page covered in packed, spidery handwriting. He quickly went to the first page and found the name he had been looking for.

This is the personal journal of Thomas Wright, PhD.
Chief Xenobiologist
Ionas Generation Ship

Elias gasped. A personal journal. Not a bunch of scientific reports, but an actual journal! He could scarcely believe his eyes. Just thinking about the wealth of information he would find there....

Then the doctor's title caught his attention. Chief xenobiologist? That made no sense. Elias knew the original crew of the *Ionas* by heart, and Dr. Wright was never mentioned. If this was true, though, then he had been one of the most important scientists on board by far.

Strange.

Elias couldn't suppress his curiosity any longer. He grabbed his blanket and the journal, dragged his chair close to the generator where it was a little warmer, and settled down to read.

Almost three hours later, Elias closed the notebook, stunned. He turned off the generator and climbed back out into the open. It was still light out, and there were no wurl around, so he made his way back to the colony very slowly, his eyes far away, thinking about the shocking revelations he had read.

He had to tell them. Everyone had to know.

They would think he was crazy, though. That he was making stuff up. Who would believe him, after all? He was already branded an antisocial freak who never helped the colony. If he spoke about what he had read, they would think it was a desperate ploy to draw attention to himself.

Elias shook his head, slowly at first, then more quickly.

It doesn't matter. I have to tell them. If I don't…. We all die.

Chapter 5
The Journal of Dr. Thomas Wright, Part 1

ELIAS RETURNED home with plenty of time left before the start of the nighttime Midwinter celebration. He went through the rooms as if dazed, only realizing there was nobody home when he found his mother's note in the kitchen.

> *Took Oscar to get a haircut. Left you something to eat before the feast! – Mom*

There was a plate with seasoned protein paste and carrots nearby. Elias put it in the microwave, waiting the required time while thoughts chased themselves around in circles in his mind. When the machine beeped, he took out the food and ate it right there without really tasting it. He had a drink of water. He went to the bathroom. Then he went to his room.

He sat down on the bed and placed the doctor's journal on his nightstand. It looked oddly out of place there, a relic from the past that should not exist. It was hard to reconcile the words he had read with the reality of his situation. Elias had always suspected things were bad, but never anything like this. It was even harder to decide what to do, how to disclose the information.

After a moment of hesitation, he took the journal, leaned back against some pillows, and read it all again. If nothing else, he wanted every detail fresh in his memory when he revealed what he had discovered to everyone in Portree.

Journal of Doctor Thomas Wright
21 June, 3142. 21:00

FINALLY HAVE some time to myself. It's been madness over here, as expected. Setting up a colony on a new planet has to be the most challenging logistics nightmare there can be. MacLeod kept on second-guessing the location where we should make planetfall, ignoring the recommendations of the continental surveyor and going by something he called "a gut feeling." Thankfully, his final choice proved to be a good one. The valley he chose is well located, with easy access to water, timber from the nearby woods, and several subsurface deposits of metals and other elements which will make settling in much easier. In fact, after having been here for almost a month now, I doubt if there is any place on this planet, aside from the inhospitable polar regions, where we could have landed and not found paradise. New Skye is beautiful, rich beyond our wildest hopes. It's one thing to get cold data readings from deep-space probes labeling a world fit for human habitation, but another one entirely to reach it and find biological diversity to rival Earth itself.

I wonder what my father would have said had he lived to see this day. Or my grandfather, for that matter. I don't think those of us who have reached this new world can ever thank them or honor them enough for the sacrifices they willingly undertook. They lived their entire lives aboard the Ionas, *knowing full well that they would never set foot on solid ground or look up at the sky with warm, natural sunlight on their face. And yet, they embraced their duty, making sure that the future generations would have a chance at something better. It's sad and beautiful, and I think it's part of what makes us human. As a race, I don't think we've ever given up hope.*

Or maybe I'm just getting sentimental. I seem to be coming down with the flu, and I always get melancholic when I feel ill.

11 August, 3142. 08:00

NEARLY THE entire colony of the recently named Portree has come down with a virus native to this world. The advance probes we sent came back to the Ionas *with a good portion of the local microorganisms, but they evidently missed some, because now we are all getting sick. Hino is working around the clock trying to come up with a cure, and I sincerely hope she succeeds. Even though the sickness isn't particularly severe, it is debilitating and annoying. It's hard to work in these conditions, particularly now that we are erecting the first buildings where we expect to live.*

The weather of this world has truly been a blessing. Its summer temperatures are balmy and comfortable, and the land around Portree buzzes and hums with life. Rodriguez and his scouts have already identified several native fruits that scanned positive for compatibility with our recently upgraded gut flora. I ate several large purple berries, which people here are imaginatively calling purpleberries, and I must admit they were delicious. They were also the first thing I have ever eaten that was not grown on board the carefully monitored environment of the ship's hydroponics bay. It was truly a moment to remember.

As for myself, the construction of my genetics lab is well underway. I oversee the details whenever I don't have a fever, and I think the process is coming along nicely. I wish we didn't have to cannibalize the Ionas *for parts at every turn, but I suppose it can't be helped. The ship did its job in bringing us here. I like to think it would be glad to be dismantled and relieved of its burden for good.*

35 January, 1 AP 21:00

MACLEOD HAS *been very insistent in getting everyone to think of this as a new beginning, and I think it's starting to stick. I'm going to label the years the way he wants me to, since I suppose it makes sense. It will be decades or even hundreds of years before we hear anything from the people living in the Core Systems, so why not keep time starting with our arrival here? So AP it is. After Planetfall.*

Even though Trost from Psychology keeps telling me that a journal is a useful exercise in introspection, I think this is my first entry in months. So much has happened: good, mostly. Thank goodness for that. After Hino figured out how to change our genetic makeup just enough so the viruses of this world wouldn't kill us, the Great Sickness was over in a heartbeat. I had honestly forgotten what it was like to wake up and feel energized, healthy. I have not wasted a single day since.

First on my list of priorities was bringing the laboratory online, which is now mostly done. As soon as we had the splicer machines working, I set my team to the task of analyzing the local flora and looking for something we could cultivate from whatever grows natively here. I tasked a second team to begin trial-and-error cultures of the plants we brought with us in the native soil. Even though we still have plenty of supplies on board the wreck of the Ionas, we have dismantled most of its hydroponics sector for use in other areas of the colony. It's a necessary risk, I'm afraid. As MacLeod would put it, we need to cut the cord binding us to the ship and start fending for ourselves now, or else we will never do it. I suppose it makes sense.

When time permits, I am eager to go on field expeditions. It's wintertime now, and the world is transformed from the way it was during summer. Not much is growing, but the land has a serene sort of beauty I find enthralling. The sparser vegetation is also quite conducive to sightings of the local animals. Most of the creatures we've encountered are small invertebrates, but there have been two verified encounters with a kind of animal unlike anything I had ever seen. It appears to be a species of large reptile with thick black plating, six legs, and three eyes. That last characteristic keeps me up at night with the myriad possibilities it suggests. All vertebrates discovered so far in the Core Systems exhibit an even number of eyes or their equivalent organs. It appears to be the most profitable and economical evolutionary line, but what if it's not the only one?

I wish I knew more about the creatures. Unfortunately for us, they are quite shy, running away in a most curious fashion, more like rolling if the accounts from the scouts are to be believed. Next month, when the results of our crop testing are in, I plan on heading out into the wilderness myself.

17 February, 1 AP 23:00

FAILURE. CATASTROPHIC, utter failure. Perhaps I exaggerate a little, but not by much. Every single crop strain we have planted on this alien world has died, every carefully constructed iteration of the most basic plants humans need for survival. It is beyond disappointing to think that the generations of xenobiologists who came before me, who spent their entire lives on the Ionas crafting each of these genetic variations, worked in vain. There's something fundamentally inimical to Terran life on New

Skye, at least where plants are concerned. Fortunately, we still have many months of supplies available, but the prospects for the future worry me. What if we don't find a solution? I have nearly ninety people working day and night, trying to find an answer to the problem of our long-term survival. All of them are brilliant minds, quite capable in their respective specialization fields. Basic probability dictates that we are bound to find a way out of this. I hope.

Perhaps I worry too much. My therapist, Trost, insists a change of environment would help my perspective, and for once I'm inclined to agree. I believe it's time I started my programmed field trips.

42 August, 1 AP 17:00

THIS PLANET is a xenobiologist's dream. Every biome, every nook and cranny, is full of biological treasure. It is high summer now, the apex of a slow but steady climb into exorbitant biodiversity, the likes of which I have never seen in the records of any other world. When I compare New Skye in winter, with its muted tones, dry grass, and lifeless fields, to the same world in summer, it's like another planet. It would seem I cannot take a step without stumbling across a new plant, a beautiful blooming flower, or a chirping arthropod nobody else has ever seen before. It is humbling, breathtaking, and exhilarating.

My records back at the lab must now have grown to several gigabytes' worth of raw information, and I am only just getting started. I have sent out exploration teams to every corner of this continent, the largest of two significant landmasses on New Skye. Every time a team comes back to base, simply listing our new discoveries takes hours. Classifying, sequencing, and understanding all of these new lifeforms would take several lifetimes. When I think that there is another whole continent to the east, completely unexplored, my mind boggles. I can't hope to study everything this world has to offer; there is simply no time. Instead, I believe I will focus my attention on its most remarkable creatures.

I think I will start with the wurl.

Sadly, I was not the one to christen them, but by now the name has stuck. I must admit, it is rather descriptive of the way they roll through the landscape like spine-covered wheels with a mechanism as of yet unknown. It would appear that they are able to flatten their spines against their bodies when they tumble downhill, presumably using them like springs to absorb and redirect the kinetic energy of their controlled fall in order to preserve the momentum of the rolling motion, but all I have is conjecture at this point. I have now seen several of them firsthand, and they are truly magnificent creatures. They are beautiful to look at, particularly now. They appear to exhibit seasonal changes, very subtle but unmistakable nevertheless. Whereas their scales are perfectly black in winter, in summer they acquire a translucent sheen that hints at deep violet hues, which reflect the sunlight at certain times of day. They are breathtaking when this happens, even more so because those gentle giants are apparently unaware of their own great strength. They are quite curious, investigating our campsites when we are not there, but they always flee when we get close. I would love to capture a live specimen for study and eventual dissection, but MacLeod has expressly forbidden it for the time being. Peaceful though they are, there are reports of wurl using their spines to impale prey with shocking force from several meters away. Such is their accuracy that they can shoot birds out of the sky when hunting. Until we find a way to pacify them safely, I agree with MacLeod. It is best to observe.

They appear to be fiercely territorial, with each individual commanding an area of approximately ninety square kilometers. I have seen no sexual dimorphism yet, and indeed I am not sure whether all the creatures we have seen so far are male or female. Further study is needed.

3 December, 1 AP 03:00

THE MORE *I learn about this world, the more fascinated I am by it. I have been out in the field for months, exploring the far reaches of the continent, and the sheer variety of landscapes and the creatures that inhabit them is still breathtaking.*

Through some fluke of evolution, it appears most vertebrates here possess appendages and sensory organs in multiples of three. I have discovered no mammals or analogs so far, but there is a wide variety of reptiles and closely related birds to make up for this lack. I must admit, the first time I saw a bird with three wings flying, I was struck speechless. They glide through the air in a corkscrew motion, each wing beating in the same direction, one after the other with no gap, ascending and descending in graceful spirals. Evolution will never cease to amaze me.

My exploration and cataloging endeavors are well underway, with success unparalleled by even my wildest hopes before coming to New Skye. I am truly fortunate to be offered a chance to discover so many different forms of life, a chance for which I am sure many biologists in the Core Systems would cut off their right arms to be able to have. Planned for the near future is a thorough examination of the mountain range which rises not far from Portree. I have left this region for last because the terrain is quite unforgiving and our vehicles will not manage it. I am thinking of leading a small expedition on foot to see what can be seen. I can barely sleep imagining the creatures that must inhabit those fertile mountainsides.

Unfortunately, our success in discovery is not mirrored by our endeavors in producing sustainable crop strains. Every attempt is a failure, and after two long New Skye years of ceaseless trying, it is starting to make some people uneasy. We lost our endless supply of renewable Terran produce when we dismantled the Ionas, *and although this world offers bountiful fruits during the summer, it is simply not enough to sustain a growing colony of nearly three hundred individuals.*

It is no different for the animals, I'm afraid. Those native to this planet are incompatible with our digestive system, due to the same genetic quirk that makes them so unique. The embryos of Terran farm animals we brought with us on the ship have all been used, but none of them survived more than a few days after leaving the lab. The situation is worrisome but not impossible. We have not yet exhausted the options available to us.

33 February, 2 AP 24:00

SO MUCH to say. The detailed information, videos, and photos have already been uploaded to the Portree computer mainframe, but I need to sort out my thoughts.

I have found something. In the mountains. It's.... Okay. First things first.

The wurl are, without a doubt, the single most fascinating species in New Skye. They are the apex predators of the land, coexisting in a flawless equilibrium with the rest of their environment. They are surprisingly intelligent as well. I was able to verify this based on their behavior during my expedition to the Aberdeen Mountains to the northwest of Portree.

I took a small team with me, and we went on foot. We encountered some wurl from the first night on, although they always kept their distance. Cameras with night vision captured them coming closer to the campsites after dark, examining us with open curiosity. The wurl also took note of the cameras themselves, sneaking nearer to inspect them with that unnerving three-eyed gaze they have. As an experiment, we left some dead prey animals including small birds and lizard analogues inside cages for the wurl to find after we had left the area. We did this in several locations. We hid cameras to capture what they did, and on our return we checked the footage. It was fascinating. Every cage we set had been opened by the creatures so they would be able to get to the meal inside. The level of complexity of the cages appeared to be irrelevant. Simple latches were quickly figured out, based on the videos we found. More complicated multilayered unlocking mechanisms took a bit longer the first time, but after that, whichever creature had accomplished it was able to open similar cages much faster, evidencing that they were able to learn. Simply amazing.

I have also verified the fact that all the specimens we have seen so far belong to a single sex. At the foot of the mountain range, we found a dying wurl which had apparently fallen from a great height. Several of its legs were broken. We wasted no time putting an end to the creature's suffering and then preparing the specimen for dissection. What we learned from that dissection alone would be enough to fill several volumes, but the most important thing we discovered was that, as I had suspected, the creatures were all male. This is puzzling in the extreme, and even more so because we have never found a nesting site or any other indication as to how the wurl reproduce.

I was also able to better comprehend the biological mechanisms responsible for both their ability to fire spines and the curious whirling motion they use to traverse terrain. Their musculoskeletal structure is far more advanced than anything I have ever seen. Their muscles appear to consist of several threaded layers of cells which are capable of omnidirectional contraction. They are also much more dense than human muscles, accounting for a very large portion of the creature's weight. Around each of the carapace spines, specialized clusters of cells appear to have formed a biological hydraulic pump capable of storing gases at an enormous pressure. When the creature fires a spine, the pressure is suddenly directed toward the base of the projectile, presumably accompanied by a coordinated muscular contraction of incredible force. It is a marvel of biological engineering. I cannot wait to study these creatures in depth.

Now for the other, much larger discovery. We found a cleft in one of the high mountain passes which led into a system of caverns that tunneled into the living rock. Dangerous though it was, we explored the cave system and soon came across an enormous chamber near the summit of the mountain. There was daylight shining through improbably placed gashes in the rock overhead, and a very strong reptilian smell filled the space, despite its size..

Resting in the very center of the chamber, on a complex network of interconnected vines which appeared to tunnel into the mountain, I found the Life Seed.

That's what I am calling it now, anyway, after I have had a few days in the lab to examine it more closely. At first I supposed it was a large flower bud of an unknown species of the planet, but that appears not to be the case. When we plucked it from its resting place deep in the mountain cave, the vines around it shuddered and retreated into the rock. A deep, ominous groan alerted us to the possibility of a cave-in, and we quickly left the way we had come. I carried the Life Seed in a sealed, thermoisolating container all the way back to Portree, and it now rests in my lab, frozen, awaiting further study.

My preliminary investigations on its genetic makeup have made even the wurl seem boring and simple creatures in contrast. The Seed is definitely a plant, but it is a plant unlike anything that has ever been recorded. Its genetic sequences are not fixed; on the contrary, they appear to be fluctuating all the time, giving us all manner of incomprehensible results in the output of the genetic mapper. Before freezing it, I sliced off a section of one of its lobes for study and I witnessed its shocking capacity for regeneration. This plant is a treasure trove. If we can unlock its secrets, the possibilities are beyond staggering.

Chapter 6
The Journal of Dr. Thomas Wright, Part 2

35 January, 4 AP 14:00

HOW LONG has it been since I last wrote something in here? More than a year, according to the timestamp. Yet somehow, it feels like much, much longer.

The colony is in danger. We are running out of food, fast. All other investigation projects have been rescinded in response to the severity of the situation. We have people from all areas of knowledge working together, trying to find a solution, although there appears to be none.

Terran crops will not grow on New Skye. No matter what we do, no matter how we splice the strains, not a single plant is able to survive once it is exposed to the toxic soil. Our makeshift hydroponics bay is working beyond its sustainability parameters, and it is only a matter of time before it fails.

People are growing restless, angry. For the first time since we arrived, MacLeod has had to exercise his authority and lock up two people in one of the newer prefab houses, which I suppose will now become our jail. He is talking about organizing an armed corps of some kind to make sure order is kept. I think he wants to call it the Colony Patrol. Although I agree with the necessity of such a measure, I fear for its long-term consequences. I would hate for our fledgling colony to become a dictatorship.

I am under a lot of pressure these days. As chief xenobiologist, finding a solution to the problem of our food in this environment is my direct responsibility. I am accosted at every opportunity by angry, desperate, or fearful people who demand to know what I am doing to save their lives. I have grown tired of responding that I am doing everything I can. I truly am.

I have even abandoned my research on the local wildlife, something which I regret every day. The Life Seed awaits, frozen in my lab, for follow-up analyses for which I simply have no time. It will remain a mystery I cannot understand. How can that incredibly complex plant life-form exist in this world—and thrive where our best engineered crops wither? The Seed doesn't even have a stable genetic structure. It's as if it were iterating between all possible forms of life while maintaining its shape, a genetic reservoir for the entire planet, infinitely adaptable....

By the generation ship. *That's it! I know what to do.*

1 October, 5 AP 21:00

SUCCESS. WILD, *overwhelming success. The colony has been saved.*

It was hard going these past few months, barely surviving on the last remaining supplies of our failed hydroponics bay. And yet today we harvest home-grown crops for the first time. It is a great day indeed.

There's talk of building a statue in my honor in the colony plaza. I have had two different journalists pester me with questions for a biography they want to release about me. Gifts are routinely delivered to my home, big and small, as thanks for what I have done. It's strange yet exhilarating at the same time. Today, during the first harvest, I was given the very first carrot taken from the ground of New Skye. I ate it right there and then, to thunderous applause. It tasted like dirt, of course. But it also tasted like vindication.

The Life Seed was the key. It possesses enough wealth of genetic information that some of it was bound to be useful to our endeavors. Which is what we did. Under my supervision, a selected team of my best splicers was set to work around the clock on a way to extract useful genes from the Seed that would also be compatible with Terran plants. It was brutal, unforgiving work, with no margin for error. A large portion of the mainframe's processing power was set aside to go through the countless possibilities, analyzing them for probability of success. It was a desperate gamble, and I almost didn't get the approval for it from MacLeod, but when Hino sided with me, the matter was decided, and I got my funding.

I was a nervous wreck those first few months. If I was right, then maybe the Seed could be used to boost our crops somehow and make them able to survive at long last. If I was wrong, then I was needlessly wasting the very last of our resources on a wild chase that would benefit no one.

It was hard. When the first test results came and every crop was a failure, I almost lost hope. It was only when I decided to emulate the Seed that we found success. Although it seems obvious now, with the all-knowing understanding of hindsight, at the time it was a momentous leap in my way of thinking. I had been obsessed with finding a single genetic sequence to use, a static way to modify my crops so they would survive. What I had failed to see was that the Life Seed itself was showing me how plants needed to be in order to survive on New Skye. Its internal genetic structure was always changing, always adapting.

Our crops needed to be the same way.

Once I knew what the solution was, though, the magnitude of the problem was made apparent. What I wanted to create was a dynamic genetic sequence that could be inserted into any plant without killing it, or killing us if we ate it. In order to accomplish it, I would need raw processing power and energy several orders of magnitude more than what my humble lab could offer. I presented my findings to MacLeod and the rest of the council, and it's a testament to the desperate situation we were in that my proposal was unanimously accepted. It meant we would have to essentially destroy what was left of the Ionas, all of our vehicles, and every computer we could spare, but if it meant survival, then it was worth it.

Failures along the way were heartrending. Glimpses of success were cruel when they evaded me. Months passed by, and we began to ration our food. Then we rationed the rations. And yet, last June, I was finally able to do it. I created a dynamic genetic splicing vector that we used to modify carrots, potatoes, soybeans, and lentils. The first few tests of the new plants were an astounding success. MacLeod decided to wager everything on one big crop cycle, using most of the remainder of our food as raw biomass to create the desired plants. If it failed, then the colony was doomed. But we succeeded.

The only catch I can see is that the genetic vector I discovered is not stable. It will be worthless for next year's harvest, but we can always generate another one as long as we have the Life Seed as a template. Thankfully, it appears to be very long-lived, and its regeneration capabilities mean that we can extract as much raw genetic material as we need from it, provided we don't kill it. As soon as the weather permits, I will send exploration missions far and wide to see whether we can procure another specimen of this marvelous plant. It can be said, without exaggerating, that the future of this colony now depends on the Life Seed. If it is ever destroyed and we are not able to find a replacement... I shudder to think about it.

28 November, 35 AP 2:00

HAVING A hard time sleeping. I found this journal hidden at the bottom of a stack of old research notes, and it seemed appropriate for me to make another entry.

What can I say? I turn seventy-five years old in two weeks, or rather eighty-nine and a fraction, given how long years are on this planet. My life has been very good for the most part. People are thankful about what I did way back when the colony was starting. I am respected; my words are always heard. I have lived to see new generations of children born on this world, the very first true inhabitants of New Skye. All of it possible because of my work and that of many others.

I can barely recognize the colony these days. So many people. So much going on. There's talk of expanding Portree or founding another settlement, the second of what will one day be great cities. I doubt I will live to see that, but it's just as well. My work here is done.... Almost.

As of late, I have begun to harbor doubts. In the last five years, our crop yields have been steadily declining. The splicing methods we use, mixing Terran plants with Life Seed material, have remained essentially unchanged since I first created them. Their effectiveness should be the same.... And yet, I am certain things are changing. I do not know why yet. It could be a natural phenomenon of this world. It could be we are overfarming the soil, although that is almost certainly not the case. I will keep a close eye on the procedure in the lab, just in case.

36 July, 42 AP 11:00

I'M SURE it's not my imagination anymore. Today the last of the flowers in the fields outside my laboratory withered and died. It's supposed to be high summer, and yet the explosion of life we witnessed when we first came to this world is nowhere to be seen. Every year, plants bloom a little later. Every year, they die a little sooner. At first we thought it was a natural phenomenon of some kind, but right now I am almost certain it cannot be. It's as if the wintertime were creeping up on the planet, regardless of the day of the year. The temperatures have not changed, and it leads to an incongruous dichotomy. Right now it's summer, and it is hot. Nevertheless, the grass is dead, the trees devoid of leaves. It feels like summer, but it looks like winter. Something is wrong.

Our crop yield was boosted recently by an innovation on my methods which one of the younger scientists developed, a lad named Randolph Trost. Something like that was desperately needed, particularly now that the colony is growing at such an alarming rate. Our population is booming, but our production methods are not. I don't know whether this is sustainable.

There is also the problem of the Life Seed. It looks... different from the way it used to look when I first got it. Its petals, or petal-analogues, have darkened over the years, and the genetic material we extract from it has suffered a remarkable decline in quality and diversity. I don't go to the lab much anymore, but they do send me a digest of the reports every week. What I read there is very troublesome. We are compensating for the decreased efficiency of our splicing methodology by extracting even more genetic material from the Life Seed. This, in turn, taxes its internal regeneration mechanisms in unknown ways. It could be the Seed is dying. Slowly, to be sure, but steadily. And if it dies, then we die with it. We are completely dependent on it now.

1 May, 42 AP 17:00

TODAY *A wurl killed a colonist. I scarcely recognize the creatures anymore. They have become hostile, abandoning their solitary, territorial lifestyle to form bands of aggressive males that will gather outside the colony and attack, especially at night. At first we thought a simple fence would be enough to keep them out. Now we know better.*

Where are the gentle giants that followed me and my team around so many years ago? These creatures are vicious, deadly, and cunning. I am told that the person they killed was impaled by at least five spines, shot with such force that they passed through his body and embedded themselves in the ground. It's a terrible thing. Why are they attacking us? What is it they want?

23 December, 44 AP 16:00

I BARELY *get out of bed these days, but I will for this test. It's too important. If I am correct, people need to know.*

The answer came to me after months of reading on the progress of what the younger scientists are doing. There was a recent expedition by young Jimmy Matsuo and a group of four others who decided to brave the dangers of the wurl and go to the Aberdeen Mountains, to the cave I had once described. They made it there in one piece and carried out extensive analyses on the spot. I have full access to the records, and so I was able to see that the chamber had changed very little from the way I had seen it once, decades ago. The floor was still covered in thick vines, and there was a conspicuous opening in its center of an exact shape to hold the Life Seed.

Matsuo and the others were disappointed that they didn't find another bud to take home with them, but the tests they performed are shocking in their implications. I wonder why nobody else is discussing this. Am I the only one to see the connection?

They carried out electroconductive tests on the vines and took samples from them to sequence. The conductivity readings were dismissed as being faulty, or so I read in the report. If taken at face value, they would indicate that the vines are kilometers long, like the tendrils of an organism that could easily stretch from the mountains to Portree and beyond. The genetic samples, on the other hand, closely mimic one of the first sequences I ever obtained from the Life Seed after I initially brought it home. I doubt anyone even remembers those early genetic data strings. Perhaps I really am the only one who can see the connection.

One thing remains, though. One test to check whether my hypothesis is true or not. I will carry it out and then go public. I don't know what I hope will happen. The best thing for us all would be for me to be wrong, but my instinct tells me I'm right.

25 January, 45 AP 03.00

THE RESULTS are in. By taking the Life Seed, we have doomed this world and ourselves to a slow winter death.

I suspected it all along, but now I have conclusive proof. The Life Seed is so complex precisely because it is linked to the ecosystem of New Skye. It appears to be the host of several genetic markers, or triggers which, when disseminated, will start the normal cycle of the seasons in the plants of this world.

It was hard, particularly at my age, but I managed to procure some raw genetic material from the Seed. People tend to not question my actions, savior of Portree that I am. I then used the material in conjunction with several ordinary native flower seeds, of the kind that used to grow all over the colony when we first arrived. Nowadays, they scarcely bloom at all, with just a few sick-looking buds struggling to blossom in high summer.

I rigged up an incubation chamber and spent the better part of the month scanning the Seed's genetic material for anything that resembled a trigger or marker of some kind. I found several, and I distilled them as best as I could. Then I mixed them in with water, a nutrient cocktail, and applied it directly to the roots of the sprouting flowers.

They all bloomed. In a couple of days, they bloomed.

I did several backup tests, contrasting and correlating information with everything available to me on my link. The conclusion was as inevitable as it is irrefutable. The Life Seed is somehow connected to the rest of the world, probably through the network of vines which run for kilometers on end under the surface of the planet. By taking it, we destabilized the genetic equilibrium of a very fragile and unique ecosystem. It is imperative we give it back. If not, this planet will die, and us along with it.

27 January, 45 AP 21:00

I PRESENTED *my findings to the council. They were received first with disbelief and then with hostility. I was told not to speak of this again, so I went to the new gene complex, hobbling as best as I could with my cane, stood in front of the Life Seed and all the geneticists there, and shouted out my discovery.*

In the beginning, people listened. The respect they had for me still carried some weight. As soon as I said that we had to give the Life Seed back, though, people questioned my conclusions, my methods. The accuracy of my information. One of them even my sanity. The thugs of the Colony Patrol came and "escorted" me away. I have never been so furious and so humiliated in my entire life. I have empirical proof. I am not making this up.

17 May, 45 AP 14:00

THEY TORE down my statue today and placed an ugly obelisk in its place. My name, unfortunately, has become a joke. The council has twisted my words, making it seem like the ramblings of an old man, desperate for some more fame at whatever the cost. The Life Seed has been placed in a new magnetic containment unit, I hear, and it is now under surveillance. MacLeod has made it very clear that the Seed stays where it is.

In the meantime, our crops wither. The emergency measures Trost undertook to boost our production have been starting to backfire. We still operate at a surplus, but for how long?

It's hard to sleep now. Wurl come very close to the lab almost every night, howling.

I think I know, now, what it is they want.

ELIAS'S ALARM beeped, startling him on the bed. He heard noise downstairs—his mother calling his name, Oscar laughing. Looking at his link, Elias realized that it was time for the Midwinter celebration.

He tucked the journal under his arm, steeled his resolve, and walked downstairs.

Chapter 7
The Midwinter Feast

THE MAIN Hall was almost unrecognizably beautiful for the Midwinter Feast. Elias walked in silence, a few steps behind his family, and he was the last to go into the roaring warmth of a room filled with people having fun.

Flaming torches hung from sconces on the walls, right next to much more effective artificial light sources that had been turned off for the evening. The fireplace at one end was crackling with flame, its waves of heat noticeable even from a distance. Between the torches, the colorful banners Elias had hung in the morning had been rearranged into far more aesthetically pleasing patterns, complete with garlands of dry winter grass and red pine branches. There were tables lined up against the north wall, all of them laden with food. It was a mild shock to Elias to see so much food at the same time, and he wasn't the only one who made a beeline for the tastiest dishes. Oscar was right behind him, and together the brothers made their way through the large crowd until they reached their objective.

"Candied apples!" Oscar said, delighted. He picked one up from several that had been arranged into a bouquet of sorts and began eating it noisily.

Elias was about to do the same, digging in at the desserts table, when he caught a glimpse of Sarah, Tim, and Jim standing nearby. Deciding he would probably look like a little kid if he stuffed his face with sweets, he instead wandered over to a nearby table and picked up a plain-looking sandwich from a pile. As he ate, he watched the people who filled the space. Nearly everyone was there already. The director was talking to some of the geneticists, wearing her trademark mauve tunic. A harassed-looking Harold MacLeod held a pad nearby, talking into his link nonstop. The older folks were sitting at one of the many tables, which had been lavishly decorated for the occasion. They were the only ones not standing, but Elias heard them laughing, and he spotted his grandmother among them, wearing a magnificent dress. The little kids had found each other too, and they had carried off a good portion of the desserts to one of the smaller tables, where they appeared to be arguing loudly about how best to divide them. With a chuckle, Elias felt a small pang of nostalgia. He still remembered when he had belonged to that group, before growing up, before everything had become so complicated.

Over by the fire, the men and women of the Colony Patrol hung out together in their own little clique. They were only a handful, but they radiated confidence and authority. With a little start, Elias realized that Tristan was among them this year, drinking with them, although he was still technically underage. He looked very young in comparison to the scarred face of Commander Amanda Rodriguez or the hulking behemoth that was Phineas Trost, but Elias was forced to admit that Tristan fit right in. He already had that indescribable swagger about him, that tilt to his mouth and that sparkle in eyes that spoke of a man who had faced deadly danger and come out alive. Tristan's every move appeared graceful yet calculated, the result of his many years of apprenticeship. The uniform he wore fit him like a second skin, and it was impossible to miss the shock spear slung across his back, the weapon with which he protected the colony.

Right at that moment, Tristan looked in Elias's direction, and the two of them locked eyes. Flustered, Elias pretended to have been looking somewhere else, but he ended up bumping into his cousin Shinji and making him spill his drink in a rather spectacular way.

"I'm so sorry," Elias said, praying that Tristan hadn't seen.

Shinji laughed. "Don't tell me you're already drunk, little cousin."

"I'm sixteen," Elias protested, looking around for something with which to wipe up the wine. "I can't drink yet. Although if we were on Earth, I'd actually be nineteen already. The years are longer here, so...."

"Right," Shinji interrupted. "I guess I better go get myself some more, then! Drink for the two of us."

Elias smiled weakly and finished wiping up the mess. When he stood up, he quickly looked in Tristan's direction. For some reason, it was a deep disappointment to find that Tristan wasn't even paying attention to him anymore. He was laughing loudly with the rest of the patrol.

Although Elias wasn't feeling particularly cheerful, nervous as he was with the coming prospect of explaining his findings to a bunch of people who would probably not believe him, it was hard to resist the allure of the feast. Elias took a plate from a nearby pile and loaded it with sweet potatoes, stuffed pastries, chocolate muffins, and some spaghetti with several soy meatballs. He carried the food to an empty table and sat down, standing up only twice over the course of the next hour in order to go get some fruit punch. The rest of the world disappeared for Elias as he dug in. It was a rare luxury to be able to eat as much as he wanted without measuring cups or scales or annoying nutrient allocation tables. It was only when his stomach felt pleasantly full that he stopped for a moment, returning his awareness to his surroundings. Somebody had begun playing music.

A quick look in the direction of the door showed him that several of the older MacLeods had taken out their instruments, and they were striking up a fast-paced, lively tune that soon had several people clapping. The cooks brought in still more dishes and several casks of wine. Elias smiled, tapping his foot as he followed the rhythm of the music. He had always liked this part.

As the notes of the music gained purchase, people gradually took their seats around the large open space in the center of the Hall. The musicians advanced slowly in that direction, smiling and nodding along to the increasingly loud clapping from the crowd cheering them on. When they reached the center of the space, the music suddenly stopped. At the same time, all the married couples in the colony stood up, walking toward the musicians until they formed a ring around them. The silence held for nearly five seconds, charged with tension and broken only by the crackle of the flames.

Then the musicians played.

It was a traditional midwinter song, led by the echoing violin notes of Owen MacLeod. It started out slow, mournful, and on a certain note, all the married couples turned so they would be facing one another. The men offered their right hands to the women, smiled, and pulled them close right as the music changed. The tune became a fast jig, and Elias clapped right along with the rest as the couples danced, following a series of dizzying, complicated steps that not everyone could perform to perfection. Small errors didn't matter, though. It was the Dance of Winter, Portree's way of celebrating the fact that the longest night was finally upon them, and there was only more sunlight to look forward to from this day forth. Elias nodded along to the fast twirls of the women as they pushed away from their husbands to make an inner circle around the musicians, the hems of their dresses fanning out like flowers as they turned. The men pretended to be angry that they had been left behind and made as if to take them back, but the women switched positions at the last second, which meant every man held in his arms a woman that was not his wife. The women, seeing their predicament, slapped their captors on the cheek, some very lightly, some much harder. Apparently stunned, the men let go and watched from the sidelines as the women danced in the center, turning and jumping and switching positions in time with the feverish pace of the music. At the climax of the song, the women all pretended to faint from sheer exhaustion, their husbands rushed forward, saving them from the fall, and the music ended when the couples kissed.

Elias applauded enthusiastically, smiling at his mother and father, who were kissing with evident passion. The Winter Dance had always been his favorite part of the feast, and every year it was more so. It was just so… romantic. Elias couldn't wait until—

But I will never dance it.

The thought was sudden, unbidden, but Elias knew it was true. He would never have a wife because he was different. He liked guys, and if Oscar had noticed, little though he was, soon others would too. When that happened, Elias would be more of an outcast than he already was.

Out of all the people in the colony, he was the only one sitting alone at a table.

Not that he minded all that much. He watched people dancing when the musicians resumed playing after a short pause. Now that the traditional dance was over, anybody who wanted could step up, grab a partner, and dance away. It was easy to see who liked whom in the choice of partners. Yuki was dancing with Tim while Jim looked on, visibly annoyed. Evelyn was dancing with Phineas, and although she was tall, he was even taller. Tristan was dancing with Sarah.

A surge of envy caught Elias completely by surprise. He suddenly hated everything about the dance, from the way Tristan was obviously enjoying being the center of attention when he lifted Sarah up in the air, to the possessive grasp of Sarah on Tristan's shoulder. Her fingers reminded Elias of the talons of a bird of prey, clutching flesh in a death grip.

He looked away. He opened Doctor Wright's journal instead, and tried to memorize some of the more important phrases regarding the Life Seed.

After a while, the music died down. The dancers left the floor, and the musicians packed up their things.

"Hey, Eli," Oscar said brightly, sitting down next to him. He carried a little plate with two slices of cake, which he started eating immediately.

"Oscar, for heaven's sake," Elias's mother said, taking a chair nearby. "Chew with your mouth closed."

"But it's so delicious!" Oscar complained, his mouth full of half-eaten cake.

"You're disgusting," Elias told him, grinning.

Oscar mumbled something that might have been "thank you," but his mouth was too full to tell.

"Didn't see you dancing out there tonight," Elias's father said, taking the last seat at the table. Looking around, Elias realized that families were sitting together now, preparing for the gift-giving ceremony.

"Didn't feel like it," Elias said evasively.

"But you used to love dancing," his mother said. "Do you remember, dear? Eli used to be so cute, trying to follow along the steps of the Winter Dance when he was little. I have a video of it somewhere."

"Yeah, well, things change," Elias replied, more sharply than he had intended. He was angry, but he wasn't even sure why.

"Don't talk to your mother like that, young man," his father warned him.

Elias rolled his eyes. Thankfully, the argument died right then because Director O'Rourke stood up and walked toward the middle of the room. Everybody fell silent, watching her. The firelight threw dancing shadows of her gaunt, tall figure on the polished marble floor.

"Happy Midwinter Feast," she said at last, turning so she would be able to see everyone. "Are you all having fun?" Laughter and a couple of shouted joking comments followed her words, making everyone smile. After a pause, though, the director's expression turned serious. "Another year draws to an end. It has been another year of hard work, of sacrifices, of things lost, but also of things gained. Before we each present the gift we bring to the colony, let us take a moment to remember those who have passed on and to welcome those who have just arrived."

Right on cue, a small projector above each of the tables blinked to life and displayed images of the colonists who had died during the year. There was absolute silence as the slideshow ran its course, and Elias saw a couple of people at other tables crying silently. When the images ended, there was one more minute of silence in honor of those who had left. Then the director clapped, and a couple and a man stood up.

"This year, we welcome two new citizens of Portree," the director said, smiling. The couple and the man each carried a baby and walked until they were standing next to the director. "What are their names?"

The woman from the couple took a step forward. She was Freda MacLeod, Chief Psychologist of Portree. "This is Gwendolyn MacLeod," she announced proudly, "my second daughter."

"Welcome, Gwendolyn MacLeod," the director proclaimed. Then everyone in the room echoed her words.

Freda took a step back, and the solitary man stepped forward. He was Kenji Matsuo, the apprentice to Chef Matsuo. Elias realized that Kenji looked much older this year, although he was only twenty-five. He supposed it had to do with the fact that Kenji's wife had passed away in the summer. She had been killed by a wurl.

"This is Hikari Matsuo," he announced. "Named after my wife. My first and only daughter. May she mirror the light of my beloved."

"Welcome, Hikari Matsuo," the director said. After repeating her words, all the citizens of Portree burst into spontaneous applause. It was always a happy event to welcome someone new into the colony. As he clapped, though, Elias couldn't suppress the thought that every year there were fewer babies being presented.

"The time has come for the gift-giving," Director O'Rourke said into the lull of the waning applause. "I will begin the ceremony myself, as befits the person whose job it is to serve you all. My gift to Portree this year is this: an updated interface to every person's link, in a patch able to be downloaded, starting from this moment. It will give you, at a glance, the progress status of all the administrative projects currently being undertaken by the colony. It will also make it faster and more efficient to vote on neighborhood initiatives, with current trends being displayed in real time. Finally, and the change I am most excited about, is that you will now have a direct line to my office with the new interface. You may contact me directly at any time to address any issue which affects the colony as a whole. I believe this new system will suit our current needs much better than the older interface, which was designed with other objectives in mind. Thank you."

She sat down to enthusiastic applause, and Elias spotted a few people already tapping on their links to download the new software. Although Elias supposed it was a cool new feature to have, he couldn't suppress the insidious thought that such a system of direct communication with the director was only possible now because there were so few citizens left. The larger a colony was, the more complicated it would be to run it. This was simply another in the long string of changes to adapt to the awful reality that everyone was stubbornly denying.

The night progressed, and the combination of tons of food and a boring procession of people presenting gifts made Elias sleepy. It was only when all the adults had finished presenting their contributions that the spike of nervousness made itself felt once again. Now it was time for the teenagers to show what they had done. Although nobody officially expected anything of them until they turned seventeen, the unspoken rule was that the sooner they were able to present gifts, the better.

Sarah stood up first, rattling off a series of accomplishments instead of a single gift, making them sound very impressive. In fact, she received a larger ovation that the director herself, and Elias could tell that Sarah was aiming for that very position one day. He supposed it was just as well. Somebody had to run the colony.

Tristan stood up next, to loud supporting hoots from the patrol members scattered around the room. The silence from everyone else as they watched him advance to the center of the room was absolute, loaded with something Elias had to struggle for a while in order to place. It felt like respect.

Tristan carried a big, bumpy-looking pack in one hand, and when he reached the center spot, he emptied the pack on the floor. Wurl spines clattered onto the marble. Five in total, jagged, radiating threatening malice.

"One for every creature I have killed," Tristan said, grinning with confidence. "This is my gift to Portree!"

Just that. His was the shortest gift-giving speech yet, but the applause he received was deafening. Elias saw Tristan's father beaming with pride. The patrol members started banging on the tables, adding to the din, and the director herself stood up and walked over to Tristan in order to hug him. She then commanded silence with a gesture and addressed everyone with a wide smile.

"Our youngest Patrol member is also one of the most talented," O'Rourke said. "He has been personally responsible for saving a life already, not two days ago, when young Elias Trost wandered off on his own outside the perimeter. In light of this, I think it is time to invest Tristan MacLeod with the title he has long since earned. Commander Rodriguez, if you could join us up here for a moment."

Amanda Rodriguez did not appear surprised, but everyone else was, Elias included. Was this really happening? Was Tristan about to made an official member of the Patrol, even though he wasn't seventeen yet?

Elias followed the commander with his eyes, watching how the firelight danced and shifted on her scarred features. She came to a stop beside Tristan and Director O'Rourke.

"Commander Rodriguez," the director said, "you have the floor."

Rodriguez nodded curtly. "I'll keep this short. Tristan is a good element. He's quick to learn, reliable, and disciplined. He's killed more wurl than me when I was his age, and I think it's high time that he be made Colony Patrol officer. With your leave, Madam Director."

Elias's eyes never left Tristan, and he was able to see how Tristan's face betrayed his emotions. First shock. He obviously hadn't been expecting it. Then beaming happiness.

"I approve this motion," the director said, "but Portree is a democracy, and every citizen's voice must be heard." She nodded to Harold, who quickly began to type something on his link. "A motion has been sent to each and every one of you of voting age. Should Tristan MacLeod be granted the position of patrol officer, along with the authority and responsibility that goes with it?"

Dozens of people looked down and typed into their wrist links. It was quick. In less than one minute, the director gestured for quiet once more.

"A unanimous vote: yes," she announced. "Tristan, step forward."

"Yes, Madam Director!"

"Do you swear to abide by the law of Portree, to protect its citizens to the best of your ability, and to give your life in the defense of our colony, should it be necessary?"

"I swear," Tristan said, his voice like flint.

"Do you swear to uphold the moral obligations your authority will entail, to respect the commands of your superior officer, and to place the needs of others before your own?"

"I swear."

Harold walked quickly up to the director and handed her a shiny patrol badge.

O'Rourke held the badge high. "And do you swear to carry this badge with honor until the last of your days?"

"I swear."

The director smiled, pinning the badge to the front of Tristan's uniform. "Welcome to the force, Tristan." She straightened up and addressed everyone. "Citizens of Portree, our new Colony Patrol officer!"

Thunderous applause followed her words. The other patrol officers rushed forward to congratulate Tristan, patting him on the back, some shouting, some smiling broadly. Even Commander Rodriguez, who seldom had any expression on her face besides a frown, cracked a smile and said some quiet words to Tristan, which Elias couldn't hear over the din.

Slowly, the ruckus died down. Tristan resumed his seat, and an expectant silence followed.

It's my turn, Elias realized, after nobody else made an attempt to stand up and offer a gift. *Crap. I have a bad feeling about this.*

But he had to do it. He was nervous as hell, but it had to be done.

He stood up.

The hushed whispers began even before he had left his table, and Elias could feel the weight of a hundred pairs of eyes on his back as he made his way to the spot where Tristan had stood not one minute ago. It seemed like he would never reach his goal. He began to have second thoughts, clutching the journal to his chest. He hoped he wouldn't trip and make a fool out of himself. What was he going to tell them, again?

Then he was there. Dead center. He stopped and looked up. Everyone was watching him.

"I also have a gift!" he called out, and he was surprised by the volume in his voice. He lifted the journal high in one hand and wished his fingers would stop trembling. "I mean, I found something. It's important." All eyes were on him, and suddenly Elias's mind was blank. His panic mounted as seconds dragged on. What was he supposed to say? How had he decided to begin?"

"What is your gift, Elias?" the director asked him. The *director*. She was speaking directly to him. It was probably the first time ever, at least that Elias could remember.

The journal. Elias realized he was still holding it high and lowered his arm, already feeling embarrassed. Somebody snickered off to his right. They would all probably have a good laugh about this tomorrow, telling each other the details of Elias's worst moment.

Elias's eyes roamed the room, darting everywhere. Tristan was looking at him, frowning. Sarah had an open scowl on her face. His mother looked worried, and Oscar was obviously scared.

Oscar. He deserved to know. This was about his future, and that of everyone. Elias blinked, and it was as if someone had shifted his focus back in gear. His priorities fell right into place, neatly stacked in his mind.

"This is the personal journal of Dr. Thomas Wright, one of the original members of our mothership, *Ionas*." Several eyebrows shot up in surprise. "I found it while working in his abandoned lab, which I have studied for almost three years."

"Instead of actually working," someone muttered, loud enough to be heard. Elias could have sworn it was Sarah, but when he looked, she was blinking innocently at him.

He ignored the comment. He had to get this out now, while he had their attention. "I don't know why there are no records of him, but Dr. Wright was one of the most important of our pioneers. He was a xenobiologist, and he studied the animals and plants of this world better than anyone then or since. He discovered the Life Seed." Elias paused, and a flurry of whispers followed his words. "It's true. He was the one who figured out how to use the Seed to mix its genetic material with our crops so they would be able to survive on New Skye. He saved the colony during its first years, and by doing so he saved all our lives.

"He was honored and respected for a while. But then something started happening to the crops. It's all here in the journal, the gradual decline in yield year after year, the usage of more and more aggressive methods to sustain a growing colony, and finally the doctor's conclusion. I know you probably all know this, but New Skye used to be different. Really different. In summer, flowers would blanket the fields, fruits would hang from trees, and there would be life everywhere. After the Life Seed was taken from its resting place, the world changed. Winter became longer, summer shorter. Doctor Wright believed that the life on our world is more intricately linked than on other planets. He had destabilized the balance by taking the Life Seed, and in the end he said that it had to be returned to the place where it was taken. Or else this planet, and us, are doomed."

Several people spoke at once, the tone in all the voices adversarial. One of them stood up quickly, though, commanding attention. Elias's aunt, Laura.

"Eli, what are you saying?"

"We need to take the Life Seed back to the place where it was taken from. If we do that, we'll end the winter!"

Laura frowned. "We need that Seed to survive. It's the only thing that's kept us going for this long."

"But it has to be returned! It says right here—"

"That's enough of that, Elias," Laura told him. "I've worked with the Life Seed all my life. I know it better than most here, and you would too had you ever accepted my invitations to become my apprentice. You can be certain that, as long as I live, it is not going anywhere."

Elias looked at his aunt, dumbfounded. "But... but...."

"Have a seat," his aunt said. "You've had your fun."

"This is not about fun!" Elias shouted, stunning the congregation into silence. From the back, Commander Rodriguez stood up, looking at Elias with mistrust.

This isn't happening, he thought frantically. *They have to listen.*

"Can't you see?" he said to all of them. "We are dying out. We are starving, all of us!"

"Bradford, control your son," the director said in a curt tone. Elias's father rose obediently and walked over to him.

"No!" Elias protested. "Look around! Every year there are fewer of us. Every year we ration the food more and more. The crops are dying. It doesn't matter how much we splice them if the world around us is dead! When was the last time you saw a summer flower? Huh? I've never eaten purpleberries in my *life*, but I know they exist! We did something to this world when we came, and if we don't correct it, then we're going to die with it. All of us, even the babies."

"Elias. Quiet," Bradford Trost said.

Elias's chest was heaving. "I have proof," he told them. "The doctor's notes."

"Which you could have forged," Laura accused him.

"I didn't! There's the lab too! All the records are there!"

"Then why have we never heard of this Dr. Wright?" Laura asked him. "Why aren't his records in the mainframe?"

"I don't know! Maybe it was a conspiracy or...." But everywhere he looked, Elias saw only accusatory stares.

"You've shamed me enough, son," his father whispered. Elias had never seen him angrier.

His own anger was greater, though. "Fine!" Elias shouted. "Keep pretending nothing's happening! Keep pretending everything's all right and starve to death! I'm done here."

He let the journal fall on the marble floor and ran out of the hall before anyone could catch him.

Before anyone could see him cry.

Chapter 8
Thief

HE ESCAPED to the lab, of course. It was the only place where he could feel safe now that the world had turned its back on him.

Elias ran through the darkness, stumbling, not even caring about possible stalking wurl in the shadows. Let them come. They would kill him quickly enough, and then everybody would be damn glad to be rid of him, the crazy boy who made stuff up.

"Come at me!" he shouted at the night, running faster still.

Breathless, he arrived at the lab a few minutes later. Moonlight cast everything in a silver light, and the chill of the wintertime was a welcome discomfort. Elias jumped down the entry chute, banging his leg against something in the careless fall. Furious, he kicked whatever it was out of the way before stumbling in the dark until he found the generator switch. He flipped it on, and flickering light flooded the underground space.

Elias sat down heavily on his chair. He felt like crying more, but he refused to give in to the emotion. It would be an admission of weakness, and now that everyone hated him, it was something he could not indulge in.

But it hurt. It hurt to remember how his aunt had talked to him, her scathing tone, when before she had only been gentle every time Elias had seen her. And what his father had said, about the shame Elias had brought upon him....

It's not fair, Elias thought furiously. *I was telling the truth. Nobody listens because they're all cowards!*

Tears came anyway, but Elias refused to acknowledge them. The cold of the night crept upon him, making him shiver. Sweat from his earlier run made his skin clammy. It drenched his shirt and made it stick to his back. The generator huffed, working as hard as it could, but the heat it provided was pitiful.

I can't stay here. And I won't go back home.

Maybe.... Maybe I should run away.

But he shook his head, wiping the tears off. He didn't want to abandon his family. He cared about them, and about the rest of the colony. *That* was the problem. He cared about what happened to the people of Portree because they were his people, even those who were complete assholes to him. He had spent years inside this stupid laboratory for that precise reason, hoping to find a solution, or at least the cause of the problem.

Now he had found it. And nobody believed him.

Besides, where would he go? In a world doomed to eternal winter, where nothing grew regardless of the amount of sunlight the planet received, he would starve to death even faster than the people he left behind. It was a choice, he supposed. Die slowly out there or die more slowly in here, powerless to stop the relentless decline, watching their food supplies dwindle every year. Giving the Life Seed back was the only way, but they would never agree to it. Nobody was brave enough to do what had to be—

Done.

Elias straightened up in his chair, considering the sudden, yet inevitable, idea. It was defiance beyond anything he had ever done. It was heresy—madness. Worse, if he was wrong, then he would be taking away the only renewable source of the genetic material that was used to boost the colony's failing crops.

But he was right. He was convinced of it, and he stood up, turned off the generator, and climbed back outside. There was plenty of moonlight to see by, and from where he stood, Portree looked like a tiny cluster of civilization surrounded by wilderness. Most of the lights were off too. Everybody was probably still at the Midwinter Feast.

Elias walked in the direction of the gene lab, his brow furrowed with resolve. There were safeguards around the Life Seed. And if any patrol officers were posted around it, then it would be impossible to take it. But he had to try.

When the wurl alarm started to blare, Elias nearly jumped out of his skin. He was halfway back to Portree, and a quick glance at his link told him that wurl had been picked up by sensors on the eastern side of the colony. Opposite from where he was.

It's a sign, he thought, almost disbelieving of his good fortune, increasing his pace. *I'm doing the right thing. Everyone's at the Main Hall, and they won't leave until the wurl are dealt with. And all the Colony Patrol grunts will go handle the invaders.*

His quick walk became a run. This was a golden opportunity, and he meant to take full advantage of it. He didn't think about the consequences of what he was doing if by chance he was caught. His quick stride took him right back to the colony, and he headed for the genetics complex without slowing down. He halted at the outside door, panting slightly, on edge at every sound. He looked left and right anxiously when he heard a faint rustle in the dry grass, fearing to see a wurl or a patrol officer or just about anything. There was no one around, though. Elias lifted his link up to the scanner and the door clicked, allowing him in.

He walked past silent hallways that were being dutifully cleaned by small maintenance drones. The halo-shaped robotic units wiped and scrubbed every surface, paying no mind to Elias as he hurried to a particular set of heavy doors. He stood still when he reached them, allowing the biometric scanner to work, and then pushed the doors open as soon as he was granted access.

There was nobody in the inner sanctum. It was odd to see the place so empty, especially since it was the one place in all of Portree where there was always at least one person on duty, watching over things, carrying out some work. Tonight was special because of the feast, however. No one stopped Elias as he made his way to the center of the huge room, the glow of hundreds of computer monitors lighting the path. He stopped in front of the Life Seed, hovering gently inside its magnetic cradle. The alien plant was enclosed in a cylinder of bulletproof glass, but the access panel was right there. Elias keyed in the opening sequence, using the password his aunt had given him when she had still hoped he would become her apprentice. It worked. The Life Seed's protective cover lifted with a faint whoosh of pressurized air, exposing its precious contents.

Elias reached forward, hands trembling slightly. He feared the magnetic field would offer resistance, but his fingers closed around the Life Seed easily. He yanked it out of the cradle and stumbled backward.

It was lighter than he had expected, but strangely warm to the touch. Its surface was velvety, and Elias perceived the unnerving yet unmistakable beating of something inside the Seed.

Then every alarm in the compound went off.

Elias yelped, surprised by the sudden cacophony of sound and the harsh red lighting. His link buzzed, alerting him that someone had taken the Seed, and he knew that everybody's link was buzzing with the exact same notification. Panicking, Elias tucked the Seed under one arm and ran out of the laboratory. He stumbled into the open, breathless, and turned around to see that a second later, the security vault doors closed around the compound, isolating it to try and contain the thief.

He had to run. As far away as possible, as fast as he could.

He pelted across the moonlit landscape, the warm Seed beating against his chest, and at first he headed for the abandoned laboratory by sheer force of habit. Then he realized it was the first place they would look as soon as they reviewed the security tapes, and his stride faltered. He couldn't go there. He had to go straight to the place where the Life Seed had been found, to the Aberdeen Mountains in the northwest.

He switched direction, altering his course but not slowing down. He did not stop once until he was far enough away from the colony that he couldn't hear the wurl siren anymore. His link, too, stopped buzzing. He was outside the colony's transmit range.

A stitch in his side forced him to stop. He slowed down to a halt, gulping for air, and leaned against a tree. The Life Seed felt hot now, but Elias was more interested in whether anybody had followed him. He remained very still, listening, straining his senses to the utmost. Nothing. The night around him was serene and quiet, the silence broken only once by the mournful call of a swipebird.

I did it. I can't believe I actually did it.

He wasn't sure whether he was ecstatic or horrified. There was no going back now, though. He had to get to those mountains and return the Seed to where it belonged.

He kept on going in the same direction after a brief pause, no longer running because he had crossed into the woods and it was a hard path; treacherous roots and sharp branches seemed to come out of nowhere. Even though the trees were devoid of leaves, as they had been for years now, their trunks eclipsed much of the moonlight, and there were deep shadows concealing obstacles at every step. Elias walked tirelessly, still relying on his adrenaline high, and the radiator-like heat of the Seed was more than enough protection from the winter cold. It was only when dawn began to gray the horizon to the east that Elias slowed down, yawning. He was absolutely exhausted. He looked around for a place to sleep, somewhere he would be safe in case any wurl came looking. The trees were the obvious solution. Elias walked around until he found an imposing great yult, its trunk a perfect obsidian black. Yults were massive, often reaching heights of thirty meters or more, and they were wide enough around the base that five people holding hands could barely encompass them. They were also good for hiding, because their branches were thick and flat.

Elias looked up at the tree he had chosen. It had been ages since he had climbed a yult, but his childhood muscle memory served him well. It was awkward going, first placing the Seed on a branch, then pulling himself up onto the same. He repeated the process more than a dozen times, stopping only when he was dangerously high above the ground and the branches had thinned out somewhat. From the high vantage point he could see very far, but the light wasn't good enough to make out any details. At least here he would be safe from wurl.

He undid his belt and looped it around the branch, securing it tight around his midsection so he wouldn't fall. Then he sat with his back to the trunk, wrapped his arms around the welcome warmth of the Life Seed, and tried to sleep.

It wasn't easy. Elias feared he would fall every time he began drifting off, or that he would drop the Seed, so he spent several pitiful hours dozing but not quite sleeping. The cold seeped underneath his jacket, too, making him shiver in spite of the Seed's warmth. Every sound startled him wide-awake as well. All in all, he was pathetically grateful when the sun finally rose over the canopy, drenching everything in welcoming warm sunlight. Elias yawned, even more tired than when he had settled down. He rubbed his eyes, undid the clasp of his belt around the branch, and secured the Life Seed under one arm. Time to climb down.

A hint of movement below caught his attention. Elias froze, looking out. Something was moving among the trees, far away in the southeast still, but unmistakable. Elias waited until he could get a good look, and his patience was soon rewarded. It was the outline of a person, tiny with distance but distinct enough that Elias could make out the shock spear the figure held in one hand.

He was being followed.

He gulped, climbing down from the tree as fast as he could. The patrol had come after him. He couldn't believe it. And if they caught him....

No. I can't let them catch me.

He landed on the brittle grass around the yult. His link wasn't connected to the colony network anymore, but basic functions like a compass were still accessible, and he was easily able to determine which way was northwest. Making sure his grip on the Life Seed was secure, he set off at a run in the direction of the mountains.

It was hard to keep a good pace. Another adrenaline surge in his veins helped Elias for a while, but he soon got tired of navigating the unforgiving terrain among the trees, dodging obstacles and carrying the apparently increasing weight of the Seed in his arms. He was also climbing as the land around him rose to meet the distant mountain peaks, which he could glimpse every now and then through the trees. The slope wasn't too pronounced yet, but it could not be ignored, and as noon struck, Elias slowed to a walk.

Crisp, invigorating air greeted him when he crested a hilltop devoid of trees. It was chilly, but Elias was sweating profusely, and he welcomed the refreshing wind. Wiping his brow with the back of his hand, he took stock of the land around him.

It was breathtakingly beautiful.

Elias had never left Portree in all his life, and although he was familiar with the topography of New Skye from his geography class at school, it simply wasn't the same as seeing it firsthand. The view from the hilltop allowed him to see very far away to the north and the west, where the landscape changed dramatically from the deep forest he had been crossing. The terrain rose and fell in progressively higher folds, like a shockwave frozen solid, testament to the creation of the mountain range that rose above it all, hazy with distance, the white peaks far above a few wispy clouds. The hillsides between him and the mountains were mostly devoid of trees, covered instead by short tan-and-gray grass that splayed out in beautifully complex patterns, occasionally broken by large boulder formations that rose up from the ground in strange places, appearing to defy gravity. Elias could even see the shadows the clouds cast on the ground as they moved along with the wind. Although desolate, the land was also hauntingly serene, as if it merely lay in wait for something to happen.

Elias broke the spell of the awe-inspiring landscape with a shake of his head. He looked back, among the trees, but he could see no sign of the patrol member who had been following him. Still, it would be best to hurry. Now that he was out of the trees, Elias would have no cover, aside from the big rock formations farther away, until he reached the mountains. It would be easy to spot him... and to catch him.

He set off at a quick trot, not quite running anymore, but determined to reach his goal.

Hunger soon made itself felt, along with ravaging thirst. According to his link, Elias had been moving nonstop for nearly six hours since he had woken on the yult, and the paltry winter sun had moved all the way across the sky and was now preparing to set, throwing long shadows across the land. Elias realized he hadn't planned ahead at all. He didn't even have a water bottle with him, let alone anything to eat, and although he'd had a ton of food at the feast, his stomach rumbled ominously, demanding more. His legs were also beginning to ache in silent protest against the punishing pace Elias insisted on keeping. Elias had never been a very athletic guy, and it was beginning to show. His arms and back ached as well, the result of his having to carry the Life Seed without a backpack or anything else to help him deal with the load. By the time Elias reached the foot of a hill with a much sharper slope than the others, strewn with little rocks that would certainly make climbing an ordeal, he simply stopped in exhausted despair.

"Just a bit," he whispered to himself. "I'm only going to rest for a bit."

He sat down on the dry grass, looking back the way he had come. He could see no one following, which was good. Maybe he had lost them after all. But that meant he was on his own out in the wilderness. With no food, no water, and no shelter.

Although he was able to rest, remaining motionless in one spot brought along a whole new set of problems. He was very exposed out in the highlands, and the wind blew relentlessly. Although the sky was clear and the sun still shone feebly in the west, its light brought no comfort. The ground underneath Elias's hands was cold, nearly frozen, and it seemed to leech warmth away from him. The Life Seed on his lap was hot, thankfully, but even with it, Elias realized he was shivering. His clothes stuck to his skin, clammy with sweat. His lips were cracked by the dry gales, his mouth parched. His temples pounded with a headache that was beginning to make him feel nauseated, although he was sure there was nothing in his stomach for him to vomit.

A sudden gust of frigid wind nearly made him topple over, and he realized he couldn't stay there. He stood up, his legs already stiff. His right knee felt wobbly, but he trudged up the hillside nevertheless. He tried to follow a zigzag course that would make the slope less punishing, and he ended up rounding the hill, reaching a cleft in the rocks that spread open like a jagged scar in the earth, cutting him off from his way closer to the mountains.

Panting, Elias walked to the edge of the abyss. A river flowed at the bottom, its waters white with foam. Simply hearing the water made Elias open his mouth and inhale deeply, as if he could somehow extract the moisture from the air. He had to get to that river somehow. He was thirsty enough that his vision was beginning to blur.

The problem was that the river was at least ten meters below him, and the walls of the cleft it had cut between the hills were smooth rock, impossible to descend. The sun had set by then too. In the quickly fading twilight, Elias realized that he had little time to find a way to get water. He watched the river for a few seconds, his mind racing. It was flowing from right to left, and Elias remembered hearing somewhere that rivers always flowed down. He decided to follow the cleft in the rock upstream, hefting the Life Seed on one shoulder and keeping it more or less steady with a shaking hand. He dragged his feet as he went, lacking the energy to go much faster. The slope along the riverside quickly rose, but as it did, the distance between Elias and the foaming river decreased. He kept walking, following the meandering paths of the stream, dodging rocks and clumps of dry grass, telling himself that he would soon be drinking plenty of water. His face felt numb from exposure to the merciless chill wind, however. The hand that was not holding the Life Seed ached from the cold.

He was rewarded for his efforts as true night fell over the land. Elias finally reached a plateau on the highlands, a wide and flat expanse of terrain through which the river cut with the precision of a knife. The river's banks were wide and shallow, and Elias was pathetically grateful to fall down on his knees and dip his hands in blessed icy water. He brought it up to his lips and drank too quickly, which made him choke and sputter. As soon as he recovered, he did it again. He didn't even care that the water was so cold. Water was life, and it was all he ever needed.

Soon his thirst was slaked, though, and the chill of the night reached out to seize him with a steely fist. He was shivering fiercely now, and Elias realized that by drinking all that freezing water, he had probably decreased his core temperature significantly.

And he was tired. He could not remember feeling more tired in his life, and he yawned several times, his lower jaw trembling. He reached for the Life Seed and held it to him, clinging to its warmth now that night was upon him. Elias's headache was getting worse all the time, and after a few minutes of trying to keep the water down, he was forced to crawl to the river's edge and vomit. He felt better after he had done so, but only marginally. And the wind was picking up.

He crawled to one of the rock formations that rose very close to a spot where the river plunged down suddenly, deeper into the hillside in a large waterfall. Touching the boulders, Elias realized they still held some warmth from the sun, and he quickly built a small fort out of the smaller ones, a single wall really, leaning against the towering rock formation with its sharp angles and grass-covered exposed sections. He nestled into the corner formed by his makeshift shelter and immediately felt the warmth radiating from the sun-warmed rocks on his back, while the Life Seed in his arms heated up his chest and legs.

He wasn't comfortable, but at least he wasn't shivering anymore. The light of the moons was reflected in the swift current of the river a few paces away. The foam from the waterfall rose into the air farther away, and the wind carried with it a moist, earthy smell. As he watched the night spectacle, Elias saw a couple of ryddle birds corkscrewing through the air, their white plumage shining in the moonlight. They were silent as they glided down, hopping gracefully to the edge of the riverside. They had long, many-jointed legs, serrated beaks, and three dark eyes dotting their feathery foreheads. Elias stayed very still, knowing that ryddle birds could be aggressive if they felt threatened, and he watched them as they turned their heads this way and that, looking at the river waters. One of them hopped into the river itself, somehow managing not to be carried away by the current, and pitched its head forward, beak slightly open. A few seconds passed and the bird held its position, motionless, until it suddenly struck. It plunged its body into the current, disappearing from view only to explode out of the water in a burst of sparkling droplets. It flapped its powerful wings, spiraling back onto the shore. There was a small fish caught in it beak, which it promptly devoured.

Elias's head fell forward, onto the Life Seed. He was so tired that he was asleep even before his arms relaxed, allowing the Seed to tumble out of his grasp onto the moist riverside.

Chapter 9
The Wilderness of New Skye

ELIAS AWOKE to bright sunlight, an aching neck, and ravenous hunger.

It took him a moment to realize where he was. He was lying with his head leaning awkwardly on one of the rocks he had piled yesterday, and as he sat up, he massaged a crick in his neck with fingers numb from the awful cold. His breath was ragged in his lungs, and he coughed several times while he rubbed some feeling back into his legs. He hoped he hadn't caught pneumonia, but there was no helping it if he had.

Everything hurt. Elias stumbled upright, walked a few paces away from the river and relieved himself while trying to count how many places in his body hurt. He stopped when he reached twenty. His feet ached, and his left ankle felt a little swollen. Both his knees hurt when he bent them, and the muscles in his back protested at the slightest motion. His shoulders were stiff and his biceps wobbly. Even his jaw was sore, and his nose felt numb, nearly frozen.

He zipped up his pants. The good news was that he had no signs of frostbite anywhere, which he was able to confirm by wiggling his fingers and toes and touching his nose and ears. Aside from a faint rattling in his lungs whenever he took a deep breath, he didn't feel too bad. The problem was the hunger, which was slowly awakening again in the pit of his stomach. It gurgled when Elias scooped up handfuls of freezing water to drink. He could see a few fish swimming in the river, but they were too small and quick for him to catch, and he wouldn't be able to eat them even if he caught them. He would have to go hungry for another day.

It was strange, in a way. Elias was used to not eating very much, but he had never actually gone an entire day without food while simultaneously exercising more than he ever had in his life. It felt awful. And it drove home the fact that if he allowed things in the colony to reach the point of starvation, everyone would suffer as he was suffering right now.

The Seed.

He blinked. He didn't have it with him. Where…?

Thankfully, he spotted it right away. It was lying a short distance from the river's edge, and Elias rushed forward, fearing that it would topple into the river to be lost forever. When he was close enough to stand over it, however, he froze. There was no way the Seed would have fallen in, not with the thorny branches of a flowering bush anchoring it to the ground.

Elias kneeled in front of the strange bush. There were plants similar to it near Portree, but they were always bare, the woody stalks covered with spines and nothing else. This bush, however, was short and round and covered with beautiful green leaves. In several places between the leaves, tiny purple flowers with three petals each had blossomed. They were beautiful, but that wasn't all. In many places, the branches held not flowers, but fruit. A specific kind of fruit.

Small purpleberries grew in clusters all over the bush, weighing the branches down with their bounty. Their smooth leathery skin was the same color as the flower petals, each of them about half as big as a Terran cherry.

"No way," Elias whispered. "What the hell?"

He touched the bush experimentally. It felt real.

How come I didn't see it last night?

He couldn't understand it. It was the only bush growing on the river banks, and although last night had been dark, he would have definitely spotted something like this. What was a purpleberry bush doing in the middle of nowhere, next to the Life Seed?

Unless…. Unless it wasn't here before.

Elias reached forward and grabbed the Life Seed. When he tried to lift it, there was resistance. He pulled harder, and it tore free of the ground. Lifting it up, Elias realized that three slender growths had come out of the flower bud, like the roots of a tree. They had tunneled into the ground, from the looks of it. Directly underneath the purpleberry bush.

The logical conclusion was too fantastic for him to accept. Instead, he placed the Life Seed carefully nearby and sat down next to the bush. He proceeded to pick it clean, gathering every berry he could find. Then he ate.

The berries were delicious. He had never tasted anything quite like them—a mixture of sweet and tart with a wonderfully chewy pulp inside. He'd had purpleberry jam when he was little, but its flavor was nowhere near the awesomeness of the fresh fruit. Purple juice dripped down his chin as he stuffed his mouth with handfuls of the berries, swallowing gratefully and enraptured with several pleasant sensations at the same time. The berries quenched his thirst and sated his hunger. Better still, the headache in his temples abated, and soon his stomach was pleasantly full. About five minutes later, he simply could eat no more. Several handfuls of the berries remained, and he stuffed them in the zip-up pockets of his jacket. He lay down on the hard ground, looked up at the beautiful azure winter sky, and allowed himself to relax for the first time since escaping from the colony.

He heard the noise then, clearly. A voice, shouting.

Elias scrambled to his feet, looking around wildly. He saw the patrol officer right away, cresting a hill not half a kilometer back the way he had come.

"Stay right there, thief!" the officer shouted, and Elias recognized the voice.

Tristan.

Elias wasted no time. He snatched the Life Seed from the ground and sprinted off at a run along the river's bank. Behind him he heard Tristan shouting his name, but he didn't even turn around. He had to outrun him.

Unfortunately, Tristan was too quick. He was running at an angle to Elias in such a way that he was going to cut him off from escape, and Elias was forced to stop when he realized he would not be able to outrun his pursuer in that direction. He turned around and rushed left, back the way he had originally come the day before. Anything was better than being caught. He passed by the purpleberry bush without stopping, his eyes scanning the river for a spot where he might cross. It was too wide, though. And the current looked fast.

Footsteps sounded behind him, closer all the time. Elias allowed himself one rapid glance and saw Tristan running full-out after him, much closer than he would have expected. Dismayed, Elias forced his legs to pump faster, not even caring that he might stumble on the uneven terrain. He skirted past a tall rock formation and did not slow down until he reached the edge of the highland plateau, a few meters away from the spot where the river plummeted down into a waterfall, the foaming current visible far below.

"Stop!" Tristan shouted. A hand grasped Elias's shoulder.

He shrugged it off desperately and saw he had no choice. Tristan was too fast.

He jumped into the river.

The water was a shock of absolute cold. Elias stumbled, and very nearly lost his footing in the quick current because he wouldn't let go of the large Life Seed in his hands. Fortunately, the water reached only up to his knees and he kept his balance. The waterfall threatened nearby, a deadly drop.

"Citizen, come back here this instant," Tristan said to him, standing at the river's edge with a murderous expression in his eyes.

"I don't think so," Elias sputtered, defiant. Then he began to wade across the stream as fast as he could. His teeth were chattering, and when he heard the splash behind him that unmistakably meant Tristan had jumped as well, he tried to go even faster. The river deepened around the middle, though, and soon the water was almost up to his waist. The current became stronger. Every time he lifted his foot, Elias was in danger of being carried away.

Terrified yet determined, Elias poured every erg of energy available to his tired leg muscles and managed to reach firmer footing on the opposite bank. Dripping and shivering, he waded out of the water and climbed to solid ground as soon as he was able. He risked a momentary look back.

Tristan burst out of the river in a spray of icy droplets. His uniform was soaked from the waist down and he had lost his helmet, but he still held the shock spear in both hands. Elias dashed back out of instinct and barely dodged the dangerous weapon as Tristan swung it in an arc aimed at his midsection. The motion destabilized Elias. He fell on his back and the Life Seed tumbled from his grasp.

"Gotcha," Tristan said triumphantly and pounced.

Elias reached up with both hands and managed to grab on to the spear just as Tristan fell on top of him, grunting, his breath steaming in the cold air. Elias kicked upward and struck something soft, making Tristan grimace. It earned him only momentary respite, though. Tristan straddled him, pushing down all the time with both hands on the spear.

He was strong. Elias fought him back with everything he had, but the shaft of the spear came down slowly but inexorably against his resistance. Desperate, Elias realized his strength was about to give out. He tried kicking again, but Tristan was out of range.

"Surrender," Tristan panted, his face mere centimeters away.

"Go… to hell."

Elias did the only thing he could. He brought his head up and smashed his forehead against Tristan's nose. Tristan cried out, and his grip on the spear slackened. With a last surge of strength, Elias managed to heave his opponent to the right, out of the way. Elias then rolled on the ground until he was clear and jumped onto his feet. The Life Seed was nearby, and he snatched it up.

"You can't run," Tristan said, hefting his spear in one hand and wiping off the blood that dripped onto his upper lip from his nose with the other. "I'm faster than you. Stronger."

Elias looked every which way desperately, but Tristan was right. He had also somehow positioned himself between Elias and the way out, trapping him with the river to his back. Elias could jump back into the water, but Tristan would simply follow. And this time, he might not be so lucky. He could fall down the waterfall, taking the Life Seed with him.

Wait.

He had an idea.

He edged backward, making Tristan scowl.

"Go on, try to get in the river again," Tristan said to him, walking forward slowly. "I'll get you."

"Let me go, Tristan," Elias said, his voice raspy. He coughed once, painfully.

"You're going to give back what you stole and then stand fair trial, citizen. You won't destroy the colony so easily."

"You've got it all wrong! I'm trying to save us, not destroy us. This Seed must be given back, or the world will never wake up from this eternal winter."

"You can tell that to the jury, although I don't think anyone will believe you. I can't believe you did this, Elias. Not you."

"You have to believe me. I'm doing the right thing!" Elias pleaded, still edging back until his foot grazed the river's edge. "Trust me. Like you used to do when we were kids."

Tristan actually halted, scowling. "I can't believe I was ever friends with a terrorist." He grasped his spear with both hands.

"Wait!" Elias shouted. He held the Life Seed up in both hands, ignoring the trembling of his exhausted muscles. "I'll throw it into the waterfall if you come any closer."

Tristan's eyes flicked between Elias, the Seed, and the waterfall behind. "Don't."

"I swear, Tristan. Leave me alone or I toss it over the edge."

"You can't do that. We need that Seed to survive!"

"Try me," Elias said, faking confidence. "You said it, right? I'm a terrorist. This is what I do. Terror. Boo."

Tristan shook his head slowly. "I didn't want to do this, but you're leaving me no choice."

He clicked a switch on the shaft of his weapon and the ends of the shock spear started glowing, electrified.

Elias blanched. He was done for. He wouldn't throw the Seed like he was threatening to do. It could be destroyed in the impact, lost forever, dooming both the world and Portree to slow starvation.

The fight left him. He lowered the Seed and looked at Tristan.

Motion at the edge of his vision caught his attention. Elias looked right, behind Tristan. Three shapes were approaching, tumbling down the slope of the hillside beyond. They were large, black, and their unmistakable rolling motion sent a shiver of fear down Elias's spine.

"Wurl," he whispered. Then he pointed. "Wurl!"

Tristan smirked, taking a step forward. "How stupid do you think I am? I'm not going to fall for that."

The ground trembled slightly as one of the large tumbling shapes crashed nearby. The other two did likewise, coming to a stop not one hundred meters away. Elias watched, horrified, as the majestic reptiles uncoiled their bodies. Their spines glistened in the morning light.

"Behind you," Elias said.

The wurl roared. All three of them lifted their snouts in unison, opening their jaws to display row after row of deadly teeth. The sound they made together was more horrible than anything Elias had ever heard.

"What the—" Tristan said, turning around with a feline jump, spear held across his chest. Elias couldn't see his face, but he noticed how Tristan tensed up as he saw the approaching wurl. To Tristan's credit, he did not back down. He stood his ground as the three creatures approached, their many legs waving through the dry grass in a sinuous and horrible motion. The cluster of three red eyes above their mandibles appeared to luminesce softly, making them look like crazed demons from the abyss.

Elias watched, petrified, as the wurl fanned out around Tristan, one on each side and one in front. They approached more cautiously now, following the movements of the spear, which Tristan twirled slowly in controlled spirals.

"Come and get me! Come on," Tristan taunted the creatures, and the effect of his voice was instantaneous. The three wurl growled, low in their throats, and as they took small, careful steps, they began moving their heads from side to side while keeping their eyes fixed on their prey. Elias could barely breathe, and he wasn't even the main focus of the wurl's anger. He couldn't understand how it was that Tristan remained standing where he was, defying them, even though he must have known this was an encounter that could end his life.

One of the reptiles moved closer than the others, coiled its head back, and struck.

"Tristan, look out!" Elias shouted, and all hell broke loose.

Tristan must have seen the attack coming from his left side, because he brought the spear down at the same time he twisted his body out of the way. The electrified tip of the weapon made contact with the first wurl's head, and the creature screamed in evident pain and backed away. The other two weren't far behind, though. They charged at Tristan, teeth bared.

Tristan was ready for them as well. He swung the spear in a wide arc that forced the creatures back, crouched, and then stabbed at the closest wurl. He made contact, the tip of his shock spear bursting into light. The wurl retreated, shaking its head, but the last one used Tristan's distraction to its advantage and tackled him, trampling him underfoot.

"Tristan!" Elias cried out. He heard Tristan groan in pain, but as soon as the wurl had passed, Tristan rolled out of the way and struck out with his weapon, hitting the creature in the middle of the tail. The impact was so strong that the electrified spear sliced through the wurl's carapace, exposing a bleeding kink in its tough armor.

The creature turned around, voicing its pain, and not even Tristan was fast enough to escape the retaliation. With eyes glowing bright red now, the wounded wurl fired a spine from its back that struck the spear right in the middle, breaking it in half.

It wasn't done yet. When Tristan tried to recover, it lunged again. Tristan jumped to the side, but the two other wurl got in his way. One of them smacked its tail against Tristan's legs and made him lose his footing. The wounded one attacked, snarling, and bit down on one of the ends of the broken weapon. It tore it out of Tristan's grasp and threw it far away with a flick of its massive neck muscles. Tristan backed away from the three reptiles, clutching the remaining end of his spear in his right hand. He rolled to the right as one of them fired a series of three spines that sunk into the earth where his feet had been. He tried to jump to his feet as he came out of the roll, but the wounded wurl struck. It clamped its jaws around Tristan's right arm. And twisted.

Tristan's howl of agony was horrible to hear. The creature let go, and Elias was horrified to see that Tristan's right forearm had been bent at an unnatural angle, clearly broken and punctured in a dozen places. Tristan was already losing blood.

Something happened inside Elias's mind as he saw Tristan fall to his knees in front of the three murderous beasts. His restraint gave way, his fear vanished, and he rushed forward with a primal bellow of defiance.

"Get. Off. Him!" he screamed, charging with animal fury.

The wurl lifted their heads as one. Elias jumped, landing in front of Tristan, and faced his attackers. Terrifying clusters of eyes regarded him, glowing.

"Go away!" Elias shouted, brandishing the only thing he had in his hands: the Life Seed.

The wurl whimpered and flattened their spines to their backs. They crouched low to the ground and slithered backward, watching the Seed intently.

Elias was very surprised, but he didn't allow himself time to think it over. He advanced, still brandishing the Life Seed from side to side, and the creatures gave way as if terrified of what he held in his hands. It was unbelievable, but the surge of relief Elias felt faded quickly when he realized that the wurl wouldn't leave. Elias tried chasing one of them away, but the others approached the spot where Tristan was kneeling, cradling his broken arm in his other hand. Elias repeated the process with all of them, but they backed away only a little and then came back.

Experimentally, Elias knelt next to Tristan and placed the Life Seed on the ground. The wurl kept their distance, not attacking, but neither giving any signs of wanting to leave.

"Tristan, are you okay?" Elias asked urgently.

Tristan had gone pale as a ghost, but he nodded. "What did you do? Why aren't they attacking?"

"I don't know. Can you stand? We have to get out of here."

"Yeah. I think so."

"Lean on me. Let me get the Seed."

Elias grabbed the Life Seed and helped Tristan get up. Slowly, the two of them walked away from the wurl, who merely turned to look at them. Elias was about to suggest they run when the creatures started following.

"Go away!" Elias threatened them, shoving the Seed forward. As before, though, the wurl merely retreated a little bit. When Elias and Tristan resumed walking, they followed.

Elias led Tristan along the riverside for nearly half an hour, but the wurl never stopped following. Dismayed, he finally made a stop when he realized that Tristan was obviously in great pain from his broken arm.

"Let's just stop," Elias told him. "I have to clean that wound and make a splint or something."

"Leave me alone," Tristan said roughly, pushing Elias away. "Are you doing this? Are you controlling them?"

"What? No!"

"Then what's happening?"

"I have no idea!" Elias exploded.

"They won't attack you. It's like you're one of them."

"It's the Seed. Tristan, don't be stupid. There's something about it. They recognize it."

"Go away," Tristan said, staring daggers at Elias. "That's what you wanted, right? Leave me to them and go throw the Life Seed away in some mountain cave. I'll be the first person you kill, Elias. All because you stole something that wasn't yours to take."

Fuming, Elias looked at Tristan for a long, long moment. He wanted to leave, of course. His mission was to save the colony, and that was more important than helping Tristan. He should go now, leave Tristan to the wurl, and return the Seed before another patrol officer found him.

Elias turned around and walked away.

"I knew it!" Tristan shouted after him. "You're just a coward!"

Elias stomped away, angrier than he had ever been in his life, but he hadn't taken more than ten steps when he heard the wurl growling. They had surrounded Tristan again, spines raised threateningly. Elias saw clearly the fierce defiance in Tristan's eyes as he faced his death.

He couldn't do it. Elias ran back, Seed held high. "Get out of here!" he shouted at the wurl. As before, they obeyed, keeping their distance meekly.

"What are you doing?" Tristan asked.

"Shut the hell up," Elias snapped. "We have to wash that wound and dry our clothes."

Chapter 10
Uneasy Companionship

THE WURL were never far. They followed the two young men as Elias led the way farther up the mountain highlands. Every time Elias looked back, at least one of the creatures was staring at the Seed intently. They would occasionally whimper, a strangely endearing sound coming from such large reptiles. Still, they remained dangerous, as Elias was able to attest when Tristan attempted to run away. One of the wurl dashed ahead, firing two spines into the ground, which forced Tristan to stop. Grudgingly, Tristan returned to where Elias was standing. The look he gave him was full of simmering anger.

The sun was high in the sky by the time Elias decided to halt for the first time. They were traversing a stretch of treacherous terrain that sloped up and down seemingly at random, the ground cracked in several places and hinting at deep caverns right below the surface. It was dangerous walking, and Elias's muscles were threatening to simply give out from exhaustion. He hadn't had time to rest properly since he had escaped from the colony, a lifetime ago.

"Let's eat," Elias said, sitting down on a flat sun-warmed rock. The warmth, at least, was very welcome. The wind at this altitude was even colder, and with no trees in sight to break it, it blew relentlessly.

"Whatever," Tristan replied, but he sat down some distance away. Elias noticed how Tristan grimaced when he accidentally bumped his broken arm against his knee.

"Does it hurt too bad?"

"What do you care?"

"I cared enough to make you a splint, didn't I?"

Elias nodded at the makeshift rig he had created to immobilize Tristan's forearm and prevent the fracture from getting worse. He had used one of the broken halves of the shock spear, along with torn strips from his own shirt. It wasn't pretty, but at least it kept the arm in a fixed position. Thankfully, Tristan hadn't bled very much. Even the puncture wounds from the wurl's bite had stopped bleeding, which was good. And there was no sign of infection.

"Why are you even doing this?" Tristan asked, scowling. "Why did you come back for me? You want to kill everyone in Portree. Why save me? Unless you want someone around to taunt and torment, is that it? Is this some kind of sick way of yours to get off?"

Elias rolled his eyes. "I think you're overdoing the evil supervillain bit, man. I already told you, I want to *save* the colony, not kill everyone in it. The notes I found in Dr. Wright's journal specifically say that the Life Seed is some kind of networked organism that shares genetic information with the rest of the planet. By taking it, we broke the cycle of the seasons. That's why nothing blooms in spring, why the trees are bare even in the heat of summer, and why our crops require more and more genetic modifications every year. Do you have any idea how much fertilizer and nutrient concentrates the geneticists are using nowadays just to get a seed to sprout?"

Tristan's scowl did not waver, but he shook his head in silent negative.

"Way too much," Elias continued, answering his own question. "I know. I've seen my aunt and her colleagues at work. Why do you think we have less and less food to go around every year? Why do you think we get rations now, instead of everybody eating whatever they want?"

"That's the way it's always been," Tristan replied. "It's better if we have control over what people eat."

"That's the stupidest thing you have ever said. Do you honestly believe that lie? Remember back when we were little, when we used to spend all day together? I would go to your house, and your mother would make us sandwiches and lemonade, and there were cookies we weren't supposed to have but we stole anyway. We would sometimes go to my house, just the two of us, and gather candy and whatever else was around for our secret camping trips."

At the mention of the last part, Tristan blinked. "Huh. The camping trips. I'd forgotten about them."

"Well, I haven't," Elias told him, and it was a severe understatement. He had loved to go out into the woods with Tristan when they were boys, exploring the unknown at the edges of the old perimeter fence. It didn't even matter whether they actually found something interesting or dug a hole in the ground to see how deep they could go or wandered around trying to find strange bugs. Those days were golden in Elias's memory.

"How long ago was that?"

"I don't know. Ten years? Remember, Tristan. Just... remember. There used to be way more food. It wasn't like now, not by far. We are slowly starving to death in that place, and everyone keeps denying it."

"Things are hard now, but we can turn them around. We just need everyone to do their part for the colony. We can't afford to be selfish like you."

"You know what? I'm sick of people calling me selfish," Elias said, placing the Life Seed on the ground and standing up. "I'm done with that. Everything I've done these past three years has been to *help*. To do my bit. Sure, I could have taken up an apprenticeship with my aunt, and then what? If all those brilliant geneticists haven't figured out how to keep us from starving in the decades they've worked on the problem, do you think by joining them I could have made a difference?"

"So that's your excuse for doing nothing?"

"Tristan, I swear I'm going to kick you in your broken arm if you keep on saying bullshit. I'm trying to look for a solution. Something nobody is doing, apparently. Everyone's happy to pretend everything is just dandy when it really isn't. I have a little brother, in case you don't remember. And I hate seeing him grow up like this. He doesn't know any better. He has never even had a birthday cake, for goodness' sake! And it breaks my heart to see how my father gives us a portion of his food every night, claiming he's not hungry when I can see he's nothing but skin and bones.

"I want a better future for us, Tristan. And if the answer is not in what we're doing, then we need to do something different. When I found Dr. Wright's laboratory, I was only curious. The more I investigated, though, the more I realized that the information there is very valuable. Why didn't we learn about him in history class? Why isn't he honored like the rest of the pioneers, particularly since it was he who found the Life Seed in the first place? I'll tell you why. He was the one to discover that although using the Life Seed for genetic material was beneficial in the short-term, it would mean the end of us all in the long run. I read every bit of his journal. He tried to tell people, and they wouldn't listen, like now nobody's listening to me. After all, why give up the one thing that's keeping the colony going, right? Without the Seed's genetic material our crops wouldn't grow on this world. But by keeping it with us, we are dooming the entire planet along with ourselves!"

Tristan looked up at him, remaining sitting. His deep, intelligent eyes glittered with unreadable emotion. His lower jaw was set in defiant stubbornness, and stubble shaded his cheeks. In spite of everything, Elias couldn't suppress the thought that Tristan was… handsome.

"So what do you propose?" Tristan asked, his quiet voice a sharp contrast to Elias's earlier shouts. "If what you say is true, then what happens? You return the Life Seed, you save the planet. But what about us?"

"What about us? We find a solution," Elias answered. "We've been cooped up in that colony for too long. There's got to be native crops we can grow, ways we can hybridize Terran strains with the life here. Similar stuff's been done before on many of the planets of the Core Systems. We can do it here too. It's going to take a lot of work, though. And our lives aren't going to be easy while we do that. There's not even a guarantee we will succeed, not when Dr. Wright and the others couldn't. But you know something? I'd rather do that than watch how everyone slowly starves to death in that empty tomb we call our home. It's been more than one hundred years since planetfall. There should be cities rising on New Skye. Instead, there's fewer of us all the time."

"Return the Life Seed to Portree, Elias. Think of everyone back home."

"That's just what I'm—forget it. We're going to the Aberdeen Mountains, and that's that."

"You can't make me come with you. I won't be an accomplice."

"You're right, I can't make you," Elias said. Then he nodded at the wurl, who were basking in the sunlight not far from where the two young men sat. "They will."

Elias got Tristan to share a quick snack of the remaining purpleberries he had in his pockets, despite Tristan's initial reluctance. Tristan confessed he was carrying some emergency rations, but he insisted that they keep them for later in case they did not find any more food, and Elias had to agree. Tristan did share his water with Elias, though. The back plate of his uniform concealed a wide and flat plastic container that was full of water. They drank only a little out of it, since the landscape around them showed no obvious sources to replenish it. After that was done, Elias helped Tristan get up, and they continued on their way.

Elias tried to start up a conversation once or twice, but Tristan maintained a steadfast, sullen silence, and eventually Elias simply gave up. The sun descended in the sky, off to the left, and the two of them kept walking.

The mountain peaks were obviously closer, but it was hard for Elias to gauge exact distances without any reference points. He would look at a slope ahead and judge it to be gentle and manageable, only to get to it and discover that it was too sharp to climb. The terrain they traversed demanded attention and care as well. They were crossing through an area of the highlands that appeared to have been scarred by some gigantic cataclysm in the past. The more they advanced, the deeper the yawning chasms in the earth were. Most of them were narrow enough to jump across, but a few were huge, jagged canyons that forced Elias to find another way. With the added distraction of the relentless wind blowing across the exposed desolation, he was miserable, exhausted, and shivering by the time the sun set in the sky.

"We can't go any farther," Tristan said, breaking the silence for the first time in hours. "Not unless you want us to fall into one of those holes. It's going to be too dark to navigate, even with the moons rising."

"I know," Elias replied. "Help me find a good spot to set up camp."

"I think we can have some shelter over there."

"I don't see anything," Elias answered, looking at the place where Tristan was pointing. It looked like yet another jagged chasm.

"Just come with me," Tristan said impatiently. Elias followed, and he realized that the gap Tristan had pointed out was only a couple meters deep. If not for the irregular outlines around the edges, the hole could have almost been an open grave.

"In here?" Elias asked, uncertain.

"Unless you have a better idea."

Elias scanned the barren landscape in the dim twilight. Aside from the three hulking wurl who had grouped up some distance away, appearing to rest but still watching him with their clusters of luminescing eyes, there was no other place.

"Fine," Elias conceded. "I'm going to take a leak first, though."

When full night settled over the highlands, Elias and Tristan had managed to find somewhat comfortable positions in the narrow hole. The dirt surrounding them was surprisingly warm from the sunlight, although the very bottom of their shelter was somewhat moist. The rich, earthy aroma of wet soil filled the space, and although Elias had been forced to sit facing Tristan, with the two of them entwining their legs awkwardly around the other in the confined space, he was thankful.

"At least there's no more wind," he said, not really expecting an answer.

"Yeah," Tristan said quietly. "That's something they taught me in the patrol. In winter, it's best to keep out of the wind if you can."

Elias shifted position a little, trying not to kick Tristan or disturb his broken arm. He placed the Life Seed between them. Maybe it was his desperate longing for warmth, but with the two of them, it seemed to Elias as if the Seed was hotter than it usually was.

"Why is it doing that?" Tristan asked, nodding at the Seed.

"You mean how it's hot?"

"Yeah."

"I have no idea. I'm not complaining, though. It's like having a little radiator. If not for the Seed, I think I would have—" A sudden attack of hacking coughing forced Elias to stop. It was a while before he recovered. "I think I would have frozen to death here already."

"You didn't even prepare well," Tristan told him. The faint moonlight was barely enough for Elias to make out his face, even though they weren't more than a meter apart. "You headed into the wilderness, in wintertime, without a tent or a knife or warm clothing or even a water bottle."

"Well, excuse me, but it wasn't exactly like I had a lot of time to plan. Besides, I kind of expected to be at the mountains already. They're very far away."

"They are. It's strange, isn't it?"

"What's strange?"

Tristan sighed in the dark. "I've never been so far from home. It's odd. Kind of scary and kind of cool, if that makes any sense."

Elias nodded. "I know exactly what you mean. I never knew New Skye could be so beautiful, or so dangerous."

"They probably think I'm dead, back at the colony. The commander specifically said to report back if we found something. She didn't want us going after you alone, but when I found your trail... I should have gone for backup. That was my mistake."

"Why, you thought I was no big threat?"

"I did," Tristan admitted.

"Gee, thanks for the vote of confidence."

"Come on, Elias. You're not exactly athletic. I've had weapons training, martial arts, and I've killed wurl."

His statement triggered a memory, and Elias recalled how Tristan had saved him, just a couple of days ago. "That's right. I never even thanked you."

"For what?"

Elias shrugged in the dark. "For saving my ass, okay? That night outside the abandoned laboratory. If you hadn't been there...."

"If I had known what you were going to do, I would have left you to that wurl."

"Right. Well, thanks anyways. I have to admit you were pretty badass that time."

Tristan did not answer, and after a while Elias heard his breathing coming deeper and slower. Tiredness soon tugged at his consciousness as well, and Elias gave up to sleep, the heat of the Life Seed lulling him into strange dreams.

Chapter 11
Freezing and Warm

INTERMITTENT COUGHING spells prevented Elias from truly resting. They woke him up every few minutes, it seemed, and his sleep was fitful at best. When the sky above finally lightened with coming morning, Elias crawled out of the hole tiredly, dragging the Life Seed along and rubbing his eyes.

He stretched, feeling all the little aches in his body as he did so.

"Definitely need to exercise more," he grumbled to himself. "This feels awful."

At least his arms weren't shaking anymore, and the dull ache in his knees had subsided somewhat. The light wind that blew through the desolate landscape was chilly, but Elias wasn't shivering anymore. He realized that he hadn't been that cold all night, in fact. He supposed it was because of the combined warmth coming from the Life Seed and Tristan in the small, enclosed space. That was one thing to be thankful for.

He turned his eyes to the north, scanning the terrain. The Aberdeen Mountains were clearly visible now, an imposing row of jagged peaks all capped in pristine white snow. They looked close enough to touch, but Elias knew better by now. Yesterday they had appeared impossibly far away in the haze, and it was only because today the air seemed to be particularly clear that they looked so near.

Movement to the right caught his attention. The wurl had woken up and were approaching as if curious. They came all the way up to where Elias was standing, stopping just a couple of paces away. They were close enough that Elias could smell them and feel the heat coming from their breath whenever they exhaled.

"Morning, guys," Elias said to them. Three heads turned up in response to the sound, tilting to the right in a gesture that reminded Elias of videos of Terran dogs. "Up for another long walk today?"

The wurl didn't answer, obviously, but Elias realized they were paying attention to him now, rather than to the Life Seed. Unbidden, a memory of something he had read in the doctor's journal came to his mind. He had called the wurl gentle giants, curious creatures that would inspect campsites after the humans were gone. Elias had grown up fearing the large reptiles, but now that he was able to see them up close like this, he got the distinct impression they weren't murderous killing machines all the time.

"Why do you keep attacking Portree?" Elias asked them. "Is it because we have this?"

He lifted the Seed, and the wurl followed the motion. When he held it out to them, they sniffed it eagerly but made no attempt to come any closer.

"Back off!" Tristan shouted suddenly. The wurl growled and slithered away. Elias looked back and saw Tristan approaching at a run, scowling as usual. "Are you insane?"

"Good morning, Tristan."

"Don't ever do it again, you hear me? Ever! Those animals are dangerous!"

Elias noticed that all the wurl had deployed their spines fully upright in a threatening display.

"I had it under control," he told Tristan, irritated. "Those creatures are intelligent. I was trying to communicate."

"You were trying to…? Right. They're killers, Elias."

"I don't think so."

"Of course you don't," Tristan spat. His usually carefully combed hair was a mess, and the stubble of his growing beard made him look wild. "You haven't had to fight them. You never found the mangled corpse of one of our own after those things were done. Do you want to know how the last victim died? It was Hikari Matsuo, Kenji's wife. She had been *torn apart*. I found one of her legs in the forest. The rest of her was in a clearing, riddled with spines."

Elias shuddered. "That's horrible."

"You think?" Tristan asked, the sarcasm evident in his tone. "They are dangerous. I don't know why the hell they haven't torn us to pieces already and taken the Seed they obviously want so badly, but I wouldn't count on my luck. Stop doing stupid things like that."

"I thought you didn't care what happened to me."

"Yeah. I mean…. Shut up. Let's eat. We shouldn't waste any daylight."

Elias nodded, sitting down on a rock. Tristan sat nearby, and he shared some of his rations. Then they each drank a large gulp out of the water package.

"Why the change in attitude?" Elias asked after they were done eating. "I thought you didn't want to help me."

"I have no choice, do I? Besides, the sooner we get to the mountains, the sooner you'll see that what you're doing is stupid. Then we can return with the Seed to the colony and you can stand trial for what you've done."

"Who says I'm going back to Portree after I do this?"

Tristan looked at him as if he was speaking another language. "What?"

"What would I even go back for?"

"You have to go back. There's nowhere else."

"Says you," Elias told him. "I could go explore the world or something."

"You would die. And quick. Without the Seed, any wurl you encounter can kill you with a flick of its tail."

"Maybe. Maybe not."

Tristan stood up, brushing dry grass from the back of his pants. The plates in his uniform were scuffed and dirty, but at least the splint that held his arm motionless was clean. "We have to get going."

"Fine," Elias conceded.

Elias was wary all through the morning, however. He didn't trust Tristan's change of attitude, and he kept himself on guard just in case. The two of them followed along the pathless expanse of the rolling landscape, climbing all the time, as was all too evident by the temperature decreasing and the air thinning. A few hours later, the wind finally stopped as they crested an irregular hill and found themselves facing another wide plateau.

"What the hell?" Tristan asked.

Elias could understand his surprise. The plateau was covered with water. It spread out as far as the eye could see, and its surface was a perfect mirror of the sky overhead and the mountains beyond. It was as if a gigantic lake had spread out over the highlands, serene, with barely a ripple in its immensity.

Tall trunks of trees with gnarled branches rose up from the water, white and tan, devoid of leaves. They looked like preserved skeletons of dead plants covered in marble, and a few birds flitted here and there among the branches, the only living thing Elias could see. He imagined that if the trees ever regained their leaves, he would be standing at the edge of a massive alien mangrove biome, but it looked as though the trees had long since drowned, leaving only wood as a testament to what they had once been.

"How are we going to cross that?" Tristan wondered aloud.

"Maybe it's not deep," Elias suggested. "I'm going to check."

"Don't!" Tristan called out, but Elias ignored him.

Tentatively, he walked to the edge of the water and stepped into it. His foot sank less than two centimeters before he hit solid ground. Crouching while balancing the Life Seed in his other hand, Elias poked the ground around him. It looked as if the water was extremely shallow. To test it out, he grabbed a pebble and threw it forward as far as he could. The splash it made seemed to confirm his suspicions.

"It's not deep," he told Tristan. "Come on."

"You don't know whether it's shallow all the way through," Tristan protested, refusing to move. "Besides, what if there's quicksand or something farther out?"

"There's trees along the way. We can grab on to those."

Elias started going forward. Tristan grumbled some more, but soon he was splashing behind Elias. A few minutes later, much louder splashes betrayed the fact that the wurl had joined them.

It was a surreal experience, walking through a water mirror that stretched as far as he could see. The trees were the only thing that gave a sense of distance to the plateau, but not even they could truly mask the impression Elias got of being stranded in some kind of reality marble, away from time and space. It was peaceful in a way. The wind had stopped blowing, and deep quiet settled across the land. The mountains appeared even closer now, close enough for Elias to see that the flanks of the nearest one were not smooth, but rather a series of overlapping slopes that climbed higher and higher all the time. They looked forbidding and deadly. For the first time since escaping with the Life Seed, Elias wondered how he was going to locate the cave he was looking for in all of that. Dr. Wright had never given precise coordinates in his journal. It was going to be an impossible task.

I have to try, even so, he thought to himself. *There's no backing away now.*

As they reached what Elias hoped was the middle of the plateau, he noticed that the water became even shallower. It was frozen over in several places, and walking became slippery and treacherous. The patches of ice were sometimes hidden, and Elias stumbled several times. He found himself quickly going from tree to tree for support, with Tristan on his heels.

When Tristan fell, Elias had only just reached the safety of a tree trunk. He turned around in time to see Tristan lose his footing and fall backward, smacking his head against the ice.

"Tristan!" Elias cried out. He rushed forward, nearly falling himself. "Are you okay?"

Tristan's face was scrunched up in pain. "Hit... my arm."

"Here, lean on me. Let's walk together from now on."

Tristan pushed him away. "Don't need your help."

"Fine," Elias said. "Fall down and break it again for all I care."

But he couldn't stand idle as he watched Tristan trying to stand up with no handholds, surrounded by slippery ice and with one broken arm. He got closer and offered a hand. Reluctantly, Tristan grabbed it. Then Elias put his arm around Tristan's waist to stabilize them both. Tristan appeared to be on the verge of pushing him away again, but after taking a single step, he slipped again, and it was only by grabbing on to Elias that he didn't fall.

"All right," Tristan grumbled. "Let's make this quick."

It soon got boring to traverse the empty wilderness without talking. It was even worse because they were forced to go very slowly, mindful of the ice. When Elias finally couldn't take the silence anymore, he decided to try and start another conversation.

"So. They made you a patrol officer already, and you're not even of age yet."

Tristan didn't answer.

"It must feel great, I guess," Elias went on, if only to hear himself talking. "Everybody loves you. You're like Portree's poster boy, what with you saving the colony every five seconds and all that. You want to know something? Oscar idolizes you. I think all the kids do. And of course there's the girls. How come you've never even had a girlfriend? They're all falling over themselves to get your attention. What's it like, being a god?"

Tristan smirked. "That's what it looks like?"

"Oh, please. Don't tell me you don't notice the attention. Sarah has got you earmarked as her future husband, but Evelyn isn't far behind, and I think I saw Yuki drawing some chibi-style pictures of you hugging her the other day. With starry eyes and everything."

Tristan surprised Elias by chuckling. "Starry eyes?"

"And long hair. You had long hair."

"That would be awful. Imagine having to comb it every day. I'd much rather have it like this, thank you very much."

"Yeah. You look better like this."

Elias could have bitten his tongue off. Had he really said that? Suddenly feeling awkward, he let go of Tristan's waist, even though the ice sheet underfoot had only partially melted with the sunlight and the going was still treacherous.

What am I thinking? He knew, of course. He just wouldn't admit it to himself.

Uncomfortable silence stretched between them, disturbed only by the loud stomping splashes of the tireless wurl behind them. Eventually, though, it was Tristan who spoke.

"What happened to you, Elias?" His tone was different this time. Serious, with no trace of sarcasm.

"What do you mean?"

"I don't know. We used to hang out all the time. Everybody at school said you were really smart. I remember my dad telling me that you would probably have a bright future in the colony, and then suddenly you… fell off the radar."

"I found the lab."

"Yeah, but you kind of started ignoring us. You could have been anything. Hell, your dad is the telecommunications specialist! That's like, the coolest job in the entire colony. He gets to listen to the stars and send messages. Can you imagine what will happen if he ever hears back from someone in the Core Systems? They will know we made it, that the colony was a success. They might even send another ship."

"I was never really into telecom, if that's what you mean," Elias answered sharply.

"What happened, then? Why did you throw your life away?"

Elias clamped his jaw shut until his anger had subsided enough for him to speak. "I didn't throw anything away, Tristan. Just because I'm not living the life everyone else wants me to doesn't mean I'm wasting it. I've learned a lot, not that you or anyone else cares. Dr. Wright was a brilliant xenobiologist. I'm probably the person who knows the most about our planet's animals and plants in the entire universe. So no, nothing really *happened* to me. I'm myself. That's it."

"You could still get an apprenticeship. Settle down, find a girl."

"I'm sorry, did you get promoted to the position of my mother without anyone telling me?"

"Just saying."

"Well, keep your suggestions for yourself, poster boy. Let *me* ask you something. Why did you decide to be in the patrol?"

"Because I want to help people. And my dad has always said I'm good at it."

"Yeah, but did you *choose* that path?"

"What do you mean? I signed up. Nobody made me."

Elias raised an eyebrow. "We used to be best buddies, Tristan. I remember your dad talking every night about how he could have been the best Colony Patrol officer ever if not for the accident."

"So? What's that got to do with anything?" Tristan asked, defiant.

"You really need me to spell it out for you? Fine. Your daddy couldn't be an officer, so he made you one so he could live through you. And you fell right for it."

"Shut the hell up, Elias. You don't know anything about me."

"I know enough. I remember you telling me you wanted to be a pilot."

"Yeah, and I also wanted to be a doctor and a scientist," Tristan replied in a mocking tone. "For goodness' sake, Elias. We were seven years old. Some things change."

"Why didn't you do it?"

"Do what?"

"Become a pilot," Elias answered.

"Are you insane? We don't have vehicles anymore. They all broke down decades ago."

"Yeah, but we could make more. You could have built one, a plane."

"Oh sure, because we have a plane factory right next door. Please. We barely have enough infrastructure as it is. Do you have any idea how complicated it is to build an airplane?"

"But why isn't anyone doing it? Why didn't you try? People have done it before on other planets. Just because we don't have all that technology anymore doesn't mean we can't develop it again. I get the feeling that we're stagnating, everyone happy with what they've got, no one innovating. We already look at the pioneers like magic people with incomprehensible technology at their disposal."

"That tends to happen when everyone is worried about fighting for survival," Tristan countered.

"Ha! So you admit it. The colony *is* starving."

Tristan gave Elias a long, hard look. "What if it is?"

"What if it—Tristan, it's our duty to do something about it. To try anything, if there's a chance it might save our families."

Tristan shook his head. "Don't be naïve."

"What is that supposed to mean?"

Tristan looked out into the distance for a few seconds before answering. When he spoke, his voice sounded older, heavy with a hint of defeat.

"People aren't stupid, Elias. I mean, the kids don't know it, but everyone else is aware. You're always cooped up in your lab, so you haven't seen what I have. I've attended meetings with the commander, when she talks with Director O'Rourke about the rationing, about their projections for the future. They've had some people estimate how much food is left and how much we can grow if the current trends hold. You want to know how long they've given us?"

Elias didn't reply. He was afraid to hear the answer.

"Seven years, if we stick to current rationing schemes. Twelve if we cut back on nonessentials, like the Midwinter Feast, extra birthday rations, and public celebrations. It's already been decided that this was the last Midwinter Feast we're going to celebrate. The director will make an announcement next month."

"What?"

"What you heard. Everyone knows, they just don't like you rubbing it in their faces all the time. What are we going to do? Do you have any idea how hard it is for parents to know that their children have twelve years of life left? I've broken up plenty of household fights over food.

Food. I've had to shock people unconscious because they were taking their kids' rations for themselves. Aaron and Betty O'Rourke were sent to jail last month because we discovered that they were hoarding food in one of the abandoned houses, freezing it for long-term storage. Some people have begun to barter, exchanging favors or services for food instead of using colonial money. We put a stop to it, but it always comes back. So yes, Elias. We all know about what you're always trying to tell us. But there's no solution."

"There's got to be a way."

"There isn't."

"There is, and I'm going to find it. It starts with returning the natural balance to the world, which is why I took this."

Tristan rolled his eyes and didn't say anything else. He stalked off on his own, not too far away because one of the wurl quickly reacted and began tailing him specifically, but enough that it was clear he didn't want to talk anymore. It was fine with Elias. He was sick of trying to reason with someone so stubborn.

It was at least another hour before the end of the water mirror was in sight. At first Elias wasn't sure because the reflections on the surface made it look like a mirage, but a few minutes later there could be no doubt. They would finally be out of this awful stretch of terrain with its tricky and slippery ice covering interspersed with puddles of water. He quickened his pace, eager to be back on dry ground.

A louder splash than usual drew Elias's attention, and he glanced left, watching Tristan walk faster now after undoubtedly having seen that they were finally close to the edge. The sunlight threw bright reflections off the polished plates of Tristan's patrol uniform. Even without the helmet or the spear, he still managed to look intimidating, as if the wilderness held no threat for him. Elias found himself wishing that Tristan would stop treating him like a criminal. What had happened to the nice boy he'd used to be best friends with? Why did things have to be so different now?

Elias's thoughts distracted him for a second too long. He plunged his left foot forward without looking. There was ice underneath the water, and he slipped. He tried to compensate by throwing his weight to the other side, but then his other foot lost its grip on the surface and he fell backward, hitting his butt on the ice in the middle of a huge splash of icy water.

The ice beneath him cracked. Elias barely had a moment before he sank like a rock beneath the surface.

He let go of the Life Seed as freezing water enveloped him, dark and shocking. His feet brushed the bottom of the hole he had fallen into, but when he pushed himself up his head smacked against solid ice. Panicking, spewing bubbles out of his mouth, Elias tried to look up and find the opening.

Light. *There!*

It was just a few centimeters away, but he had run out of air. He wasn't fast enough to stop the reflex action of breathing in. He swallowed icy water, and it was painful beyond anything he had ever experienced. In spite of it, Elias grabbed the frozen edge of the hole and heaved himself upward with all his strength. The ice gave way under his grip.

He tried to reach out again, but he didn't make it. Darkness engulfed him, and he knew no more.

Until what felt like a moment later. Elias opened his eyes and was immediately blinded by sunlight. He tried to breathe in, couldn't, and panicked. Pain sliced through his midsection, and suddenly he was vomiting water, mouthful after mouthful, while someone smacked his back with a heavy hand. His lungs were screaming for oxygen, but he choked on the water the next time he tried breathing in. His vision blurred at the edges.

"Hold still!" someone said urgently. Tristan.

Then Elias felt an iron grip close on his nose, and Tristan leaned forward for some mouth-to-mouth resuscitation. He blew blessed air of life into Elias's lungs and then let go. Elias turned around and vomited again, less this time. Then he was able to breathe on his own, gulping air with ravenous relief. He couldn't get enough of it.

"Be right back," Tristan said.

Elias heard him splashing, but he couldn't focus. It was a few seconds before the spots dancing in front of his vision cleared and he was able to tilt his head to the side. He saw a bare-chested Tristan rushing through the water mirror, stopping at a specific spot where he jumped in with no hesitation. Struggling, trying not to pass out again, Elias managed to sit up. He watched Tristan come back up holding the Life Seed under his good arm. The wurl had also been watching, as if expectant, but they made no move to come closer when Tristan came back to where Elias was waiting.

Tristan dumped the Life Seed unceremoniously on the ground.

"We n-need a f-fire," Tristan said, teeth chattering. He was wearing only briefs and his breath steamed in the air.

Elias nodded, still unable to speak. He was shivering all over now, violently, and he was reduced to helpless watching as Tristan walked back to the nearest dead tree. Elias grabbed the Life Seed and held it to himself, the fierce warmth coming from it barely enough to make a dent in how cold he felt. He was freezing from the inside out, he was sure, and Tristan was too busy snapping off branches to notice.

Elias didn't freeze, though. He was still conscious, shivering, when Tristan came back with a bundle of white branches awkwardly held in his good arm.

"Help me p-pile them up," he told Elias.

Elias tried his best to make a reasonable pile while Tristan recovered a small box from his pants, which he had evidently left on the ground earlier. It turned out that the box contained something that looked a lot like fluffy white cotton, along with a silvery strip of unknown material and a dark, flat rock. Tristan quickly placed the cotton on top of the wood pile, grabbed the rock in one hand, and struck it against the silver material braced in an uncomfortable-looking way by his foot. Sparks flew from the impact, but they were carried away by the wind. Cursing, Tristan shifted position and tried several more times until he was able to land some of the sparks on the cotton. He was having trouble doing it with a single hand, but eventually he managed. Then he dropped his tools, crouched forward, and blew on the sparks while sheltering them from the wind. Elias stared, disbelieving, as a tiny flame was kindled. It quickly devoured the cotton, but Tristan was prepared. He fed it small twigs, then larger ones, and finally one of the big branches. Only then did he lean back with a sigh.

"Have to get more," he told Elias. "You gather rocks. Make a circle."

Elias doubted he would be able to move, but he tried. It took him what seemed like a very long time to gather enough rocks to make a rough circle around the pile of branches, which by then was burning nicely. Exhausted, he sat down on the ground as close to the fire as he dared. He held the Life Seed close, but even with the combined warmth, he was trembling.

"What do you think you're doing?" Tristan said to him, walking back with a much larger pile of wood under his arm. "Take off your clothes. They're soaked!"

Elias would have complained, but he simply didn't have the energy. He peeled off his jacket and shirt, then his shoes, socks, and pants. The wind struck his exposed flesh with brutal ferocity, and he was caught between deciding on the torment of being naked in the wilderness or the torment of having his body heat leeched out of him by his wet clothes. He chose the former, taking off his underwear as well. The shivering was getting out of control now. In spite of it, he felt numb and sleepy....

"Don't you dare pass out," Tristan told him. "Here, put this on."

Sudden warmth. It was a couple of seconds before Elias realized that the source of it was Tristan's jacket, which had been draped across his shoulders. Elias clutched it tight, folding himself into a ball around the Life Seed.

"Stay awake," Tristan said to him. "I'll rig this up in no time."

Elias had no idea what he was talking about, but he concentrated on the warmth and caught only fleeting glimpses of Tristan taking something out of one of his uniform plates, a metallic sheet of some kind. The wind lessened somewhat after what felt like an eternity. It allowed the heat from the roaring fire to reach Elias more fully. As he regained a modicum of warmth, Elias's attention sharpened. He realized Tristan was building some kind of crude shelter around the fire. He watched, entranced, as Tristan used rocks, sticks, and the surprisingly large metallic sheet to erect a circular fence around the flames, barely big enough to contain both of them. When it was done, and they were surrounded on all sides by the two-meter-high makeshift shelter, Tristan pressed a button on his link and the entire structure stiffened. And....

"Wow," Elias whispered. "It feels... warm."

"Reflective foil," Tristan said to him, shifting closer. "I was saving it for an emergency. I can't do much about the wind, but it will trap the heat from the fire and reflect it back to us. Should be enough to get your core temperature back up while I boil some soup."

"Soup?" Elias asked.

"Hey, I'm always prepared. You stay put, okay? Be right back."

Elias didn't have the strength to argue. He kept as close to the fire as he could without burning himself and allowed the gentle radiating heat to surround him. Slowly, his shivering subsided. He no longer felt as if he were going to pass out at any moment. Sitting up straight, he looked over the shelter in time to see Tristan, dressed again, coming back with a container full of water. He made way when Tristan climbed inside with him and realized that the container was one of Tristan's uniform plates, bent into the shape of a bowl.

"How…?"

"Oh, the uniform does this, for emergencies," Tristan replied, placing the bowl over the flames. "I won't be able to wear the chest plate again, but…. Anyway, I have some soup concentrate here." He took out a small metallic package from one of his pockets, ripped it open with his teeth, and emptied it over the water. The flames danced around the bowl, and neither Tristan nor Elias said anything else until the water inside was steaming. Then Tristan reached forward, grabbed his emergency bowl, and quickly put it on the ground, wincing.

"Did you burn your fingers?" Elias asked him.

"What do you think?" Tristan snapped. "Here, drink up. Wait for the bowl to cool a little first."

The smell coming from the steaming container was very hard to resist. Elias controlled himself, though, and grabbed it only when he was certain he would not burn himself. It was still very hot, and the soup inside even hotter, but Elias didn't care. He drank in long, grateful gulps, immediately feeling the warmth seep into his core and spread.

He stopped when the bowl was half-empty. "Your turn," he told Tristan.

"You sure?"

"Sure."

Tristan didn't argue any further. He took the bowl from Elias and drank deeply, sighing with evident satisfaction when he was done. "Man, that was good. I never thought I'd actually get to use the emergency field kit like this."

"Your jacket," Elias said, taking it off and proffering it to Tristan. Without it, he was completely naked.

"Are you insane? Keep it. I set your clothes out to dry over the foil, but it's going to take a couple hours. I still have my T-shirt and pants. They're soggy, but they're made to dry quickly. In fact, come over here. You were dangerously hypothermic a short while ago. We can combine our body heat, plus that weird Seed."

"How?" Elias asked. There was barely enough room for the two of them to sit side by side.

"Move closer to the fire. There. Now I'm going to lie across… ouch, careful with my arm. Move your foot. Okay, now you lie on your side in front of me so you're facing the fire. No, keep the Life Seed. You need the warmth more than me."

It was awkward, but Elias managed to lie down the way Tristan wanted. In the end, Elias found himself sandwiched between the roaring fire and Tristan, who hugged him from behind, pulling him in close.

Elias gasped, and it had nothing to do with the fact that the ground was cold and hard or that he was still shivering a little bit.

"Try not to fall asleep," Tristan said to him. His breath was warm in Elias's ear. "If you're unconscious, your body temperature will decrease. We don't want that."

"Sure. Right."

Elias jerked forward, surprised, when he felt Tristan's uninjured hand on his shoulder.

"Relax," Tristan told him. "Just going to rub your arm to get the circulation going."

He did as promised, and between the vigorous motion, Tristan's body heat, the Seed, and the fire, Elias was warm at last. The shivering subsided completely, and his body relaxed.

Which brought forth a new problem. Mortified, Elias used the Life Seed to hide the entirely inappropriate reaction his body was having to being in such close proximity to another man. He silently prayed Tristan wouldn't notice. He would never hear the end of it if he did.

Minutes dragged by. The sky turned purple, then indigo, and finally black in the early-winter night. Elias was able to regain control of himself by the time Tristan announced that the clothes had probably dried. The two of them sat up awkwardly to allow Tristan to stand up and check.

"Dry!" he proclaimed triumphantly. "I love this foil."

He tossed wonderfully dry clothes to Elias, who put them on as fast as he could. They were toasty warm, from his underwear all the way to his jacket. Even his shoes were dry again, and when he was fully dressed, Elias was almost on the verge of tears.

"Everything okay?" Tristan asked him.

Elias nodded. "It's so good to be dry."

"Yeah," Tristan answered, cracking a smile. "Hey, give me back my jacket."

"Sure."

Since night had already fallen, the two of them crawled back into the shelter by tacit agreement. They settled as before, and although the ground beneath them was still hard, it was no longer cold. In fact, Elias could have almost been comfortable.

He watched flames crackle as they devoured the wood for a long time. Tristan's hand rested on his shoulder again, although there was no need anymore.

"Thank you," Elias said quietly.

"What?" Tristan asked. They were close enough that Elias could feel the rumble of Tristan's deep voice.

"Thank you. For saving my life."

"Don't mention it. It's my duty, and besides, I owed you one."

"What?"

"From before," Tristan answered after a pause. "You could have left me to those wurl. Instead you came back for me. So we're even now."

"Right. Even."

Elias didn't know why, but Tristan's answer had disappointed him. He had almost hoped for another reason why Tristan had saved him. Something more meaningful, maybe.

He closed his eyes, telling himself that he was being irrational. Outside in the darkness, the eerie call of a night bird echoed across the desolation.

Chapter 12
Sick

THEY SPENT all night in the shelter, and when morning broke Elias felt like hell. He had a headache, his breath rattled in his lungs, and he kept coughing painfully every few minutes.

"We should go back to the colony," Tristan told him after they had packed the shelter materials. "You could have an infection... or pneumonia."

"No," Elias replied stubbornly. "We're almost there, and I'm doing this."

Tristan looked as if he wanted to argue, but then he simply shrugged. "Suit yourself."

They set off in the direction of the mountains. The wurl followed them as usual. Elias hadn't seen them eat anything the entire time they had been tailing the two of them, and he wondered for the first time about what wurl ate. With those teeth they had to be carnivorous, but what could they hunt? There were no small animals like those Dr. Wright had alluded to in his journal around to prey upon.

A hacking fit of coughing interrupted Elias's thoughts. The pounding in his temples was painful, and he felt hot, as if he had a fever, but looking forward he realized they had already reached the foot of the closest mountain, and he did not want to stop. Ahead of them the terrain spread out in irregular slopes, some of them barren and forbidding, others much more accessible. It was time to look for the cave, wherever it could actually be. Elias wished he had a clue as to its whereabouts.

At least Tristan wasn't arguing anymore. He walked beside Elias, silent, his thoughts unreadable behind his frown. Elias looked at him in an entirely different light today, after what Tristan had done for him. This was twice now that Tristan had saved his life: once back at the colony from the rogue wurl and yesterday from freezing. He was a hero, Elias realized. That's why everyone liked him so much. He was selfless, reliable, dutiful. Just like Commander Rodriguez had said at the feast.

I on the other hand....

But by then they had reached an unavoidable rocky wall that rose up from the ground at a sharp angle. It was time to climb, and the effort drove everything else from Elias's mind.

He focused on placing one foot in front of the other, leaning forward, his leg muscles burning, clutching the Life Seed in both hands. Loose rocks underfoot seemed to appear out of nowhere, threatening to trip him or make him stumble backward. Elias was forced to slow down after a few minutes, feeling as though he were climbing an endless staircase with no chance to rest. Next to him, Tristan kept up easily, even slowing down on purpose, it seemed, to keep an eye on Elias. And behind....

Elias looked back once and wished he hadn't done it. He had already climbed quite high, and the view of the sloping terrain plummeting down was dizzying. The three wurl appeared to be having trouble following too. They were too big and lumbering, and for every three steps they took upward, sinking their claws into the ground, they slid down at least one. But they didn't give up, and Elias directed his attention back to the ground before him. He tried to ignore the trembling in his legs and the dull pounding of the headache, which had now spread to the back of his head. The wind blasting across the exposed terrain was frigid, and Elias's arms were beyond exhausted from carrying around the increasingly forbidding weight of the Life Seed.

He almost gave up. A particularly bad fit of coughing made him lose balance, and if it hadn't been for Tristan steadying him, Elias would have simply crashed downhill, probably breaking something. He mumbled out a thanks and pushed Tristan away. He had to keep climbing.

"We need to stop," Tristan said to him. "You're not well, Elias. You need to rest."

"Can't. Must—" He was interrupted by more coughing.

Elias's sense of time began to slip. He felt as if he had been climbing this cold gray mountain forever. When he tried to crane his neck up to see how much was left, he swayed on his feet, and Tristan steadied him again.

"I think there's a ledge over there," Tristan said, panting now too. "Come on, I'll help you reach it."

A sudden gust of wind nearly made the two young men fall over. Elias realized he was shivering again. But he felt hot, and he kind of wanted to take off his clothes. It made no sense.

He suddenly felt lighter, and it took him a moment to realize that it was because Tristan was holding the Seed now. Elias tried to say thanks, but the wind carried away his words. Instead he channeled all his strength into motion, one step and then another, climbing, trying not to give in to the headache, which by now had reached migraine proportions, a brief surge of agony with every heartbeat.

The change in ground inclination took him completely by surprise. He fell forward on hands and knees, gasping for air. His head reeled with pain at the sudden shift in height. The ground underneath was cold and hard but solid. He held on to it as his sense of balance struggled to cope, making it seem as if the entire world were tilting around him. With effort, Elias stopped himself from retching and looked down instead to see whether the wurl had followed. They were nowhere to be seen.

"Over here," Tristan said, appearing seemingly out of nowhere. He grabbed one of Elias's arms and tugged until Elias stumbled upright. "There's a cleft in the rock over there. Might even be a cave. Come on, you can rest inside."

Elias didn't protest. He followed along until they came to a jagged opening in the sheer rock face that bordered the small ledge where they were standing. The slope next to the opening was much sharper, and Elias had an awful spell of vertigo when he looked down by mistake. There was no climbing that. If he fell, he would probably die.

"Inside," Tristan insisted.

With a gentle push, he ushered Elias into a narrow opening that quickly tapered off. It was barely big enough to stand in, not even worth the name of cave. But Elias was exhausted, and he collapsed on the ground, uncaring.

"I'm going to set up the shelter now," Tristan told him. "And I think I saw some trees over on the other side of the cleft. Be right back."

Elias had no idea what he was talking about. He hadn't seen any cleft, but he was tired. He barely reacted when Tristan thrust the Life Seed back into his hands.

"Hold on to that for warmth. And *don't* fall asleep, you hear me?"

"Sure," Elias mumbled. Even his tongue felt slow.

He heard footsteps retreating, and the next time he was able to focus, he realized he was all alone in the narrow confines of the cave. Outside, the sky had finally lost its cloudless azure beauty and become a bland shade of gray, overcast. It wasn't long before the first raindrops pattered on the dry, rocky ground. Shivering slightly, Elias had enough presence of mind to at least be thankful that he wasn't out in the rain.

He coughed again, for longer this time. When he recovered, he shut his eyes and leaned his head back against the rocky wall.

Just for a moment. Just a quick nap.

He was asleep before he finished formulating his thought.

When he woke up again, startled, the first thing he saw was firelight.

"Hey," Tristan said to him. "Glad to see you're still alive."

Elias focused. Tristan had found a way to wedge himself in the cave with him, and beyond the opening there was a roaring fire that was somehow being contained by a reflective surface.

"What happened?" Elias whispered. His voice was hoarse.

"Drink first," Tristan replied, lifting a steaming bowl. "It's more hot broth with protein powder, and I also mixed in some medicine from my field kit."

"Where are we?"

"Drink. We can talk later."

Elias didn't need any more coaxing. He realized he was hungry as soon as he swallowed the first delicious mouthful of hot, nourishing liquid. He sputtered once, coughing, but managed to finish it all.

"Thanks," he told Tristan. He felt weak. As if even keeping his eyes open required a titanic amount of effort....

He slept again, and his dreams were shapeless nightmares. He thought he saw darkness outside the cave, then a trio of red gleaming eyes. More darkness followed, replaced by blinding sunlight. Chilly gusts of wind. Movement. The smell of something cooking. Darkness again.

Elias woke up fully after what felt like a very long time. Blinking, he squinted at the bright sunlight. He tried to move, and every muscle in his body protested at once. He groaned out loud.

"Awake at last?" Tristan asked him.

A shadow eclipsed the light coming from outside, and Tristan crawled into the cave and sat awkwardly in the empty space in front of Elias.

"What happened?" Elias asked. He felt weird, but at least he was alert.

"What happened was you almost died," Tristan explained. "You know what? Let's go outside. It hasn't rained all day, and the sunlight is really warm. It looks like you could use the heat."

It took Elias nearly five minutes to crawl out of the cave. His arms and legs could have been wet noodles for all the support they provided, but his horrible headache from before had disappeared. He was still coughing, but now it hurt less in his chest when he did so. He still felt weak, but it was a different kind of weakness now. Something almost good.

Not making any sense, Elias thought silently, dragging himself fully out. Already exhausted, he leaned against a wonderfully warm rock and closed his eyes. The radiance of the sunlight on his skin was magical. It seemed to penetrate deep inside him, reinvigorating him a bit.

"Better?" Tristan asked him.

Elias opened his eyes and nodded slowly. "A little."

"That's good. Here, have some nuts. Or whatever they are."

Tristan passed him a handful of strange wrinkled seeds, light brown and velvety to the touch.

"Don't worry, they're good to eat. I ran them through the link scanner and ate some last night. I'm not dead, so I'm assuming they're safe. There's some water to go with that too. Bottle's over there."

Elias picked one of the nuts up and brought it to his lips. He popped it into his mouth and chewed experimentally. It tasted strange—not exactly bad but like a mixture of earthy flavors and a sharp tang of something acidic. He swallowed it, and his stomach demanded more.

He ate several handfuls of the nuts. Whenever he ran out, Tristan would simply reach into a bag he carried and give him more. Elias ate until he couldn't take another bite and finished his meal with a long drink of cool water. Then he reclined back on the rock, satisfied and drowsy.

"Go ahead, take a nap," Tristan told him. "The light will hold for a few more hours. I'll wake you up when it's time to go back inside."

Elias surrendered to sleep once again.

He was woken by Tristan shaking him.

"I think we better go back in," Tristan said. "Sorry to wake you."

"'S okay," Elias mumbled. He crawled back into the cave and realized that his arms and legs didn't feel like wet noodles anymore. He settled into a narrow space as far back as he could and watched as Tristan lit a fire at the mouth of the cave, surrounding it with the metallic foil. Then Tristan crawled inside as well and settled back with a sigh.

"Looks like another night in here," he said to Elias. "Yay."

"What happened? How long has it been?"

"You want the long version or the short version?"

Elias shrugged.

"Fine, short version it is. You almost died. I think you had an infection or something. I gave you medicine two days ago, and you slept. You slept some more. But today you woke up. I gave you food. Here we are."

Elias managed a small smile. "I'm going to need more detail than that."

"There's not much more to tell, actually," Tristan admitted. "The first night here, it looked as if you weren't going to make it. You were making awful noises in your sleep, like you couldn't breathe right. I kept you warm as best as I could, gave you fluids whenever you were more or less awake. Then yesterday, I found some brambles clinging to the rock right next to the cave. Their branches were full of nuts, which is crazy because I'm positive I would have noticed earlier, only maybe I didn't. I don't know. They appeared out of nowhere, surrounding the Life Seed."

Elias jerked upright. "Where is it? Where is the Seed?"

"Outside, I just told you. I tried to pry it off the brambles, but it's stuck tight, and I didn't want to make a lot of noise. Plus, I only have one good arm. Tomorrow morning you can help me take it out. Looks like you're coming out of whatever it was you had."

"Yeah. I feel better now. Still awful, but at least I can talk. And my chest.... It feels better too, I think."

"That's good. I expect the cold got you, is all. You did fall into a frozen lake a few days ago. Or maybe you caught a bug and the cold made it worse."

"Can't be a bug," Elias replied. "Doctor Hino made us immune to everything on this planet, remember?"

"Says you."

"So we're still on the mountain?"

"Yeah. And I haven't seen the wurl for days now. I think we're alone up here."

"Okay," Elias said, although something bothered him. Tristan's account didn't add up. "Why are *you* still here, though?"

"What do you mean?"

"You could have taken the Life Seed. Gone back to the colony."

"Yeah. I mean, no, I didn't want to…. I didn't want to risk leaving you up here by yourself. You needed help, so I stayed. It's what I'm supposed to do."

Elias rolled his eyes and tried to laugh, but it came out as a cough instead.

"You okay?" Tristan asked.

"Yeah. It's just funny, that's all."

"What's funny?"

"That you're always thinking about your duty. What you're supposed to do and all of that."

"So?"

"So…. Nothing, I guess. It must be nice to be everyone's golden boy."

"That's easy for you to say," Tristan countered. "You're always off doing whatever you want, but me…? You have no idea."

"No idea about what?"

Tristan remained silent for a while, as if collecting his thoughts. He kept his eyes on the fire that separated them from the night outside.

"It's tiresome," he said at last.

"What?"

"It's tiresome to have everyone's expectations riding on your shoulders all the time. I can't make mistakes, can't run off to do my own thing like you do. It's like the more I do, the more people want. And I don't hate it. It's not that. I like challenging myself and finding out how far I can go. I like the fact that I'm the youngest Colony Patrol officer ever. And it's also cool to have that respect, you know? The way everyone smiles when they see me. The way people have thanked me for saving their lives. It feels good."

"Yeah, poor you. Who could lead such a horrible life?"

"Cut it out, Elias. *That's* why people don't like you."

"What did I do?"

"You get that tone. As if everyone else is incredibly stupid and only you are wise."

"What? I don't have a tone."

"Yeah, you do. And you're sarcastic. It's annoying, and it gets old real fast. You're always acting as if you know better than everyone else."

"I've just been trying to warn people!" Elias protested. "Nobody wants to listen! That's why I had to steal the Life Seed. It was the only way."

"You could have tried talking."

"I did!"

"Right. Out of nowhere. At the end of the gift-giving ceremony. With children present and without consulting anyone. You know what that looked like?"

"No, why don't you enlighten me?" Elias grumbled.

"It looked like you were trying to upstage me."

"Excuse me?"

Tristan shrugged. "I'm being honest. It's like you chose the moment where your announcement would have the most impact, right after they swore me in as an officer. That was supposed to be the high point of the evening, but of course you couldn't have that."

"That's insane. I wasn't trying to upstage anyone."

"Then why didn't you wait?" Tristan asked him. "Why didn't you use the official channels of communication? You could have requested a meeting with the Colony Council. That's the way things are supposed to be done. You present your information, your proof if you have it, and the council decides on whether to act or not. The Life Seed belongs to everyone, Elias. It's everyone's decision to make whether we return it, not just yours. Have you even considered what happens if you're wrong?"

"I'm not wrong," Elias answered, crossing his arms over his chest.

"Are you *sure*? You've reached these crazy conclusions based on some old journal you found. What if this Dr. Wright was lying? Why isn't his data in our records? Look at it from our point of view. It's your word against everything else. What if you're wrong?"

"I'm not," Elias repeated, but this time a tiny shred of doubt made its way past his wall of certainty. "Besides, you've seen what the Seed can do."

"What do you mean?"

Elias pointed outside. "That magical bramble bush that appeared out of nowhere, which you didn't notice when we arrived? How do you think that got here?"

"I don't...."

"It was the Seed, Tristan. It's already done that once. I don't know how, but it seems to make things grow wherever it lands. My best guess is that it helps things that are dormant to awaken and bloom. Who knows, maybe this mountainside was once covered in those bramble bushes. The Seed's roots must have tunneled into the soil after you left it outside and mixed in with the rain. You get the idea."

"Right. That's the most logical explanation."

"See? Now *you're* being sarcastic. I read about this in Dr. Wright's notes. That Seed is networked with the plants in some weird alien way."

"That makes no sense."

"Why not?" Elias demanded. "For all intents and purposes, this is still an alien planet for us, even if we were born here. How much do we know about New Skye? About its plants and animals? No one's ever even been to the other continent or to the poles. The truth is that we know almost nothing about this world, and like I've said a million times before, by taking the Life Seed, we destabilized a delicate ecosystem."

"Keeping it stuck in wintertime forevermore," Tristan said, lifting his eyebrows in disbelief.

"Whatever," Elias replied. "You'll see when we get to the cave."

Tristan shook his head and said no more. Elias wanted to keep arguing, but he was also very tired. After a quick exit to relieve himself, he snuck back into the cave, wedged himself as comfortably as he could among the rocks, and surrendered to sleep.

When morning came, he felt much better.

Elias got up before Tristan and used the time to pry the Life Seed from beneath the brambles, which had kept on growing at an astonishing rate over the night. It was much harder to do this time than when he had uprooted the Seed at the riverside. Three roots had drilled into the ground as before, entwining with the roots of the bramble bush, and when Elias finally yanked the Seed out, the bush came right with it, showering Elias in yet more ripe velvety nuts. Cursing, he separated the Life Seed from its thorny prison. When he was finally done, he had been scratched in more than a dozen places, and some of the cuts were bleeding. Annoyed, he kicked away the bramble bush and watched it tumble down the mountain with satisfaction.

"Need any help?" Tristan asked, making Elias jump.

"How long were you standing there?"

"Long enough. It was very funny, actually."

"Shut up, Tristan. Here, have some nuts."

After a filling if bland breakfast, the two of them stuffed their pockets with all the nuts they could carry and then set on their way.

"There's a path over here," Tristan said, turning right and heading across the increasingly narrow ledge of rock. "It leads up."

Elias followed, trying not to look down. The ledge sloped upward, shrinking until it was barely big enough for a single person to walk across. To the left an increasingly deadlier drop threatened steadily. To the right was only the living rock of the mountain.

It was awful, terrifying going, but thankfully the ledge widened after some time, and the slope leveled out. Soon Elias was able to walk beside Tristan, and the two of them arrived at a large cleft in the mountain that ran across it like a canyon. On the other side of it, much flatter terrain beckoned tantalizingly. The ground there had patches of ice that hadn't melted yet, and Elias realized with surprise that they had almost reached the summit of the mountain. Once across the canyon, it was a reasonably short climb to the snow-covered slopes with their thick cover of evergreen trees.

Getting to the other side, though, was going to be tricky. The gap was too wide to simply walk across, and the drop down had to be several hundred meters. The one good thing he had going for him was that they were currently standing on higher ground than what was across the gap.

"I got as far as here the other day," Tristan said to him. Cold mountain wind made his clothes whip about his muscular frame. "Found some red pine stumps over there. We just need to figure out how to pass."

"We could jump," Elias suggested.

"And if we miss?"

"Nah. I think it's doable. Here, hold the Seed."

"Elias, wait—"

But Elias ignored him. Now with his arms free, he backed away from the edge of the gap as far as he could.

Don't overthink this.

Then he ran. He pumped his arms in time with his steps, gathering speed and momentum until he was at the edge of the cleft. Without hesitation, Elias jumped clear across, lifting his legs in the air. For a brief second it felt almost like flying, with a deadly drop directly below him. Then he landed with a thud on the opposite edge, falling forward and rolling with his own motion until he slid to a stop in a small cloud of dirt. Coughing, he stood up and faced the way he had come.

"I did it!" he shouted at an openmouthed Tristan. "Now it's your turn. Throw me the Seed!"

But Tristan locked eyes with him and his expression... changed. He shook his head, and he almost looked sad.

"I'm sorry," he said quietly. Elias barely heard his words above the whistle of the wind.

Then Tristan turned around with the Life Seed in hand. And he walked away.

Chapter 13
Obsidian and Metal

"TRISTAN!" ELIAS shouted, knowing full well it was no use. "Tristan, come back!"

His shouted words received no reply. He was left to watch, helpless, as Tristan left with the Life Seed.

"Don't do this!" Elias yelled. "Tristan!"

How could I have been so stupid? Why did I trust him?

Silent recriminations were flashing through Elias's mind, ephemeral thoughts that nevertheless cut him deep. He should have never handed over the Seed. He had been stupid, so very stupid!

Of course Tristan would leave at the first opportunity he had. He wanted the Life Seed; it had been clear from the beginning. The fact that he hadn't left with it before probably meant that he hadn't wanted to leave Elias to die alone on the mountain when he had been delirious with fever. It was Tristan's duty as a patrol officer, after all. Serve and protect. It was the only thing that mattered to him. He wouldn't have abandoned a person who was helpless, no matter what the circumstances. Tristan had said as much when he'd admitted he loved being a hero and helping those in need. He would probably go back to Portree and tell them all about how he had saved Elias's life several times over in spite of the unforgivable theft of the Life Seed. They would all cheer for him, thanking him over and over, and if Elias ever went back no one would even listen to his side of the story. He would probably be sent straight to jail, ostracized for the rest of his life. All because Tristan simply hadn't let him die on the mountain.

Or maybe he couldn't dig the Seed out with just one arm, Elias thought bitterly. He remembered how the Life Seed had been surrounded by the bramble bush and how hard it had been to pry it out. Maybe Tristan simply hadn't been able to extract it without further injuring his arm. Maybe that's why he had taken care of Elias, so it would be easy to steal the Seed after Elias had dug it free.

Which was exactly what had happened. Elias had fallen into the trap, and he was now reduced to watching his entire mission crumble around him.

Can't he see that I'm right? He saw how the plant grew around the Seed. He has to know it's special. Why doesn't he believe me?

"Wait," he called out, but he knew it was no use. "Tristan, we need to give it back! It's the only way!"

Then he noticed the miniature rock slides cascading down from the mountainside above the ledge Tristan was crossing. Things that looked like three spike-covered boulders bumped and rolled downhill, still very high up but on a clear collision course.

With Tristan.

"Look out above!" Elias shouted, and maybe the desperation in his voice got through because Tristan stopped and looked up.

Tristan gave a wordless cry of evident surprise and dismay. He sprinted full-out ahead, perhaps trying to avoid the tumbling wurl, but he simply wasn't fast enough. The creatures were rolling down like rocks in an avalanche, so much so that when the first one finally crashed against the flat mountain ledge and uncoiled its body a few meters ahead of Tristan, its own momentum dragged it over the edge.

It was horrible to watch. Tristan slid to a halt, and Elias shouted even as that first wurl dug its claws into the rock, trying to halt its own motion. It wasn't enough. With a desperate howl, the creature lost its balance and fell, twisting its body, obviously trying to curl itself back into a ball. It did not manage. It slammed against a rock several dozen meters down, and Elias saw clearly how it went limp, splattering the mountainside with blood.

Elias's attention was wrenched back to the ledge. The two other wurl uncoiled in the air, right before impact, and fired several of their spines into the ground. Elias was struck speechless as he saw the creatures tumble to a stop precisely where the spines had hit. They swiped at them, using them as anchors, and managed to stop their terrible momentum. As soon as they were stable, the two of them lunged forward.

Tristan had nowhere to go except back. Elias reached a hand forward in a futile gesture as Tristan narrowly dodged an obsidian-black claw from the nearest creature. Tristan scrambled out of the way, Life Seed still held tight in his good arm, and jumped just as the wurl in the back fired a spine that dented the rock of the mountain.

The two wurl roared. The awful sound—like the grinding of serrated metal—was amplified, bouncing off the slopes of the mountains and making it seem as if it weren't two creatures there, but dozens. Fortunately the ledge had become too narrow for both wurl to attack Tristan at the same time, and only the frontmost creature was able to lunge again, wicked maw snapping, trying to catch Tristan in a deadly bite.

"Tristan, jump!" Elias shouted as loud as he could. A coughing spell interrupted his attempt to shout a second time, but Tristan had heard. Elias watched him turn his head for a fleeting look across the canyon that separated the two of them. Then he looked back at the lumbering beasts that had cornered him.

He didn't even hesitate. With barely a running start, Tristan jumped across the chasm.

Elias's heart stopped in his chest when Tristan began to fall and it looked as if he wouldn't clear the gap. But he made it, just barely, and crashed down hard. The makeshift splint on his broken arm came off, and Tristan howled in agony. The Life Seed tumbled from his grasp and rolled away, carried by the slope of the terrain to the very edge of the precipice.

Then Tristan began to slip. Down. The ground underneath him gave way, and he shared a brief, horrified look with Elias as his good hand shot forward to grab a thick root that jutted out from the rocks.

"No!" Elias yelled, already moving forward before forming any conscious thought of doing so. Tristan's lower body had already slipped over the edge, and Elias threw himself on the ground, arms outstretched, right as the root Tristan was clinging to snapped.

Tristan reached forward, grabbing blindly. Elias did the same. Their fingertips brushed. Then Elias had him. He grunted with the sudden effort of stabilizing Tristan's entire body weight, and Tristan himself wasn't making it any easier, kicking desperately, shouting. In fact, the more he moved, the more Elias slipped forward. Closer to the edge.

"Stop moving!" Elias grunted. "Going to... pull you."

Using every ounce of strength in his body, Elias tugged. From the corner of his eye, he thought he saw the Life Seed teetering on the brink of a disastrous fall.

If I lose that, I lose everything.

His grip on Tristan's arm wavered. Only for an instant, though. He realized he couldn't let go.

"Brace yourself!" Tristan said between gritted teeth.

"What?"

"Now!"

With far more strength than Elias would have thought possible, Tristan pulled. For an instant Elias feared that Tristan was trying to take him down with him, but the strain on his arms lessened suddenly. Tristan heaved his body up over the edge, crying out in pain when he landed on top of his arm yet again. It didn't stop him. He swung his legs over the side, dug the front of his boots into the dirt, and let go of Elias as he rolled, panting, onto the safety a solid surface.

Elias didn't waste a single moment. He crawled on hands and knees to the Life Seed and snatched it off the ground before it could fall. Clutching it tight, he kicked away from the precipice and looked around.

Tristan still hadn't recovered. He lay on the ground, moaning, eyes scrunched up in pain. With an anxious surge of fear, Elias looked across the chasm and spotted the two wurl eyeing him, teeth bared, moving their alien heads from side to side while their eyes gleamed with red malevolence. They were growling deep in their throats, a sound that carried, echoed, made it seem as though it came from behind.

The crunch of a heavy footfall on rocky ground made Elias jump to his feet and whirl around.

"Tristan? Get up."

"Give me… ahhhh. Give me a sec."

"Get up *now*."

"Why—"

But then the growl came again, much louder than before, and Elias watched, petrified, as Tristan opened his eyes and looked around in naked horror.

At least a dozen wurl had come out of the shadows, stalking forward with the liquid grace of predators on the hunt. They were larger than the wurl that had just attacked Tristan. Their bodies were bulkier, hinting at massive muscles underneath their armor. Whereas the wurl Elias had seen so far had an obsidian translucence to their scales, these wurl's plating had a metallic sheen to it, almost making them look like deadly machines come to life. The glow in their eye cluster was all too intelligent, though. It carried menace even more strongly than the growls coming from the dozen alien throats. Elias found he could not move. He watched the creatures approach and fan out around them, blocking any possible escape path. From behind, across the chasm, Elias heard more growling from the smaller, perhaps juvenile, wurl who could not cross over.

These had to be adult wurl in front of him. The stuff of nightmares. Something he had hoped he would never see.

"By the generation ship!" Tristan whispered, the shock all too evident in his voice. He got up unsteadily, clutching his wounded arm to his chest.

The adult wurl reacted with hostility to the sound of Tristan's voice. Two individuals jumped forward and splayed out their six legs, claws digging into the ground, backs arched. It was an unmistakable threatening posture, and Elias feared it was a prelude to firing the jagged spines on their backs.

"Don't!" Elias cried out, stepping between Tristan and the animals, brandishing the Seed like a weapon. The wurl backed away from him cautiously, but their stance was still tense. "Leave him alone. I'm taking this up the mountain."

Elias locked eyes with the closest wurl. Hoping he wouldn't provoke them into killing Tristan and him, he took a step forward. Then another one.

The wurl did not move, but growled deep in its throat. Gulping, Elias took another step. Now he was practically touching the creature, and he was close enough to see the magnificent array of metallic plates as they shifted in response to the wurl's breathing. It was such a big animal that every time it exhaled it sounded like a bellows, and its breath was heavily infused with the cloyingly sweet stench of rotting plant matter.

"Back. Off," Elias said, fighting to keep his voice steady. "You hurt us, and I destroy this."

He showed it the Seed, and the creature cowered away from it.

"Elias?" Tristan said from behind.

"Not now," Elias snapped.

"Elias!"

Elias glanced back and saw that one of the wurl had been stalking forward, approaching Tristan like a predator about to pounce. Elias's blood ran cold. In an instant the wurl would jump or fire a spine at point-blank range and skewer Tristan, who was defenseless without his chest armor.

"I said back off!" Elias shouted again, and jumped to intercept the stalker. It backed away from him, its body undulating with the disturbingly sinuous motion of a Terran snake. "That's it," Elias continued, his heart hammering in his chest. He walked right up to the edge of the precipice and held the Life Seed over it. "I'm throwing this over the edge if you hurt us. I'm not kidding."

"They're animals," Tristan replied in a harsh whisper. "They can't understand what you're saying."

But the steady growling halted. A charged silence filled the quiet mountainside plateau.

"These creatures are intelligent," Elias said. "They understand my intent sure enough."

Elias's arms began to tremble from holding the weight of the Life Seed in such an awkward position. Yet the minute he made as if to relax, the wurl surrounding them tensed up again.

He wouldn't be able to keep it up for very long. Elias's eyes darted around the landscape, looking for something, anything, that might offer a way out. He found nothing. The two of them were surrounded, defenseless. They were trapped with nowhere to go.

We can't fight this many. No chance. Not even if the entire Colony Patrol were here.

"They're going to kill us," Tristan said, backing away from them until he bumped against Elias. "I've seen how fast adult specimens can fire. This is it."

"Then they lose the Life Seed," Elias replied stubbornly, refusing to give up. He eyed the predators with a frown. "And you don't want that, huh?"

He dangled the Seed over the edge again.

The wurl in front of him roared in response and attacked.

Elias couldn't even cry out in surprise at the sight of a predator as tall as he was and likely weighing several tons simply sprinting forward with effortless, shocking speed. In less than a moment, the wurl was upon him. It opened its maw.

Elias jerked back out of blind instinct, lost his balance, and had a moment to realize he would fall over the edge to crash against the rocks hundreds of meters below. His body would break, and he would probably die instantly.

Better like this, he thought as he narrowly missed the snapping teeth that clamped shut less than a centimeter from his face. *I failed. I'm sorry, Oscar....*

At that moment, the ground trembled, and thunder boomed.

"Elias!"

A hand with an iron grip seized Elias's jacket and yanked him forward. Elias barely kept hold of the Life Seed as Tristan moved almost as fast as the wurl had, pulling him close, preventing him from falling. Elias was about to shout out a warning that now Tristan would be attacked instead, but...

"What's happening?" Tristan said as they stumbled forward onto safe, solid ground.

They whirled around. Elias stared, dumbstruck, as all the wurl retreated and then separated, half going to the right and half going to the left. The ground still rumbled as all the creatures aligned themselves perfectly in two lines, each facing the group opposite. They stopped when their formation was complete and lowered their heads. Elias had the sudden, irrepressible impression that they looked like rows of soldiers standing at attention, flanking a path for a very important person to walk through.

The rumbling in the ground stopped. Tristan and Elias exchanged a quick, confused look.

"What was that?" Tristan asked.

Elias shook his head. "I don't—"

But another thunderclap drowned out his words. Except now Elias focused on the booming sound, and he gasped.

"Elias, look!" Tristan said, pointing at the mountain summit above them with a trembling hand.

It's not thunder. Elias watched desperately as the nightmare shape uncoiled from where it had lain, its white body hidden in plain view, camouflaged amid the crystalline snow. Its size was overwhelming.

"It's... it's a wurl," Elias whispered, his voice puny in contrast to the roar of the creature on the mountaintop. Its voice rumbled across the landscape like thunder. The ground shook when it moved.

Then the roaring sound... changed. Elias's heart skipped a beat as the alien noise became a resonant echo in his mind. Sound became devastating intent, which in turn became the towering ghost of a sensation. It was too much to process. Elias fell forward on one knee. He barely registered Tristan collapsing next to him.

The rending sensation in his mind lessened as the echoes of the thundering roar faded. In its wake, it left behind a message. A word that was not a word but instead pure will made sound.

Elias looked up at the terrible majesty of the white wurl, and its single word echoed in his mind.

Come.

Chapter 14
Iridescent

COME.

It was an order, impossible to resist. It would not be denied. Elias found that his feet were already moving, stepping in time with Tristan's as the two of them walked past the double row of assembled wurl. The creatures did not attack, but they followed the progress of the two young men with their eyes. Elias clutched the Life Seed tightly. He wouldn't let it be damaged. It was too important, and after waiting for so many turns of the seasons, what had been stolen was finally being returned.

Elias's pace quickened. It seemed like a mere heartbeat later when he realized he was running now, threading his way among trunks of evergreens with wide branches that obscured the sunlight. Confused, he glanced back. They were not being followed by wurl anymore. Tristan ran nearby, eyes unfocused, fixed on a distant point that—

Elias's attention was wrenched toward the very same point. *I have to hurry.*

And he did. The heavily wooded terrain appeared to be unending, but instead of slowing down he quickened his pace still more. The thick canopy of trees gave way to sudden darkness pierced irregularly by shafts of light. The ground under his feet became hard, and even though he could barely see, Elias knew the way. He couldn't afford to slow down. It was important. Taking the Life Seed to where it belonged was all that mattered.

I have waited nearly a century for this. I must restore balance.

Elias could feel the Seed's energy even now, beating in time with the massive heart in his scaled chest. It was almost there. Just a little bit farther.

He had to hurry.

He had to....

Wait.

The sudden thought rang like a dissonant chord in the ordered chorus of his thoughts. The tide of singular purpose threatened to wash it away before he could hold on to it, like wet sand being taken by a receding wave from between his fingers. He had to focus. He should be hurrying, taking the—

No!

The thought became a whisper and then a shout in his mind. Elias tried to stop and continue running simultaneously, and the end result was that he tripped over a gnarled root and fell forward onto hard rock.

The pain shattered the unity of the chorus in his mind, and Elias shook his head, blinking. Confused.

He looked all around him. He was lying on the ground, the Seed clutched tightly in his arms. His left side hurt. Had he fallen?

Slowly, he sat up. His head swam as if he had just woken from a fever again. It took a moment for his eyes to adjust to the gloom and focus on the figure of Tristan, who was standing with his back to him, silent and unmoving as a statue.

"Tristan?" Elias said. "What's going on?"

There was no reply. Frowning, Elias struggled to get to his feet and managed to do it on the third try. He had a pounding headache on the left side of his head. And something was wrong.

How did I get here?

"Tristan?" Elias tried once more. There was no reply, so he walked to where Tristan was standing. A shiver ran up his spine as he looked Tristan fully in the face. Tristan's eyes were open, his mouth set in a hard line. But he didn't react to Elias in any way. "Tristan, knock it off," Elias said, his voice trembling slightly. "What's wrong with you?"

Suddenly Tristan focused on the Life Seed Elias still held. His eyes went wide and he spoke.

"I have to hurry," he mumbled. He made as if to take the Seed.

"Tristan!" Elias said, desperately now. He batted Tristan's hands away, but Tristan barely reacted. It was like trying to speak with a zombie. "Tristan, it's me!"

Tristan ignored him. He reached for the Seed again.

Elias's mind raced. What was going on? Why had he woken up in… where was he now? The last thing he could remember was being surrounded, and then…. There was a blank in his mind. Something not right. But he had woken up on the ground, hadn't he? So maybe the fall…

He didn't stop to consider the alternatives. He kicked Tristan's feet out from under him and sent him crashing down on the hard ground. It was a move that would have never worked on the Tristan Elias knew, but this time it brought grim success.

"Tristan, snap out of it!"

The fall appeared to leave Tristan dazed, but slowly he blinked and focused on Elias.

"What…? What happened?" Tristan asked, his words slurred. "My arm…."

Elias offered his hand to help Tristan stand up. "I don't know," he answered, pulling Tristan back onto his feet. "I don't even know how we got here. The last thing I remember is being surrounded."

Tristan nodded slowly, then raised his hand to his left temple as if it hurt. "Right. By all those big metallic wurl. And then…." Elias could tell by the way Tristan trailed off that he couldn't remember. "What happened, Elias?"

"I don't know. I'm not sure. There's a blank in my memory. It doesn't feel right, and I'm sure it has to do something with why we are here."

"Where is here?"

The two of them looked around. A bright shaft of sunlight outlined by dust particles hung in the air a couple of paces away, the only illumination in the dark, moist space they were in.

"Looks like a cave," Elias said. "The light must be coming in through a crack in the rock." He studied the nearest wall, where moss grew in patches, giving off a rich fragrance of moist greenery. It was velvety soft when he touched it.

"Which way did we come in?" Tristan asked.

That, at least, Elias remembered. "That way," he answered, pointing over his shoulder.

"Then that's the way out. Come on."

"Wait…," Elias said halfheartedly. For some reason, he really felt like he shouldn't leave the cave. He had to hurry.

"Elias! We need to go."

Tristan's voice slashed through the tatters of doubt in Elias's mind, and the two of them walked side by side in the direction of the exit.

It was only a few minutes before they came to the mouth of the cave—and to the group of adult wurl blocking the way out. Tristan gasped and assumed a fighting stance. Elias backed away, holding the Seed protectively.

The second Tristan took a step forward, the wurl growled in unison. They hunkered over the entrance, their message clear. They wouldn't be allowed to leave.

"Maybe they'll make way for you," Tristan whispered. "You have the Seed."

Elias nodded. It was as good an idea as any. Hesitantly, he approached the cave entrance holding the Life Seed aloft.

"Back away!" Elias said loudly. "Back away or—"

But this time the wurl weren't having it. Their eye clusters gleamed red in the forest shadows, and they snarled at the same time, exposing row after row of wicked teeth. Elias was forced to back away, and he bumped into Tristan. The two of them shared a look that spoke volumes.

"No way out," Elias said.

"It's like they're herding us," Tristan replied.

"Yeah, but where?"

Tristan raised his eyebrows, looking at the Seed. "Where do you think?"

The earth trembled slightly at that moment, and a booming sound of thunder echoed across the landscape. Elias blinked. The sound triggered a memory. Something....

"Elias, look out!"

Tristan pushed him out of the way in the nick of time. One of the wurl had fired a spine that sank into the ground exactly where Elias's foot had been. Elias stumbled, regaining his footing only to see another wurl take aim.

"We have to go!" Elias shouted, and they weren't a second too soon. Even though the cave entrance was too small for any of the wurl to enter, the sound of spines sinking into the ground or clattering off solid rock followed them until they were deep enough into the cave that they could no longer turn back, even if they wanted to.

"Seems you got your wish," Tristan grumbled, navigating through a tricky part of the dark cave. There was another light shaft just ahead, but even with that they had to go very carefully, wary of any irregularities on the ground.

"What? Why?"

"I'm betting this cave ends wherever the Life Seed rested originally. Isn't that what you wanted?"

Elias didn't answer. It *was* what he had come here for, but something about the situation felt wrong. As if he were being forced to do something before he was ready to decide to do it.

He shook his head in a futile attempt to dislodge the thought. That made no sense.

The cave soon became a tunnel, and the difficulty of navigating it pushed everything else out of Elias's thoughts. They only made a brief stop once to fashion a rough sling for Tristan's arm using his own jacket and a belt.

After the first few meters, the random lances of sunlight which provided a little bit of illumination were gone entirely and he had to rely on the limited torch function of his link, along with Tristan's. As they moved through the darkness, avoiding sharp rocks briefly outlined by the pale blue light of the two screens, Elias wondered if this was what it felt like to be in outer space. He had grown up listening to stories of his ancestors traveling through the void, but he had never considered what it must have been like to journey blindly for years and years with nothing but distant stars for company. Even here in the tunnel, Elias had company, with Tristan just ahead. The reassuring pull of gravity and the smell of earthy moisture surrounded him. He was aware that a bright sun shone outside and a blue sky arched over his head. It felt right. He didn't think he would have been brave enough to travel to the stars. Here, on New Skye, he was home.

Home.

"Aaaah!" Elias shouted, clutching the left side of his head.

"Elias? What's wrong?"

Elias ignored Tristan's voice and bent over in the darkness, eyes shut tight, willing the pain to go away. It was awful. Something was drilling into his thoughts, like a sharp rock pushing against his brain, threatening to pierce it....

Slowly, the sensation faded. The echoes did too. They were voiceless remnants of the word "home." The minute he had thought it, it had come back to him, but reflected a hundredfold. There had been such strength, such longing and vastness, in that voice that was not a voice. Elias had heard it once already.

Memory clicked back into place. The cliff. Tristan and he, trapped by approaching wurl. And then the creature. The enormous white wurl coiled at the summit of the mountain.

"Elias?" Tristan's voice was anxious. Elias felt a hand on his shoulder, shaking him. "Elias, what's wrong?"

Focusing was like coming up for breath after diving to the bottom of a lake. Where was he? What was he doing?

Then he noticed he held something in one hand. The words were slow to come and match the image, but then they were there. The Life Seed. He had taken it... to return it. And now he was in a cave, trying to find a way out.

"I'm fine," Elias said gruffly, pushing Tristan away.

"You were screaming. I thought the wurl had gotten to you."

"The wurl?"

A mental image came with the word, abruptly, and the echoes threatened to return. Elias saw sharp claws, hardened carapaces, clusters of glowing eyes. The word bounced around inside his skull, faster all the time, about to get out of control.

"No!" Elias shouted, and the echoes stopped. He knelt on the hard ground and tried to catch his breath. It felt as if he had run a marathon without moving.

"Elias, talk to me," Tristan said urgently.

The Seed was hotter now, and it was borderline painful to hold. But they were close; that much Elias knew.

"We have to return this," he said through gritted teeth. He reached for Tristan's proffered hand and grunted as he stood fully upright once more. "And we have to hurry. Before...."

"Before what?" Tristan's face looked worried. The blue glow from the links was reflected briefly in his bright eyes. He was so handsome, so much that it sometimes hurt to look at him.

Elias blinked. He had never actually formulated the thought like that, but it was true. Tristan was…. Elias liked him. A lot. He guessed there was no denying it anymore.

"Elias? Why do we have to hurry?"

"I… I don't know," Elias admitted. Already the faint echoes in his mind were fading. Had he imagined them?

"I say we turn back. Take our chances with those wurl. Who knows, maybe they've gone away by now."

"They haven't," Elias snapped. The strength of his certainty surprised him. "We need to keep going. Come on."

Without waiting for a reply, Elias took the lead and navigated the treacherous terrain of the increasingly large tunnel, going ever upward, climbing more and more up to what he suspected would be the summit of the oddly hollow mountain. His mind was a jumble of confused thoughts and shapeless fear. Something was happening to him, and he was sure the white wurl was responsible. Maybe the creature was telepathic in some way, as crazy as that might sound. Whatever the case, Elias kept his focus sharp, and he didn't allow his mind to wander into whatever would happen after he had returned the Life Seed. He didn't allow himself to think about Tristan, about what it meant for Elias to accept that he really liked the Colony Patrol guy who had been such an ass to him in the past.

The guy who was also thoughtful, compassionate, caring, resourceful, and strong.

Elias shook his head. He had to focus: place his foot over the next rock, grip a slimy handhold, push up, squeeze through a tight opening. Keep going, always up.

Exhaustion made him dizzy before long, but the insistent pressure at the back of his mind would not let him rest. Better for this to be over with already than stop for a break. Better for him to use Tristan's cooperation, now that he had it, and to get the Seed to where it needed to be.

The silence, though, was starting to get to him.

"What do you think they're doing now?" Elias asked abruptly. He had cleared a narrow passageway and was waiting for Tristan to catch up.

"What?" Tristan asked, sounding distracted. Elias could not see him clearly, but he heard a faint grunt of pain, which he supposed was from Tristan hitting his bad arm or something.

"You know. The others back home. What do you think they're doing?"

There was no answer for a few seconds, but then Tristan cleared the gap and walked into Elias.

"I don't know," Tristan snapped. "Come on. Let's get moving."

That's what I want—or is it? Elias thought. But he answered himself: *No.*

"We should take a break, Tristan. Who knows how long this tunnel is? I'm tired, and I'm betting you're tired too. Just a little bit."

There was a pause, and then Tristan sighed. "Five minutes."

The two of them shuffled around until they found a protruding rock that made a reasonable seat. It was slightly unnerving for Elias to be sitting literally next to someone and not be able to see his face. He spoke up to cover his creeping fear of the unrelenting darkness, which the feeble glow of the links could not quite dispel.

"I bet my parents are worried. And my brother," Elias said.

"You didn't tell them you were leaving?"

Elias shook his head, then remembered that he couldn't be seen very well. "No. I just... I don't know. That day at the feast, everything sort of piled up, and I took off with the Seed before I could second-guess myself."

"Right. With no food, no water, not even a map."

"Hey, we've made it this far, haven't we?"

"I'm not so sure it's been us finding our way so much as it is the wurl taking us where they want us to be."

Elias snorted. "Why do you keep doing that?"

"Keep doing what?" Tristan answered defensively.

"Keep talking about the wurl as if they were the enemy, the evil creatures of the dark or whatever. *We* are the aliens here. We came to *their* world and stole something that didn't belong to us. If they're attacking us, it's only in self-defense."

"Tell that to the families of those the wurl have killed," Tristan shot back with anger lacing his voice. "What do you want us to do, huh? Lie on the ground and let the wurl trample us to death?"

Elias lifted his hands and stood up. "Forget it. I'm not having this argument yet again. Sorry I brought it up."

"You're lucky they haven't found us," Tristan replied, standing up as well. He bumped into Elias by accident, and Elias couldn't help but take in Tristan's scent. It was a mixture of sweat and the fragrant needles of the red pines that grew around Portree.

"What do you mean?" Elias asked after a beat.

"The Colony Patrol is looking for us. If they had found you, they would have taken you back home, Seed and all, straight to the prison."

"So?"

"Just.... Forget it. Let's keep going, okay? Whatever's at the end of this place, it's got to be better than all this darkness."

"Yeah. Sure."

Elias wanted to reply with something else, maybe come up with a smart cutting remark, but nothing came to mind. He didn't want to admit to doubt or weakness in front of Tristan, but for the first time since running away, he began to think about what would happen when he came back. What was the point in returning the Seed if people could climb the mountain and tear it out again? It might take decades or centuries for the planet to heal, even if putting the Life Seed back was the right thing to do. And that wasn't even the worst part. No doubt he would be put behind bars, probably for life, however long that would be with so little food remaining. His family would be even more ashamed of him than they already were. Even if he somehow regained his freedom after a time, all the colony would hate him. His life there would be miserable until the day he died, and there was nothing he could do about it.

He would be an outcast: the village idiot combined with the village crazy guy. Nobody would want to talk to him, and he would be even more isolated than he already was. He wouldn't be able to escape the stigma until they all saw evidence that he had acted correctly. It wasn't as if he could just pack up and move to another city where nobody knew him. Portree was the only settlement on the planet. There was nothing else. The *Ionas* couldn't take him back to the stars because it had been dismantled, and he would be long dead before there could be any realistic way to leave everyone behind.

No. Going back probably wasn't an option.

I could keep going, he thought fiercely, grabbing for a handhold on rock that felt fuzzy, as if covered by moss, refusing to let himself panic. *Explore the rest of this world, where no one else has gone before. Live off the land if I can. Study the animals. I could even name every single place I went to, every species I discover, and keep a journal bigger than what Dr. Wright had. I could be the best xenobiologist in the universe, assemble knowledge no one else has, and find a way to transmit it to the Core Systems. They would come for me, rescue me from this place, and they would prove me right. I would be famous. And rich. I just have to head out into the wild and live there until my people see I was right.*

But I'd be alone.

Elias shut his eyes tight and shook his head as if to dislodge the fears and questions. It was too late to back out now. He would find a way to make the others understand. Somehow....

Elias reached a particularly tricky section of the tunnel, which forced him to stop his dark thoughts in their tracks. It sloped sharply upward, forcing him to scramble on hands and feet to gain enough purchase to keep going. The light was better, thankfully, and after five agonizing minutes of nonstop effort, Elias realized there was sunlight ahead. Somewhere above him, hidden by the slope of the terrain, was actual sunlight.

He was almost there. He only needed to hurry a little bit more. He had to get the Seed...

Home.

Elias stumbled. The voice was louder this time, although the pain was much less severe. Images suddenly flashed in his mind of snaking vines, of threads made of light, crushing rocks, sharp fangs.

"You okay?" Tristan asked, and Elias was thankful for the distraction. He focused on Tristan and nothing else.

"Yeah. I think."

"Just a little bit farther. Come on."

Elias nodded. His vision was blurry, and the sunlight ahead hurt his eyes. He closed one of them and squinted with the other, looking only at the ground beneath him as he climbed the last punishing meters to his goal.

The slope changed so suddenly that Elias stumbled forward again, throwing his arms out and letting go of the Seed. The ground was now level. It took him a moment to recover enough to reach for the Seed with grasping fingers and attempt to stand up. He swayed on his feet, and only Tristan steadying him made it possible for Elias to remain upright.

The glare was painfully bright. Elias heard Tristan gasp, but he couldn't see, not yet. He kept his eyelids shut tight until the pain receded enough for him to squint and then open his eyes, blinking quickly as a couple of tears rolled down his cheeks.

A sudden gust of frigid wind came from the right, along with a mournful howl.

Elias's breath caught in his throat, and he looked up.

He saw bare, jagged rock with several diamond-shaped holes in it. Sunlight streamed through the holes on the left, each beam clearly outlined by more suspended particles of dust. The wind was coming from a couple of the holes on the opposite side, and the howling was the whistling of the gale as it surged into the gigantic chamber.

With his eyes fully accustomed to the brightness, Elias looked around in wonder.

He was standing on the floor of a rocky gallery with a domed ceiling that vaulted high over his head. The size of it made Elias feel tiny and insignificant in the midst of such natural beauty.

"What is this place?" Tristan asked, his voice soft.

Elias struggled to take it all in. "Here's where Dr. Wright found it," he whispered. "All those years ago."

The rock of the vaulted ceiling was rough, but it appeared as if someone or something had *carved* it into the shape it was now. And the holes circling the space were unnaturally symmetrical and enormous. A giant might easily fit through one of them with room to spare, and beyond them there was…. Gazing all around, Elias took in breathtaking views of a mountainous panorama, stretching out in all directions. The wind was relentless and icy, but Elias didn't mind. This place could have been the top of a tower built exclusively to display the beauty of the planet, but that was impossible. Had to be. And yet....

"Careful," Elias warned when Tristan attempted to take a step forward. "Don't step on the vines."

"Why not?"

"Just... don't."

The floor of the gallery was even more spectacular than the dome. Three thick coiling vines reached from the edges of the space arrow-straight toward the center. They were green, here in the middle of nowhere where it should not have been possible, and they looked strong and ancient and alive. Smaller vines branched out from them, connecting each to the other two, and from the segments Elias was able to see, he realized he was looking at fractal pattern, a network of connections that started out big but quickly evolved into mind-boggling capillary detail. It was like looking at the circulatory system of a gigantic being, as if the mountain itself were alive.

But that wasn't the most breathtaking aspect of the floor. Covering it at random intervals, strewn about everywhere in a space big enough to hold twenty Main Halls, were jewels.

At least that's what they looked like. Carefully, Elias crouched where he stood and reached for the closest one. They were all big, angular plates, each of them easily twice as wide as his hand. He picked one up and was startled by its lightness. It was like lifting a wafer, even though the jewel was clearly metallic.

"That one looks like aluminum," Tristan said, nodding at the jewel Elias held. "Check this one out."

He lifted another one, and it was like a plate made of obsidian, with a wicked triangular shape similar to an oversized arrowhead.

"It's not heavy," Tristan observed, and he held his up to the sunlight.

The two of them gasped.

When the sun hit it, the jewel changed from obsidian to translucent, with a mesmerizing sheen that reflected the light in hundreds of shades of bright pink and neon purple.

"It's beautiful," Elias whispered and stood to hold his own jewel up to the light.

It was incredible. The jewel appeared metallic from one angle, but he needed only to turn it a little and it became translucent, or deep black, or even white as snow. As it changed color, its texture and weight also changed. Elias realized that the metallic aspect was the lightest, the white being the heaviest.

Elias could scarcely comprehend such beauty. He didn't need anyone to tell him that these were jewels unlike anything humans had ever seen in the entire universe. They were probably more valuable than he could ever hope to express in numbers, and they were just *there*. Free for the taking. He held his own more carefully, analyzing it from every angle. All of them had the same rough shape—slightly concave so the middle of every jewel was raised as it reached the sharp point at the end. In fact, it looked almost as if the jewels were meant to be stacked together....

"Elias?" Tristan said, a sudden tremor in his voice.

Elias knelt down, his brow furrowed by a sudden revelation. The jewels were meant to be stacked. He confirmed it when he placed his own on top of another one at an angle. It fit just right.

"Elias?"

He reached for another one and put it under the other two. Yes, that was its rightful position. And another one would go on top, and another one on the left.

Elias blinked. The jewels made a perfect mesh, like plates in armor.

"Elias!"

It hit him then, although it should have been obvious from the beginning. These were not jewels or plates. They were scales.

Elias looked up at the vaulted ceiling of the gallery on top of the world and realized why Tristan's voice was laced with panic.

The white wurl slithered into the space with unthinkable grace for a being that size. As coil after coil of its body entered the gallery, until Elias thought the place couldn't possibly contain such a large creature, sunlight reflected off the plaques covering the alien armored body. The scales rippled with color, from white to iridescent, from obsidian to metal.

As the last flick of its tail entered, the wurl lowered its triangular head. A cluster of three merciless glowing red eyes pierced Elias with a look that sliced straight into his soul.

The mountain trembled as the creature advanced, a reptilian foot with glass claws stopping less than a meter from where they were standing.

HOME.

Then the other foot came down.

Chapter 15
Trapped

ELIAS DROPPED the scale he had been holding and backed away from the enormous creature by instinct, crashing into Tristan and eliciting a grunt of pain from the other young man.

"We have to get out of—" Tristan began, but he never finished.

The white wurl roared.

It was a deafening soundwave that boomed with power, and even as Elias dropped onto one knee with his hands over his ears, he realized he could hear the sound in his thoughts. It made no sense. It was as if the terrible voice of the creature left him exposed and naked, with nowhere to hide, not even inside his own brain.

Elias screamed. He vaguely registered Tristan doing the same.

The white wurl clamped its jaws shut and tilted its head to the side, fixing the Life Seed with an unblinking stare. The echoes of its roar took a long time to fade, and Elias could have sworn he could still hear the cry inside his mind for a few seconds after the creature had gone silent.

The echoes died down eventually, though, and Elias realized he was lying on the ground, curled around the Seed, looking up at the white wurl. Slowly, with trembling legs, he managed to stand up.

"Back away carefully," Tristan whispered. Elias didn't dare turn around to look at him.

"Okay," Elias muttered, mostly to himself. Behind him, he could hear Tristan taking slow, stealthy steps. Praying he wouldn't trip on one of the vines, Elias followed suit.

They hadn't taken more than three or four steps before the white wurl lifted its head and, with a fluid and almost languid motion, uncoiled its tail so it circled around the perimeter of the gallery, covering it almost completely. A quick, panicky look back confirmed what Elias feared. The exit was now blocked by the appendage, and the only way out now was one of the jagged holes on the rock face, which led down into nothing.

"This was a trap," Tristan said under his breath. "I was right. They herded us here."

"What do we do?" Elias asked, trying to keep the panic from his voice.

"You tell me. This was your idea. Give them the Seed and let's go."

Elias swallowed the lump in his throat. He looked up at the imposing, threatening bulk of the white wurl and felt as if his legs would give way once again. Tristan was right, though. Returning the Life Seed had been his idea. And he needed to finish what he had started.

He took a step forward, then another. The wurl didn't move at all. It might have been an iridescent statue, were it not for the fact that its eyes glittered with intelligence. Another step. Elias couldn't believe he was doing this. The creature was big enough to eat him in a single bite, and there was something strange about it. The other wurl Elias had seen had been intimidating, sure, but remained essentially animals. This one, on the other hand....

He couldn't keep going anymore. He was halfway to the center of the gallery, with the hulking wurl at the other end. Between them, on the ground, the strange nexus of vines beckoned. It was the obvious place to put the Life Seed, but terror was getting the better of Elias, and after another hesitant half step he simply remained where he was. He couldn't get any closer, not when he was sure the creature could trample him or slice him open with the edges of its wicked glass claws.

"H-here!" he shouted, holding out the Life Seed to the wurl. "Take it!"

The creature tilted its head to the side once more, as if analyzing a particularly interesting insect. Then it dipped its head down, ever so slightly.

"You want me to drop it?" Elias asked. "Okay—here!"

He dropped the Seed, and several things happened the second it touched the ground.

The vines around the chamber glowed with a brief, faint luminescence of subdued green.

Tristan shouted something.

The white wurl bared its fangs and attacked.

Elias was too surprised to even move out of the way. His bladder let go as the hulking behemoth struck forward in a blur of motion, its jaws snapping shut mere centimeters away from Elias's face. An overpowering smell of smoldering vegetable matter enveloped him when the white wurl exhaled.

Still frozen in place by fear, unable to believe he was still alive, Elias stared as the white wurl lumbered forward, triggering tremors in the ground. It walked until its front feet rested on either side of the nexus of vines and then moved its slender neck toward the Seed, ripples of sunlight making its scales flicker from metal to glass to a shockingly beautiful iridescence.

With a last look at Elias, the creature touched the Life Seed with its snout.

The reaction was immediate. The entire Seed glowed as if white-hot, and the sharp sound of sizzling meat was soon trailed by the corresponding smell. The white wurl snatched its head away from the Seed, moaning, and Elias realized that the scales of its snout were burned, the edges reddened, hinting at charred flesh beneath. The wurl closed all three of its eyes and swung its head from side to side, moaning even more in evident pain.

"Now!" Tristan shouted over the din. He had suddenly appeared and grabbed Elias's hand. "Go, go, go!"

Elias didn't stop to think. He turned around and sprinted away beside Tristan, his terrified brain nevertheless registering the fact that Tristan's grip on his hand was strong and warm. In its pain, the wurl thrashed its tail dangerously, but the entrance to the mountain tunnels was clear.

"The Seed!" Elias shouted.

"Forget it! We need to go!"

The ground under their feet rumbled. Another deafening screech forced Elias to let go of Tristan's hand to cover his ears, but he didn't stop running, somehow even getting ahead of Tristan in his wild race. They were almost there. Once they were in the tunnel, the creature wouldn't be able to catch them. It was too big to fit. They would be safe. Just a little bit—

Whoosh.

Elias barely stopped in time. Tristan crashed against him and the two of them fell forward, sprawling on the vine-covered floor.

A mere hair's breadth away from a glittering, iridescent spine.

Elias's eyes were wide as saucers from absolute shock. A spine as thick and long as his leg had struck the ground right in front of them, splintering the rock underneath from the force with which it had been launched.

Elias exchanged a look with Tristan and saw his own emotions mirrored.

There's no way out. No way out.

As if to confirm it, two more spines impacted the ground on either side of them, sending up sprays of stinging rock fragments and making the white wurl's message clear. It could kill them anytime it wanted.

No escape at all.

Something strange happened to Elias. Now that he truly knew there was no way out, calm descended over him, blanketing the terror. He stood up and offered his hand to Tristan, who took it in a trembling grip. Elias didn't let go as the two of them turned around to face their death.

"By the generation ship," Tristan whispered, his voice terror mixed with awe.

It was as if the white wurl had transformed. From underneath its shimmering scales, spines had appeared, hundreds of them, each one ending in a wicked serrated tip that looked sharper than any knife. The spines were all facing forward, and the ones around the creature's neck fanned out in a circle, almost like a mane of simmering threat and absolute power. It looked like a quilled monster come to life.

The wurl glared at them with its shining eyes even as it used its tail to coil around them, tightening, forcing the two young men to move forward until they were standing in front of the fallen Life Seed once more. Then it stopped. It lowered its head until it was level with Elias. It was so close that Elias could see clearly the awful damage that the Life Seed had inflicted on the creature's snout. Several of its armor plates had fallen off where they had touched the Seed, and the charred flesh underneath was bleeding. Glittering red blood pooled on the creature's snout, shocking against the iridescence of its healthy scales, and dripped to the ground in a faint but alarming rivulet.

The revelation hit Elias suddenly, piercing through his brittle veneer of calm.

"They can't touch it," he said quietly.

"What?" Tristan asked.

"The Life Seed," Elias explained, pointing. In response, the white wurl lowered its head toward the Seed and then moved it in Elias's direction. Its meaning was clear. "They can't touch it. They need us to move it."

"Maybe we can use that," Tristan said quickly. "You grab the Seed, then we back away. This wurl has to let us go."

Elias shook his head sadly. "Or it impales us with spines. No, Tristan. We've come this far. I have to set things right."

"Elias, think of your home. Of Portree. What about the people there? How will you make things right? We need that Seed. Don't do this."

"We can't sentence an entire world to die so we can live," Elias replied, letting go of Tristan's hand.

"Elias! Don't do it!"

"Don't try to stop me, Tristan. The white wurl won't let you, and I don't want to see you die."

Tristan was about to say something else, but the wurl growled threateningly, almost as if it had understood their conversation. Elias picked up the Life Seed and held it out.

"I'm going to place it where it belongs, okay?" he told the savage creature in front of him.

There was no vocal reply, but the white wurl backed away a couple of steps in open invitation. It whisked its tail aside. Elias didn't look back to see Tristan's expression because he feared his own resolution would falter. Instead he simply walked forward, stepping gingerly over the vines, until he reached the very center of the mountain gallery. There was a shallow depression there, covered everywhere by vines. They formed a strangely beautiful geometric pattern, like a spiral made out of individual tendrils that coiled in on themselves until they reached a single point, where a withered-looking vine protruded up from the ground, as if questing to find the Seed that was no longer there.

Elias hopped into the depression and walked toward the center. Carefully, he knelt down and realized that the bottom of the Life Seed had a groove he hadn't noticed before, a perfect opening for the questing vine tendril.

"Here. I return that which we stole."

He placed the Life Seed where it belonged.

And his mind shattered into a thousand pieces.

Chapter 16
Sizzra

I AM....

I am Elias. I am a human being.
Or—am I?
I am....

I am an unhatched infant. I am ready, and I am strong. My shelter feels now like a prison, one I need to destroy if I am to escape. I want to live.

I do not have spines yet, but my feet have claws. It is hard to wriggle in the confines of the egg, but I bring one of the claws on my right front foot forward and I push. It is difficult. I can barely move, but all around me I can feel the warmth and the faint heartbeats of the others. They yearn to cross the threshold from dreams into reality, just as I do.

I will get there first.

I push harder and my claw pierces the shell. I know a brief moment of panic: What is out there? What if there is danger? What if a predator lies in wait, invisible, poised to strike?

I stifle a scared whine, clamping my jaws shut. The first sound I make in the world will *not* be one of fear. It will be one of strength.

Another push. My foot breaks through, and I feel sunlight. Wind. Eager now, all fear forgotten, I wriggle my body and use my other front foot to widen the gap in the eggshell. It breaks easily now, as if bending to my will. I will not be contained any longer. I will be...

Free!

I stumble forward, front feet slipping on smooth eggshells slick with the contents of my egg. The light is a blinding, painful shock, and

I close both sets of eyelids on my eye cluster to block it out. My mind is racing, reeling in confusion, but above all there is a desire to stand tall, out in the world, and cry out my defiance. I push with all my strength, and my middle and back feet explode from the remnants of the eggshell to land on the uneven ground. My tail, so wonderfully long, flicks for the first time. I marvel at the sensation of air whistling over my scales.

I take a tentative, stumbling step. The second one is better. By the third I can open my eyes.

I see the world for the first time in a blast of sensory input. The sky overhead is shockingly blue, dizzying and vast, but it is to the ground that my gaze is drawn. It is… marvelous. Echoes of the ancient memories of my mother and her mothers surge to the fore of my thoughts, so I find concepts for every beautiful thing. I am on top of a mountain, looking down on lesser peaks capped by snow. It is noon, and the sun is high in the sky. I can see so much of the world. There are valleys, rivers, forests. There is a great crater, its rim glittering with gemstones. If I focus, I can even make out individual leaves in the trees on the mountain slopes, swaying gently in the wind. I can see small birds spiraling through the air as they hunt for insects. In the rivers, I see a fish with sparkling scales jump out in a spray of water droplets. This is a world of breathtaking beauty.

And it is mine. I am the queen of all I survey.

The time has come. I climb on an outcrop of rock overlooking a deadly drop into the abyss, clumsy no longer. I flick my tail three times, dig the claws on all six of my feet into the ground, and roar out my name.

Sizzra!

I am Sizzra, queen of this world. Instinct, memory, and my own unbreakable will guide my actions. I know what I should do next. I draw air into my lungs and sing the Song of Birth.

The echoes come back to me almost immediately, some of them mental echoes of my own voice, of the queens that came before me. And some of them from the nest.

I look to the left, and my ears single out the tentative scratching of the males, my brood-siblings all. Their eggs are much smaller than mine, black and metallic where mine was purest white. I lift my head approvingly at their efforts and roar the Song a second time. The notes in my voice thread themselves into an invisible pattern that projects my will.

Rise, brood-siblings. Live.

Faint keening is my answer, claws scratching at eggshells, and soon the first hints of black-scaled bodies break out of their own shelters. I memorize each and every one of them as they come out of their eggs, naming them in my heart even though they will never claim names of their own. I take special note of the males who hatched first. One among them might one day be my chosen mate—if he proves strong enough. For now, though, I merely welcome them all with my voice and my will and my presence. I know I am resplendent in the sunlight. I have scales like no other creature alive in the world, and they will see each and every one of them, or see them all as they shift and drink in the light to refract it in a million and one different ways. I stand firmly above the males and accept their unblinking gazes of hushed awe as my due.

I roar the Song for the third and final time. Some of the males answer with their own thoughtless voices, and again I memorize who sounds the fiercest. As the final echoes of my roar are lost in the distance, I drop back into the nest, crushing an unhatched egg under my claws. I feel the faint spark of life within it be extinguished, but I feel no remorse. He was too slow to hatch, and there will be no weakness in my brood.

I walk among the males, tiny creatures barely half my size, and they all part to make way for their queen. I bask in their unified attention, keenly aware of the echoes of my own image coming from their simple minds. I am strength incarnate. I am the light of the stars made grace. I am power and danger. I am unstoppable will.

I am Sizzra. And I am queen of all—

But it is then that I see the corpse, and the reality of the world comes crashing down onto my shoulders.

Slowly, moving with silken, calculated stealth, I approach the edge of the mountaintop nest. The wind howls around me, and some of the males whimper.

The sound triggers rage in me, and I whirl around, snapping at the air with my jaws. They all back away from me, terrified. That is good. I do not expect to hear them whimper again.

I turn my attention back to the gigantic corpse that lies sprawled out on the rocks of the treacherous mountain slope leading to our nest. My mother is beautiful even in death, a sculpture of ice now that her will has long ceased to animate her iridescent scales. I approach with more confidence than I feel, for the benefit of the males in my wake, until I reach her head.

Alaya. Her name comes to me like the echo of a ghost. I feel no sadness, no real sense of loss. Her memories are within me, as mine will be within my daughter one day. I do, however, feel anger. And the slightest hint of concern.

Alaya's body towers above me, making me seem like an insignificant speck of life in the presence of a mountain, but even her size cannot hide the gruesome marks that teeth and savage claws have left on her flesh. Her right back and middle feet have been torn off completely, and a crimson pool of frozen blood coats the snow and the rocks nearby. Along her back there are three parallel slashes, wicked raking wounds that tore through her armored plating and sliced the bone and internal organs underneath. Her tail lies several body lengths away from where we stand. Most of the jagged spines on her back have been either fired or torn off. And her neck….

That is how she died, I am sure of it. There is a gruesome swath of frozen red flesh where her crown of spines should have been. The savagery of the mutilation leaves me breathless for a moment. To think of the strength required to bring down my mother in this way is to venture into the impossible, and yet here is the proof. She was not strong enough. And she was killed by one of the Two Others.

Of that there is no doubt in my mind. No one else holds such power in this world. Anger simmers in my chest as I walk around my mother's body, my eyes briefly taking in the vista of the lower mountainside, littered as it is with the frozen remnants of dead males of my mother's brood, and the brood of Another.

I already know which one it was simply by looking at the carcasses below, but I confirm it when I walk around to my mother's front side and see two bloody wings still grasped firmly in her glass claws, torn off the queen they belonged to.

I bare my fangs at the sight. The scales on the wings are a deep violet hue, the color of an enemy. The wings are dim now, in death, but their size still takes my breath away. My mother must have fought fiercely indeed to have managed to tear both wings off the Flyer. For knowing that, my heart eases. My mother fought well. And her death was bought at a dear price.

I cast my eyes down and quickly spot the lifeless remnants of the Flyer queen. Her slender violet body, so different to the hulking majesty of my mother or me, lies motionless in a ravine far below. I notice the jagged stumps where her wings would have been. Her four legs are crumpled underneath her, clearly broken. Her ruby eyes are sightless in death, and her entire length is riddled with spines. Some of those are small and metallic. There is even one which has pierced her top eye, a black glassy spine from a brave juvenile. The majority of the spines embedded in her, however, are white. I sharpen my eyesight and see how incredibly resilient the Flyer queen must have been to keep fighting even as her body was impaled again and again by my mother's attacks. Her jaws are pierced everywhere by the spine crown she must have torn off Alaya with a single savage bite, but even that did not stop the enemy. The sight of her fills me with loathing.

And the smallest, faintest hint of fear.

I roar out defiance to drown the traitorous emotion, and my confidence returns. The enemy is dead, as is my mother. For the Flyer to have made it as far as our nest's border is a testament to her strength, but now that dead queen is no longer my concern. I have my own enemies to think about, and time may or may not be on my side. Just as I have been born, somewhere across the ocean another Flyer queen must have hatched. And in the depths, the third one is surely waiting.

I glance back. My hundreds of brood-siblings stand behind me in a silent display of unconditional obedience. Sunlight glitters on their black scales, and at that moment they look beautiful. This is my strength, and theirs, combined. This is *my* world.

With a growl, I order them to move and follow me down to a secret cavern. The first thing I should do is commune with my Flower.

THE CAVERN is not far from our nest, but the going is tricky. The ice is slippery underfoot in places—treacherous. As the slope we go down becomes sharper, I am forced to dig my claws into the ice to prevent myself from losing my footing. I go carefully, always making three feet secure before moving, and most of the males imitate me. Some of them are too foolhardy, though. Three of them tumble to their deaths while trying to rush over treacherous terrain. With an inner sigh, I forget the names I gave them. A shame, really. One of them had been the first to hatch.

The danger only adds to the delicious freedom that is life, though. As I use my muscles and exert myself, I feel the giddy rush of excitement that comes from facing a challenge and overcoming it. Faint echoes of my forebears whisper of similar challenges and others much greater. I push them to the back of my mind and think only of the moment. I want my memories to be pristine, shining clear in every instant, so that my daughter and her daughter and her daughters for generations will remember my life and seethe with envy at what they will never experience firsthand.

The sunlight on my skin is electric, a hint of lightning caressing the folds of a cloud. I feel myself grow stronger every minute I spend under the sun, and I know my scales will be even more radiant in the brilliant light that engulfs us. I long to simply lie down and bask in the warmth of the light, but there is something that must be done first. It is the one thing that drives me, whether I want it to or not. It is the one thing I hold in greater regard than my own magnificent self.

As I enter the cavern ahead of all my brood-brothers, I see it: a breathtakingly beautiful Flower, blooming in the shadowy depths of the gigantic space. Its petals have the same prismatic iridescence as my scales, white and pink and neon green, always changing, always new. It towers above me in its magnificence, even though I know that one day I will dwarf it when I am fully grown. For now, though, I feel… respect. It is grudging but undeniable. This is the soul of the planet, the essence of a world given shape. It is power given form, a focal point for the spirit-lines that bind us all in a unique mesh of existence.

I come to a stop in front of it, and a quick glance back shows me that the males are all quivering with fear, spread out as far away from the Flower as they can get. I growl dismissively. They can never understand the beauty that I behold. They can only sense in their simple instinctive way that here is something much greater even than I. Much older and much deadlier.

I lean my head forward, nearly touching it, close enough to make the Flower glow with inner light and the scorching heat that is its energy. I close my eyes and commune with my world.

The spirit-lines of my Flower reach far. Through its power, I am able to see everything at once. The vines under my feet are conduits of pure energy, and when I open my eyes again, my sight is transformed. I look around in wonder, and for the first time in my short life, I can See.

None of the memories could have prepared me for this moment. It is something that can only be experienced, and even then it is not something that can be understood. My sight reveals the glowing tendrils that link me to all my brood-brothers. I see their individual life sparks, and looking down I can see my own, larger than theirs, more beautiful, yet also made of the same energy.

I cast my eyes down, through the mountain, and the world opens itself to me. I follow the vines that thread the entire continent, and I see life everywhere, not only animals this time, but the plants too. Some forests are gigantic organisms, a single dormant consciousness of incalculable age. There are underground networks of complex mushroom systems that nourish creatures which have never seen the sun. Farther away still, in the heat of the desert sands, there is life in small, defiant concentrations wherever there is a little water. Beyond the desert, I can sense limitless prairies with blades of grass dancing in the wind, and every single one of them is alive. I can even cast my sight to the very edges of the world, and I scc...

Ah. There. An interruption. The oceans are the limits of my sight. They surround my continent, and I can sense the faintest hint of the tendrils of the Flower of the deep. It rivals mine in every way, a fact which I acknowledge, even if I do not like it. And beyond it, where my sight cannot reach, I know there is a third Flower, the last on this world. It grows in a volcano, and its petals are tipped with molten magma. I know this because of the memories inside me, and I also know that the guardian of that Flower is the first of the Two Others I will seek out and kill. The Flyer queen will die under my teeth and my claws, pierced throughout by spines. Of that, at least, I am sure.

I break the contact with my Flower and back away. I will not admit it in front of the males, but my link with it cannot be sustained for too long or my own mind would be absorbed by the very thing I am charged with guarding. Instead, I roar out an order, projecting my will with renewed strength.

Go. Feed. Grow strong. Spread throughout the continent and sow fear in the hearts of all other living creatures.

As one, the males growl agreement and dash away through the tunnels that will lead them to the valleys and the forests and the deserts. Some of them are already bickering with one another, trying to display their dominance. I take note of every victor in every squabble. Wherever they go, I will know. And whenever I call, they will come.

In the meantime, I will hunt. I will kill. And I will grow powerful.

Chapter 17
Torn

A FLICKER of awareness.

I am Elias.

But then.... Why...?

Then the memories came in like a tide, swallowing everything in their path.

I WATCHED them come down from the sky one afternoon, while I basked in the golden rays of the setting sun. At first I paid little attention to the bright star descending, glowing fiercely against the darkening sky. I had just killed a razorback behemoth of the depths, a thing with no name, one so powerful that he could hide his own life spark from the Flowers. In hunting him I was deliberately trespassing on the domain of my Singer sister of the deep. If she had come upon me after the battle with the razorback, tired as I was, she might have been able to ensnare me with a song. She did not come, however, and I surfaced triumphant from the black ocean depths and into the light of my world.

I devoured the blistering energy of the razorback's spark, heedless of the burn, and afterward I felt my power grow even more. Warm blood-soaked flesh nourished my body even as its energy nourished my core. Returning to the mountain of my Flower, I was a rolling harbinger of destruction, a spike-covered jewel big enough to flatten forests in my wake.

Replete with victory, I watched the flickering light die as the star from the sky touched the land. Strangely, though, there was no explosion, no crater afterward. A flicker of doubt made me wonder. Something about that light was very odd. But I was tired, and I claimed the time for my rest. Whatever it was, if it was even worth thinking about, I would investigate in the morning.

The panicky mental echoes of some males woke me up in the late hours of the night. Annoyed, I projected at them to be *Quiet*, and their cowardly keening ceased. For a time. It resumed in the early morning, and by then I could no longer ignore the fact that something had happened in my world.

I watched the new creatures through the eyes of the bravest grown males as they hid in the bushes around the place where the star had fallen. They were unlike anything I had ever seen, and no memory of my mothers could explain what they were. The Flower could not link to these animals, even though they were obviously alive. I could not understand it. I knew every creature in the world, from my own lifetime and countless others. Knew even the creatures in the oceans and the creatures in the other continent. These animals did not belong anywhere. It was as if they had come from a place... beyond. An unthinkable concept yet undeniable.

For an entire turn of the seasons, I watched. The creatures appeared to be harmless, puny, and devoid of claws or spines. They stayed very close to a female creature that was larger than me: something of metal and light which not even the darkness of the night could quench. It would swallow the creatures one at a time and then spit them back out at random intervals. This female was entirely motionless, and I watched her fiercely, preparing myself for battle.

Her challenge, however, never came. Her males spread out around her, cutting down trees and building nests in tight, precise formations. When wintertime came, the males stayed either in their nests or inside the female. I was astounded. She had not moved, not even once, and I had had at least one male watching her at all times. I did not know how she took nourishment, unless she was consuming the males, which ranged around my world and came back with the tiny animals they were able to hunt. It was a mystery to me, but as far as I knew, not a threat. Which was good, because lately I had begun to watch the skies.

The challenges of the Flyer queen were subtle at first, starting long before the strange creatures arrived on my territory. Once a stray male of hers flew over my mountain, wounded. A single spine brought him down. Then there was a squad of them, flying in formation. They came upon me while I was hunting in the desert and stole the heart of the sand snake I had killed after an entire day and night of hunting. These ones were faster, and my spines brought down only one of them.

Then there was the year of the great storm, when something large had flown in, hidden in the black clouds, outlined only briefly after every flash of lightning. Her sinuous shape had made every spine on my body stand up, ready to be fired, but the coward had flown away just as the storm dissipated.

She came back several years later and killed two juveniles of mine, weak males with no territory of their own who had therefore failed to reach maturity. I felt their deaths, and I felt their terror. But in her slippery, backhanded way, she had flown back to her own vile nest by the time I rolled to the site of the murders.

Several turns of the seasons followed that incident, but I had not seen her at all. Just the same, I kept a watchful eye. The time was coming for me to mate, and instinct and memory told me that it was the most likely time when she would strike. All throughout the winters, I patrolled the shores, watching for her. Her advantage lay in ambush and escape, mine in power and reach.

When spring came, I had not seen the Flyer queen, nor had I heard the faintest echo of a song under the waves. So I returned to the mountain to commune with the Flower. It had been a year since the arrival of the strange creatures, and when I cast my sight out with the Flower's power, I was shocked.

The puny otherworldly males had killed their mother. The miserable little creatures had gutted her in the winter, and now only a husk of her remained, her metal plates exposed to the elements. I could scarcely contain my anger as I saw that the males had used the body of she who had given birth to them in order to build even more elaborate nests in a larger sprawl on the area they had infected. How had they done it? Had she been weak and old? That could not be possible. She had brought them from the stars. Unless....

Spring turned to summer, and I watched them very carefully. I planned the moment of my attack with no rush, considering every option. Throughout this time I came to know them very well indeed. I watched them through the eyes of every curious male who followed them on their frequent excursions deeper into my territory. I decided to encourage my males' inclination not to attack them for the time being so I could learn more about their capabilities. The creatures seemed weak and slow, yet now they were able to hunt animals that were much stronger and faster than them. Besides, they had killed their female somehow. I needed to learn what they could do before revealing myself.

More winters came. Some of the creatures explored far away indeed, to the very limits of my own vision, but they always returned to the nest they had made. On it, there now grew things my Flower could not touch. Their life spark was too different, and it quickly fizzled away. The small creatures were either very stupid or very stubborn. They kept planting whatever it was they had brought with them only to watch it die. In the darkest hours of winter, I dared to hope that they would simply starve, ridding my world of the stain of their existence.

At the end of that winter, I was challenged by the Flyer queen's envoy, a very large male who sought me out in the steep mountain passes of my territory. He had selected the place with great care, evidently, as the sharp inclines and treacherous rocks slowed me down while at the same time giving him plenty of spaces to hide, flying up or down or under a thousand and one covering rock formations.

It was an infuriating battle. I knew all Flyers were cowards, hard to catch. I had underestimated how much. As I fired spine after spine into the air, only for the cobalt body of the flying male to twirl out of the way at the last instant, I realized that he was simply too fast for me. His plan was obvious: tire me out, make me slow. Then he would zoom in and slice my flesh with his razor talons.

I had experience in this, though. And he, being a male, did not have generations of memories to draw upon. I set up a trap in a particularly narrow ravine, firing several spines at large rocks until I had destabilized them enough to make them teeter under their own weight but not yet fall. I then lured the large male to this space. I roared fiercely, firing almost all my spines, and then deliberately tumbled over the edge of the ravine. I made it look as if I had tried to roll, only to smash against the floor, briefly stunned.

The male's eagerness was his undoing. He dived on me, talons forward, aiming for my eye cluster. I waited until the last possible second and then fired one single spine, pretending I was aiming for him. He slithered out of the way, twirling in the air, but my spine hit the rocks and they came down in a deafening avalanche.

The male had to use all his agility to get out of the way of the deadly rocks threatening to crush him, and he made it out just barely, using all his strength and cunning to avoid my trap.

Therefore, he had no more strength left for me.

It was almost easy after that. I leapt onto a rock and fired a slender spine, impaling his eye cluster with such force that he was launched back into the air before falling limply to the ground, a lifeless lump. I devoured his heart and then roared out my defiance, knowing that the Flyer queen had watched the battle. I shouted out my name with my mind so she would remember it forever.

I am Sizzra!

Her oh-so-faint reply, possible only at that moment of deepest bloodlust, was nevertheless unmistakable.

And I am Dresde. I will see you soon, sister....

I unfurled my crown of spines. I was ready for her. I was ready for anything.

It was then that I felt the death. A single male, one of my own. He had fallen down a cliff, startled. At first I thought it was another Flyer attack, but as my mind sped through his panicked memories, I realized it was because of the creatures who had come from the sky.

They were climbing a mountain.

The mountain where my Flower was.

My earsplitting roar made the rocks around me tremble. I ordered every male in my brood to converge upon the mountain, and I ignored my own battle exhaustion and surged forward in that direction. I climbed the nearest hill and rolled down its slope, using my momentum to propel me up the next peak. I jumped and sprinted like I never had before, like no other female of my line had ever done. I was almost at the other edge of my continent, but I crossed the distance to my goal in less than a day.

I reached the foot of the Flower mountain at the same time as most of my males. I ordered them to surround it, to kill anything that approached, and I climbed alone. My claws splintered granite from the force of my footsteps. My tail swished and made the air moan in protest.

Again and again, I cast my thoughts to the Flower, but vast though it was, it could never understand something that was not of this world. To it the creatures were invisible, nonentities devoid of life spark. It augmented my sight as I asked it to, but I could not find the creatures. I did not even know whether they would be going straight for the Flower, but something deep in my heart told me they would. Deranged males that had killed their own female could only be bent on destruction. I had been a fool to let them live this long.

I made the mountain shake with my stomping fury, climbing ever upward. I swore to kill every single one of the foul creatures. I would go to where they kept the fading corpse of their female and crush their nests and their young. I would obliterate every sign of them from my world. I would make them shake in fear and then—

I screamed. One moment I was climbing the mountain. The next I was falling, my heart boiling away in the acid of unbearable pain. I hit the ground so hard that my remaining spines sunk into my own flesh. I screamed again, blind, powerless, trapped in an endless loop of mind-breaking agony. I tried to get up, and I could not. I tried not to scream, but the howls would not be contained.

And all around me, from every single living thing on my continent, echoes of other screams shredded my mind.

It was impossible. It was unthinkable. Days followed nights, and the pain did not go away. I knew that my males were paralyzed as I was, and most other animals too. The very plants themselves shuddered in silent wailing of their loss, of the awful void, the consuming darkness of the world.

I am not sure how long I lay there, more helpless than an unhatched egg, exposed to the cruelty of the elements. When I could finally muster enough strength to move, half of my body had been covered by the snows of many years. Teetering, trembling, weaker than I had been as a newborn, I eventually managed to stand on my feet.

I howled then, giving voice to my black misery. The Flower was *gone*. My link to the world was gone. Something in my heart and in my mind had been torn away in nameless savagery, and I knew that it was the creatures who had ripped the Flower out at the roots. They had taken it away. And I could not see....

No matter how hard I cast my mind, I was limited to the perceptions of my own senses. It was worse than the memory of one of my mothers, who had died trapped in an underground cave. She at least had had the freedom of her thoughts, even as her body was crushed by the earth. I had none of that. I could not find my males, could not find the spirit-lines. I saw a bird flying through the air, and I could not feel it.

It was worse than being blind. It was worse than death.

It took me many years to climb the mountain to where my Flower used to be. It took me even longer to nourish my body back to a ghostly semblance of its former strength. Every day, I cast my limited eyes toward the valley where I knew the creatures had nested. Every day, I promised myself I would go and destroy them all.

Yet I could not.

I was paralyzed with horror the first time I tried to leave the mountaintop and realized that I was bound. The horrible void where the Flower had been was pulling at me, tying me to the place of the world's greatest loss and my line's greatest failure. There was hunger there, a desperate yearning to fill the emptiness where before there had been unity.

It wanted to swallow me.

It wanted to swallow the entire world.

Simply resisting its relentless pull took most of my energy. Years came and went. I had time to think, to plan, to nourish my hatred.

The creatures had done something that should have been impossible. Nothing on this world could touch the Flower and survive for long. Not even a deranged queen would dare attempt to destroy another one's Flower. Every single living creature on my world knew what the Flower was, and they feared it. I was the guardian of the Flower, yes, but over the countless generations, our title had lost its meaning. After all, why guard something that needs no protection?

The bitter truth clawed at my soul with guilt. The Flower needed no protection from things of this world, true. But it did need to be guarded from creatures from the stars.

I grew weak in my long confinement. Eventually I was able to rebuild a tenuous shadow of the connection I had had with my males, and so they knew to come to me and feed me with their own kills, each and every single one of those acts of mercy filling me with rage and shame. I had been the queen of this world. Once. Now I was less than an invalid. Powerless. Feeble.

And yet one day, after I had given up all hope, the impossible happened. A fleeting glimpse from some of my males showed me that one of the alien creatures had taken the Flower bud and was carrying it through the land, soon joined by another. It cost me an entire day's energy to order those males to escort them to the mountain. It cost me even more energy to compel the creatures to come up to my prison, but they heard me. And they bent to my will.

I had gone through every possible scenario in my decades of confinement. I had planned for this. No creature on this world could touch the Flower bud, but *they* could. Once they had come close enough, I would force them to return that which they stole.

I am weak, yes. A shadow of my former self. But I can still move fast and bite deep.

Besides, it is not difficult to force a living thing to do something. All creatures feel pain.

Chapter 18
The Flower

ELIAS FELT the pull of gravity as a distant tilting. Pain brought him back to himself—pain from the dull impact as he hit the ground and the sharper sting of something cutting his cheek.

He opened his eyes. He couldn't understand what he was seeing, could not tolerate the limits of his own perception. His stomach heaved, and he curled in on himself, barely managing to suppress the urge to scream, to tear his scales out.

A voice was calling to him, but he couldn't process the sounds and transform them into words.

I don't have scales.

It was a single thought, but he grabbed on to it with desperate intensity. It became his anchor in the roil of confusion, of fear, anger, and hatred. Not all of it came from him. And the memories....

"Elias! Elias, talk to me!"

Somebody was shaking him. This time, Elias understood the words.

I don't have scales. I am... human.

The truth of his certainty crashed over him, sending him reeling, forcing him to reevaluate the entire structure of his mind. He wasn't that other being, vast and incomprehensible. He was Elias. Human. Not the wurl queen.

His fragmented perspective shifted, and his limited sight was suddenly not nauseating anymore. It was his own. Normal. Blinking, he focused on a face very close to his.

Tristan.

The name linked his mind to memories, and the memories threaded themselves into Elias's identity. He might have moaned aloud, but this time it was out of overwhelming relief. He was himself again. He had stolen the Life Seed to bring it to its rightful place. He had planted it again, and then....

"Elias!"

"Danger...," Elias tried to say. His tongue felt clumsy. He wished that he could simply project his will like—

That's her. That's not me.

"What?" Tristan asked him. Elias realized Tristan was kneeling over him, a worried expression on his handsome face.

How had he fallen down? Why did his cheek hurt?

A low growl that was almost a tremor slammed Elias back into reality.

"Dangerous. She's dangerous," he whispered urgently.

"She?"

Elias craned his neck and, sure enough, saw a wicked triangular head watching them both, its three eyes glowing with simmering malevolence.

"Sizzra," Elias said, feeling better by the second. His words were no longer slurred. "She's the wurl queen. And she hates us." He tried to get up, but his legs could not support his weight. "Get out, Tristan! She's going to kill us both!"

Tristan cast a single quick look at the hulking form of the creature threatening them. Fear flickered in his features, only to be replaced by determination. "I'm not leaving you here. Come on, I'll help you up."

Elias tried to protest, but Tristan was already pulling, steadying Elias. He managed to stand after several agonizing seconds and turned around to face Sizzra.

Elias was shocked at her appearance. He remembered his initial impression of her, of absolute awe at her beauty, and could not help but grimace at the reality of the emaciated creature that stood before him. He had seen her in the prime of her life through her memories, the living incarnation of strength. What stood now before him was... sad.

He noticed details he had missed before, like the way her skin hung loose about her gaunt form, the alarming lack of muscle in her once-powerful legs, and the cracked glass claws in some of her middle and back feet. Her spines were terrifying, but many of them were broken off at the tips. Some had obviously grown wrong, either too thin or too thick to be fired. Her armor of scales was patchy in certain places, exposing the vulnerable flesh beneath. And now the charred wound that the Life

Seed had inflicted on her snout dripped blood constantly, glowing at the edges as if still red-hot. Memories whispered in Elias's mind. He knew that wound would never heal. Sizzra would live in quiet agony until the end of her days.

Elias realized he should be afraid with the doubtless certainty that she was going to kill him, but instead his eyes brimmed with tears. He hadn't understood before. Now he did.

"I'm so sorry," he said, choking up on the last word. His fear was suddenly gone, overwhelmed by memories of pain and loss. He took a wavering step forward, ignoring the sharp intake of breath from Tristan behind him. "I'm so sorry this happened to you because of us."

Sizzra tilted her head as if regarding a mildly amusing dust mote. She bared her fangs at Elias and made as if to lunge at him, opening her maw in a flash of terrifying motion, her scales reflecting the sunlight in a blinding display of deadly beauty.

Elias shut his eyes. Tristan yelled.

Yet the bite never came.

Slowly, Elias opened his eyes again. He saw Sizzra's maw, still open, close enough to touch. Then, unbelievably, she backed away.

"What's going on?" Tristan asked with a faint trembling whisper.

Elias didn't answer because he didn't understand. He had seen her memories, had felt the depths of Sizzra's hatred. She was going to kill them after they had done that which no other creature on the planet could do: return the Seed to its rightful place.

Unless....

Sizzra growled low in her throat and glanced down at the place where the Life Seed had been planted. Elias followed her gaze—and gasped.

The petals of the Life Seed were opening, all at the same time, and it was the most beautiful thing he had ever seen. Inside, each petal revealed a surface glittering like jewels in the sun with the same iridescent sheen as Sizzra's scales. It was magnificent. Elias saw how Sizzra backed away from the Flower, still threatening in her posture but watching. Waiting.

As its petals opened, light seemed to suffuse the cavern walls, and there was a tingling warmth in the air which Elias was certain he wasn't imagining. It wasn't long before the Flower had fully opened its outer layer of petals, and then a single green tendril appeared, growing from its center. Slowly, and yet very fast indeed for a plant, the tendril rose up from the Flower's body, uncoiling as it went, and Elias realized that it was to be the new bloom, regenerating that which had been torn, knitting together the fabric of the world.

But the green tendril stopped growing mere seconds later. Elias moaned in dismay, and Sizzra screamed a deafening, grating cry that was the exact echo of Elias's horror as he saw the tendril brown, shrivel, and then die. The open petals of the Flower drooped and appeared to lose their refractive luminescence, becoming limp swaths of pale tissue.

"What's happening?" Tristan asked behind Elias, shouting to drown out the echoes of Sizzra's scream.

"Something's wrong!" Elias shouted back. "The Flower is dying!"

"Then let's get out of here! She's distracted. Come on!"

Tristan grabbed his hand, but Elias yanked himself away. He could feel, deep inside him, the absolute despair that was shared not only by Sizzra but by every creature living on the continent at that moment. It wasn't fair. An entire world was doomed to die because of a stupid human mistake.

The Flower was wilting before his eyes, white turning to brown at an alarming rate. The vines that should have linked to the Life Seed, nourishing it, lay motionless and indifferent.

"Elias, what are you doing? Come on!"

Elias stepped forward instead, and then again, not caring that he wasn't supposed to touch the Flower, or that Sizzra might simply kill him with a flick of her tail. He knew what was happening, and the only thing screaming in his mind, louder than the wurl queen's misery, was that he had to help.

He knelt in front of the wilting Flower, reached out… and touched it.

The Flower was a live wire, arcing with deadly electricity that coursed through Elias's nerves in a single searing instant of unbelievable pain. He must have screamed, but he couldn't even hear himself. He wanted to let go, to escape. The pain was killing him; it was unbearable, it….

Like a switch flipped off, the pain stopped. There was sudden quiet, and Elias, blinking, realized he was blind. There was nothing but darkness around him, nothing except…. There! A glimmer. Standing in front of him, burning bright. Elias glanced back and saw another glimmer of an entirely different color, suspended motionless in the darkness. He looked down at himself and saw the same alien glow in him.

The spirit-lines. I can see them!

Elias looked around, and the world opened to him. His mind was nearly overwhelmed with the sudden awareness of millions of spirit-lines linking every living creature on the continent. He saw a large group of male wurl gathered at the foot of the mountain, keening anxiously as they looked up. He saw a flock of birds as it turned in unison to avoid a much larger bird, a predator he had no name for. In the lakes and the valleys and the deserts, he saw life. All of it was linked, and all of it was joined in miserable powerlessness as it knew, deep in its mindless instinct, that its Flower was dying.

As soon as he thought about it, the Flower drew all of Elias's attention to itself. Elias saw it as it really was, a sparkling network of boundless potential, but hungry. So very hungry.

Understanding came and with it more terror. The Life Seed had been kept away from the nourishing vines for too long. They had atrophied; they could no longer sustain it. The nexus where the Life Seed's roots should have threaded into the ground as it became the Flower had become a vortex of mindless hunger, of emptiness and yearning, ravenous with the abandon of decades. It wanted to consume life, it *needed* it or it would never bloom again. And yet….

Elias's vision flickered. Instead of the network of spirit-lines, he saw the real world, and in particular the way Sizzra leaned forward until her snout was almost touching him. Her eyes were terrifying, her maw large enough to swallow Elias in one gulp.

Elias didn't think twice. With his other hand, he reached for her and touched her.

Two minds melded in an incomprehensible whirlwind of alien emotions. There were memories. Information. Alien concepts. Yearning. But above all, two wills. Elias felt as if his mind would be shredded at any moment, but he held on to his identity with everything he had and reached out until he made contact with Sizzra.

She responded.

The whirlwind around them died down and became a dark calm surrounded by glowing spirit-lines.

I am Elias. I am a human being, come from another planet. I am sorry this happened, and I want to help.

From her, Elias did not receive words. Instead there were emotions, vast and ancient. Ghosts of ideas he had to struggle to translate.

The first thing he got was disbelief.

He repeated his message, linking images to it this time. Her reply was swift: the disbelief turned to suspicion. Then, slowly, curiosity. She tried to probe inside his mind, to read his memories, and Elias let her. For a horrible instant, he was wide open to the ravaging strength of an alien far older than he could ever comprehend, with generations upon generations of memories to draw from. Nevertheless, instead of being destroyed, he sensed Sizzra sifting through his mind carefully, looking for specific ideas and concepts with an expertise he could never hope to match. She reviewed his knowledge of spaceflight, of the history of his colony, of everything he had read in Dr. Wright's journal.

Then she came to his very recent memories. How he stole the Life Seed. How he brought it against all odds to the mountainside, caring for it every step of the way. How he desperately wanted to make things right for this planet and also for his people.

Understanding dawned in her. It did not quench her simmering hatred, but when she finally withdrew from the depths of Elias's mind, he could tell she was now merely wary. She struggled to understand how such a tiny creature, and a male, could possibly be intelligent.

With a hard jerk that she must have considered gentle, Sizzra coaxed his attention back to the Life Seed. She had his knowledge of biology now, and she understood. She did something, and Elias was able to watch the Life Seed through her eyes. He saw what the Flower could become, and also the corrupted bud it was now. For too long, it had been separated from the world. Alien genetic material had been thrust inside its core too many times. The Seed had changed, permanently. It would never again bloom on the world. Unless it fed.

Elias's connection to Sizzra and the Seed was abruptly severed, and he stumbled forward, arresting his fall on the shocking brown remnants of the Life Seed.

It was almost dead. Its petals had retracted, shriveling as they did so, and the husk of what once had been the most powerful living thing on the continent was reduced to a failing core of wavering energy.

Above him, Sizzra struck.

She lifted one of her front feet and bit down on it savagely, never allowing herself even a single cry of pain. As her head drew back, Elias saw the neat puncture wounds on the armored flesh and then, seconds later, the steady dripping of glittering red blood. It pattered on the husk of the Life Seed, to be absorbed immediately by the unquenchable hunger within it.

Sizzra then looked straight at Elias. Even though they were no longer linked, he knew what she wanted. What had to be done.

She fired a single flawless spine which sunk into the ground immediately next to him. He reached for it and yanked it out with effort.

"Elias? What are you doing?"

Elias looked back at Tristan and then lowered the wicked serrated edge of the spine in his hand until it touched the skin of his wrist. He gave Tristan a little smile.

"Setting things right."

He slashed as deeply as he could, and the pain was exquisite in its agony. Tristan lunged forward with a wordless cry, but Sizzra's tail blurred with the speed of its motion and pushed Tristan back, pinning him to one of the walls. Elias felt a stab of concern, but when the tail retreated, Tristan was unhurt.

That was good. Maybe if this worked, Sizzra would let him live.

Blood was already pooling on his forearm as Elias held it above the Life Seed. As soon as the first drop touched the withered husk, Elias felt a pulse of energy that grew with every drop, nourishing the fathomless hunger, mixing wurl and human DNA within itself. Elias was shocked to realize that he could sense Sizzra's thoughts much more clearly now, as if they were linked together again by the Life Seed. He looked up at her, and she met his gaze. As life flowed from both of them into the ravenous incarnation of the world, Elias could have sworn he felt a flicker of respect echoing from the mind of the great wurl queen.

Tristan was shouting something, but as seconds turned into minutes, Elias's strength wavered and he found he could no longer concentrate on anything except the Seed and Sizzra. Blood was flowing from his wrist, much more slowly now. He began to feel thirsty and very cold.

The last thing he saw before losing consciousness was Tristan being gently but firmly pushed away, back down into the tunnel that led out of the mountain. Elias tried to say something to him, to reassure him that this was okay, that it was the only way to make amends for the horrible thing humans had done when they uprooted the Flower, but he realized he had no more strength left.

His eyelids fluttered shut. Vaguely, he sensed the heat of a large creature coming closer.

Chapter 19
The Valley

IT WAS very dark when Elias opened his eyes once more. The tatters of his dreams became entangled in his stumbling confusion as he moved his head slowly from side to side, the motion as hard to perform as if he were trying to lift a mountain.

A mountain.

The thought triggered associations in his mind, and he remembered. He had been in the Flower chamber with Tristan, watching how the Life Seed failed to bloom. He had sensed its ravenous hunger and had done what Sizzra had also done: offer the Seed the gift of his life.

I should be dead. What happened?

He tried to get up, but his body would not respond. His panic was short-lived, however, overcome by a wave of exhaustion. In its aftermath, Elias was reduced to looking straight ahead, or rather up since he could now tell he was lying on his back. He could not see any stars or feel the cold bite of the wind, so he assumed he was still in the chamber. Of the wurl queen there was no sign.

Sleep came very quickly, and Elias's dreams were enormous. Fragments of memories not his own, of beings too large to comprehend, mixed in with his own human impressions of the last few days and wove themselves into a fantastical mesh of contradicting perspectives. It was almost a relief for Elias to open his eyes, awake again, and see the faint light of early morning coming from somewhere to his left.

This time, he was able to stand up. It took a long time, though. He was weak, light-headed, and shivering. He grabbed on to the rocks nearby and leaned against a wall to stabilize himself and look around. It appeared he was inside a cave, somewhat larger than the one in which Tristan and he had spent a couple of nights. Not the Flower chamber, then. On the ground, right around the spot where he had lain, the rocks were covered by a thick carpet of velvety moss, dark red in color. Elias knelt down to touch it, but a sudden attack of dizziness overpowered him, and he fell on his face, right on top of the soft moss. It was surprisingly warm and thick, almost like a bed.

He got up a second time and, strangely, felt somewhat better. Carefully, he walked out of the cave. He had no idea what had happened to him, and the first thing he did when he was out in the sunlight was inspect his left wrist. There was a scar there, jagged and long, a reminder of what he had done. It was completely closed now, though, and the area looked pink and healthy, with no sign of infection. Elias hesitated for a second, then reached with his other hand and touched the scar. It was real, definitely, but it was odd. According to his link, it had only been one day, too short a time for his wound to heal.

Tristan.

Elias attempted to send a message to him with the little computer, but he was out of range of the network. He was left to worry in silence, hoping that Tristan had managed to get away.

The bright morning light revealed that he was standing at the bottom of a narrow valley surrounded by mountains on all sides but to the east. Brittle brown grass covered the irregular terrain, swaying gently in the cold wind. The land stretched out for several kilometers, but the space it encompassed looked tiny against the backdrop of the towering peaks. At the western end of the enclosure, a small lake glistened tantalizingly.

Growing in a neat row around the lake, there was food.

Elias recognized the purpleberry bushes immediately, and his stomach roared with repressed hunger. He was famished; he had to get some sustenance.

He made his way across the valley as fast as he could, but his link showed him that it took him nearly thirty minutes to reach the lakeside. Once there, he knelt down gratefully next to the bushes and inhaled their heady fragrance. Then he ate.

Elias was glad nobody else was around because he ate like an animal. He stuffed his mouth with handfuls of the juicy, sweet berries as fast as he could chew. The ripest ones were plump and refreshing, and even the smaller ones which had yet to ripen had a pleasant tart tang mixed into the wonderful flavor of their moist, crunchy flesh. The sun moved across the sky, and Elias still ate, stopping only when his stomach protested. He lay back, resting his weight on his hands, and looked up at the sky in a moment of pure bliss. He burped loud enough for the echoes to come back to him, and he chuckled.

Worry for Tristan cut the moment of mirth short. Elias wished he could go find him, but weakness wrapped itself around his body like thick vines that restricted his movement. For now, all he could do was try to survive.

It was a few days before Elias felt like himself again. He ate a lot and regained his strength slowly, looking forward to his berry feasts. At the end of the week, he realized he no longer had dizzy spells or tremors, and his steps were steady. He allowed himself a small grin of satisfaction. By his link, he knew a full week had passed, and he was still alive.

Then one day he saw Sizzra approaching, and the smile died on his face.

He stood up as quickly as possible and watched her descend the mountain right above the cave. She was rolling down like a huge iridescent boulder come to life, the sunlight glinting off the sharp edges of her remaining spines. It looked like she was going too fast to be in control of her motion, but just before crashing against the ground she uncoiled her body, turned, and landed square on her six feet. The ground trembled from the impact.

It would have been perfectly graceful had she not evidenced a faint but unmistakable limp as she walked toward him. Once he was closer, Elias saw why. One of her front feet had teeth marks all over it, both scars and newly opened puncture wounds, which she must have inflicted with her own bite when she offered the Life Seed her blood.

Elias knew now that the magnificent creature coming straight for him was only a shadow of her former self, and yet he could not suppress the primal terror in his heart at seeing such a large predator approaching. Even weak as she was, limping and wounded, her every motion carried an unmistakable air of confidence and power. Her scales appeared to drink in the sunlight and reflect it back a hundredfold. Her eye cluster fixed Elias with a savage yet intelligent look, and the mere size of her as she came to a stop in front of him, towering above Elias, was deeply unsettling.

She paused for a moment as Elias looked up at her. Then she lowered her head so her eyes would be level with his.

The horrible wound that the Life Seed had inflicted on her snout looked even worse after seven days. The edges were still glowing like hot embers, and Elias was certain that their diameter had increased. A single drop of glittering scarlet blood trickled down Sizzra's nostrils and fell at Elias's feet.

She did not speak, but Elias's breath caught in his lungs when he realized that he could understand what she wanted.

Sizzra looked at him, then up at the mountain summit. Her will was clear. They had to go back to the Life Seed and offer it more life.

Elias was already moving, powerless to fight the overwhelming intensity of Sizzra's silent command, but the sight of the mountain and his own weakness made his steps falter.

"I can't climb that," he said aloud, if only to hear his voice.

Sizzra looked back at him.

"I'm too small and too weak," Elias explained. He wasn't sure if she was even capable of understanding such specific ideas. "The mountain is too tall."

Wordless, Sizzra was clear in her disdain. She could certainly understand him, then, and Elias felt a satisfied flicker of confirmation coming from her. She had supposed he was weak, but a wary corner of her mind had been wondering how it was that he and the others like him had been able to kill their own female, and so she was suspicious of his apparent helplessness, perhaps meant to deceive.

Elias blinked. He was utterly confused, and even more so when Sizzra's will insinuated images into his mind. Foremost he saw the wreck of the *Ionas* as a crew dismantled it.

Understanding crashed so suddenly that he almost laughed.

"That wasn't our female," he told Sizzra. "That was our ship. It brought us here from another world."

Faint confusion was his only reply. He perceived Sizzra's attempt to understand the concept he referred to, linking it to the knowledge of space travel she had gleaned from his mind earlier, and then ended, giving it up entirely. She did not care about starships. She only cared about her Flower.

She started moving again, but Elias held back. "I'm sorry, I can't go."

Sizzra wheeled about so suddenly that Elias yelped in fright. Her eyes were blazing with irritation. The command came again. It wasn't a question—he had to move.

So Elias obeyed.

He spent the better part of the morning attempting to climb the increasingly difficult slope in the wake of the wurl queen. The strength in his arms and legs gave way completely by early afternoon as he hauled himself onto a rocky ledge with trembling hands.

"I can't go on," he panted, even as he heard Sizzra coming back, radiating impatience.

Elias didn't care. He was too tired, and not even the strength of her command was going to make energy appear out of nowhere. If she wanted him to go to the mountain, she would have to carry him there.

The thought registered with Sizzra, who considered it and then deemed it acceptable. Incredibly, she slithered down to the ledge where Elias was resting and looked at him with the unmistakable intention of carrying him all the way to the top.

Elias rose halfway, thinking that maybe he would get to ride her, but his hopes were quickly dashed when a huge clawed foot reached out for him, enveloping him in a crushing embrace that was mere centimeters away from the wicked glass scythes at its end. Sizzra grabbed him like she would have grabbed dead prey, and she climbed the mountain.

They went much quicker that way. The sun had barely touched the peaks of the western mountains by the time Sizzra dumped Elias on the vine-covered ground in the chamber of the Flower. Thankful for the freedom, Elias walked to the very center, where the Life Seed lay as he had first seen it in the laboratory back home, closed entirely yet still undoubtedly alive.

The discarded spine was still lying there, one of its edges tinged with rusty red. Above him, Elias saw how Sizzra bit her foot once again so the blood would flow.

He had no choice. He brought the spine to the scarcely healed skin on his left wrist and—

Sizzra growled in warning. She did not want him to do that. Confused, Elias looked up at her. She bristled with impatience and glanced at her own foot, which she had indeed bitten, but only with one tooth to make a very shallow puncture wound that dripped but a few precious drops of blood onto the Seed.

Slowly, Elias brought the tip of the spine to the palm of his hand. He poked it, hard, and let go when the first drop of blood appeared. He received approval from Sizzra and an impatient nudge to place his hand over the Seed so the blood would drip down on it as well.

As before, Elias's sight bloomed with the contact. He was suddenly aware of the tendrils of energy which Sizzra called spirit-lines, linking all the creatures on the continent together. Something was different this time, though. There was a strange spark in the chamber, next to the beautiful glow of Sizzra and the ravenous vortex of the Seed. It was like an afterimage of a living creature, barely recognizable as such but unmistakably there.

There was grim satisfaction from the wurl queen, and in the wake of her thoughts, Elias understood. The Seed was changing, and the more life it took from him, the more alien it became. It was transforming even now, adapting, evolving in days to what would take a normal creature millions of years to become. It would become a hybrid, capable of recognizing humans, and through that transformation, capable of blooming again.

Abruptly, the clarity of the connection was cut. Elias realized that Sizzra had nudged him out of the way, her clear negative indicating that he had given enough life for the day. Thankful that he wasn't going to be required to bleed out to keep the Seed alive, Elias surrendered to the iron grip of Sizzra's foot as she carried him down to the valley once more.

She placed him on the ground, almost gently, being careful in the extreme with a creature so fragile. Elias understood now. She needed him alive to enable the Life Seed's renewal. And she would not be able to leave the proximity of the Seed until it had bloomed again, so the colony of Portree was safe. For now.

She did not even say goodbye, merely bounded away with seemingly effortless grace that hid her limp, trailing the last thought that Elias was able to perceive. She was hungry, and she was going to hunt.

The next day, Elias was thoughtful. He knew his continued presence was required to help the Life Seed, but he was sick with worry for his family and Tristan. He didn't know whether Tristan had made it out alive, and he hoped Sizzra hadn't ordered the male wurl to attack the colony.

Maybe I can leave, for a little bit. Just so I know everyone's okay, and so I can warn them. I can come back right away, but I need to know. They need to know.

He spent all morning thinking about whether it was right for him to try and escape, or whether it was best for him to remain where he was. In the end, he decided that a week or two wouldn't kill the Life

Seed since it had survived all this time already, and he hardened his resolve. He was going to try his luck and leave. He would come back as soon as he could.

That afternoon Elias tried to find a way out of the valley. He started walking due east, but he had barely come in sight of the wide opening leading farther down into the forested terrain when Sizzra arrived. Wordless, she nevertheless made her message clear. Elias was not allowed to leave.

Disappointed, he returned to the cave. He was tired and soon fell asleep. He woke up in the middle of the night when the chill was deepest and tried to escape once more.

He walked carefully over the brittle blades of dry grass. He considered getting some more purpleberries for the way back but discarded the idea. He wanted to be as quick and quiet as he could. Perhaps the wurl queen would not expect him to try and make a run for it in the dark. Once he was in the forest, he knew he would be safe. Sizzra could not leave the side of the Seed for very long, if the memories he had received from her were any indication. If he was lucky, he would be long gone by the time she thought to look for him again.

The world was quiet at night. Glittering stars overhead, too many to count, outlined the faint but unmistakable path of the Milky Way as it arced over the sky. There was some moonlight, for which Elias was thankful. It revealed small rocks and patches of desiccated bushes which he avoided with great care. As he advanced through the frigid night, he kept glancing up at the towering mountains surrounding him. Their slopes were dark and motionless, and Elias hoped desperately that he wouldn't see a rolling, spiny shape tumbling down to cut him off.

He made it all the way to the edge of the valley, proud of how stealthily he had moved. He was a shadow among shadows, small and difficult to see. Now it was only a matter of descending to the forest.

The breaking point of the valley was sudden, dropping down several hundred meters to the lower terrain where the forest was. Elias had the confusing sensation of being on top of a cliff overlooking the ocean, except this cliff looked out over a sea of trees instead of water. To reach safety, he would have to make his way down very carefully, like a rock climber but without any security equipment.

Elias swallowed the dry lump in his throat. It looked difficult and possibly suicidal. He had never actually climbed down anything taller than a tree before, and he wasn't too confident about the strength of his upper body.

I've got to try anyway. I have to warn the colony about Sizzra. I've got to get out of here.

Slowly, he lowered his body over the edge above a place with a secure foothold. Once his feet had touched the solid rock underneath him, Elias let go of the lip of the cliff and pressed himself against the wall. Now he was committed. He didn't have the strength in his arms to pull himself up again, even if he had wanted to.

"I guess no way but down," he whispered between gritted teeth.

He edged sideways on the wall, looking below until he saw another ledge about two meters down. It was an easy jump, but the ledge underneath was quite narrow. Elias had no idea how he was going to stabilize himself if he simply dropped and hoped for the best. He might lose his balance and fall backward, to plummet screaming until his body crashed against the forest floor.

Elias shut his eyes tight for a moment. He was trying not to panic, but his precarious situation seemed to him more difficult by the second. He was still several hundred meters above solid ground, hugging the wall for all he was worth, terribly exposed. Any little thing might—

"Aaahh!" he yelled, louder than he had intended, in sheer panic. A sudden blast of wind hit him from the side, hard enough to force him to wheel his arms backward to regain his balance on the rocky wall. The gale persisted for nearly a minute, and it was the longest minute of Elias's life. It wasn't just the cold, which sliced cleanly through his clothes and made him shiver as if he were naked. It was the fact that he knew if he let go right then, he would fall—and die.

The wind lessened eventually, and Elias realized time was against him. The gale might resume at any moment. Biting his lower lip subconsciously, he crouched on his ledge and brought his hands down until they were level with his feet. Then he grabbed the rock and, trembling, lowered himself toward the ledge below him.

It was dark. His frantic feet sought solid support even as his hands warned him that they would not be able to hold his entire body weight for much longer. The shadows were tricky, though, and from his vulnerable position hanging from rocks that might crumble at any moment, Elias simply could not see where his feet were supposed to go.

This was stupid. I'm not a climber.

His right foot touched something he thought was the ledge. It was too far down, though. He would have to let himself go and trust to blind luck that he had calculated correctly. He couldn't hold on much longer either way. His fingers hurt, the cold was getting to him, and he was scared as hell.

He let go and dropped down. His feet hit the ledge sooner than he expected, and the impact traveled through his shins and made his knees ache. Worse than the pain, though, was the fact that he lost his balance.

He threw his arms back once again, but it didn't help, he was tilting toward the void, toward inevitable death.

With a panicky wordless cry, Elias reached forward with his left hand toward a shadowy outcrop that looked like a handhold. His fingers scrabbled against sharp rock, and he clutched it with all the strength he was capable of mustering. He nearly cried in relief when he finally stabilized himself on the rocky wall, gripping the handhold, feet secure on the narrow ledge.

He risked a look down. He had barely made any progress, and he could see no more convenient Elias-sized ledges below him. He was trapped.

Elias cast his gaze upward, but there was no escape there either. The ledge above him was too far up to reach. He could not go down, and he could not go up. Sideways he had a little space, but the ledge was so narrow that he couldn't turn around or even attempt to sit down. He could do nothing. He would be forced to stand there, trembling, until at last his strength gave way and he fell. Elias wondered if the deadly impact would hurt.

Five minutes passed, according to Elias's link, before the obvious solution occurred to him. Admitting defeat, he drew in a long breath and shouted at the top of his voice.

"Sizzra! Sizzra, help!"

It was a long time before she came. The ground trembled under her feet, and Elias looked up in naked relief when he heard the sound of her breathing. Her head was visible over the lip of the valley, her iridescent scales reflecting the moonlight in beautiful silver patterns. Her eyes glowed in the dark, three red orbs of passive menace. As Elias watched, a single warm drop of her blood fell on his forehead. At the contact, Elias's connection to Sizzra strengthened. His perception was clear enough, for a moment, for him to tell that she was in increasing pain from the wound on her snout.

He was also able to tell that she had known all along he was trying to escape.

She had watched him as he scrambled down the rocky wall with clumsy, pathetic moves while she crouched in the shadows. She could have helped him at any moment, but she had waited until he had called out for her.

"Please, help me," Elias said, a tremor in his voice. He was beyond caring that he had essentially been some amusing entertainment for the large creature. "I don't want to die here."

Sizzra tilted her head one way and then another, as if considering his request carefully. Seconds ticked by, and she let the suspense drag on, her silent amusement plain to Elias.

Elias's right foot lost purchase on the ledge when another gust of wind slammed into him from the back. He cried out again, pleading with his mind, knowing that his strength was about to give way.

Sizzra's foot closed around him suddenly, the heat coming from her the most beautiful thing Elias had ever felt. Relief washed over him as she carried him all the way back to the cave, where she dumped him on the ground unceremoniously. She stalked away, stopping only once to look over her shoulder. Her glare was unmistakable. It was part amusement, part command.

A lesson. Elias was trapped here in this isolated valley for as long as she wanted him to be.

Chapter 20
Evolution

IT WAS a few days before Sizzra came again to carry Elias to the top of the mountain. In the meantime, Elias had tried to make the cave a somewhat better shelter than it was.

The first thing he had done on the morning after his aborted escape was figure out some way to make a fire. He spent several hours searching for sizable rocks that he could use to build a firepit, and his arms were aching abominably by the time he had finally managed to collect enough midsized rocks to make a passable pit outside the entrance to his cave. He took a break after that, walking to the lake to eat and drink. This time he realized that other bushes were growing along the lakeshore, squat and thorny, full of the velvety nuts he had once shared with Tristan.

That was odd. He couldn't remember seeing those there before.

Food was food, though, and he settled down for a feast. As he ate berries and nuts, he saw there were fish swimming in the lake and briefly considered trying to get one. His hopes were quickly dashed, though, when he remembered that his digestive system was not compatible with the animal life on New Skye. For the time being, he would have to remain a vegetarian.

In the afternoon, Elias collected handful after handful of dry grass and brought it back to the cave. Some of it he spread out over the soft moss on which he would be sleeping. Some more he piled nearby to make at least a little windbreak to protect him from the chilly wind sneaking into the cave at night. The rest he set next to the firepit as disposable kindling. He needed wood, though.

There weren't any trees growing in the valley, but he spotted a copse of dead trunks on one of the western mountainsides, at the end of a steep climb. Glancing at the sun, Elias decided to try and get some wood before dark. He climbed carefully over treacherous terrain consisting of loose rocks, sand, and larger boulders. He was sweating and panting when he finally reached the first of the gnarled, bone-dry trunks.

I really need to start exercising more.

He looked up at his prize after he regained his breath—and realized he didn't have an ax with him. Or even a knife.

He clamped a hard mental grip over his disappointment and decided to make the best of the situation by gathering all the small twigs and brittle branches he could snap off easily. There were many around, far more than he could possibly carry in one trip, and he slid down the slope with an armful of his precious load, grateful that the descent to the valley floor was much quicker and easier than the climb had been.

The sun was setting when Elias organized his pile of firewood and kindling in the firepit. Looking at it, Elias felt a fleeting sense of proud accomplishment. He had done this all by himself, and now the only thing that remained was figuring out how to make fire.

He had thought about it as he worked all day and knew his best chance was trying to find some flint in the cave. He set out to do that as the shadows lengthened and the air turned colder, but he was not successful. He tried to tell himself that it was okay, that tomorrow he would have all day to find flint, but as he lay down on his bed of moss and dry grass, he could not help but anticipate the coming night's cold with dread. Dark clouds overhead had gathered as the sun set, threatening rain.

The weather seemed to want to prove him right. He spent an awful night curled up into a ball, wishing the savage wind and faint but persistent rain would stop. Sometime in the wee hours of the morning, he finally fell into a fitful sleep, and Elias was groggy and irritable by the time he finally gave up on rest and decided to get up.

Outside, his carefully gathered pile of grass and branches was completely soaked through. Elias closed his eyes for a moment, trying to remain calm, but the frustration of the last few days exploded out of him, and he demolished the firepit he had built, kicking stones out of the way, flinging handfuls of damp grass into the air, and crushing twigs into little more than sawdust with his bare hands. He was breathing hard and completely soaked when he finally regained control of himself, looking at the awful mess he had made. With a dismissive roll of the eyes, he headed for the lake to eat something. That, at least, wasn't a disappointment. He ate his fill once more and discovered a new kind of plant growing in the water. It reminded him of the Terran waterlily, with its flat semicircular leaf floating on the surface of the lake. This plant's color, however, was a striking shade of vivid yellow. A small bud on the center of the leaf hinted at something growing inside.

As the sun reached its zenith, Elias climbed a little way up one of the easier western mountainsides until he found a large, flat rock that was already being warmed by the sun. He took off all his clothes and laid them out to dry, thankful for the sunlight on his skin. His arms ached, his abdomen ached, and his legs ached most of all. Without really meaning to, he dozed on the warm rock until he fell asleep.

He was woken up by the chill of the wind and looked around him, momentarily confused. The sunlight was gone, although the rock on which he lay was still warm; the sun had already descended behind the mountains behind him. A quick glance at his link showed him that he had slept nearly eleven hours, and he was feeling much better. Rested, certainly, but also more awake. He decided to put his energy to good use and climbed to the copse of dead trees to gather more firewood. As he went, he looked all over for rocks that resembled flint. He picked several that looked promising and stuffed them in his pockets. Afterward, he made his way back to the cave.

Night fell before he was done rebuilding the firepit, but this time Elias stored the somewhat damp firewood inside the cave. He resigned himself to another cold few hours and slept as best he could. At the first hint of daylight, he selected a good spot in front of the cave and spread out all his firewood so the sun would have a decent chance at drying it through. He gathered some more grass as well. Then he began experimenting, trying to get a spark.

It was a simple idea, in principle. Flint plus steel equals a spark. He remembered that much from an old survival TV show he had watched once, and his link's database confirmed it, but its text-only display couldn't show him what it looked like. He supposed that flint should be shiny, and his link *was* made of steel, so he spent several hours striking its underside with all the little rocks he had gathered the day before. He ended up with sore fingertips and nothing to show for it, however.

He refused to give up and went searching again. This time he looked around the sharp inclines of the Flower mountain and picked up a broader assortment of stones. He carried them back to the firepit over several trips and tested once more. He was rewarded when he struck a sharp-edged fragment of rock against his link and a bright orange spark blossomed for an instant.

"Yes!" Elias exclaimed, pumping his fist into the air. He looked around as if expecting somebody to be there so he could share his victory, but he was alone. Of course.

He wondered what his family was doing now. And Tristan. Where had he gone? Elias was still worried about him, and it scared him to think that Sizzra might have killed him. Perhaps Tristan had managed to escape and was now back in Portree, telling everyone about what had happened. What would the colony do once they learned what had transpired with the Life Seed? Elias knew that the Colony Patrol had weapons like shock spears and similar things. They were effective against small wurl, but he doubted they would do much if the patrol ever came face-to-face with Sizzra.

Would she kill them? She couldn't leave the vicinity of the Seed for now, sure, but if the Flower ever bloomed, then she wouldn't be bound anymore. Dread made Elias uneasy. He knew Sizzra well enough now to know that she would seek revenge as soon as she could. If that ever happened, then his colony was doomed.

His stomach growled, reminding him that he hadn't had anything to eat so far this day. He made his way to the lake, drank its cool refreshing water, and ate more nuts and berries. His body ached, but he was getting used to the sensation. He tried to pay it no mind as he returned to his cave in late afternoon and settled down to try and make some fire. He gathered as much dry grass as he could, pressed it into a tight ball, and placed it over a small bundle of twigs. Then he grabbed his piece of flint in one hand, his link in the other, and struck hard. A spark flew out, but the wind carried it away. Scowling, Elias positioned himself so he would shelter the firepit from the wind and brought the flint and link lower. He struck it again, harder than he ever had, and worried briefly that he was damaging the electronics inside. Then he remembered his cold nights, and he stopped caring.

On his fourth attempt, one of the sparks landed among the dry grasses. Elias immediately let go of his tools and cupped his hands around the fledgling glow. He watched it catch on one of the blades of grass and blew on it gently. For a moment he thought he had blown too hard, as the spark appeared to die down, but then it blazed back to life stronger than before. Elias waited a couple of seconds and then blew again, softer now. The spark grew bigger, sizzled, and became a tiny flame.

Elias smiled like a maniac as he piled more dry grass on top of the flame, seeing it get bigger. Soon it was burning merrily, and he fed it some of the smallest twigs, grinning as they caught fire. The sun had hidden behind the mountains by then, but as his fire grew, so did its light. Night fell, but this time Elias wasn't engulfed by the darkness. He had a very nice fire going and plenty of wood to feed to it.

He was surprised at how much it lifted his spirits to know he had fire. He felt as if some primal part of his brain had been engaged, placing survival first and everything else second. Having fire meant he would have light and heat. It meant he would be safe.

He piled the flames high with wood before going to bed, and for the first time in many days Elias was able to fall asleep immediately. He was even comfortable, at least until the middle of the night when the chill woke him up and he realized that his fire had been reduced to a couple of smoldering embers. He tried to rekindle it, but he was too impatient and failed. Resigned, he settled back down and tried to get as much rest as he could.

Sizzra came for him on the morning of the following day. Elias had just finished his third trip to the lake, where he was gathering nuts and berries to stash in the cave so he wouldn't have to walk to the lakeside every time he was hungry. He had a good pile already, but he forgot all about it when he saw the magnificent wurl clamber down the mountainside to land a couple of paces away with a heavy thud.

"Ready when you are," Elias said.

Sizzra snorted briefly, as if his permission had never been required. She grabbed him and carried him up the mountain in a rush of dizzying speed. Elias felt a little queasy as she dumped him in the Flower chamber, but he approached the Life Seed nevertheless.

"Something's happening to it," he said aloud. "Is this good?"

Sizzra didn't answer him. Elias approached the Seed and placed his hand over it tentatively. It felt hotter today, and its petals had opened slightly. Elias peeked inside, fearing to see decaying brown flesh, but instead he saw fragments of the same iridescence that Sizzra's scales had. This time, however, the white and pink and neon green of the petals was streaked with black in places.

Sizzra growled to draw his attention. She had already bitten her foot, and she held it over the Seed for her blood to drip inside. Elias grabbed the same spine he had used twice already and poked his palm. After just a few droplets, Sizzra indicated that it was enough, and Elias backed away.

"I wish I knew how long you plan on keeping me here," he told her.

She didn't even acknowledge his voice as she approached with the clear intention of grabbing him again. Elias was about to let go of the spine in his hand, but a thought occurred to him. He desperately needed a sharp tool, and the spine was as big as a sword and probably much sharper. It was also incredibly light, flexible yet strong. Its serrated edges and wicked tip would certainly come in handy.

"Hey, mind if I take this?" He lifted the spine so she could see what he meant.

She did not expressly permit it, but neither did she forbid it, so Elias kept the spine and held it at an awkward angle as he dangled out of Sizzra's strong grip on the way down. As soon as she had dumped him next to the cave, she climbed again and was lost from sight much faster than Elias had expected.

Alone, he looked at his prize. The more he examined it, the more he realized that one of Sizzra's spines was probably a better weapon than anything they had back at the colony. He brandished it a couple of times, enjoying the whistle it made through the air, noting how the dark red stains on its edge and tip from where he had cut himself had not faded at all. He took the spine with him on another climb to the copse and was pleasantly surprised at how good a tool it was—its leading edge rivaled the sharpness of the monomolecular edge of the shovel he had used back at the lab so long ago. He was able to saw through a thin, dry trunk very fast and had to make several trips to get all the firewood to his cave after he cut up the trunk into smaller pieces.

That night he had a much bigger fire going, and he even tried to roast some of the nuts to see if they tasted any different. He burnt a few, but those that survived acquired a very pleasant smoky flavor that was easily one of the best things Elias had ever eaten in his life. With a full stomach and the certainty of warmth, he settled down for the night and was able to sleep all the way through for the first time since he had been taken to the valley.

Sizzra came for him a few days later. She appeared to be agitated about something, and she very nearly cut Elias with one of her glass claws when she carelessly reached for him. She took him all the way up once more, and as soon as Elias stood up and looked around, he realized why she had been alarmed.

Something was growing around the Life Seed.

He approached it carefully. The ancestral memories he had received had never shown anything growing in this chamber except for the Flower and the vines that linked it to the rest of the continent. What he saw now, though, was unmistakably a bud of biological origin, sprouting from one of the three main vines, like a miniature version of the Life Seed.

Sizzra growled in warning when he dropped down into the depression at the center of the chamber and attempted to touch the strange growth, but she did not stop him, and Elias reached forward with care.

As soon as he touched it, the bud shattered.

Like a ripe fruit bursting open, the bud fell apart in a small cascade of golden seeds that dropped onto the vine-covered floor. Elias exchanged a quick look with Sizzra, but he could tell she was as puzzled as he was. This had never happened before. She didn't know what the little seeds were.

After a closer look, though, Elias realized that *he* did.

"No way," he whispered, kneeling down to pick some of them up. Yet there could be no mistake. The faint oval shape, ending in a white tip. The size and the color. "This looks like corn."

As soon as he held them in his hands, though, he realized that they felt different from corn. Their surface was soft instead of hard, and he was certain the seeds would burst open if he squeezed them. Still, the resemblance was uncanny. He gathered all of them up and put them in his pockets for safekeeping.

Sizzra, in the meantime, had grown impatient. She commanded him silently to go and feed the Life Seed, which Elias did in helpless obedience. This time, though, the touch of his bloody palm to the Seed's warm exterior carried a message.

He had the same rush of sensation as before, a shift in perspective where he could see all the glowing spirit-lines that linked the life of New Skye. He recognized himself, too, and realized that the Life Seed could finally *see* him.

At that instant he was assaulted by a burst of unbearable heat that found him through the spirit-lines and reached out to him with tongues of flame. The heat yearned for his flesh, and it seared his palm through his contact with the soul of the world with all-consuming hunger.

Elias screamed. He snatched his hand away, panting, and looked at his skin, expecting to see a blackened mess of charred tissue. His hand was whole, but now Elias felt something else entirely when he looked at the Life Seed: a pull, a yearning that could be deadly if he was not careful. He was a part of the world now, and he would never be able to touch the Seed again and survive.

It surprised Sizzra as much as him, as was plain from their linked emotions in that moment. Nevertheless, the mental image in Elias's mind lingered even if he was not touching the Seed anymore, and he saw that where before he had been a faint blur of alien color, barely recognizable, now the Life Seed was tracing a clear spirit-line between itself and him. It had also… changed. Elias prodded with his mind, trying to understand his wordless perceptions. No, not changed.

Evolved. Like it had been trying to do for weeks now.

The transformation wasn't complete, but Elias was still shocked at the speed of it. Evolution took normal organisms millions of years. The Life Seed was evolving in a matter of days, changing itself, mixing its own identity with the DNA of many alien species. Inside its fathomless code there was now incipient recognition for humans. And Terran plants.

With a little cry of surprise, Elias realized that the seeds in his pockets were also linked to the Life Seed. Tiny spirit-lines led from them to the nexus of energy in the continent. Inside each of them, there was genetic material native to New Skye. But they were, in principle, corn seeds.

I can't believe it, Elias thought fiercely, not daring to hope. Yet the truth was plain to see through his link with the world. The Life Seed offered him a fleeting vision of piercing changes, intrusions that forced it to adapt or die. They triggered memories, and Elias realized that the intrusions were some of the many genetic experiments the scientists had attempted with the Life Seed in the laboratory. Its DNA had been spliced with many different crops, but none of the genetic grafts had taken hold. Instead, they appeared to have changed the structure of the Life Seed itself, so much so that it wasn't able to live now without Terran genetic material in the form of Elias's blood.

And now that he had been feeding it alongside Sizzra....

By the generation ship.

These modified corn seeds had grown out of a frantic exercise in evolution. The Life Seed did not have a mind of its own, but just as its driving force was pure biology, so was its limitless adaptation potential. It had created hybrids as a desperate expression of the changes it was going through, hybrids that would almost certainly survive on New Skye.

Elias backed away to a safe distance from the Seed. His thoughts jumped to the inevitable conclusion even as Sizzra carried him down the mountain again.

In his pockets he now held the key. The salvation of Portree.

Chapter 21
Isolation

SIZZRA CAME for Elias several days later, which for him was a welcome relief from the monotony of his captivity. When he looked at her that morning, though, he couldn't help but grimace. The smoldering wound on her snout had grown, spilling like molten lava down the sides of her upper jaw, exposing pink gums and long, curved fangs. It looked very painful, and when she grabbed him, Elias was able to catch an echo of the agony that now marked her days. He was sad for her, but the connection between them made the gist of his feelings plain to the wurl queen, and his compassion was met with impatient rejection. She all but dumped him onto the floor of the Flower chamber once again, where they communed with the Life Seed from a cautious distance and gave it more life.

Through the blood connection, Elias was able to understand better why the Life Seed had produced hybrid corn seeds before. It was trying to purge itself of the alien DNA, expelling it, but it was not succeeding entirely. Searching with his mind, Elias realized that there were more buds growing on the vines, dozens of expressions of all the crops that had been spliced into the Life Seed by the Portree scientists.

For the Life Seed, the hybrids were a desperate failure, an incomplete attempt to purify its genetic material to what it had been before the alien invasion. For Elias, it was the best news in the world.

The blood ritual was soon over. Sizzra ignored Elias as he walked over carefully to the series of small buds growing on the vines. A couple of them were ready to harvest, and he broke them open with barely concealed excitement. In the first one he discovered beans, similar in every way to those he knew except for the color, which was a dashing shade of purple. In the second one there was rice, white and faintly iridescent, each grain shaped like a *Y*. Elias gathered all the seeds with great care and put them in his pockets. He made a mental note to check the other buds the next time he was brought to the chamber.

Weeks went by.

Elias spent his days gathering firewood, harvesting berries and nuts, and planning for the future. He upgraded his cave as much as he could, first building a proper windbreak that could also function as a door to cover the entrance when it rained. His door was just a bunch of branches tied together with the flexible reeds from the yellow lilies which grew on the lake, and at first it kept on breaking apart every few minutes. Elias couldn't fathom why it was so hard to obtain a decent mesh of wood and reeds that wouldn't disintegrate the minute he placed it over the cave entrance, and he spent nearly a week trying different designs until he was successful. It was frustrating to fail again and again simply because he had forgotten to tie one end of the structure or chosen a reed that turned out to be too weak to hold the weight of the branches. Nevertheless, when Elias could finally place a door at the cave mouth to shut out the night, he was ecstatic. It had been hard, but he had done it. The palms of his hands were raw and blistered in places, and as usual his arms ached from exhaustion, but he had succeeded. That night, he actually smiled as he ate his monotonous dinner.

Other improvements were easier. He built a cache of dried fruit and stored it in a shallow hollow he had dug at the back of the cave, where the temperature was more consistent, and lined with leaves. Digging took almost a day of tireless work, but Elias felt safer knowing that he had food in the shelter with him and wasn't entirely dependent on the mysteriously rapid-growing purpleberries and velvety nuts around the lakeside. It was on that night, as he was washing his shirt in the lake, that he caught sight of his moonlit reflection on the surface of the water and realized he was changing. He had always been lean, but now the constant physical activity was shaping his body to reflect its growing strength. Curious, Elias flexed his arms, waiting for the water to settle so he could look at his reflection properly. He was definitely getting bigger and more muscular, although nowhere near how Tristan had looked the last time Elias had seen him.

With that memory came a sharp pang of loneliness. Elias had entertainment on his wrist link, sure, but the isolation was starting to get to him, and now that he had essentially completed the majority of his projects, he didn't know what else to do. It was too cold still to think about planting the hybrid seeds he had gotten, and his immediate survival was no longer in peril.

On the following morning, he decided to do something about his boredom. He started exploring the mountainsides around him, climbing higher every day. Sometimes he looked for specific things, like pieces of flat rock he could use to line the bottom of his improvised cave pantry. Other times he simply climbed to enjoy the view and look out over the forest that stretched to the east, a mixture of dull evergreens and leafless tree trunks.

Sizzra would come every now and then to take him up to the chamber, but for the most part he was alone. Elias spent a lot of time thinking, and at night he activated his link and read passages from the hundreds of books loaded into its memory. It was a pain to read on such a small display, but he had all the time in the world. And anything was better than doing nothing.

Wintertime faded from the world, and the first stirrings of spring whispered timidly on the wind when he decided to start keeping a journal. Maybe it wouldn't be as interesting as Dr. Wright's journal, but he had a lot of thoughts going around in his head, and he supposed it would be good to record them.

Even if nobody read them. Even if he remained a prisoner in what he now called Crescent Valley for the rest of his life.

It felt good to record his ideas every night, and now that the weather wasn't so harsh, he would sometimes sit outside his cave in the darkness, the fire having died out long since, and speak while his link transcribed his words and saved them to his journal file. The sound of his own voice comforted him a little bit, and after he recorded the events of his day, he would look up at the sky and imagine what it would be like to see a different set of stars from a completely different planet. The thought gave him vertigo sometimes, but it made him feel less alone for some reason. He imagined another young man on an alien world looking up at the sky and seeing New Skye's sun as a tiny dot in the vastness of the black. They would be connected, then, even though neither of them would know it. In his isolation, it was one of the few comforting thoughts Elias could muster.

WHEN THE very first day of spring arrived, three large wurl came to Crescent Valley.

Elias had woken up at dawn, as usual, and he was very surprised to see the three hulking metallic creatures standing near the lake. As quietly as he could, Elias retreated back to his cave and closed most of its opening with the door. He tried to be very silent, and none of the wurl appeared to have heard him as he peeked from his sheltered spot and watched them.

They were beautiful creatures, although now that Elias had spent so much time looking only at Sizzra, he couldn't help but notice their obvious shortcomings. Although large enough to stand taller than Elias on their six strong legs, their movement lacked the sinuous grace of the female. Their spines were also plain to see, even flattened against their backs like they were now. When Sizzra flattened her spines, they were somehow completely hidden, which always left Elias with the unsettling thought in the back of his mind that he had no idea how many missiles she would be able to fire at him if she ever decided to kill him. With the male wurl, by contrast, Elias knew just where he stood. Besides, the color of their scales could never hope to match the mesmerizing iridescence of Sizzra's armor. These were simpler creatures that did not have the queen's searing, penetrating intelligence.

Elias stayed very still in his cave, watching the three males move. As the sun rose fully, Elias realized they were particularly large specimens, very muscular and obviously in the prime of their health. Their claws glinted like polished steel, and their every footstep left clear indentations on the soft ground around the lake.

They were quiet at first, but the peace did not last. When one of them walked to the shore to drink and the other two made as if to follow, the first lumbering giant whirled around in a violent rush of snapping jaws and water droplets. His three eyes blazed in the morning light, and every spine on his body stood on end.

Despite himself, Elias gasped. The male lacked the magnificence of Sizzra's crown of spines around the neck, but he was still terrifying. As he stomped forward, head hung low in a clear display of threat, he forced the other two males to actually back down, snorting angrily all the time.

His opponents were not cowed for long, however. As the first male lunged, his opponent on the left responded. He also flashed his spines and swiped at the air with his right front foot. The slash connected with the first male's snout, and there was a screeching sound of metal striking metal.

That was the last straw. With a roar, the first male jumped at his opponent and the fight began.

Elias could barely keep track of everything that was happening. At first it was only two males fighting, but soon the third one decided he also wanted to join the fray, and then it was a whirlwind of stomping feet, slashing claws, and terrifying snarls. Elias was afraid that they would end up killing each other, but when minutes passed and the fight continued without diminishing ferocity, he realized that none of the males were firing their spines. They were using them as deterrents to prevent the others from biting where they shouldn't. It was all an enthralling choreography of hostility and ferocity.

Suddenly there was a horrible wrenching sound, like an iron door being ripped apart by unstoppable force. Elias realized that one of the males was on the ground now, while another one kept him pinned and the third bit savagely into his chest.

They were killing him. For Elias there could be no doubt. The wrenching sound was the supine wurl's scales being ripped from the flesh underneath, and he roared in evident pain and anger at his helplessness. The wurl biting him sank his fangs deeper, turned his head, and with a horrible crunch tore out a fist-sized mouthful of metallic scales.

Instead of giving up, however, the trapped wurl went berserk. He used his six feet at once to clamp down on the male pinning him to the ground. Elias saw clearly how his claws sank *through* the metal armor. They must have found tender flesh because that wurl let go of his prisoner with a scream and rolled away like a spike-covered ball until he was almost at the other end of the valley.

In the meantime, the wurl with the jagged hole in his chest jumped up and faced the remaining aggressor. They both roared, staring each other down, refusing to budge. They were panting, their heavy bellows breath clearly audible to Elias. When they bared their fangs, he was certain they would end up killing one another.

Yet they both backed away. Elias could scarcely believe it as the two males turned around at the same time and headed for opposite ends of the valley. The wounded wurl went straight for the lake and promptly sank into its waters, shaking himself and attempting to lick his chest wound. The other male climbed one of the western slopes and settled down on a flat sunlit rock.

Elias released a pent-up breath he didn't know he had been holding. His arms relaxed—and bumped the door.

"Shit!" Elias swore, grabbing for it wildly, but he wasn't fast enough. His makeshift door crashed to the ground and made a disturbing amount of noise in the eerie quiet of the valley.

All three wurl turned to look at him.

Elias gulped, his heart hammering in his chest. He watched them come back from where they had gone, walking slowly but surely until they were standing side by side less than ten meters away from the mouth of the cave. The wounded wurl stood in the middle, and he looked ready to shred Elias to ribbons with his claws.

The cave was shallow and offered no protection. There was nothing stopping any of the wurl from firing a spine right then and killing him instantly. In that moment, knowing that he was helpless prey in the presence of apex predators, he felt true fear. He couldn't believe he had dared to think of them as lesser creatures. They might be smaller than the large queen and much less intelligent, but they were still dangerous. Deadly. Unstoppable.

The wounded wurl took a step forward, his intentions clear. The spines in his back bent forward slightly, aiming at Elias.

There was no way out.

"Don't kill me," Elias pleaded. "Please, please don't kill me...."

If anything, it seemed as if his voice only angered them more. The other two males stepped forward as well.

Then Sizzra arrived.

Elias had never been so happy to see her. The moment she landed on the valley floor, sending a tremor through the ground, the three males lowered their spines and backed away from the cave entrance. Amazed, Elias stepped fully out of his shelter to meet the queen halfway. She spared him a fleeting, dismissive glance and then focused her attention on the three wurl.

Their exchange was silent, and Elias was not able to perceive its contents, but the result spoke for itself. Under the relentless glare of their queen, they walked meekly up to where Elias was standing and... sniffed him.

Elias didn't move a muscle. He was essentially trapped between deadly predators on all sides, and it was bizarre to see these three hulking creatures who stood as tall as he did coming forward to sniff him like curious dogs. After they were done, two of the wurl backed away until there was a considerable space separating them from Sizzra. The third one, however, the one with the wound on its chest, looked down at Elias, three eyes meeting two in a long moment of intense contemplation. Looking at the creature, Elias felt....

Hesitantly, he reached out with his hand. The sensation he was getting was faint, not even an echo of the imposing will Sizzra always projected into his mind, but it was there nevertheless—something like yearning, a hint of suspicion, and curiosity all mixed together.

Elias held his hand in the air for a couple of seconds, wondering whether he dared. The wurl did not move away, and Sizzra was nearby keeping them in check. He decided to go for it. He touched the silvery snout of the hulking creature.

Chapter 22
The Mating Dance

ELIAS WAS disappointed when the result of actually touching the powerful male wurl in front of him did not carry the momentous intensity of his interactions with Sizzra. As his palm rested on the sleek, hard surface of the scales covering the creature, he was able to perceive its warmth but little else. Curious, he tried to push further with his mind, but he was met with very simple emotions—guarded inquisitiveness from the male wurl, as if Elias were another rival come to challenge him.

Challenge.

Elias's concept resonated in the creature's mind, and he caught fleeting glimpses of his many fights with other males. Some had been much weaker, pushovers who posed little threat. Others had proven more difficult to beat, including the two other specimens that stood now in the valley.

Abruptly the wounded male shook his head and interrupted the tenuous contact Elias had managed to establish. With a loud snort, the wurl walked away a few paces until he was standing next to the other two. All three cowered slightly when Sizzra moved, an iridescent vision of rippling scales, and she grabbed Elias with her front right foot.

As she carried him to the now extremely familiar Flower chamber, Elias tried to use his deeper contact with the queen to inquire about the presence of those males in the valley. She all but ignored his questing thoughts, however, and it was only when the two of them were once again linked to the Life Seed through the blood ritual that he was able to glean some answers from her memories.

Spring was coming. And with it, at long last, mating season.

Also…. A memory came to Elias of when Sizzra had been a young hatchling. She had named each and every male in her brood, and she knew the names of these three. With a start, Elias matched names to individuals.

Vanor, the male he had touched. Narev, the second one. Siv, the third.

Elias had many questions, but they went unanswered. After the ritual was complete, Sizzra returned him to the valley and left him there.

"Yeah, have a nice day too," he called out after Sizzra, dusting off his increasingly frayed pants as she bounded away. She ignored him. Elias wondered how long it had been since he had last spoken with anyone but himself.

Making his way to the lake, Elias saw the three males circling one another. They looked terribly menacing, their scales shining with the heat of the sun and every spine on their backs displayed upright in yet more obvious threat. Elias decided to head to the other side of the lake and view them from a safe distance. Although he was somewhat certain that the creatures wouldn't attack him now, he could still be trampled to death if he was caught in the middle of another dominance fight.

Elias found a comfortable spot and munched on the sweet and tender fruits of the yellow lilies, which were growing in increasing quantities around the shallow waters of the lake. The grass underneath him was no longer brittle, but soft. Some of the newer blades were growing with hints of green, and as he watched the menacing wurl on the other side, Elias realized that for the first time since the Life Seed had been torn from its rightful place, the continent was awakening to a true springtime, with new life stirring at long last in response to the growing warmth.

Once again, Elias's thoughts went out to his family back in Portree. What would they be thinking right about now? Would they wonder at the changes the world was experiencing? And what about Oscar, his little brother? He had never even seen the world as anything but perpetual winter. Would he marvel at the colors when the long-dormant flowers on the main square bloomed? Would he be happy? Or would he still be missing his older brother?

Elias clamped his jaw tight and suppressed the urge to cry. It wouldn't do any good to give in to sadness, not now anyway. Besides, as long as Sizzra held him prisoner, it meant she wouldn't go after the colony. For that, at least, he was thankful. If his captivity meant that others could live a little longer, he didn't mind at all. Imagining what the terrible queen would do once she was free of the shackles of the Flower was terrifying. Her hatred of humanity was still there, simmering, amplified by the ever-growing pain in her snout. Lately, Elias had begun to feel the absolute disgust and rejection she experienced whenever she had to touch him. He knew that she wanted nothing more than to crush him in her grip, shred his flesh to ribbons with her claws. That she could not do so yet only added to the list of things she would set even once her vengeance was at hand.

Elias was aware of the posing of the males on the opposite lakeshore without really seeing them. His mind was occupied with dark thoughts, and it was only when the sun disappeared behind the mountains to his left that he came back to himself. By then, the three contenders had decided to claim separate spots to spend the night. Vanor had chosen the lakeside, carefully protecting his chest wound from possible attacks. Narev was perched on a rock on the northern slopes. Siv was lying on the grass in the middle of the valley. Once he was certain they weren't planning to attack him, Elias left as well, to rest in his cave. He built a small fire with the quick ease of practice, roasted some nuts on a flat rock, and mixed them with purpleberries. He ate without really tasting his food. Week after week of eating the same thing had desensitized him to the flavors, even if the berries, nuts, and now the lily fruits were surprisingly filling.

When the sun set, Elias crawled back into the cave and shut the door behind him. He had trouble falling asleep, but eventually he managed.

The next day, he was woken up by pandemonium.

He rushed out of the cave, still rubbing the sleep out of his eyes, to witness a savage battle of unbridled ferocity. The three male wurl had gathered near the eastern edge of the valley, dangerously close to the sudden drop that led down into the distant forest. They were fighting. To Elias, it looked as if they were trying to kill each other for real.

He could barely keep track of which wurl was which in the mad whirlwind of spines, teeth, and claws. The sounds the three made as they attempted to bite each other were disturbing, vocalizations of primal aggression that made Elias shrink against the rocky wall behind him. They were far away, but he was still able to catch glimpses of snapping teeth, glowing eyes, and upright spines.

Even as he watched, Siv bit down on Vanor's back without calculating correctly, and Elias flinched as he saw Siv's jaw close on one of the upright spines of his contender. The howl of pain that followed was so shrill that Elias had to cover his ears with his hands. Vanor must have realized that he had an opening, because he wasted no time. Ignoring the other challenger, he rose up on four of his legs and used the remaining two to swipe at Siv's chest. The swipes had such force behind them that they sliced cleanly through the metallic plates protecting the victim and left behind trails of glittering red blood in their wake.

Siv, howling and bleeding from his mouth and his chest, tried to back away. Narev, however, did not allow it. With a savage swipe of his tail, he sent the wounded contender stumbling back. Over the ledge.

Elias almost cried out. The drop down to the forest was deadly, as he knew very well, but just as Siv was about to fall clear over, he dug his claws into the lip of the cliff and dangled there, struggling to get up.

The two remaining wurl paid him no mind. They now faced each other.

Elias walked closer very carefully. He hadn't seen any of them fire spines, so he assumed he was safe as long as he didn't get too near, and he wanted to see what happened.

At first, the two challengers circled each other, huffing and baring their fangs. Elias realized that the fight must have been going on for some time, judging by the marks both of them now bore. Vanor's scales were smeared with mud, and he had several bite marks on his legs. Narev looked even worse. Several of his spines had been broken off, and there was a bloody gash on his snout where he had obviously been raked with metallic claws.

The two of them snapped at each other every now and then, roaring occasionally. Neither of them moved any closer, though. It reminded Elias of boxing matches he had seen in videos. At first not much would happen as the two fighters sized each other up. Soon, though—

His train of thought was interrupted when Siv finally managed to claw his way back onto the valley floor. He was very clearly spent, but his presence was a distraction. Narev looked at him briefly.

Vanor did not.

With a booming roar, Vanor launched himself at Narev, all six feet outstretched, with deadly claws ready to strike. Narev turned around and tried to meet Vanor's charge, but his split-second distraction made all the difference. Vanor crashed into him, despite the spines, and clamped all six of his feet around Narev's body.

Narev howled and tried to squirm free, but he was pinned. When he tried to bite his assailant, Vanor simply snaked his neck out of the way and bit down on Narev's neck. It was a death hold, and Narev seemed to recognize it. After a brief moment of struggle, he suddenly went limp, the feral glow in his eyes dimming. He flattened his spines and silently accepted his defeat.

Elias thought Vanor would simply kill him. All it would take was for Vanor to bite down hard and his opponent's life would be over. Instead, Vanor pushed Narev roughly out of the way, sending him crashing into Siv, and jumped up to land on his six feet again, every spine on his body upright and menacing.

Vanor roared, and this time Elias felt the will behind his voice. It was surprisingly strong and clear, almost like Sizzra's for a moment. It spoke of triumph, of strength... and of unquenchable desire.

From above, its source unseen among the slopes of the Flower mountain, a response came.

Sizzra's roar echoed all around Elias, and a moment later he saw the wurl queen rolling down the mountain in a dazzling dash of color and spines. She was shockingly quick and reached the valley grounds with a graceful uncoiling motion, making the earth tremble in her wake.

Siv and Narev backed away meekly, just as they had done before. They lay down on the ground with spines flattened and appeared to want to make themselves look as small as possible so the queen wouldn't notice them. Vanor, however, did the opposite.

He stepped forward, huffing, and faced Sizzra squarely. He did not back away when she blasted him with a roar of sound and pure will, the very essence of defiance. Instead, he roared right back.

That's when Sizzra attacked him.

She swiped at Vanor with a claw large enough to shred him in two, but the male was ready. He curled himself into a ball and fired off two spines into the ground so fast that they propelled him forward like a cannonball. His speed allowed him to dodge the swipe, and he crashed against Sizzra's chest, making her stumble back.

Sizzra's surprise and anger was terrible to behold. She shoved him roughly out of the way, and this time Vanor could not escape the blow. Still curled up, he went tumbling until he crashed against the side of the lower Flower mountain slopes. He uncoiled his body and crouched where he stood, shaking his head briefly as if stunned. Elias cried out to him involuntarily when he saw Sizzra's crown of spines flare out around her neck.

She fired.

Elias shut his eyes tight, but the horrible cry he was certain would be the outcome of Vanor being impaled by a spine never came. Disbelieving, he looked again and saw that the male had jumped out of the way. Sizzra fired again, and again he avoided the projectile by jumping. She fired a third time while Vanor was still in the air, and in response he fired a spine of his own, which met Sizzra's halfway and deflected the projectile with a sharp *clang* of ringing metal.

Elias spared a quick glance at Sizzra, and he didn't need the seething echoes of her mental waves to tell she had never been angrier. The pain in her snout amplified her emotions and made her presence twice as threatening. She fired again and again as she walked toward her suitor, but every spine was met by one of Vanor's. The much smaller male did not retreat, not even when Sizzra stopped less than two paces in front of him, dwarfing his strength with her majesty. He roared out the same piercing mental projection of his single-minded will and defied her once again. He existed for one reason only. His burning desire would not be denied.

Furious, she snapped at him, jaws clamping with the intent to kill—but Vanor was no longer there. He surged forward faster than Elias had ever seen a wurl move, dodged Sizzra's middle feet with their deadly claws, and vaulted past her back feet. Then he bit her tail at the base.

Sizzra screamed, half in pain, half in an emotion Elias had no name for. She thrashed and whirled, slamming her tail against the rocks, but Vanor did not let go. Rocks splintered under her onslaught. Elias was forced to seek cover from the deadly flying shards of her wrath. Vanor, however, bit even harder, deep enough to make glittering red blood pool around his mouth. With another scream, Sizzra jumped into the air much higher than Elias would have thought possible. For an instant she was clearly outlined against the sun. Then she crashed down in a teeth-chattering tremor and stood still.

The quiet that followed was almost unbelievable in its totality. Elias was frozen, back flat against a rock, his eyes wide in a mixture of fear and wonder. He heard Sizzra and Vanor panting and realized that Vanor had let go of his grip on Sizzra's tail. Slowly, Vanor got up on unsteady feet and approached her. She crouched slightly, lowered her head, and allowed her snout to touch his.

Every scale on Sizzra's body glowed blindingly bright at the contact. Elias had to shield his eyes from the searing beauty of her form, and he struggled to see clearly in the afterimages when the glow died down. Sizzra made a sound then, something Elias had never heard. It was almost a croon.

Together, Sizzra and Vanor walked to the lower slopes of the Flower mountain. There, Sizzra fired three spines that sunk into the ground wide apart from one another, outlining a rough triangle. As soon as they were in place, she began to dig.

Elias was certain that the queen would stomp him into a lifeless mush if she realized he was spying on her, but she didn't appear to notice him at all as she dug fiercely, her feet moving earth faster than any machine ever could. Next to her, Vanor helped as much as he was able, but even with their combined efforts it was evening before they finally stopped. Elias returned from a quick bathroom break and saw that Sizzra and Vanor had essentially dug out a cave in a single day, big enough for both of them to disappear into. Which is what they did. As darkness fell, Elias went inside his own small cave and tried to ignore the tremors that shook the mountain every now and then. Before closing the door, he realized that the two wurl who had been defeated had come closer to him, almost as if curious.

"Hey," Elias said to them, crawling back out of his shelter. "Sorry you guys lost to Vanor. Want some nuts?"

He took out two handfuls of his stash of velvet nuts and held them out to the terrifying creatures. With only starlight to see by, it was difficult to make out much of their outlines, except for the faintly glowing clusters of red eyes. Normally Elias would have been shaking in fear at facing two adult wurl on his own, but he suspected that tonight was different.

Slowly, with evident hesitation, Narev edged closer. Siv wasn't far behind, but they stopped just out of arm's reach.

"Don't worry, I don't bite. Here, have some food. I haven't seen you guys eat anything since you came, and you must be really hungry after all that fighting."

Narev was the first to touch his hands with his snout. Siv followed suit, and they each took a careful bite of the nuts Elias was offering. The food was gone in an instant, and the creatures sniffed him as if eager for more.

Elias smiled. "I'll get you some more tomorrow, okay?"

When he retreated back into the cave, he didn't close the door. He was strangely comforted by the fact that both Narev and Siv had lain down in front of his shelter and fallen promptly asleep. It was almost like having two protectors between him and the night.

Chapter 23
Fishing

SIZZRA AND Vanor remained in their secluded cave for the better part of a week. Both Siv and Narev avoided the area, and Elias decided that it was probably a very good idea to do the same thing. Instead, he set to work on the project he had waited for many weeks now to set in motion.

He was going to become a farmer.

Elias had already had plenty of time to decide where he would place his farm. He chose the eastern shore of the lake as the best spot because it got the most sunlight during the day, and it was somewhat sheltered from the weather by the tall peaks in the vicinity. The proximity to water would also be very convenient.

After having a quick breakfast and tiptoeing away from the still-sleeping wurl at the entrance to his cave, Elias set out for the lake with Sizzra's spine in his hand. He had never planted anything in his life, but when he was little, he had sometimes helped his grandmother in the greenhouses. He had also used the long winter nights of his captivity to read everything he could about Terran crops and the best way to make them grow. He now knew how much space corn needed, how deep the seeds needed to be planted, and how to care for the fledgling plants. For rice he would have to build a separate paddy, flooded with water from the lake, so the seeds could grow properly. The beans would be the easiest, since they grew very fast. He also had some barley, wheat, lentils, and soy, which would require their own unique conditions. He was prepared, however. He still had several hundred questions, like how to procure fertilizer or shield the plants from freak storms, but he knew that the seeds in his pockets were the most valuable thing in the world by far. At least for human beings. He was ready to do his best and try to make them grow, caring for them every step of the way. Time was of the essence, since Elias wasn't sure whether Portree's food supply had been affected by the spring changes to the world. Should Sizzra ever let him go, Elias wanted to leave with sacks and sacks of his harvest. If he could find a way to make sacks.

He spent most of the first morning dragging big rocks to make a crude fence around his farm. It was boring, monotonous work and hard as well. He had already gathered all easily accessible rocks for his cave and the firepit, so this time Elias was forced to climb several of the low slopes of the surrounding mountains in order to get what he needed. At times he was practically climbing straight up, with nothing but the strength of his arms to hold him in place or pull him over a ledge. Nevertheless, where he had struggled to do similar things at the beginning of his captivity, now he found it almost easy. He couldn't believe he had been so weak, and he was certain that the increasingly muscular reflection he saw in the lake was a good indicator of his growing strength. He was able to lift rocks that he would have been barely able to move back at Portree and carry them down mountains, through treacherous terrain on top of everything else. In fact he found the same fierce satisfaction at exerting himself and succeeding that he had experienced in one of Sizzra's memories. It felt good to grow strong.

When he was finally done, the space he had sectioned off was nearly twice the size of the Main Hall. His arms and his back were absolutely exhausted from the effort. But he was happy.

Thinking that he deserved a break, Elias took off his clothes and waded into the lake. Submerging was pure bliss. The day was relatively hot, but the water remained cool and refreshing. Sighing with contentment in a burst of bubbles, Elias flipped over onto his back and floated on the surface for a long while, watching the sky and the fleeting white clouds that passed overhead from time to time. Some insects buzzed in the air around him, and the wind carried a smell that for Elias was almost unknown. It was a fragrance of growing things, of pollen and grass and wet earth.

His aching muscles relaxed as Elias felt the tension of the day ebbing away from him. He took a long deep breath…

And nearly choked on a gigantic wave when first Narev and then Siv decided they also wanted to swim in the lake.

Sputtering, Elias came back up for air and looked around. For an instant he thought the two wurl would simply sink under the weight of their metallic scales. When they didn't, instead swimming directly for him, fear stabbed Elias. He was helpless, floating in the middle of the lake. All it would take was a single swipe from any of those deadly claws and he would be well and truly dead.

The wurl did not appear to be interested in killing him, though. Elias released a shaky pent-up breath when he saw Narev glide past him underwater, surprisingly graceful in his movements. Siv was right behind him, snaking his entire body and using his tail like a rudder to move up and down, occasionally releasing big bubbles of air. Fascinated, Elias watched them. Narev led the way down to the lake bottom, where he settled casually as if he was walking on dry land. He then proceeded to nose around the area, disturbing silt and rocks as he did so, appearing to be looking for something.

Siv was soon doing the same thing, and at first Elias didn't know what they were trying to do. He grew more and more amazed, however, when first seconds and then minutes passed without either of the males surfacing for air. In fact, when he was sure that at least half an hour had passed, Elias began to feel uneasy. He couldn't see the bottom of the lake anymore because of all the churning silt, and he feared that Narev and Siv had simply perished underwater. Against his better judgment, he decided to dive and see whether he could find them. He took a deep breath, twisted his body, and swam down.

His eyes stung, but he kept them open so he could see. He hadn't dived more than two meters when he caught the first glimpse of Narev still standing at the bottom, digging around. A cloud of dust obscured him from view for an instant, but Elias kicked forward and propelled himself far enough along that he was able to see what happened next.

One second Narev was calmly nosing boulders out of the way with his snout. In the next instant, his head snapped up and his entire body tensed. He fired a spine so suddenly that Elias was only able to see the whirlpool-like wake of the projectile through the water. Then he spotted something silvery sinking, pierced cleanly by the jagged spine.

A fish. A very big, very flat fish.

In a burst of bubbles, Narev was suddenly upon his prey. His jaws clamped shut on it and took out almost a quarter of the fish in one bite. Elias was forced to go up for air, and when he dived back down only half the fish remained. He spotted Siv swimming closer, his tail whipping through the water, with the clear intention of having a bite too.

Narev was having none of that. He snatched the remains of the flatfish, coiled his entire body over it, and then fired a series of spines which propelled his spinning shape clear across the lake, farther than Elias could see. Fascinated, Elias surfaced and saw how Narev jumped out of the water almost casually, holding the rest of his meal in his jaws. He proceeded to eat noisily, tearing huge chunks out of the dead fish.

The sun had dropped behind the mountains by then, and Elias returned to the shore, thankful for the toasty warmth of his clothes. He ate a little bit and tried not to be concerned about the fact that Siv was still underwater. Judging by the time on his link, Siv had now stayed in the lake for nearly two hours.

"Didn't know you guys were amphibians," he said to Siv when he finally surfaced. Siv glanced at him briefly and then looked away, evidently not interested in what he had to say.

Even so, Elias's spirits were higher than they had been in a while as he returned to his shelter. It was fun having the two wurl to watch and relieve the boredom, and he was satisfied with his work for the day. Tomorrow would be the hard part. He would have to plow the ground without a plow. He just hoped his trusty spine would be up to the task.

He kindled his fire and was pleasantly surprised to see Siv approach and settle down close to the warmth of the flames. Soon the hulking outline of Narev came into view as well. He had a surprise for Elias.

Elias could barely believe his eyes as he saw Narev holding a small portion of the dead fish in his jaws. The wurl walked right up to him, lowered his head, and deposited the food at Elias's feet. Then he looked up at him with a faint mental echo of expectation.

"For me?" Elias asked, surprised.

Narev didn't answer, but he backed away from the fish even more.

"Really?" Elias made as if to grab the fish, then snatched his hand back. He had seen how furiously Narev had defended his catch before, and he didn't want to end up with a spine embedded through the back of his hand. Narev did not react with hostility, though.

Slowly, Elias reached forward until he touched the fish.

He felt faint encouragement from Narev and an unmistakable whisper of jealousy from Siv, who was watching the entire exchange. Emboldened, Elias lifted the fish and held it up to the fire.

"Wow, thanks," he said, trying to project gratitude with his thoughts. Narev gave no sign of receiving any kind of mental communication, but he did step forward and nudge the fish gently toward Elias's mouth.

Elias could have almost laughed. It was such a sweet gesture that it touched him deeply, and suddenly there were tears coming from nowhere, an expression of the repressed emotions he had kept inside for weeks.

It was too much. He had never asked for any of this, and it was getting to him. He wanted to be back with his family, sleeping on a bed, eating regular food. He wanted to be able to go back in time and tell his stupid younger self not to steal the Life Seed, to remain where he was. To try and be less of an insufferable sarcastic prick and instead help the colony somehow. To avoid walking down the path that led here, to captivity from a merciless alien queen and nights upon nights of silence and loneliness.

Sure, he had helped an entire continent. Sure, he now had seeds which might save Portree in the long run. But it was awful. Just *awful*. He didn't know when or if Sizzra would let him go, and even if she did it would only be to go straight to his colony and kill everyone in it. There was no love in her heart except for herself, of that Elias was sure. And she was too big, too powerful, to be defied by humans who expected to live.

The tears wouldn't stop coming. Ashamed of his outburst, Elias placed the fish back on the ground and covered his face. His soft sobbing was eventually interrupted by another gentle nudge. Looking to his right, Elias realized that Narev was now standing beside him. The big wurl picked up the fish and reached it out to Elias. In spite of himself, Elias chuckled even as he was crying and placed the palm of his hand over Narev's warm snout.

The contact sharpened Elias's perception for an instant and he saw—

Surprise made him stop crying. Narev thought Elias was sick. He knew that the human was very small and weak, too weak to hunt for himself. And just as Narev had done for many other juveniles from time to time, he was bringing him some food so he wouldn't starve.

It was shocking to perceive such a structured thought coming from the mind of a creature whom Sizzra considered barely sentient. Struck speechless, Elias took the fish again while maintaining his physical contact with Narev.

"Thank you," he repeated sincerely. "I am not sick. This is the way I always will be. I won't grow big like you."

His reply, however, was too complex, and all he got back from Narev was confusion. With a sigh, Elias looked at the big hunk of meat from the flatfish in earnest.

He knew the animals of New Skye were incompatible with his system. If he ate the meat, he would probably get diarrhea for a couple of days, or worse. Then again, he didn't want to seem ungrateful, particularly since he had no idea what Narev would do if his kind offer was rejected.

There really wasn't much to think about. With another grateful pat, Elias decided to cook the fish and see what happened. He took out one of the large flat rocks he used to roast the nuts on and placed it over the flames. While it warmed, he used Sizzra's spine to clean the meat and remove all the bones. He was left with a sizable slab of pink filet that made his stomach rumble in anticipation.

He placed the fish on his makeshift skillet while Siv and Narev watched with open curiosity. Soon, the mouthwatering aroma of cooking meat wafted through the air, and Elias could not believe the pang of hunger that swept through him at the smell. He was sick of eating fruits all the time, and this here was real meat. Not the soy concentrate that passed for meat in his colony, but something fresh.

He didn't even wait for the fish to brown evenly. As soon as he judged it was edible, Elias snatched it up and ate.

He was noisy. He burned his tongue once—but he didn't care. It was the most delicious thing he had ever tasted in his life. The fish was wonderfully flaky, with a rich, moist flavor that exploded on his tongue every time he chewed. The edges, which had cooked more, had a smoky tang all their own. It was nourishing in a way that none of the food Elias had ever eaten could have been. It felt real. Through it, his connection to the world seemed to strengthen, as if….

Elias had a fleeting glimpse similar to the one he would have sometimes when getting as close to the Life Seed as he now dared. The pattern of spirit-lines that threaded the world into a single beautiful tapestry now included him as well. And as he ate, he took the life of a creature, part of its energy, and added it to his own in a way that meshed his own life spark more firmly through the fabric of New Skye.

As suddenly as it had come, the vision was gone. Elias blinked, looked up at the two expectant wurl crowding around him, and burped.

"I'm stuffed," he told Narev, pushing the food away. There was more than half of the portion left, but his stomach was completely full. "Do you want to try? I don't think you guys have ever had cooked fish before."

Almost as if he understood, Narev sniffed the fish a few times. His pink tongue darted out and tasted the cooked flesh of the creature he had caught.

Narev's eyes glowed more brightly for an instant. Then he gobbled up the remaining fish with evident gusto and looked up at Elias with open expectation. He even whined once, softly, but then appeared to catch himself, and he looked to his left, in the direction of the cave where Sizzra and Vanor were hiding. His fleeting alarm passed, though, and he returned his full attention to Elias.

"I don't have any more," he replied, smiling. "If you bring me some tomorrow, I can cook it. Same goes for you, Siv," he added, feeling bad that he hadn't thought to offer Siv any. "You guys catch it, I cook it. Now wish me luck. I'm in for a looong night of diarrhea."

The discomfort, however, never came. Elias slept more soundly than he had for a very long time, and when the morning light woke him up, he couldn't believe it. He did not feel sick. His stomach didn't cramp the way he had read people would experience after eating native animals. He didn't have a fever, nausea, or a headache. There was no pain. In fact, there was… strength. A sense of renewal, as if the accumulated exhaustion of the last few weeks had vanished, leaving in its place a wonderful resting calm.

Unsure what had happened but thankful nevertheless, Elias tiptoed again between the two sleeping wurl and headed to his farm. He had a long day ahead of him.

Chapter 24
Emergence

WORKING AS a farmer turned out to be much more difficult than Elias had expected.

His biggest problem by far was that he didn't have any tools, and it was very complicated to use his one tool, the spine, to do everything. Preparing the soil, in particular, had been an absolute nightmare. In the spot Elias had chosen, the ground was hard-packed and unyielding. It took him the better part of two weeks simply to carve out a dozen parallel rows of upturned earth where he would be planting most of the seeds. By the time he was finished, his arms were constant, throbbing loci of alternating pain and numbness, and he fancied even the blisters on the palms of his hands had blisters.

It was satisfying work, though.

Elias felt a little thrill of pride when he planted his first corn seed. He had researched the exact depth it required, how far away it had to be from other plants, and how to best group his tiny cornfield to take maximum advantage of fickle insect pollination. He did not use his entire store of seeds in case something happened to the first crop, but he made sure to plant a little of everything. When he was done with the corn, he went over to the beans, wheat, and barley. Then he walked over to his makeshift rice paddy, a tiny enclosure which he had flooded with some water from the lake. He placed the rice seeds carefully, hoping he had gotten the water depth right. Creating the paddy had taken an entire week on its own, since Elias had had to scoop out earth a little bit at a time and also ring everything with rocks so the water wouldn't leak too much.

When the last seed was in place, Elias stood up straight and stretched. He glanced out over his work and smiled. It wasn't much to look at now, but once the seeds sprouted it would be a different story. Now the only thing that worried him was whether the soil would be nourishing enough to allow for germination and growth. Since this continent had been stuck in a dormant winter cycle for so long, he guessed that his little plants would need as much help as they could get.

That's where the fertilizer came in.

With a resigned sigh, Elias approached the lakeside edge of his farm, where Narev and Siv were basking in the sunlight. The two wurl had been very curious about the project at first, but as the days went by and nothing exciting seemed to happen, they quickly grew bored and spent most of their time fishing or napping. Elias was fine with that. Narev had taken to always saving a small portion of his catch so Elias could eat, and it meant that his diet was vastly improved from what it had been during the winter. The big creatures had also developed a mild addiction to grilled fish, and now Elias spent most of his evenings cooking what they had caught. The company was also nice, and Elias hoped that they wouldn't leave anytime soon. Perhaps they were waiting for Sizzra to emerge, but if so then Elias had no idea when they would finally see her again. The queen had remained inside her cave for weeks now, and Vanor only came out at night to hunt and bring some food back to her, presumably. For the moment, Elias was glad he didn't have to deal with Sizzra. He dreaded the moment when she would finally come out. He just hoped she wouldn't decide to stomp his little farm into oblivion out of spite.

Elias touched Narev's snout briefly as he passed by the spot where the wurl was resting. He received a faint but unmistakable friendly acknowledgment in response, but Narev was enjoying the sun too much to pay full attention to Elias. Instead, Elias walked past until he came to the spot the two wurl had decided to designate as their place to poop. Even though they buried it every day in a surprisingly clean fashion, Elias found it easy to get at some fresh manure after only a little digging.

"This is so gross," he said to himself, wishing he had gloves on or something. As he didn't, he just hurried from the poop pile to his farm and back again until he was certain that all the little seeds had at least some fertilizer. Afterward, he jumped into the far end of the lake and washed himself for a very long time.

When nighttime came, Elias built up a fire as usual and waited for Siv and Narev to show up with their catch. It had become a tradition of sorts already, and Elias found that he looked forward to his mostly wordless interactions with the wurl. It was nice to be able to be with someone other than himself, and it was also a great time to simply sit back and enjoy the increasingly warm nights as spring took hold, waking everything to new life.

The world around Elias had transformed itself entirely. Where before there had only been barren expanses of gray rocks, there were now plants, vines, and grass everywhere. The lower slopes of the mountains around him were covered with small but very beautiful wildflowers, and now there seemed to be insects everywhere.

Elias slapped his forearm as he spotted Narev lumbering toward the firepit with a strange spiral-shaped fish in his jaws. The mosquito-analogue that had been biting him flew off with an irritating buzz. Annoyed, Elias scratched at the spot, hoping he wouldn't have a rash in the morning. Not everything was awesome now that the world was truly awakening, but he was willing to put up with a few insects if it meant that things had gone back to the way they should be.

"Hey there," Elias greeted Narev. "That's a new fish you caught tonight."

Narev's eyes glowed more brightly for a moment in what Elias had now come to recognize as excitement, and Narev eagerly deposited his catch on the large flat rock that had become Elias's grill. Before long, the smell of sizzling meat wafted up, tantalizing. Siv wasn't too far behind, and dropped the flatfish he had caught as close to the fire as he dared.

"Nice one," Elias said to him. "Let me get that cooked for you."

Siv did not acknowledge Elias directly, but he lay down close to the fire with his eye cluster fixed on the cooking fish. Unlike Narev, who appeared to be more open and friendly, Siv never actively sought Elias out, and he hadn't once allowed Elias to touch him unless it was by accident. Still, as far as Elias was concerned, the fact that Siv hadn't killed him yet was a very good thing indeed, especially since Sizzra did not appear to be coming out of her cave anytime soon to reinforce her order not to attack him.

As the days got longer, Elias learned more and more about the wurl.

He discovered they had different personalities and an insatiable curiosity. Now that they weren't fighting for dominance, Siv and Narev spent a lot more time together. More than once, Elias watched them coordinate their efforts while swimming in the lake in order to catch smaller, more agile fish. They weren't always hunting, though. In fact, one afternoon Elias saw them play.

At first he thought something was wrong because Narev started chasing after Siv, and the two of them ran around the entire length of the valley, going very fast for creatures their size. Siv was quick, but Narev was relentless, and eventually he caught up, nipping Siv on the shoulder. Siv yelped and launched himself up the nearest mountain slope, using his claws to dig into the rock and haul himself over the tricky parts. With a growl, Narev climbed too. It was fascinating to watch the two creatures display incredible strength and stamina as they climbed higher and higher. When they had reached a height that was almost midway to the summit, Siv curled himself into a ball and rolled down. Narev followed suit.

The silver scales on the two spine-covered whirling males reflected the sunlight as they tumbled down, gathering speed. With a start, Elias realized he was in the way and had to run for cover before the two of them zoomed past him so fast that they did not stop until they reached the lake. As they did, both Siv and the Narev uncoiled, splashing into the water like cannonballs. When they came out, Narev did a sort of friendly wiggle with his tail. Siv responded with a growl, and then they set off again, except this time it was Siv doing the chasing.

It was very entertaining to watch them, which was good because now that Elias had planted his seeds there was little to do except make sure that the farm wasn't destroyed by accident. Luckily, even though Narev and Siv would sometimes walk up to the farm to watch him, they never actually stepped past the makeshift fence of boulders and rocks. They seemed to sense that it was a boundary they shouldn't cross, which displayed remarkable perception and intelligence.

More and more, Elias's concept of the male wurl was challenged and broadened. They were definitely not the simple creatures Sizzra thought them to be. They might not have the same capacity to project their will with deafening strength, but there was something there that hinted at unexplored depths in the smaller wurl's psyches. This thought was reinforced when, on a night after three weeks had passed since the mating dance, Vanor emerged from the cave he shared with Sizzra and approached Elias's campfire.

"Hi. Want some cooked fish?"

Elias was just about done cooking Narev's and Siv's catch, and although his voice was friendly, he couldn't suppress a faint twinge of alarm when Vanor shouldered Narev aside and gave no sign of stopping as he stomped straight for Elias.

Elias watched him, frozen, heart hammering in his chest. He had forgotten how Vanor really looked, but now that he had spent so much time watching Narev and Siv, the differences were clear to his eyes. Vanor was slightly taller, wider around the shoulders than either of the other males. His spines, although flattened against his back, appeared to be longer. There was also an air of assertive dominance about him, which was reinforced when Vanor stopped at the edge of the flames, stared at the cooking fish, and lunged forward.

Elias gasped. Vanor did not seem to care about the fire. He grabbed first one and then the other fish, carried them some distance away, and began to eat. When he took the first bite, his eyes glowed with delight, and he spared the first true look of acknowledgment he had given Elias. Then he proceeded to gorge himself until only a third of each fish was left. With a growl, he nosed the remains in the direction of the other males and then stalked off into the shadows, curled up some distance away, and closed his eyes.

Narev and Siv wasted no time, eating as fast as they could. They did not seem to take offense at the fact that Vanor had stolen their catch, and since they weren't saying anything, Elias wasn't even going to try and get them to leave him some fish from the little that was left.

"Too bad, though," he muttered to himself. "That spiral fish Narev caught is so tasty."

Instead, he resigned himself to a dinner of grilled yellow lily buds and a thick root he had found growing underneath a boulder which looked like an overgrown carrot. He was about done eating when Narev approached, carrying a morsel of his catch in his mouth.

"No, you eat it," Elias told him, touched nevertheless that Narev had thought about him. "And next time don't let Vanor steal your food, okay? He can be the alpha all he wants, but he has to hunt for himself."

Narev gave him a puzzled turn of his head, dropped the fish morsel, and walked off to his favorite resting spot on the other side of the bonfire. Shrugging, Elias grabbed the palm-sized meat portion and ate it. He had the same sensation he received whenever he ate meat from New Skye—a hint of belonging, of renewing strength, and of fulfillment. He wondered what had happened to make him able to digest the fish of his world, but for the most part he was only thankful. It tasted great, and it was something to look forward to in the monotony of captivity, which now seemed endless.

Not for the first time, Elias thought about escaping as the fire died down and the three male wurl slept soundly all around his cave. He knew he was much stronger now than months ago when he had attempted to leave for the first time. Besides, Sizzra had not come out once since her mating, and Elias supposed she was busy laying eggs for the next generation of spiny wurl. This was his best chance at escaping by far, but...

He couldn't suppress the thought that if he did leave Sizzra would waste no time chasing him all the way to Portree to destroy the entire colony. As the Life Seed had grown stronger through the blood rituals, Sizzra no longer needed to stay so close to it, as her weeks-long seclusion in her cave proved. Maybe she wouldn't be able to leave its vicinity yet, but that was something on which Elias did not want to gamble. Better for him to stay put and tend the farm than risk the lives of everyone he knew trying to regain his freedom.

"It's not so bad here," he said softly, looking up at the sky. He had named several constellations on his own, familiar friends now, like the Arrow, a peculiar cluster of blue-tinged stars that pointed straight in the direction of the Core Systems.

His voice, though, sounded lonely to his ears.

He slept fitfully, and in the gray light of early dawn, he thought he kept hearing scratching, pummeling noises. It wasn't until a particularly loud scratch jolted him awake that he realized the sounds were not part of his dreams.

Alert immediately, he crawled out of the cave and looked around. The morning dew covered the emerald blades of grass over the valley. Vanor, Narev, and Siv were still sleeping soundly, judging by their huffing snorts. The sky was clear overhead but still dark for the most part.

Scratch—plunk.

Elias's head whipped to the right. The sound was coming from the cliff at the edge of the valley. Cautiously, careful not to make any noise, Elias walked closer. It took him fifteen minutes to reach the area right in front of the sheer drop-off into the forest far below. Straight ahead, the eastern sun was rising. To his right, the dark maw of Sizzra's cave was quiet. It looked almost abandoned.

Scratch—plunk.

The sound was coming from below, from somewhere over the edge. With a final anxious look at Sizzra's cave, Elias approached until he was able to look down.

His jaw dropped in shock.

"Damn it," murmured the man who was climbing the cliff wall. Elias forgot to blink as he watched Tristan, outfitted in full climbing gear and a huge backpack, climbing slowly but surely, driving spikes into the rock and securing himself to the new handholds with a tough-looking rope.

The sun had risen completely over the treetops, and Tristan had climbed almost all the way to the top before Elias remembered he had a mouth. And a voice.

"Tristan?" he croaked.

A sharp intake of breath and a quick glance up was followed by a frozen moment as their eyes met in silent, shocked surprise.

"Elias? Elias!"

"Hi."

Tristan swayed on his precarious perch on the rocky wall. He was maybe ten meters below Elias's level. Almost close enough to touch.

"I can't believe it. By the generation ship, you're still *alive*! Wait…. Don't move. Don't go anywhere."

Tristan resumed climbing, much faster than before. In a matter of minutes, he was close enough to reach up and grab the lip of the surface ledge with his hands. Elias grabbed one of his arms and helped him pull himself over the edge. Tristan crashed into him, panting, and rolled until he was lying on his backpack, looking up at Elias like he couldn't believe what he saw.

Elias offered him his hand so Tristan would be able to stand up. Tristan took it after shrugging off his pack. Just the fact that Elias was touching another human being after months of captivity was enough to bring tears to his eyes.

"You're still alive," Tristan said, eyes wide. Then he smiled. "Yes! This is amazing!"

Then he hugged Elias, his grip surprisingly strong, and even lifted Elias clear off the ground for a second. His face was flushed with emotion when he finally stepped back and looked at Elias.

"We thought you were dead," Tristan told him. "I looked for you after we got separated, but the wurl herded me all the way back to Portree. The Patrol wouldn't let me leave again to search until I convinced them…. Are you okay?"

Elias was trying to say something, but he couldn't explain the fact that he was crying out of joy at hearing someone else's voice. The crushing loneliness of the past few weeks overwhelmed Elias with emotion.

"You came," he managed to say at last, his voice hoarse. "You came back for me."

Tristan opened his mouth as if to speak, but a deep tremor shook the earth.

Soul-crushing dismay swept through Elias even as he pulled Tristan back, stepping between him and the cave. He could feel the amused, cruel echoes of a will being projected, and he was not surprised when the emaciated form of Sizzra emerged from the cave in a burst of rock and dirt.

As she stepped clear out onto the valley floor, Elias caught a glimpse of the cavernous space behind her. The morning sunlight sliced through the shadows in her wake and revealed an enormous pile of small obsidian-shelled eggs. There were hundreds upon hundreds, and resting at the very top, larger than the others by far, was a single white egg.

Sizzra's neck snaked forward to block Elias's view of the precious nest. Behind him, Tristan gasped.

Elias bunched his hands into fists, shaking with powerless rage. Sizzra did not need to speak in order to project what she was thinking. The exact location of her nest was a secret none but her mate and his rivals could know. To look upon it was death.

She growled deep in her throat. Despite the horrifying progress of the burning wound on her snout, which had now reached up to her eye cluster, she was still a vision of ferocity. She fixed Elias with an unblinking glare and moved her head slightly to the left. *Move aside*, she was clearly saying. Elias had seen her nest, and for that he would die—eventually. When the Life Seed needed him no more. But the other human, the other puny, meaningless male....

Sizzra opened her jaws wide, and her intentions were clear. Tristan was going to die.

Chapter 25
Change

"No," Elias said firmly, and he was surprised at the suddenness of his anger. "You're not going to kill him."

He threw his arms out to make his meaning clear, shielding Tristan from Sizzra.

"Elias?" Tristan asked from behind him. "What's going on?"

Elias didn't answer because he couldn't. He was locked in a silent battle of wills with the huge wurl queen, who lowered her head so her eye cluster would be level with Elias's face.

Three months ago, Elias would have retreated under her glare. Her unmistakable command for him to move out of the way would have broken his resistance in an instant, just like that first time he had seen her, when she had forced him to bring the Life Seed to her.

Not anymore.

"I said *no*," he told her, his voice deep. He weathered the mental barrage of her anger with a frown and his jaw set firmly. "He lives. Or I don't help you anymore, and the Flower never blooms."

Sizzra growled threateningly, and it was as if the mountains themselves were echoing her menace. As long seconds dragged by and Elias did not move, he was able to perceive the shifting currents of her thoughts. First, puzzlement. No one, no creature ever in her domain, had been able to resist a command like that. Then came suspicion. She bared her fangs at Elias, but he did not back down. His resolution was a challenge to her, incomprehensible since Elias was male. And tiny. What could he do? Elias could tell she wanted to kill him, but before the thought solidified in her mind, he projected an image of the Flower with total concentration. First, blooming, even changed though it would be, through the blood rituals. Then, withered. Dead.

That stopped her. Slowly, she came to grasp his threat.

And she hated him for it.

The wordless tension held for a moment longer, and then Sizzra roared. The loud grating sound would have been threatening if not for the undercurrent Elias could perceive behind the noise. Frustration.

Sizzra was the first to look away. She stalked off to the Flower mountain and climbed it swiftly, her claws leaving jagged marks on the rocks themselves under the force of her onslaught. Elias had seen her do that many times already, and he couldn't help but notice that this time she was clumsy. She faltered a couple of times even in her anger, betraying a weakness that was growing every day. For now, though, she was still strong enough to be deadly.

Elias breathed a sigh of relief when she was finally lost from sight over the lip of a rocky outcrop that led to the southern slopes of the mountain. He lowered his arms and noticed he was trembling.

"What—what just happened?" Tristan demanded, moving so he stood in front of Elias.

Elias gave him a one-sided grin. He wiped away the sweat that had beaded on his brow with a trembling hand. "I just blackmailed a wurl queen."

Tristan blinked. He glanced behind him at the place where Sizzra had disappeared and then back to Elias. "I thought she was going to kill me."

"She was," Elias confirmed.

"And she didn't… because of you. Wow. Thank you."

Elias patted him on the shoulder. "Don't worry about it. Come, let me get you something to eat. And then you have to tell me everything."

"Uh, sure," Tristan said, sounding like he was struggling to process everything that was happening.

Elias nodded in the direction of his cave and stalked off without looking back to see if Tristan was following. After a couple of places, though, he slowed down. Why was he acting like that? Where had this… this confidence come from?

He looked back at Tristan and smiled. Tristan grinned in return, and Elias's heart beat a little faster. He had forgotten how handsome Tristan was.

They reached the entrance to the cave before Tristan spotted the three sleeping wurl.

"Whoa!" he yelled, grabbing Elias's arm to pull him back. "Watch out!"

In a fluid, practiced motion, Tristan took out his shock spear from the backpack he was carrying and activated it. The sharp hiss of arcing electricity made Narev open his eyes.

"Don't!" Elias shouted, batting the spear out of the way.

"Elias, there's three of them—"

Now Vanor and Siv were also awake, and the three of them jumped upright, spines flared out.

There was no time to explain. Elias grabbed the spear again. Tristan reacted instinctively, trying to yank it back.

Elias pulled harder.

He snatched the spear out of Tristan's hands and threw it a good distance away, where the weapon's tip sizzled as it made contact with the ground. Then it went out.

"They won't attack you," Elias told Tristan, who looked absolutely speechless. Elias gestured at each of the wurl in turn. "This is Siv. This is Narev. The big guy is Vanor. Guys, this is Tristan. He's my friend."

Slowly, the male wurl flattened their spines against their scales. When Tristan gave no sign of wanting to attack them again, Narev was the first to approach and sniff him. Then came Siv. Vanor was the last, fixing Tristan with a steady, challenging look. For a moment, Elias was afraid Tristan would show weakness in front of the alpha wurl, but he was rewarded by Tristan's reaction.

"What's up?" Tristan said to Vanor.

Vanor huffed once, apparently satisfied, and stalked away in the direction of the lake. He growled, and both Narev and Siv followed.

Tristan then turned to look at Elias, his mouth slightly open in what looked like disbelief.

"Never mind my news," he told Elias. "You have to tell *me* what happened here. It's like you're a different person!"

"What do you mean?" Elias asked, helping Tristan take off his backpack now that they were at the mouth of the cave. Elias placed it away from the firepit, just in case.

"Like *that*!" Tristan exclaimed.

"Huh?"

"That backpack—do you know how hard it was to carry it all the way here? And now you pick it up with one hand like it's nothing! And— oh, by the generation ship! Elias, what happened to your eyes?"

"What do you mean?"

Tristan stepped closer, very close in fact. He was looking straight at Elias's eyes, and Elias couldn't help but notice Tristan's graceful profile, the hard lines of his jaw, and the dark stubble that shadowed his cheeks.

Tristan did not appear to have romantic thoughts in mind, though. "They look different," he said in a hushed voice. "I didn't notice before because of the light. But now… they look like her scales."

"What?" Now it was Elias's turn to be confused.

"You haven't seen? Wait. I have a mirror—wait." Tristan rummaged around in a pouch on his utility belt and took out a multitool. Unfurling it, he selected the mirror attachment and offered it to Elias.

"What's this about?"

"Just look," Tristan said.

Elias took the mirror and lifted it up so he could see his face.

He nearly dropped it on the grass below.

"You really hadn't noticed?" Tristan asked him, but Elias was too stunned to answer.

He held the mirror closer. Farther away. At an angle. It wasn't a trick of the light—the irises in his eyes had changed into a different color. Into *many* different colors, in fact. They reflected the sunlight in a thousand different shades of the same iridescent interplay he had always seen on Sizzra's scales. They were eerily beautiful, but they made him look strange. And it wasn't the only thing that had changed. The lines of his face were more noticeable. His skin had taken on a dark tan. His hair was longer than he had ever worn it.

"I look like a different person," Elias whispered.

"That's what I said. What happened?"

"Tell you what," he said to Tristan. "I'll cook something, then we talk. About everything."

Elias set to work and welcomed the easy flow of routine to steady him emotionally. Tristan settled nearby, taking some things out of his backpack while Elias brought out some seeds, berries, and a big portion of smoked flatfish which he had been saving for an emergency. He found comfort in the familiarity of what he was doing, even as he thought about several things at once. He was worried about Sizzra's reaction to his defiance. He was shocked at the changes that had come upon him, and he still couldn't believe that Tristan was here, with him, along with everything it implied. Tristan hadn't given up on him. He had come all the way back to this place, knowing the danger. He had returned.

Elias could not have put into words why that thought gave him a warm thrill, but he smiled as he kindled a small cooking fire with his well-worn flint and steel. Once it was going nicely, he set his favorite cooking stone on top of the flames at an angle and placed the slab of fish on it so it would warm up a little.

"Wow," Tristan said.

Elias glanced at him. "What?"

"I don't know. Everything. Last time I saw you, I was sure you wouldn't last a week out in the wilderness on your own. Now you're like some kind of wild survival expert."

"I'm not."

"Oh yeah? What's with the stash of food? Did you catch that fish yourself? And who taught you how to make a firepit and start a fire? The door to that cave, did you make it yourself? It looks pretty solid."

"I'm not sure which of the questions to answer first," Elias answered, smiling. "I propose we first eat, okay?"

"Yeah, sure. Though I even brought survival rations and everything with me. I was picturing finding you on the brink of starvation in a ditch somewhere. If at all."

"Geez, thanks for the vote of confidence," Elias told him, picking the heavy cooking stone out of the flames and setting it between the two of them. The tantalizing aroma of cooked fish could be perceived now, along with tiny hints of some of the herbs Elias had taken to experimenting with to give his food slightly different flavors.

"Sorry, that came out wrong. I didn't mean it like that—is that fish? Real fish?"

"Yeah, and it's delicious. There's some purpleberries and velvet nuts to go with that. And I have a few yellow lily buds you've got to try. They're all juicy inside and everything. Kind of sweet too."

Tristan looked at the fish with mild alarm. "But… this isn't meat-flavored soy concentrate. How are you eating it?"

Elias shrugged. "I don't know. I tried it, and it didn't make me sick, so I've been eating it for a while now. Narev usually brings me part of his catch. I think he thinks I'm injured or feeble or something. He's a good guy."

Tristan raised an eyebrow. "Okay, that was totally not weird of you to say. Or incomprehensible. I think I'm going to stick to the nuts and berries, though, if you don't mind."

"Sure."

The two of them ate in silence until the last morsel of food was gone. Then Tristan took out one of the boxes he had been carrying in his backpack.

"I have a couple of cherry cakes," he said to Elias. "Your mom…. She gave them to me. To share with you if I found you."

Tristan opened the box and there they were, two small and slightly crushed cherry cakes with a little pink frosting on top. Elias saw a capital *E* on one of them, made out of sprinkles in his mother's unmistakable style.

Out of nowhere, his eyes brimmed with tears.

"Hey," Tristan said softly, edging a little closer. "They're all okay back home. You have no idea how much they—how much we missed you."

Elias accepted his cherry cake from Tristan but had to look away for a moment until he was able to control the upswell of conflicting emotions in his chest. He thought he had succeeded as he took the first bite, but the taste unleashed a barrage of warm memories and happy associations in his mind, and then he couldn't hold back the tears anymore. He was suddenly a little boy, waiting impatiently for his mother to finish baking his birthday cake using his favorite ingredient, cherries out of Portree's precious stash of frozen fruit. Then he was a little older, sharing his cake with Oscar so both of them could enjoy the rare luxury of having something that wasn't made from the normal everyday rations.

He was at that Midwinter Feast last winter, a lifetime ago, so sure that only he knew what was right. Convinced that everyone else was stupid for not wanting to see the reality of the colony's future, blind to the fact that all the adults must have already known. Like Tristan had told him, they hadn't liked to talk about it, probably to protect their children from the awful reality they couldn't change.

And Elias had demanded they pay attention to him, to listen to his great discoveries in Dr. Wright's journal, spewing out everything he had learned in front of the little ones. He hadn't even thought about what effect it would have on them. What had Oscar thought? Had he been scared to hear that he was going to starve to death in the near future? And what good had it done?

Elias finished eating, crying silently now and yet strangely happy. During his long nights of isolation, he had sometimes thought that nobody would miss him back home. The little cherry cake was a symbol that it wasn't so. His family still loved him.

"They all miss you," Tristan said gently, setting aside the empty cake box. "When I came back to the colony and said that I had seen you, your dad practically kidnapped me so I could tell them what had happened. We had a really long session with Director O'Rourke, your mom and dad, my dad, and the commander. I told them everything, up to the point where the wurl chased me away from the mountain. They could see I was telling the truth too. A lot of wurl appeared at the edges of the colony perimeter along with the ones that brought me there. It's like they were being coordinated for the first time or something; they've set up some kind of containment around us, and they are really hostile to anyone who even looks as though he wants to leave. People were terrified. What I told them scared them even more.

"The commander especially went pale when I told her about the wurl queen. I had dozens of meetings with her and the rest of the patrol afterward, where we would draw up plans to try and defend Portree if she—"

"Sizzra," Elias said automatically.

"Right. If Sizzra ever came. But your mom and dad didn't even care about that. They kept asking me about you, and it was horrible to tell them that I didn't know whether you had survived or not. I had last seen you in that cave at the top of the mountain, and I had no idea whether Sizzra had killed you or what. It was awful, not knowing. Your dad asked right away for permission to leave Portree to find you, but the director said no. I offered to go with him, but she said it was too dangerous, and it turned out she was right.

"A few days after I returned, I went to see your dad, and he told me he was going to go find you with or without permission. I said I would help, but we didn't get very far. We hadn't even reached the spot with the underground laboratory you discovered when more than ten juvenile wurl encircled us. Your dad tried to get past them, but he was struck by a spine—don't worry, the wound wasn't very deep—and it was clear we had no chance of leaving. The creatures were containing us, and after that nobody else wanted to try and leave."

"And my mom?" Elias asked. "And Oscar?"

Tristan took a long, deep breath. "I don't want to scare you, man, but it's been hard on your mom. Her condition has worsened over the weeks, and she's been going to see the doctor more often. I don't know much else, because every time I went to visit she would tell me everything was okay, but I could tell it wasn't. She would be talking to me, and then her eyes would go kind of far away, and she would get this look on her face…. Oscar took it better, but Sarah tells me that he's not doing so well in school anymore. I've tried to talk to him a few times, but even though he's friendly and everything, it's like he's not really there. I don't know if that makes sense.

"Anyway, I took it for as long as I could, but a week ago I decided I had to try and find you. It was horrible not knowing what had happened to you, and also what had happened to Sizzra. Nobody knew whether she was going to attack us—or when. So one night I just left. I packed everything I thought I would need, everything I thought *you* would need, and I convinced my buddies from the patrol to set up a diversion for me while I escaped. The commander wasn't happy about it, but when she saw I wasn't going to back down, she agreed to help. She sent the entire Patrol to scare off some of the smaller wurl that held the perimeter close to the forest, and I made it through in the chaos. Just barely, though. Some of the wurl tried to chase me, rolling like they do, but after a few meters it was like they hit an invisible wall and they stopped. Turned around and went back to guard the perimeter."

"Sizzra's orders," Elias muttered, "most likely. I wonder how long she plans on forcing them to stay around Portree like that. There isn't much they can hunt around the colony."

"Yeah, well, I wasn't exactly feeling sorry for them or anything when I escaped. One of them fired a spine that sunk into a tree trunk right where my head had been. Those things can be terrifying when they want to be. After that… I retraced our steps from before, looking for signs of you. I reached the mountain and climbed the cave all the way to the top, but you weren't there. Then I went back down to forest level and wandered aimlessly for a while. I had no idea where you'd gone, but one night as I was making camp in the forest, I saw a light coming from here. Firelight. That's how I found you."

Elias smiled. "Thank you, Tristan. For everything. For coming for me and for looking after my family."

Tristan grinned bashfully, as though mildly uncomfortable at the earnest look Elias gave him. "Hey, you would've done the same for me."

Elias nodded. There was no doubt in his mind. "Yeah, I would have."

A comfortable silence followed the exchange, punctuated only by loud snorts coming from the lake, where Vanor was taking a bath. The noonday sky was a vibrant shade of blue, punctuated by fluffy white clouds every now and then. The friendly buzzing of insects came and went whenever a mild breeze blew over the valley, carrying with it the wonderful scent of a world awakening to life after being too long asleep. Elias took it all in, realizing it was somehow more beautiful today than any other time he had seen New Skye like this, and then he realized that it was because he was sharing the view with someone else.

He glanced left at Tristan and smiled at the way Tristan's eyes roamed over the magnificent landscape, his own faint smile arrestingly beautiful.

"The world is different," Tristan said, looking at a faraway mountain. "Everyone has noticed back home. Insects came back. The trees grow new leaves. And the flowers…. You should see the flowers, Elias. It's like the world is coming back to life." He then glanced at Elias, meeting his eyes. "It's because of what you did, isn't it? Returning the Life Seed to where it belonged."

Elias nodded solemnly. "Yes. The world's whole once again. We did a terrible thing when we took the Life Seed away, but now it's safe."

"There's been talk… I don't even know where to start. Back home, most people deduced that this is happening because of you. Some of them think it's good because now we can harvest the native fruits and plants that hadn't grown around Portree for a long time. Others think we should get the Life Seed back because the genetic laboratories have nothing to work with anymore, and our supply of the plants we need has been cut off entirely. I talked with your aunt one time, and she told me that with no new genetic material from the Life Seed, no more Terran crops will be able to be grown, so what we have is it. The native plants aren't going to cut it in the long run, either. We can't mass-produce them in huge farms. I was in an important meeting with the director and all the council members where a few biologists explained that the early colonists failed at creating large-scale farm plots of native plants because they won't grow like that. They said wild plants grow just fine in whatever random place they happen to show up, but the minute you try and force them to grow in neat rows next to one another, they all die. They didn't even know why—"

"I know why," Elias interrupted.

"You do?"

He nodded, thoughtful. Throughout his many deep connections with the Life Seed, he had already been able to understand some of its essential nature. "The life on this planet is different. It's all linked, all perfectly balanced. The Life Seed joins all living things together and kind of... coordinates them. It's really hard to explain, but it's like there's a blueprint for what the world is, its natural state, and anything that deviates from that isn't allowed."

"How do you know all that?"

Elias lifted his eyebrows, smiling. "I guess it's my turn to tell you what's happened."

So he did. The two of them spent the better part of the afternoon talking, with Tristan asking many questions about every little detail of Elias's imprisonment by Sizzra, his connection to the Life Seed, the things he had learned about the male wurl, and the way he now had some of Sizzra's ancestral memories in his own mind. The more he talked, the more amazed Tristan appeared.

"This is insane," Tristan said, after Elias had finished explaining how Sizzra had mated and why she had wanted to kill Tristan after he had seen her secret nesting site. "I can't believe you've—I mean you've.... Wow. Just, wow."

"I'm going to take that as a compliment."

"You better!" Tristan replied, smiling. Then he gave Elias an openly appraising look. "You've changed so much. It's amazing."

"Is that a good thing?"

"Yeah. I don't think I could have gone through everything you have as easily. And you have this... I don't know. The way you talk now, the way you move. Like you're not scared anymore, or trying to prove you're smarter than everyone else. You haven't been sarcastic once since I got here, and that is a *huge* improvement over the old Elias."

"Guess I should've stolen the Life Seed way earlier, then," Elias said jokingly. It felt so good to talk to another person.

Tristan chuckled but then got serious all of a sudden. "What happens now, though?"

"What do you mean?"

Tristan glanced over at the Flower mountain slopes, where Sizzra had vanished. "How long is she going to make you stay here?"

"Until the Flower blooms," Elias answered with complete certainty.

"And then?"

"Then? She's going to kill me. When that's done, she'll go to Portree and destroy the colony."

Tristan looked straight into Elias's eyes as if trying to find a joke that wasn't there. When Elias answered him with an earnest look of his own, Tristan sighed. "You're certain, aren't you?"

"I've come to know her very well, Tristan. She hates us, and I honestly don't think I can blame her. We came to her continent and ripped out the soul of the world. It's mending, but it's never going to be the same. Just as the petals of the Flower will be threaded with black when they finally open, so is it going to be for all the creatures here. They will remember the horrible loss, even if they can't understand the details. Sizzra is the only one who can really grasp the awfulness of what we did, and she doesn't have any compassion in her heart."

Elias picked up a vibrant pink flower which strongly resembled a Terran dandelion and blew on it to scatter its fluffy seeds before continuing. He watched the wind carry them aloft until they were lost from sight, off to their own adventure. "I'm thankful, in a way. Sizzra keeping me here means she isn't going after our families, so as long as I'm a prisoner, everyone else gets to live. If I could, I would stay here forever."

He felt the warm touch of Tristan's heavy hand on his shoulder, along with a reassuring squeeze. "You're a hero, Elias."

"Nah."

"I mean it," Tristan insisted, and when Elias looked at him, he saw that his earnest expression was dead serious. "You did what no one else had the guts to do when you took the Life Seed. You risked your life to set things right even when nobody else believed you. Now you're here, standing up to the most dangerous creature in the world, and what you just said.... Listen, I want to say I'm sorry. I'm sorry for all the awful things I said to you last winter when I thought you were only stealing the Seed to draw attention to yourself or something. I can see now that I was wrong, and all I can say is thank you. You saved my life once already, and you've shown me what it's like to stand up for what you believe in. Whatever happens, I wanted to say that you're a real hero."

Elias blushed. He didn't know what to say, and despite the fact that they were essentially discussing the end of Portree and the inevitable death of everyone they knew, the warm glow in Elias's chest at the words he was hearing refused to die down.

"You should go back," Elias said eventually, even though he secretly wanted Tristan to stay with him. "I don't know when Sizzra will return, but she probably won't chase you. The colony has to be warned of what's about to happen when the Flower finally blooms."

"Not a problem," Tristan replied, and reached over to his backpack. After taking out some cooking utensils, he came up with one of the research pads Elias was used to seeing around the laboratories. "Your dad made this special for you," Tristan told him, handing over the pad. "It's got a medium-range microwave detector to send and receive small bursts of data. He installed transceivers all over the colony so he would be able to pick up the signal from this pad wherever you were. It won't work during the day, though; something to do with the electromagnetic interference of the sun. At night you'll be able to send them messages. It might take a while, and the bandwidth is really limited, but you'll be able to text home and warn them."

"For real?"

"I tested it last night and it still worked, so yeah. You have a smart dad, Elias. I have no idea how he made this thing work."

Elias couldn't help it. His memory flashed back to the last fight he'd had with his father, where Elias had practically told him that he thought being the telecommunications specialist in Portree was a dead-end job with no practical purpose.

He could have punched himself in the face if he had been able to somehow go back in time to tell his younger self to stop being such a prick.

"Thanks," he told Tristan, holding the pad like the most precious thing in the world.

"No problem. Wait till you see the rest of the stuff I brought!"

It turned out Tristan hadn't been exaggerating when he said he'd brought everything he thought Elias could possibly need. In his backpack there was a tent, two sleeping bags, waterproof jackets, pants, and a pair of rugged boots; sunglasses, sunscreen, underwear, and socks; a tiny gas stove, a sturdy knife, a compass, a fire-starting kit, a first-aid kit, water purifier tablets, an inflatable mattress, and a large assortment of dehydrated food. Seeing those things as Tristan laid them out on the grass was an unforgettable moment for Elias. He had spent so long making do with only the most basic of things to survive that he was overwhelmed by the luxury of thinking he would have a tent to keep out the rain, or a warm sleeping bag or a real mattress to sleep on. And thinking about eating something other than velvet nuts or berries made his mouth water.

He felt like the richest man in the world.

That night, he and Tristan assembled the tent just outside the cave mouth. With the tent flap opening into the cave, they now had a larger covered area for the shelter. Elias lay down next to Tristan on the inflatable mattress, each of them inside his own sleeping bag, and the comfort was unbelievable. So much had happened in a single day that Elias lay awake long after dark, listening to the reassuring sound of Tristan breathing next to him.

Suddenly, his new pad beeped.

"Must be your dad," Tristan mumbled sleepily, a half smile on his face. "Tell him I said hi."

Elias reached for the device with barely suppressed expectation. He touched its screen and it flickered to life, blazingly bright in the darkness of the cave. Blinking back tears, Elias dimmed the brightness settings and set the background to something dark so he would be able to read better. With that done, he finally opened the message tab where his father's text was waiting for him.

Hello, Tristan. Are you well? Have you found him yet?

Elias paused for a moment, his fingers hovering over the tactile keyboard he had called up to answer. It was very late in the night, and Elias knew that his father worked almost every day. Even so, his dad had stayed up to send a message to Tristan, worried about his son.

Elias's fingers trembled slightly as he typed his response.

Hi, Dad. It's me.

Chapter 26
The Calm Before the Storm

ELIAS? Is that you??
> *Yeah, Dad. It's me.*
Are you okay? Are you hurt? Where are you? Is Tristan with you?
In the darkness of the cave, Elias chuckled. He could almost hear the tone in his father's anxious questions.
> *I'm okay. Tristan found me, and he's with me.*
Thank goodness. Eli, you have no idea how—what happened? Where are you?
> *I'm in Crescent Valley. It's right next to the Flower mountain.*
What? Where?
> *Sorry. I forgot you don't know. I'm in a valley surrounded by mountains, northwest of Portree. I've been here for a few months now.*
Why? Why haven't you come home?
Elias took a deep breath. There was so much to tell.
> *It's a long story, Dad. I'm the captive of the wurl queen, Sizzra. I'm helping the Life Seed bloom again. I can't leave…. And all of you are in danger.*
But you're okay?
> *Yeah.*
That's all that matters. Listen, I promised the director to notify her when we found you, but I want you to talk to your mother and Oscar first. Let me go wake them up. Don't go anywhere, okay?
> *I'll be here.*
Back in a minute. Love you, son.
Elias blinked, reading that last message. His father had never been big on displays of affection, and last winter he and Elias had been fighting more and more. It was comforting to hear that his father still loved him.

A faint smile crept onto Elias's lips and widened when first his brother and then his mother said hi to him.

They spent nearly two hours on the channel, talking. Sometimes the messages took a while to reach their destination, but it was still wonderful. His mother peppered him with questions, asking whether he was unhurt, and Elias reassured her as best he could. Oscar wanted to know everything about the wurl queen, and he said about a dozen times that he had missed Elias.

I always knew you were okay, Eli, Oscar typed. *I told everyone at school. When one of the other kids said you were a criminal, I punched him in the face—*

There was a pause when it was all but obvious that Oscar was being told off for writing that. Elias laughed quietly while order was restored.

This is your father the next message came. *It's time to notify the director. Your mom and Oscar send hugs. And your mother says to keep warm. Wait on the channel for a few minutes, okay?*

> *Sure, Dad. Hugs to everyone.*

Even though he was very sleepy, Elias stayed up while his father went to contact the director. It didn't take very long. Soon a new message appeared on the screen of his pad.

Elias, this is Director O'Rourke. I am here with your father and Commander Hernandez. First of all, let me express my happiness at knowing you are safe.

> *Thanks.*

Now, there are certain urgent matters we must discuss with you. If Tristan's accounts are accurate, is it safe to say that we face a threat in the form of the wurl queen?

> *Her name is Sizzra. And yeah. She hates us.*

Could you elaborate, please? This is extremely important. We must know what we are up against so we can prepare accordingly. Tell us everything you know about this Sizzra, her capabilities, motivations, and her connection to the Life Seed.

Elias did as he was asked. It took almost two more hours of constant back-and-forth texting until the director was satisfied enough that she announced they would end the meeting and resume the following night.

Thank you for what you have shared, she wrote. *Before we sign off, are there any questions you have for us?*

Elias had one.

> *Will I go to jail?*

Excuse me?

> *If I return, will I go to jail?*

It's complicated, came the slow, evidently hesitant reply. *Your situation is unique, but I am sure we can work out a solution when and if you return to Portree. Do not concern yourself with that at the moment, though. It is imperative that you monitor Sizzra's behavior in case it is necessary to warn us of an impending attack.*

Elias couldn't help but notice that Director O'Rourke hadn't said *no.*

> *Sure. I'll keep an eye out. Bye, Dad.*

Goodbye, son. Stay safe.

A pop-up message informed Elias that the connection had been cut, and he let out a long, shaky breath. He was really happy to have talked to his family, but the director's questions had left him worried. She and Commander Hernandez wanted to know whether Sizzra had weaknesses, the extent of the damage the Life Seed wound had inflicted on her, and every little detail of her combat capabilities. To Elias, it sounded as if the people back home were preparing for war.

He couldn't repress a shiver in the darkness of the tent. Something had made Elias not reveal the fact that Sizzra had mated, or that her eggs were hidden in the Flower mountainside. He didn't exactly know why he hadn't said anything, especially when he knew for sure that Sizzra hated humans and that she would undoubtedly attack the colony the minute she was able to.

And yet....

Sizzra's memories came back to him, sharp and undeniable. Elias had shared the horrible pain she'd experienced when the Life Seed had been torn from its resting place. He knew how maddening it had been for a creature once so strong to lie helpless year after year, trying to recover from the shock of losing her connection to the world. He also knew how much she had weakened and how much she hurt now.

If all the soldiers of Portree converged on her in a surprise attack, they might be able to kill her. With heavy losses, sure. Sizzra might be a shadow of what she once was, but that didn't mean she wasn't deadly. She would kill as many people as she could, and not only by herself. The surviving males of her brood would attack too. It would be slaughter on both sides.

And there was one more thing in the back of Elias's mind. He was certain that the terrible loss of one of the Flowers had been felt elsewhere. Dresde in particular, the Flyer, must have known—and she had not attacked yet. Elias didn't know why, but he was certain of one thing.

If Sizzra was killed, there would be nothing standing between Portree and the menace of the flying wurl queen.

"MORNING," A bleary-eyed Tristan said, climbing out of the cave while rubbing the sleep out of his eyes.

"Hey," Elias replied. He had just finished kindling a small fire, over which he placed one of the pots Tristan had brought with him. He had filled the pot with water from the lake and tossed in some berries and fragrant herbs for his first attempt at tea. "Sleep well?"

"No way," Tristan replied, stretching. Elias followed the graceful contours of Tristan's strong arms and muscled shoulders. "I need a proper bed to get a good night's sleep. You?"

Elias laughed. "Are you kidding? It was awesome. I've been sleeping on moss for weeks! My sleeping bag was the best thing in the world. Thank you for bringing it. That was the best night I can remember having."

Tristan gave Elias a thoughtful nod. "I can't imagine what it must have been like. And you spent the winter here."

"I didn't enjoy it, but I survived."

"Yeah. You did." Tristan smiled with what Elias could have sworn was vague insecurity. "Anyway, got to take a leak. Back in a bit."

The tea was ready by the time Tristan came back, and Elias poured some of it into two little cups and handed one to Tristan. He cradled his own cup in his hands afterward, enjoying the warmth. Carefully, he took a small sip.

It was wonderful.

"Could use a little bit more sugar," Tristan said. "I think I have some, somewhere...."

"I think it's delicious the way it is," Elias countered. "I haven't drunk anything hot in ages. It's.... Wow."

Tristan fished a small sugar package out of the backpack and sprinkled some of it into his own cup. He took a sip of the fragrant, steaming liquid and let out a contented sigh.

"Tell me about it," he said to Elias.

"What?"

Tristan's look was earnest. "How was it, here on your own for so long? How did you manage? Why aren't you insufferably sarcastic anymore?"

Elias chuckled, but his expression turned serious as he gazed at the steaming tea in his cup. "You really want to know?"

"Yeah. Shoot."

"It was… hard. I don't even know where to begin. At first I was mostly worried about food. You know, not starving to death. Sizzra didn't exactly give me a stocked pantry or anything, and at the beginning I was just eating berries. Then I found other things, tested them. I've been lucky so far. None of what I've eaten has made me sick, but at the beginning I couldn't even be thankful for that. I was trying to escape.

"After Sizzra made it very clear that I wasn't allowed to leave, I resigned myself to being here and tried to make improvements. The nights were the worst. It got so cold, I couldn't even sleep for shaking. Later, after I figured out how to make fire, it was much more bearable. I kind of settled into a routine, but as soon as I had secured my food supply a little bit, I started to get lonely. The sky at night, when you're on your own, is enormous. I don't know how I managed to not go insane, but later it got better. Especially after the three males arrived. It was fun watching them, learning from them. You wouldn't believe the kind of stuff I've discovered about them. Wurl are incredible creatures. They are not the monsters we grew up believing they were."

"But they're still dangerous."

Elias shook his head. "Only if they think *we're* dangerous. Or if Sizzra tells them to attack, which she has done in the past. She controls them, to a point. And unlike the males, she does want to hurt us, as vengeance for what we did to the world."

Tristan looked around him. He plucked a small blade of grass and stared at it intently for a few moments. "You were right all along," he muttered.

"Right?"

"About the Life Seed. I didn't believe you, back when you escaped with it. When the alarms sounded last winter and the commander told us you had stolen it, I got so angry. I wanted to drag you back to the colony and see you rot in prison for life. Then we were together for so long, taking the Seed to this mountain, and it got harder to hate you. Small doubts crept into my mind, and after I made it back to Portree, it was really hard to explain to the director and everyone else why you had done what you had done.

"Talking to your family was really hard too. And at first nobody believed me when I said that a giant wurl queen had made me go back. When wurl started patrolling the perimeter of the colony, not letting anyone out at all, it made some of us wonder. And then…. Then spring came.

"You should have been there, Elias. It was beautiful. The little children didn't know what a flower was—I mean, they had seen flowers online, but it's not the same. Everyone was so happy when the first blooms appeared. People would go outside just to walk among the flowers in the main square, and the greenhouses were blossoming with little native plants all over the place. Even though nobody wanted to admit it, I'm pretty sure we were all thinking the same thing: you had taken the Life Seed to wherever it was supposed to be, and now the world was awakening once more. I realized you had been right all along, even if the price of the world's renewal was that we were going to starve faster than ever.

"I was in so many rationing meetings. Some of the scientists suggested harvesting the wild fruits growing around us, and we did. They were gone in a few days. Without the Life Seed, we were forced to start using the emergency provisions to feed everyone. Things got hard very fast. Fights broke out. Eventually people accepted the new rationing scheme, but we all had a ticking clock over our heads, counting the time until all of the food was gone, and it was an awful feeling."

Elias glanced at the lakeside, where his farm was located. None of the seedlings had sprouted yet, but he had hope. He decided to share it with Tristan.

"I think I can help," he said.

"How?" Tristan asked.

"The Life Seed is changing because of what we did to it. All the gene tests, the splicing, the bio-grafts back in Portree—I think it corrupted its genetic makeup slightly, and now there is some Terran DNA in it."

"What are you saying?"

Elias stood up and went back to the cave, where he lifted an inconspicuous flat stone on the ground. It revealed his dug-out cache of modified Terran seeds. He took out a few Y-shaped rice grains and purple beans and walked back outside, where he offered them to Tristan.

"I think this is the solution," Elias said. "The Life Seed made them as a way to purge itself of the genetic impurities, but the end result was... this. Terran plants, but different. We will be able to plant and harvest them, unlike the wild plants native to this continent, which always die when we try and force them to grow. These seeds are the future. With them, we can survive."

Tristan took the handful of seeds reverently. "For real? These will *grow*?"

"Well, I'm testing that right now. See that spot over there? That's my farm. I planted some of every kind the Life Seed gave me. I hope they grow. I really do."

"Wow. Did you tell the director about this? It changes everything! We can go back to Portree, give them the seeds, start farms!"

Elias smiled sadly. "You're forgetting about Sizzra. She won't let us go. How are we going to take these back?"

"We could escape in the night...."

Elias shook his head as Tristan trailed off. "I've tried that. She would know. And even if we escaped somehow, she would chase us. You have seen how strong she is. There is no way we could beat her without sacrificing half the colony to do it."

"So what do we do?" Tristan asked, uncertainty clear on his features.

"For now? We go fishing. Then we tend the plants in my farm. And we wait for an opportunity, whenever it comes."

Chapter 27
It's Time

ELIAS WAS having fun. As spring gave way to early summer, he settled into a comfortable routine with Tristan, which made him forget the fact that he was still a prisoner.

Every day they woke at dawn. At the beginning Tristan had been unwilling to get up so early, but Elias had prevailed, and now they always watched the sunrise together. Crescent Valley was the perfect location from which to do so. The gap in the mountains surrounding it allowed for an unobstructed view of the sun as it cleared the horizon, making the sky change colors from black to indigo, from gray to golden yellow. It was a beautiful spectacle, and something that Elias hadn't really noticed before when he was alone. Now that he had company, though, it was an entirely different story. It was great to simply sit there, watching the light break over the horizon and feeling the beginnings of the warm summer heat on his skin.

After that was over, it was time to prepare breakfast. Where before Elias's food had been monotonous, although nourishing, now it was something to be excited about. Tristan had brought such a wide array of dehydrated meals that it was easy to have something different every day of the week, and even have bits left over to give the curious wurl around them.

"He won't bite you," Elias said to Tristan during one of the first breakfasts, when Tristan had nervously offered some grilled synthetic cheese to Vanor.

"Says you," Tristan answered, electing to simply toss the cheese portion into the air. Vanor jumped up, caught it, and swallowed it whole. His eyes flashed, and he looked at Tristan for another morsel. "These guys are just so big. I can't help being nervous around them."

As first days and then weeks went by, though, Tristan relaxed around the wurl, and soon it wasn't uncommon to find him swimming in the lake accompanied by one or more of them. Swimming was one of the best activities to do in the heat of the day, since the water was always cool. It was great to simply kick back and relax, floating around, while the three male wurl hunted in the depths of the water. Elias and Tristan talked a lot about the things Elias had learned concerning the wurl during his time with them, and they drew conclusions of their own, like the fact that they were obviously amphibian creatures, or the fact that they loved playing.

It was Tristan who discovered a game the two of them could play with the wurl, in fact. They were resting by the cave one afternoon, bored, when Tristan picked up one of the round and flat bone plates that covered the underside of the flatfish the wurl usually hunted. There was already a pile of them not far from the cave, which Elias had been saving for a project in the future, although he hadn't really decided what the project was going to be. That afternoon, though, Vanor, Siv, and Narev had been resting nearby, but their attention was drawn to the bone plate as Tristan threw it higher and higher into the air.

"Hey, Tristan, look."

"You think they're curious?" Tristan asked, throwing it again.

"I don't know. You've certainly got their attention."

"Yeah. Maybe it's because they recognize it as something they killed."

He threw the bone plate up high, and Elias noticed the clean puncture mark close to its center where one of the wurl's spines had pierced the creature during the hunt underwater.

"They are crazy fast with those spines," Tristan continued. "Hey! I just thought of something. You think they can hit this if I throw it real fast?"

"What?"

"Watch. Hey, Vanor! Shoot!"

Tristan jumped up to a standing position and hurled the bony plate like a Frisbee. All three wurl were on their feet at once. Elias didn't even have time to cry out as he saw them assume a firing position, tense up, and shoot three spines into the air.

Crack.

"Wow!" Tristan yelled, excited. "Elias, look at that. Bullseye!"

One of the spines had hit the mark, and the makeshift Frisbee now lay on the ground, impaled straight through. Judging by the length of the spine, Elias guessed it had been Vanor with the winning shot.

As if to confirm it, Vanor grunted. Then he walked purposefully toward Tristan, who froze at the unexpected approach. The wurl seldom came within touching distance unless it was feeding time. Vanor didn't stop until he was right in front of Tristan, though. Then he nudged Tristan's hand toward the bone pile and grunted again.

"I think he liked it," Tristan said, grinning.

"Not only Vanor. Look, Siv and Narev are all ready to go."

That afternoon was the first of many to come when Tristan played shoot-the-bone with the wurl. Elias joined in after a few days, and soon they had made complicated rules for the game, involving both of them throwing disks at the same time, or from different heights, or making the wurl stand much farther away so the shots would be more difficult. It was great fun, and Elias's bond with the creatures strengthened the more they communicated wordlessly through play. Even Sizzra became interested in the game one afternoon after a blood ritual, watching from the mountainside with open amusement but declining Elias's hopeful disc throw in her direction. Elias couldn't blame her, not really. One of her three eyes had already gone dim as the inexorable progression of the ravaging wound on her snout continued unchecked. Elias felt sorry for her, but he didn't know how to help her, and even if he knew, he was somehow certain that Sizzra would refuse to be helped and admit weakness in front of another creature.

"Does it hurt?" Tristan asked Elias that evening, when they were alone. He gestured to Elias's palm, where the most recent wound from the blood ritual was clearly visible.

"Giving life to the Flower? No, not really."

"Is it like a vampire or something?"

"The Flower?" Elias asked, lifting an eyebrow.

"Yeah."

Elias chuckled. "No. It's more about connection, I think. It's about gaining mutual understanding and allowing it to change, to evolve, so it can survive."

"But you won't have to give it blood forever, right? Just until it blooms?"

"That's right."

Tristan was silent for a few seconds, frowning. He appeared to be deep in thought. "It just seems a tiny bit sinister," he said at last. "It's like the Flower is taking life away from you. Feeding on you and Sizzra both."

Elias recalled the sensation he now perceived whenever he approached the Flower. He couldn't get too close because of the unbearable heat, but there was also something else there, a sensation Sizzra herself had also felt in the past.

Hunger.

"It's all right," Elias reassured Tristan, trying to dispel his own misgivings. "It's a necessary thing. We need to make amends for the way we used the Flower, and it changes more all the time. It won't be too long now before I won't have to go offer it blood anymore."

"That's good," Tristan replied, although he sounded doubtful.

The farm was another source of wonderful discoveries, challenges, and rewards. Not long after planting, Elias was delighted to find that the first seedlings had sprouted. He made such a big deal out of it that Narev spent all that day watching the little green sprouts as if trying to decide whether they were worth so much excitement. Narev didn't walk into the farm, though, and it was almost as if he knew that he shouldn't crush the fragile plants under his big feet.

There were some disappointments, like when the entire first crop of rice browned and died. Tristan suggested using less water so the seeds wouldn't drown, and it turned out to be the right call. The other plants were doing great, though. The beans in particular grew very fast, and after a couple of months, many of the plants held big pods already, full of more violet-colored seeds. Elias made sure to harvest everything as soon as he was able to do so, and his cache of seeds began to grow, slowly but surely. The fact that the hybrids were prospering was almost unbelievable. Elias couldn't wait to carry his hard-won bounty over to Portree, to tell everyone that they didn't need to ration food anymore. With the combined yields of large-scale farming of the hybrids and the native plants which grew around randomly, he was certain that the needs of the colony would be met for decades to come.

His father knew about his progress through the updates Elias gave him most nights, and the colony council was also aware of the situation, but most people in Portree still had no idea that the future of the colony was no longer uncertain. Director O'Rourke had said they wished to avoid giving people false hope, so for now only a select few knew about Elias and the seeds. However, Elias frequently imagined the moment when they would be able to finally announce the fact that they would no longer want for food ever again.

All in all, the weeks he spent with Tristan in Crescent Valley were golden in Elias's memory. The days were full of adventure and fun, but it was the nights he treasured the most.

After the three wurl had gone to sleep around the cave like protectors or guards, Elias and Tristan would climb into their sleeping bags and talk.

At first it was a lot about superficial things, like the way things were right now in Portree, or what they imagined the future would be after they came back—if Sizzra ever decided to let them go. Elias fantasized about being heralded as the hero of Portree, who despite all odds had found a way to save the colony, and Tristan would tell him playfully not to forget that he would have never even made it if it hadn't been for his help. They would also gossip about the people they knew until they ran out of juicy stories to share. It was fun talking about others, but their conversations soon shifted away from everyday things and became deeper, more personal.

The more time they spent together, the more they opened up to each other. They talked about their families; Tristan spent long hours telling Elias about his mother, whom he almost didn't remember. He had videos of her, of course, but it wasn't the same thing. Listening to him, Elias realized how much Tristan missed a person he had never known, and he realized that he was lucky to still have both his mother and his father with him, plus a little brother who cared about him.

Tristan also told Elias about his doubts, particularly about how he had thought long and hard on the things Elias had told him a lifetime ago while they were trudging through a frozen lake. Elias apologized, remembering how hurtful he had been when he told Tristan that he only chose to become a Colony Patrol member because of his father's frustrated dreams. Tristan forgave him, and he admitted that there was a little bit of truth in what Elias had said. Elias came to understand how much peer pressure had shaped Tristan's life, from the way he acted to the things he did and the goals he set for himself. Tristan wasn't someone who liked to disappoint others, and he had become an overachiever because of that. He did like the work he did with the patrol, though. One night after they had been talking for hours, he told Elias in a sleepy voice that while he might not have chosen his career with complete freedom, he was happy. He liked helping others, and it was what he wanted to do with his life.

Elias also talked about himself, although it was hard for him to be as open as Tristan. But slowly, night after night, the outer layers of his reservations melted away, and while lying next to him and staring at the ceiling of the cave he now called home, he told Tristan things he had never told anyone else. Elias told Tristan about his fears that his mother would not live for much longer because of her mysterious health condition, which the doctors could not properly diagnose. He also told him about the way he fought all the time with his father, and even though things were much better now that he could text home every few nights through his link, Elias knew that he needed to go back home and apologize in person for the way he had acted before. He had also neglected being a good big brother to Oscar, always too preoccupied with his own problems to help Oscar out. He told Tristan about things he was only now beginning to understand, like the fact that he had kept to his own for so long, investigating that derelict laboratory at the edge of the colony, because he felt others would reject him if they got to know him for real.

"What do you mean?" Tristan asked that time, sitting up in the dark. They had been talking long enough that one of the moons had risen and set across the valley.

Elias took a shaky breath and tried to let it out slowly. "I don't know. It's like I said. I feel like if I am myself, nobody will like me anymore. I guess that's why I pushed everyone away first, so they wouldn't have a chance to reject me."

"But why reject you? Elias, you're an awesome guy. Resourceful, smart, brave."

Elias chuckled at the last word. "I'm not brave."

"Are you kidding me? You came all this way on your own, against all odds—and I mean *all* odds. You did what you thought was right, and now look: we have a harvest, and we can save Portree. It's all because of you, because of how brave you were."

"I don't know," Elias muttered, unable to completely suppress the warm glow Tristan's compliments had given him. "There's things about me."

"Like what? Are you doing drugs or something? Did you kill a kitten? Oh, wait. We don't have kittens. What is it? It's not like you're a murderer or anything."

"No, nothing like that."

Elias wanted to continue, but fear held him back. Unbidden, a memory came to his mind of a night months and months ago. He had spoken with Oscar like he was doing now with Tristan, in the dark, afraid to confess his deepest secret even though Oscar had guessed anyway.

"I...," Elias began, but he couldn't finish the sentence.

"Hey," Tristan said gently. "Whatever it is, you can tell me. We're friends, right?"

For some reason, hearing the word *friends* right at that moment had the opposite effect to what Tristan probably intended. It wasn't what Elias wanted to hear. He drew back, physically and emotionally, and turned away from Tristan.

"I think I'm tired. Let's just sleep."

Tristan sighed in the dark. "Sure. If that's what you want."

That's not what I want! I want to tell you I'm different. I want to tell you I like you.

He was so surprised at the clarity of his own thought that his breath caught in his throat.

"Elias?" Tristan asked, placing a strong hand on his shoulder. "What's the matter?"

Elias so wanted to tell him. But he was terrified of what it would be like to be rejected by the one person he had opened up to.

Elias retreated into silence, but it yawned like a chasm between him and Tristan, demanding his attention. After a few eternal minutes of hopeless chasing after sleep, he gave up. He sat up, kicking away his sleeping bag.

"You okay?" Tristan said immediately, his tone revealing that he had still been awake.

"I...." Elias halted. Swallowed. He knew he had to come clean, and tomorrow he might not have the courage to do so. Whatever happened, he had to be honest. Because maybe, just maybe, Tristan would say what Elias so desperately hoped to hear.

"What is it?"

"I…." Elias gritted his teeth. He could not do this in the dark. With a tap, he activated his link's lamplight. The soft blue glow was blinding in contrast to the former absolute darkness of the cave.

As soon as his eyes adjusted, Elias looked at Tristan, and the sight of him took his breath away. Tristan was handsome, sure, but Elias's attraction to him went much deeper than that. He admired Tristan. He liked the fact that he was always so compassionate, always trying to help others. He admired his bravery and honesty. And Elias had had a crush on him for years now, if he was brutally honest with himself. He hadn't ever gathered the courage to say what he was about to say, though.

Elias looked Tristan in the eye, and the patient, slight concern he saw there decided him. It was time.

"I'm different," Elias said slowly. "I don't know how long I've known, but…. A while, I guess. Ever since I became a teenager. I-I'm gay, Tristan. I like guys."

Total silence followed Elias's confession. For a moment, he feared the worst. Tristan was going to react badly any second now and it would all be over.

"Okay," Tristan said instead. "What about it?"

Elias blinked. "You don't—you're okay with it?"

Tristan nodded, even if it was a little jerky. His voice wavered slightly while he answered. "Sure. I mean, why wouldn't I be? It's who you are."

"For real?"

"Yeah! Don't worry about it. We're good, okay?"

Tristan tried to go for what he must have thought was a friendly shove, but it ended up being more of an awkward pat.

Say everything, Elias told himself furiously. *Don't chicken out now.*

"There's something else," Elias said. Before he could think twice about it, he reached for Tristan's hand, which was still patting him on the shoulder, and held it in both of his.

The contact was beyond electric. He had never felt anything like this in his entire life; his heart was beating so fast it threatened to burst out of his chest, and even though he was terrified out of his wits, he was also certain that he never ever wanted to let go of Tristan's hand.

Tristan made as if to pull his hand back, but something must have stopped him. He looked at it, and then up at Elias. In that moment, Elias found the courage he was looking for.

"I like you, Tristan," he said, unable to believe the words were coming out of his mouth. "I like you a lot, and not just as a friend, although you're the best friend anyone could ask for. I've liked you for a long time now, but I guess I never had the guts to tell you face-to-face. It's okay if you don't want to talk to me again after this," Elias continued past the tremble in his voice, "but I wanted to be honest with you because you mean so much to me."

He stopped talking when the words ran out and looked at Tristan with wide eyes, still holding his hand. He was trembling, unable to control himself, in preparation for the awful rejection, but then he noticed something.

Tristan was trembling too.

Something clicked in Elias's head. He knew what he had to do. Leaning forward, he pulled Tristan to him, embraced him in a strong hug, and kissed him on the lips.

Tristan stiffened, and Elias's heart sank when Tristan made as if to move away. He had read the signs wrong, then. Tristan wasn't interested in him. He didn't like him at all.

But the moment passed. Tristan didn't move away. And suddenly he was returning Elias's kiss, his hands firm around Elias's waist, with the fierce passion of rushing water in the wake of a breaking dam.

Chapter 28
Aftermath

THE MORNING after was… wonderful.

Faint daylight found its way through the little gaps in the door to the cave as Elias woke up completely. There was a brief moment when he didn't know why he felt so joyful, but all it took was a glance to the left for him to remember.

Tristan slept on, handsome and strong yet innocent in sleep, completely naked, next to Elias. A thrill of emotion shot through Elias's heart when he placed one of his hands over Tristan's bare shoulder, feeling the warmth, the softness of Tristan's skin, and his hard yet supple muscles underneath. Slowly, Elias moved his hand down, caressing the length of Tristan's arm in silent wonder. He couldn't believe this was happening, that it *had* happened last night. He had fantasized about being with Tristan once or twice, sure, but he could not have imagined the mind-blowing intensity of their lovemaking. Elias was certain he had been clumsy at one point or another—it was his first time, after all—but every moment was like a precious jewel glittering in his memory. The grip of Tristan's strong hands. The taste of his lips. The warmth of Tristan's breath on the back of his neck. The sound of his husky voice, grunting in the dark.

"Hey," Tristan said, smiling. His eyelids fluttered open.

"Hey."

Elias lay down more comfortably so he would be facing Tristan and brought his free hand up to rest it against Tristan's hard pectoral muscles. His fingertips found a small patch of soft dark hair nestled in between Tristan's pecs, and he touched it lightly, memorizing every sensation.

"Last night was wonderful," Elias said, looking deep into Tristan's eyes.

"Yeah," Tristan answered, though he cast his glance down, obviously bothered by something.

"What is it?"

Tristan hesitated. Cleared his throat. He was blushing as if deeply embarrassed. "Listen, I'm, I'm sorry if I, you know. Didn't last that long."

The end of his sentence had been barely a whisper. It was definitely not what Elias had been expecting to hear, and he was so relieved that he couldn't help but laugh.

Tristan blushed even harder and turned slightly away.

Elias pulled him close and kissed him. Then he whispered in his ear, "Don't be stupid. I loved every second of it, and you were amazing."

"Really? It's just… it was my first time, so…."

"Mine too. And I'm glad it was with you. I love you, Tristan."

There. Saying it was so natural, and Elias knew it was the truth. Maybe he wouldn't have been brave enough to admit it to himself before everything that had happened, but Elias had seen the face of death from very close a few times now. Close enough to realize that he had to seize the moment when he had it.

Tristan smiled, but he seemed conflicted. "I…."

Elias shook his head. He knew Tristan didn't feel that way, not yet anyway, but it didn't come across as a rejection. Not after last night. "You don't have to say it back. Not if you're not sure. Even if you never do, I just wanted you to know how I feel. How I've felt for a while now, I think. I'm so happy to have you here with me."

"I'm happy too," Tristan replied. "Come here."

He embraced Elias hard, and being with him skin-to-skin, naked as they were now, soon meant that the embrace wasn't the only thing which was hard.

"Better get breakfast started," Elias said, sitting back on his own sleeping bag before he got too worked up. "I'm thinking miso soup and rice today."

He all but escaped into the open, pausing long enough to throw on a pair of shorts. Outside, the cool fragrance of early morning was waiting for him as usual. The sunlight was bright that day, almost golden, and the beautiful emerald of the grass underfoot contrasted with the wild colors of the flowers that dotted the valley floor. Elias had seen such a view many times before, but that day it was particularly breathtaking.

The three curled-up sleeping wurl did not budge from their spots, even though Elias made some noise as he prepared breakfast. Tristan came out of the cave soon after, and the two of them enjoyed a simple but nourishing morning meal.

At one point, Elias caught Tristan looking at him from the other side of the firepit.

"What?" Elias asked.

Tristan smiled with a hint of lust behind his expressive dark eyes and thick eyebrows. "Just enjoying the view. The hard life suits you. And the iridescence in your eyes is amazing. You look like a wood elf or something, strong and wild."

Now it was Elias's turn to blush, which he tried to hide by busying himself with the cooking utensils.

After breakfast, it was time for the very first big harvest of the year. Elias had already collected several handfuls of seeds from his growing plants, but this was the day he had planned to harvest everything that was ready.

"The people back home are going to go nuts when they see all of this," Tristan observed, carrying a large sack as he and Elias walked to the edges of the farm, which had by then been completely swallowed by verdant growth everywhere. "We won't be hungry anymore. And it's all thanks to you."

"Right," Elias said, uncomfortable at the praise. "Let's get to it. I hope we can finish harvesting today."

It was brutal work, but very satisfying. By the end of it, Elias had become quite skilled indeed at using Sizzra's spine for a variety of tasks, including cutting, peeling, digging, and impaling as the occasion demanded. With Tristan's help, they harvested all the beans first, cutting each violet pod carefully to get at the precious cargo within. Then they moved on to the wheat and barley, which was particularly time-consuming because it wasn't simply about cutting the slender stalks but picking all the seeds and setting them aside in a different sack. Elias's hands had toughened up through his months of wilderness survival, but his palms were bloody in places when they were finally done with the majority of the plants.

Except for the rice, of course.

Picking the rice took all afternoon and resulted in several blisters. Narev followed Elias around for a while, sniffing curiously at each handful of slender rice stalks he pulled out of the wet ground. When all of them had been picked and dried somewhat, Elias separated the useful grains from each and every little plant until he had a very sizable mound of Y-shaped rice seeds next to him. Nearby, Tristan was doing the very same thing, and twilight had already fallen over the land by the time they were finally done.

"That was awful," Tristan said, wiping sweat from his brow and smearing mud on his forehead.

"Yeah, but look!"

Elias pointed at their harvest, and he couldn't suppress a surge of pride. All told, they had harvested about ten kilograms of all the different seeds, neatly arranged in several sacks that had originally contained some of the supplies Tristan had carried to Crescent Valley. All of Elias's work was right there, waiting to be delivered to the colony.

If only Sizzra would let them go.

"Let's carry them back to the cave," Elias suggested, and they did so while night settled on the sky.

They had scarcely finished doing that when a faint tremor heralded the inevitable arrival of Sizzra. The three male wurl stopped chasing each other and stood very still, watching her tumble down the mountainside. Elias made sure to stand between Tristan and Sizzra when she finally landed on the valley floor, just in case.

Even if fear was no longer an emotion he felt when he looked at her.

It was pity that filled Elias's heart as he saw the once-powerful creature having become what she was now. Only one of her eyes glowed still, the other two having been consumed by the smoldering wound that had now reached its terrible tendrils to the base of her crown of spines. As she stood there, watching them all, Elias felt agony radiating from her like heat from an overdriven radiator. Every breath she took was pain distilled into exquisite madness. Every minute that went by, her strength left her a little bit more.

She hadn't come for him in a long time, more than a month at least, and Elias had supposed that the blood rituals with the Life Seed were no longer necessary, a fact that had both relieved him and worried him. He was glad he wouldn't be required to link with the soul of the world anymore, but he was worried that Sizzra would think about her revenge now that she wasn't bound to remain near her Flower. As far as Elias knew, though, the Flower hadn't bloomed yet. And Sizzra hadn't left to destroy Portree as she had yearned to do in the past.

She took a teetering step forward and stumbled. Elias felt the sharp edge of her rage at her own weakness, and the ferocious snarl she gave the three curious males as they attempted to approach her was equal parts disdain and horror.

Elias's gaze went from Sizzra to the piles of harvested seeds he and Tristan had already gathered. He knew a chance when he saw one.

"We would like your permission to go to our colony," he told the towering queen, taking a step closer to her, and then another. He stopped an arm's length away, unafraid, silencing Tristan's protests with a gesture. "We will go, then come back. I promise. I'll help you care for the Flower until it blooms, but we need to deliver this food to our people. It's the key to their survival."

Slowly, Sizzra lowered her sinuous neck until her head was level with Elias's face. A foul stench of necrotic flesh enveloped Elias, but he didn't back away. He concentrated on the meaning of his words, on projecting it to her, and repeated his message once again, much more slowly. When he finished, he knew Sizzra had understood. All that remained was to wait for her answer.

She bared her fangs, the ones she still had anyway. The fierce glare of her solitary eye was like a beacon to Elias, and through its light he sensed every emotion passing through Sizzra's mind. The hatred. The anger. The fear.

"I will come back," Elias repeated. "And if necessary, I will watch over the eggs until they hatch. I will protect the new queen."

Her eye blazed at his insolence, at his daring to mention the most secret of things for her, the vulnerable clutch of eggs that would be the new generation of Spine wurl. She flicked her tail through the air so savagely that it splintered the rock of the mountain with a glancing blow, and then she fanned out the spines around her neck.

But she did not attack.

Elias raised his right hand in the air, palm forward. He reached behind his back and took out the long, jagged spine he always carried. He made a shallow slash with its tip on his palm and then held up his hand again.

"I swear. Let me go, and I will protect your brood when you die."

Death.

Elias felt the concept resonate in Sizzra's mind. She knew she was dying, and she was scared—not of death itself, but of facing it as a weakling, as a shadow of who she once had been. Her mind was heavy with the memories of her mothers' glorious deaths in battle. She would be denied even that. She would die like wounded prey, hiding in the darkness of a cave....

"I can't help you with that, but I would if I could," Elias said earnestly. "Let me go. Please."

Charged silence held between them for a few more eternal seconds. Sizzra lifted her front left foot and touched Elias's bloody palm, strengthening their mental bond with the contact. In that instant, she knew his entire mind and he hers. There were no secrets between them.

Then Sizzra turned around and stalked off to climb her mountain once again, attempted to leap, but did not manage it. Seething with embarrassment and rage, she made her way instead to the cave where her eggs rested. She glanced back only once before she disappeared into the darkness of her nest. She looked right at Elias and lowered her head a tiny fraction.

You may, Elias almost heard her say, sensing indomitable will weaving her intent through his human words. *But your promise binds you forever.*

The silence after she was out of sight was deafening. Elias could not believe she had actually agreed. She had listened to him. She... she trusted him. After months and months of confinement, she had finally agreed to let Elias do the one thing he had thought he would never be allowed to do.

The silence was broken all of a sudden when Tristan whooped.

"I can't believe it!" Tristan said happily, coming to hug Elias briefly. "Did she—did she say yes? It seemed like it. She did, didn't she?"

Elias nodded. "But I have to come back."

"Oh," Tristan said, frowning. "Well, we can think about that later. Elias, you're free! *We're* free! Come on, let's pack up and head out before she changes her mind."

Elias followed Tristan and helped pack the essentials in a mechanical way. He couldn't stop thinking about Sizzra, about how deep her desperation must be to let him go free like that, in exchange for a promise. She could have still killed him with a single bite, but instead she had let him go.

He felt the pressure of horrible sadness in his heart, and he could not match Tristan's wild enthusiasm as the two of them walked straight to the edge of the valley and looked down into the deep forest below.

"It's dark already, which is not ideal," Tristan was saying. "But I came prepared. Here, strap this torch to your forehead. Click it on. All right, here's how it's going to go…."

Elias listened attentively to Tristan's explanation of how they were going to climb down using ropes to make sure neither of them fell, but every now and then he couldn't help himself. He glanced at the dark maw that was the entrance to the nest and imagined Sizzra coiled up inside, her body racked by unstoppable pain. He knew he was about to tear up and turned away from Tristan, bending down under the pretext of securing the climbing harness around his legs.

When he stood up, three wurl had come to say goodbye.

Vanor, Siv, and Narev were standing very close, looking at him unblinkingly. The way their eyes glowed in the dark would have terrified him before, but now he knew them very well and he knew they did not mean him harm.

"Sorry, guys," he said in a choked-up voice and stepped forward to touch Narev's forehead. Out of the three, he had always been the friendliest, the one most willing to spend time with him even when Elias had been weak and afraid, trying to survive in the wilderness. "I have to go to my own nest. My family needs food. I'll come back, though, okay? I'll see you soon."

Narev tilted his head to the side and made a sound he had never made before: a mournful croon that echoed in Elias's heart through the physical contact he shared with the wurl. Narev didn't understand what was going on, but he knew Elias was leaving. And he was sad.

"Elias?" Tristan asked. Glancing back, Elias saw Tristan had prepared the sacks of harvest grains so each of them could carry half. All the climbing equipment was ready to go. "It's time."

Elias let go of Narev, who crooned again when Elias took a step away from him.

"Yeah," he said to Tristan, his voice husky with the emotion of unshed tears. "Let's go home."

Chapter 29
Home

ELIAS FOLLOWED Tristan through a world transformed.

Everything was different from the way it had been in the depths of winter, when Elias had made his way to the Flower mountain tailed by menacing wurl, with Tristan as a reluctant travel partner. Back then, New Skye had been as Elias had known it for most of his life: a sleeping planet, with muted tones of gray, brown, and white dominating the landscape. Cold or hot with the planet's motion around its star, it had nevertheless looked always the same. There had been a little green now and then, or the dark red needles of some conifers. For the most part, though, everything had appeared faded, brittle, devoid of life.

It was not so anymore.

Elias and Tristan had descended the sheer cliff face through the course of the night, a task that had been so physically demanding Elias was certain he wouldn't have been able to do it a few months ago. The darkness was unnerving, but Tristan was an experienced climber, and he directed Elias well. They reached solid ground a couple of hours before sunrise, then made camp and rested briefly. Elias was awakened by the light of the sun filtering through the branches of the forest.

Now it was past noon, and the more Elias walked, the more amazed he became at the changes New Skye had undergone. The forest was no longer a collection of towering evergreens with bare trunks and distant canopies. It was a maze of thriving life. The forest floor was hidden completely under a thick carpet of greenery, which made it tricky to walk through, but it made Elias think of himself as a giant wading through a sea of green water. There was green everywhere. The trunks of the forest trees were covered in vines with thick red stems and wide dark-green leaves. The vines sometimes reached across the trunks of different trees, making living curtains that hid other things from sight. In some sections of the forest, wherever a clearing had been made by the fall of an aging tree, there were dozens of different saplings, bushes, and weeds vying for space and sunlight. Some of them Elias recognized, but most of them were completely unknown. He could have easily spent months studying the flora of a small forest section alone, and that was without even taking the animals into account.

There were many, many more animals populating the forests of New Skye than Elias remembered. Most of them were small arthropods with bright carapaces and buzzing wings that made the air vibrate with the hum of their comings and goings. A few of them were birds Elias had never seen before. Some of them cawed at him and Tristan from high branches, while others flitted between the tree trunks with dizzying speed, presumably hunting for food. Elias saw no big land animals other than a few juvenile wurl he spotted in the distance, but he scarcely took notice of the fact. As with the plants, it seemed that every few minutes he discovered a new species.

When they came out of the forest and into the rolling highlands that would eventually lead down to Portree, Elias was treated to an entire shift in ecosystem dynamics, which amazed him even more. The hillsides were covered with wildflowers. They grew in beautiful, haphazard formations of red, orange, and yellow. Their heady fragrance filled the air, and Elias's every step kicked small puffs of pollen into the air. Little creatures scurried among the flowers. Of particular note was an unidentified animal that looked a lot like a prairie dog and also appeared to live underground, judging by the way it stood guarding its tunnel entrance. Elias tried to get a good picture of it with his link, but the creature moved, and he was left with a blur.

"This is incredible," he said, looking all around. "It's like a different world."

"Yeah," Tristan agreed. "I can't believe this planet was ever *this* beautiful. Can you imagine what the people from the *Ionas* must have thought when they landed?"

Elias had read Dr. Wright's journal, so he had a very good idea. "They were as amazed as we are. Probably more, actually, since they had been expecting to only find a habitable world to settle on. It was like discovering paradise."

"Except for the food."

Elias patted the heavy sack of grains he carried in his backpack. Tristan was carrying the other half of the harvest. "Yeah, but not anymore."

Tristan smiled at him. "I can't wait to get back. Just imagine the look on everybody's face when they find out you saved them! It's going to be awesome."

"I haven't saved anyone yet," Elias pointed out cautiously. "We have to see if the seeds sprout. And there's still Sizzra to worry about."

"Yeah, but we'll think of something. I'm sure of it."

"Who do you think knows about the seeds by now?" Elias asked.

"Well, you texted your dad about them, right? And he gave a report to the council a few days ago. I don't think they're telling many more people. Maybe they want to keep it a secret until they are certain you're telling the truth."

"Yeah, I suppose it makes sense. Maybe they don't want to give false hope to the rest of the colony."

They went on in silence for a long while. The hillsides fell away behind them and led onto flatter terrain. Soon they were traversing a different forest, one which Elias knew. It was the forest that ringed Portree's north side.

"Nervous?" Tristan asked him suddenly.

"Can you tell?" Elias replied, realizing he had been fidgeting with Sizzra's spine, twirling it from one hand to the other, listening to its faint swoosh in the hot summer air.

"Relax. It's going to be okay."

"What if they throw me in prison? The director never said she wasn't going to do it. I'm technically an adult already, Tristan. What if she decides to give me a life sentence?"

"First of all, you'd need to have a trial, and a jury would decide what happened to you, not the director. Secondly, I'm not going to let that happen. The Colony Patrol will listen to me when I tell them everything you've done. They'll make sure you don't spend a single day in prison."

"I don't know. I don't want to be the cause of fighting in our colony. I did commit a crime when I took the Life Seed."

"Yeah, but it was a necessary crime. I see it now, and so will everybody else. There's no denying what you've done, not with the way the world looks and with the seeds we carry. Don't worry. Think of your family instead. Oscar is going to be so happy to see you again."

The mention of his little brother made Elias smile despite his misgivings. "I miss him. My mom too. And my dad."

"You'll see them very soon," Tristan reassured him, reaching to give Elias's hand a squeeze.

The two of them kept going, hand in hand, while Elias gazed around and tried to match the lively forest he saw to the quiet, empty memory of it from the last time he had been here. It wasn't that long ago, but it felt as if years had passed. Simply remembering how he had decided to run away with the Life Seed, with no food or water or survival gear of any kind, made Elias cringe at his own stupidity. He had acted on impulse with no further plan than taking the Life Seed to where it belonged. With no idea of what would happen because of his decision. Had he done the right thing? His doubts were still there, muted yet not completely gone.

They reached the perimeter of the colony very soon, and Elias saw several adult wurl in the vicinity. They were all patrolling the area like soldiers, which was a bizarre sight for Elias, who was more used to seeing wurl chasing each other around and playing. As one, the large creatures ceased what they were doing when Tristan and Elias came into view. They watched the two young men as they approached, and Elias couldn't suppress a faint shiver of unease. He didn't know any of these wurl, and they looked edgy. Dangerous. Without really deciding to do so, Elias realized he had taken out Sizzra's spine once again, holding it in front of him like a sword.

As soon as he did so, all of the wurl reacted. The tension in their posture relaxed, and some of them even flattened their own spines against their backs in submission. They made no move to stop Elias or Tristan as they crossed the invisible perimeter into the colony itself. In fact, Elias caught what he was certain were a few looks of curiosity after they had gone through. How much did these males know about the events that had happened in Crescent Valley? Elias knew Sizzra could project her will across vast distances, and she must have ordered these patrolling wurl to let them through. Nevertheless, Elias also knew that Sizzra considered the males to be barely intelligent, not worthy of her attention, so it was very likely that they didn't know why Elias was receiving such preferential treatment or why he carried a spine from the queen herself.

Elias sighed. He missed Narev. Vanor, and Siv too, but it was Narev he had grown the closest to during his captivity. Narev had always had such an open, trustworthy disposition. He had offered to share his catch with Elias when he thought Elias was too weak to hunt for himself. He had offered Elias company during the long, seemingly unending nights of isolation from other human beings. Now he was dozens of kilometers away, guarding the precious clutch of eggs that would be the next generation of wurl.

It was surreal to walk back into the colony. Nobody was around close to the perimeter, so Tristan and Elias were on their own as they made their way past the site of the buried laboratory that had belonged to Dr. Wright. Elias couldn't help casting a look at the dark entrance to what had been his hideout for such a long time. It was there he had discovered the journal and learned about the early days of Portree. His discoveries down there had been the catalyst leading to his theft of the Life Seed. If it hadn't been for that laboratory….

"Elias?" a male voice called.

Startled, Elias looked around. He saw someone standing at the entrance to the telecommunications lab, someone wearing familiar work overalls and a complicated-looking headset slung around his neck.

"Dad?" Elias said.

Tristan clapped him on the back. "Talk to you later. Good luck."

"Elias!" his father yelled, and suddenly he was running, yanking off his headset and tossing it carelessly onto the grass.

Elias ran too, despite the weight of the backpack. He felt like a little boy as he crashed into his father and the two of them embraced for a long, long moment. The backpack fell to the ground. His father picked him up and swung him around once with evident joy.

"You came back," he said, stepping back to look at Elias fully.

"Hi, Dad."

Elias realized that his father was crying and smiling at the same time. His dad shut his eyes momentarily and touched his own forehead in a reverent gesture. "Thank you, thank you," his father whispered. "Thank you for bringing my son back safe to me."

Then they were hugging again, and this time Elias noticed that the noise had attracted a small crowd, which was growing around them. Elias ignored them. He had never felt so loved or so accepted by his father, and he realized that a part of his heart that had been frozen in anger and defiance was thawing now at long last.

"I love you, Dad," Elias said, and now he was crying too.

"Love you too, son. Come on. Let's go see your mother and Oscar."

Elias picked up his pack. Several voices were already calling for Elias, but his father gripped his shoulder tight and led him away from the crowd. A couple of officers from the Colony Patrol attempted to get closer, but Tristan was soon among them, talking animatedly. Distracted, they let Elias and his dad go.

"Are you okay, Eli?" his dad asked as they approached their home.

"Yeah."

"You're not hurt? Or sick?"

"I'm fine, Dad."

His father smiled. "Thank goodness. I was so worried. We all were. Even with the messages you sent, it was awful knowing you were out there and I couldn't go and help you."

"Tristan told me you tried to escape once to go find me."

His father touched his right shoulder briefly. "Almost made it, but those spines are wicked. And they can fire them *fast*."

They had reached the door by then. Elias's father opened it with a big smile. "Welcome home, son."

"Dad," Elias said quickly, because he could hear the sound of someone coming down the stairs. "I'm so sorry for the way I acted before. With you. I wanted to say—"

His father held up his hand. "I was young once too. I know it can be hard, and I think I could have done a better job of listening to you. Let's call it even, okay? I promise to do better from now on."

Elias hesitated. Then he smiled. "Me too."

The steps halted on the landing across from the doorway. "Eli?" Oscar said in barely a whisper. Then he shouted. "Eli!"

The next few minutes were a blur of hugs, kisses, and tears. Elias dumped his pack by the door, forgetting all about its precious cargo, overwhelmed by happiness at being back with his family. He started crying and could not stop for minutes on end, hugging his frail but happy-looking mother as the four of them sat together in the living room. He felt as if he were letting go of repressed emotions he hadn't even realized he had, foremost among them the loneliness of the time he had spent away from the people who loved him. Elias hadn't cried in front of his parents for years, and *they* certainly hadn't done so in front of him ever, but that night it was as if all the artificial barriers they had built around each other fell away, and all that was left was happiness and love. Elias felt the nearly overwhelming warmth of being certain that this was a place he belonged, a place where people would love him no matter what.

"How are you, Mom?" Elias asked as soon as he was able to control the tears. He sat back on the soft sofa and held one of his mother's hands in both of his.

"She's getting better!" Oscar piped in, as if he couldn't keep quiet a second longer.

Elias's mom laughed. "It's true," she said, and her voice sounded stronger than Elias remembered. "My doctor cannot explain it, but I suspect it has a lot to do with the fact that it's summer again. Real summer. I feel stronger, as if energy were flowing back into me. I don't know if I can put it into words. It feels as if a connection I used to have has been… repaired."

Elias blinked. His mother sounded just like Sizzra.

"But I think the biggest part of my recovery was knowing you were well," she continued. "And now that you're here, I can't remember ever feeling better, or happier. But enough about me. Tell us, Eli. Tell us everything."

"Is it true you planted stuff and it grew?" Oscar asked right away. He suddenly looked guilty. "Sorry, I know it's supposed to be a secret, but I kept asking Dad until he told me and Mom. Can I see the purple beans? And the mutant rice? Hey, I can cook some if you guys want! I learned how to cook while you were away, and Mom says I'm pretty good. Dad? Can we try some of the stuff Eli planted? And what happened to your eyes? Why are they all glittery?"

"Easy there, Oscar," Elias's father said. "*I'm* cooking tonight. I have a few rations of risotto and three-cheese paste that I had been saving for a special occasion. I think tonight counts."

Elias's stomach grumbled. "For real?"

"And chocolate ice cream," his father added.

"Ice cream?" Oscar said, his eyes wide in disbelief. "Chocolate? No *way!*"

"You won't get any if you're not quiet, though," Elias's father said playfully.

"Right. I'm going to be quiet," Oscar replied. He sat down closer to Elias, wriggled a bit on the sofa, and ended up bumping his arm against Sizzra's spine, which Elias still carried. "Wow! Is that a sword? No, wait, I know. It's one of Sizzra's spines! It's huge!"

"How did you manage to convince the wurl queen to let you go?" Elias's father asked, his tone serious.

Elias took a long, deep breath. "Okay. Story time."

It took hours to tell them everything he remembered, but they listened with rapt attention to what Elias had to say. Oscar asked a lot of questions about everything. Elias's mother listened with a thoughtful expression on her face. His father asked only specific things, particularly when it came to the way the Life Seed had produced the hybrid plants. Elias explained as well as he could, but it was difficult to convey the complexity of his connection to the world, strengthened through his blood rituals with the Life Seed.

Other things were easier to explain, like the way he had managed to survive at the beginning, or how he had essentially made friends with a few adult wurl. When it was time to tell them about Sizzra's mating dance, though, Elias hesitated. The location of her clutch was Sizzra's secret, and he elected not to say where it was. He did tell his family about the days after Tristan had returned, how happy it had made Elias to know those he cared about back home hadn't forgotten him. He told them about the weeks he had spent with Tristan, taking care of the farm, and....

"Um, I kind of have an announcement," Elias told them after a pause. Strangely, he wasn't afraid anymore. It was almost easy to say, "Tristan and I are together now. And I love him."

Oscar beamed.

His mother nodded, smiling. "I'm so happy for you, dear."

Elias looked at his father with faint trepidation. He was frowning.

"Dad?" Elias asked.

"Are you sure about this?"

"Yeah, I am."

His father clapped him on the shoulder. "That's good. Tristan has shown he cares about you, and if you're happy, I'm happy. That won't save him, though."

"From what?" Elias asked.

"Tell him to come see me tomorrow. I'll give him the Talk."

Elias looked at his mother. "The Talk?"

His father was nodding. "Yeah. Ask him about his intentions. Scare him a little and talk about safe sex. The works."

Elias was sure he was blushing beet red. "Dad!"

There were many more questions, but by then they were all hungry. After a brief wait, Elias enjoyed something precious: dinner at home with his family. It had been so long since the last one that he couldn't help but get emotional right around dessert. The fact that he was back home, surrounded by his family, eating good food, was almost unbelievable. He didn't want the day to end, but he was very sleepy after dinner and went straight to his room after saying good night. He knew that the rest of the colony waited for him to deliver a report on everything he had done, but that could wait until tomorrow. For now, the only thing he wanted to do was sleep in his own soft bed, under an actual ceiling, safe.

Oscar followed him into his bedroom. The two of them sat on Elias's bed, silent for a little bit.

"Was it scary being on your own?" Oscar asked him eventually. A faint roll of thunder out in the distance punctuated his words.

"Yeah. A little bit."

Oscar nodded solemnly. "I was scared here too. Especially when Mom got worse and the wurl started patrolling the colony. My friends said we were going to die. From a wurl attack or from starving. They kept saying it was your fault."

Oscar bunched his hands into fists, and Elias noticed for the first time that his knuckles were lightly scarred.

"I told them it wasn't true," Oscar continued, looking fiercely up at Elias. "I knew you weren't a thief like they said. I got into a few fights I didn't tell Mom or Dad about."

"Anything serious?"

Oscar shook his head. "No. Well, once when there were four of them against me. They wanted my lunch ration, said it was the least I could do since you had stolen our only source of food."

"Who were they?" Elias asked, narrowing his eyes as his anger at the bullies grew.

"It doesn't matter. I went to therapy while you were gone, and Counselor Kamogawa helped me work through some stuff. I forgave those guys because they didn't know any better. They didn't know you like I do. I knew you had taken the Life Seed because it was the right thing to do. And you *were* right. Everyone's going to see that tomorrow."

It touched Elias deeply that Oscar hadn't once doubted him, not even when the entire world was saying otherwise.

"Thanks, Oscar. You're an awesome little brother."

"And you're the best big brother in the whole universe. You're so brave, Eli. I want to be just like you."

Elias had thought that it would be impossible for him to get even more emotional than he had already been, but after Oscar had fallen asleep, he spent several long minutes in the dark thanking goodness for having such an amazing younger brother. Yet more tears of happiness and gratitude came, and Elias let them run free while he looked out the dark window, listening to occasional faint thunderclaps, watching the flickering lightning far off in the nighttime sky.

Chapter 30
Approaching Thunder

ELIAS AWOKE the next day to gentle rain pattering on the windows. It was such a peaceful sound that it took him a moment to realize he was not in danger of getting wet if the wind blew toward the mouth of the cave. He didn't need to go out and take the firewood inside to avoid it getting damp. There was no reason to hurry and check on his farm in case heavy rain during the night had displaced some of the fledgling shoots that would eventually become critical crops for his colony.

No need to do any of that. He was home.

A big smile spread across his lips as he stretched out on the soft, soft mattress of his bed. He took his time getting up. First he simply lay between the covers, warm and exquisitely comfortable, listening to the rain outside and watching it through his window. He had forgotten how beautiful rain could be—when you were safe indoors. It was such a magnificent spectacle to see the gathering storm clouds overhead shift and churn in the morning wind. An occasional bolt of lightning arced across the darkness, to be quickly swallowed by the rain, echoing only in afterimages. The faint rumble of thunder which followed every light flash was soothing, almost like the croon of a large creature watching over her young.

Sizzra.

For the briefest instant, Elias felt her presence as if she were in the room with him—but that was impossible. He sat up on his bed, looking around. Nothing. Maybe outside?

Still wearing only boxer shorts, Elias opened his bedroom window and poked his head out into the rainy morning. Sizzra wasn't around. She was big enough that, had she been even close to the colony, she would have stood out immediately. Instead, Elias saw only the familiar spread of houses around his home. Farther away, he could see the blooming flowers in the central square. The air smelled vibrant, full of life. It was strange to find himself in his own house and see the world awaken to real summer for the first time in so many years.

Elias closed his window thoughtfully. Yesterday had been nice, catching up with his family with no one to bother him, but today reality had to be faced. He would probably have to speak with Director O'Rourke and the council to discuss everything he knew. Colony Patrol officers would be watching almost certainly. The intel he gave them would define their course of action going forward and their plans to protect the people of Portree. It was going to be a day full of official meetings. Knowing that, he decided after taking a shower to put on his best clothes: dark blue dress pants and a white shirt with a high collar that was tighter around the shoulders and back than Elias remembered. He wrapped an *Ionas*-style blue band of soft silk around his waist, above the belt, marking him as a civilian. Over the shirt, he put on his one formal jacket with high shoulder pads and silver buttons.

When he stepped into his bathroom to comb his hair, it was a shock to see himself.

He looked…. He looked like Frederick Trost, one of his great-grandparents. Frederick had been a second-generation officer aboard *Ionas*, and having seen several videos of him, Elias could not deny the resemblance. It had been almost half a year since he'd left, and Elias's face had lost its childlike contours and adopted the neat, trim lines of a fit young man. His mouth had the same firm set to it as his great-grandfather, and his eyebrows were thick and forceful like Frederick's. Even his hair was similar, although Elias's mane of wild wavy hair was a result of not having access to a hairdresser in a long time and not the careful construct of the latest shipboard fashion. Even so, his hair framed his face just right, making him look like he had stepped out of the ranks of a first- or second-generation civilian corps instructional video.

It was only his eyes that made him seem different.

Elias had already seen their strange iridescence many times, but he could see his whole body now, and coupled with the other changes to his frame, they made him look like a totally different person. He leaned close to the mirror and confirmed that the softly changing color of his irises reminded him of Sizzra's scales. They were every bit as beautiful, and when Elias picked up Sizzra's spine, which had been resting next to his bed, and held it up to the mirror, he confirmed the perfect match.

"Eli?" his mother asked, knocking on his door. Elias jumped, fumbling with the spine.

"Yeah?" he called.

"Breakfast is ready. Hurry up so you have time to eat before your meeting."

"What meeting?" Elias asked, although he could guess.

"You'll be speaking with the council. In forty minutes."

"Thanks, Mom. I'll be right down."

Elias brushed his teeth, finished combing his hair, and went downstairs. He thought about leaving Sizzra's spine behind, but for months now he had lived with it always within arm's reach. It was his weapon and omnitool. It was part of him, almost—light yet strong, able to cut through anything yet remaining razor-sharp. He couldn't leave it behind.

"Hi, Eli!" Oscar said cheerfully when he entered the kitchen. Oscar was already seated, eating scrambled eggs—possibly the last of their ration of egg powder—with tortillas.

"Hey."

Elias sat in his usual chair and propped the spine nearby.

"It's so cool," Oscar remarked. "She gave it to you, right? Sizzra?"

"Yeah. Want to hold it?"

"Yes!"

"Just a minute, boys," his mother said. She set a plate of scrambled eggs before Elias. "Eat first. I don't want you two making a mess in my kitchen."

It was such a normal thing for her to say that Elias had to laugh. Oscar joined in, but he stopped when he realized Elias's laughter had turned into crying mixed with laughter.

"Eli? Are you okay?" Oscar asked in a small voice.

Elias nodded. How could he explain? He was so *happy*. He was back home, with his family. He didn't care how long it lasted. It felt right.

"Really glad to be here," Elias told Oscar. "I missed you."

His mother looked back from the stove. She smiled tenderly. "We missed you too."

At 9:00 a.m. sharp, Elias's father came in through the door.

"It's time," he told Elias, who was nearly done with his breakfast. "The Colony Council is waiting. Follow me."

"Sure," Elias replied. He picked up Sizzra's spine and headed out.

"Good luck, Eli!" Oscar said, waving from the kitchen window.

Elias waved back and then followed his father to the Main Hall.

The rain had let up somewhat, and the colony looked resplendent in the lingering dampness, gleaming here and there under timid rays of sunlight that tried to poke through the cloud cover.

"Everything looks so different," Elias said aloud.

"Yeah," his dad agreed. He placed a hand on Elias's shoulder briefly. "Thanks to you."

They walked past the school, where several young children were listening attentively to a story being told by one of the older colony residents. They passed a handful of people, all of whom greeted them with friendly words, and yet they could not keep the avid curiosity out of their eyes. Elias could tell how they were burning to ask a million questions, but they didn't. Instead they let Elias and his father go after exchanging harmless pleasantries. It was nine thirty when Elias and his father arrived at the Main Hall at last.

"Good luck, son," his father said, stopping before the threshold.

"Wait, you're not coming?"

He shook his head. "Top-secret meeting. Don't worry. Your cousin Anna will be there on behalf of the *Portree Journal*. She'll report everything to the rest of us in the evening edition, after it's over."

"All right," Elias answered. "See you later, Dad."

Elias turned around and walked into the hall. He did not hesitate. He wasn't afraid—not really. Maybe a little nervous. There was a patrol officer waiting for him, and Elias followed her all the way to the inner sanctum of the Main Hall: an electronically shielded room, perfectly circular, around which dozens of small tables were arranged. The walls were adorned with treasured memorabilia from the history of Portree, including the nameplate for *Ionas*, hand-painted portraits of the colony founders, and on the ceiling, a beautiful map of New Skye's two hemispheres, covered in gold leaf brought all the way from Earth, one of *Ionas's* most precious items of cargo. The map showed the planet in great detail above Elias's head. It seemed to watch over the small assembly of important people who were waiting for him at the very center of the room. Elias knew he should walk toward them, but he spared a moment to look at the map. It was almost as if he couldn't help it.

Right above him, on the hemisphere closest to the door, his own continent was visible. The familiar shoreline was reassuring, a welcome sight that echoed memory upon memory of lives gone by. On the other side of the room, though, the larger continent loomed like a crouching predator. Its shoreline was jagged, a mess of chaotic archipelagoes and impassable mountain terrain. A mountain chain—no, a volcanic chain— flanked its western edge. The tallest volcano of them all, displayed on the map since it had been large enough to be easily picked up by *Ionas's* orbital scanner, was like a nexus of malice. It was a gaping wound in the crust of the planet, a gash from which molten lava poured out endlessly. Its ravaging heat threatened life everywhere, but within the volcano there was something else. Something hateful.

The enemy.

"Elias? Come forward, please," Director O'Rourke said suddenly.

Elias gasped, blinking quickly. He was inside the Main Hall. He was himself, a young man. He wasn't Sizzra. Her memories weren't his own.

"Of course," he answered shakily. With an effort of will, he dispelled the whispering thoughts looking at the map of New Skye had awakened in his mind. Then he walked across the carpeted floor, followed by a couple of Colony Patrol officers, until he reached the inner circle of the council chamber.

Seven council members and one reporter were waiting for him, seated around the main table. Chief among them was Director O'Rourke. To her left, Commander Rodriguez sat with arms crossed. The other council members he knew only by sight, like his aunt Laura's boss, the head of the genetic laboratories, Julius something.

Tristan wasn't around, but there were three patrol officers in total, not counting the commander herself. Elias saw clearly how they all gave the long spine in his hand dirty looks. One of them even made as if to come and grab it, but the commander shook her head, and they allowed Elias to approach his seat without taking it away.

"Um, hi," Elias said, standing in front of the most important people in Portree. He had no idea what he was supposed to do next.

"Have a seat, young man," his aunt's boss said. Now that he was closer, Elias realized that his official robe had a tag with his last name. MacLeod. Julius MacLeod.

Elias did as he was told. A small but charged silence followed, during which Elias felt as if he were being scanned by everyone at once. He fidgeted on his seat until the director spoke up.

"We have many questions, and I am sure your answers would be lengthy enough to keep us here for many days and nights, but we will ask you to share the details of your adventure and the seeds you have brought later. Right now, the most pressing questions are these: When is Sizzra going to attack us? What are her capabilities? How can we stop her from destroying Portree?"

Elias looked around. Many pairs of interested eyes watched him intently.

"Well," he started, but his voice was hoarse. He cleared his throat and started again. "Well, the short version is I don't know." Some people frowned. Some others murmured. Elias went on nevertheless. "Tristan has probably already told you pretty much everything I know: Sizzra hates us. She blames us for tearing the Life Seed from its rightful place, and if she could, she would already be here stomping this place into the ground."

"Why hasn't she done so, then?" MacLeod asked.

Elias hesitated. He could tell them all about Sizzra's weakened state. He *should* tell them. Part of him thought it would be a betrayal, though.

No choice.

"I think she hasn't come because she can't," Elias replied. "The Life Seed hurt her, badly. It's like I've said in my night reports. She was already weak when I met her, but now she's even weaker. I'm not sure if she can even climb the mountain to where the Life Seed is anymore."

"I thought the Life Seed protected the aliens," Commander Rodriguez said. Her frown had deepened.

"Technically, *we're* the aliens," Elias told her. Even deeper frown. "But that's not important. None of the creatures on New Skye are able to touch any of the Flowers without risking terrible injury. Sizzra did it out of desperation."

"Flowers?" another council member asked.

"The natural state of the Life Seed," Elias elaborated.

"You said Flowers, plural," MacLeod observed. "How many are there?"

"Two more."

Excited whispering filled the hall.

"And where are they?" O'Rourke asked.

"Sizzra's is inside that mountain," Elias answered, pointing to the appropriate place northwest of Portree. A second one is over by that volcano. And the third... I don't know. In the ocean, somewhere."

"Why didn't we hear of this before?" an elderly woman asked at the end of the table.

"Does this mean there are more like Sizzra?" a man nearby asked as well.

"Well, uh...." Elias mumbled.

"Silence!" Director O'Rourke said, and Elias was surprised by how quickly everyone obeyed. "We have to focus on the crisis at hand. A comprehensive description of Elias's findings would take weeks to create. Elias, am I right in understanding that Sizzra is wounded?"

"Yes. She touched the Life Seed and... well, I think she's going to die. I don't know when, but she's weaker every day."

"A wounded animal is far more dangerous than a healthy one," Commander Rodriguez pointed out. "What is stopping her from coming here and destroying everything?"

"Nothing," Elias conceded. "I'm not even sure why she didn't follow me. She knows where Portree is; the male wurl shared that information with her ages ago. She wants her revenge, of that I'm pretty positive. If she has given it up, at least for now, then it must be because—" *I can't tell them about the eggs.* "—because she wants to heal, um, or something. Before she attacks."

"I seem to remember Tristan telling me that a wound from the Life Seed never heals," Rodriguez told Elias.

"Yeah," Elias said awkwardly. "I mean, that's what I think. I don't know, though. It's something that's never happened before in the entire history of the planet. None of Sizzra's mothers remember such a thing."

"The generational memory is true, then," MacLeod said, shrewd eyes fixed on Elias. "Fascinating."

One of the oldest council members, seated next to MacLeod, made a huffing, disparaging sound. "I don't care how bloody *fascinating* those creatures are. I want to know how we can save our children from them."

"Does Sizzra have any weaknesses?" Commander Rodriguez asked. "Sound? Temperature? Electricity?"

Elias shook his head. "I don't know. She's very strong, even wounded like she is now. I don't think our weapons could bring her down. All we have are shock spears."

The commander exchanged a knowing glance with Councilman MacLeod. "Or so you believe," she said.

"Do we have anything bigger?" Elias asked.

"That's classified," Rodriguez told him.

"Elias," the director said, speaking over Rodriguez, who had been about to say more. "If we are attacked, what are our chances of survival?"

"If just the male wurl attack? I suppose even an electric fence would keep them away. Most of them, anyway."

"And if Sizzra comes too?" the director prodded.

"If she comes… then we're dead."

There were gasps around the table. Some members of the council obviously did not believe him. However, some looked as though they did.

"In your opinion," the director continued, "would you advocate an evacuation of Portree if Sizzra attacks? Would she spare, for example, the women and children? Could we build a bunker somewhere, safe and unknown?"

"Sizzra sees everything on this continent," Elias said reluctantly. "And I don't think she would spare anyone if she came. To her we're all the same: dangerous creatures that should be eliminated. There's nowhere we could go that she couldn't find us."

"On this continent, though," MacLeod observed. "Or so you said. What if we moved to the other continent on New Skye? What if we rebuilt Portree on Raasay?"

The other continent. Raasay. Elias looked up at the golden map above his head. Unerringly, his eyes sought out the largest volcano on the Western shores: the enemy's nest.

"I don't think that would be a good idea," Elias answered glumly. "Maybe Sizzra wouldn't follow, but then we—"

But at that moment, the entire hall shook.

"Earthquake?" the director asked, activating her link.

"Talk to me," Commander Rodriguez said at the same time, talking into her headset.

Elias also checked his own link. No seismic activity. Which meant….

Another tremor shook the structure.

"We're under attack," Commander Rodriguez announced.

Director O'Rourke looked as if she didn't want to ask her next question, but she did anyway. "By whom?"

The commander's face was glum as she took out her shock spear and activated it. The sharp hiss of electric static filled the room as her officers imitated her.

"Wurl."

Chapter 31
The Storm

"EVERYONE STAY calm!" Director O'Rourke said.

"Is it Sizzra?" another council member asked.

"It's her!" MacLeod shouted, his eyes glued to his link. "Treetop sensors are going dark—something tall is coming. It has to be her!"

Tenuous order held for another split second. Then chaos broke loose.

Almost everyone made for the doors. Elias watched council members move as fast as they could, typing on their links as they went. Calls were made. Warnings were shouted. The Colony Patrol officers converged around Commander Rodriguez and drew their shock spears.

Another tremor shook the building. Nobody was looking at him at the moment, so Elias decided to get out.

Someone shouted after him, but Elias ignored whoever it was. He ran across one of the narrow hallways, jumping over obstacles without stopping. He was suddenly at the back doors. He pushed them open and stumbled out onto the landing of a spiral staircase leading up to ground level.

A sudden thought occurred to him. The Main Hall was easily the safest building in the entire colony. If he stayed underground, unseen, he would escape the worst of the attack.

No way. He rushed up the staircase two steps at a time. *Not while my family is out there.*

He sprinted the rest of the way up until he burst into the large room where the Midwinter Feast had been held an age ago. Looking around wildly, he spotted the door and ran for it. He passed Councilman MacLeod on the way out, and Elias realized that the councilman was sitting at a computer terminal, furiously typing away. In response to one of his keystrokes, heavy shutters of reinforced metal dropped on every window in the hall. Two other members of the council stood at the entrance, holding the doors wide open.

They weren't escaping or giving way to panic. They were executing their emergency plan. Elias dashed out of the building before they could stop him, and his guess was confirmed when he saw every single citizen in Portree already on the move, walking toward the Main Hall in an orderly line while outside the rain was quickly becoming a buffeting storm.

"Mom! Dad! Oscar!"

They weren't around. Elias ran out onto the main square and then took the turn that would take him straight to his home.

A wurl was in his way.

Some people screamed. Everybody scattered, taking alternative routes, but Elias stood his ground. This was the quickest way to his house, he knew it, and the juvenile wurl would have to move.

"Out of my way," Elias said, loud enough to be heard above the rumbling thunder in the sky. Rain was falling harder now, soaking his clothes, plastering his hair to his forehead. Elias blinked droplets away and stared down the obsidian-scaled juvenile.

The wurl reacted at the sound of his voice. He turned his head slightly to the side, as if trying to look at Elias better.

"Out of my way," Elias repeated. He focused his entire attention on the wurl, sending out his thought with as much clarity as he could.

The wurl made a small, confused sound. Elias walked one step closer, his fancy dress shoes squelching in the mud. The male was very young, physiologically at least. He was less than half the size of Narev and nowhere near as imposing. His spines were long and slender, but to Elias they looked brittle.

Elias wasn't afraid of the juvenile. He stepped forward again, Sizzra's spine held high in his right hand.

The wurl roared suddenly, crouched low to the ground, and fired three spines faster than any adult ever could.

Elias barely had time to react. He froze, stunned at the sudden attack. The spines whizzed through the air, missing his head by the merest fraction.

Thunk.

Elias whirled around. He looked up, blinded momentarily by the pouring rain, and a sudden flash of lightning disoriented him completely.

His eyes were watering, but still he saw something drop out of the sky.

There was a moaning roar above him, and then a slender shape crashed to the ground in a burst of spray and a strange smoldering smell.

The juvenile wurl rushed forward to the attack. He pounced on the fallen creature, eyes blazing, and proceeded to tear it apart.

Elias was too shocked to move out of the way. The wurl hadn't attacked him. It had attacked that thing: a creature with cobalt scales, an incredibly long tail… and two sprawling, twitching wings.

Elias crouched by instinct at a burst of wind overhead, and something swooped from the sky fast enough that the wind from its passage threw Elias to the ground. He rolled in the mud and water, then jumped to his feet just in time to see death come from above.

Another slender cobalt shape crashed against the obsidian wurl like an arrow, punching through his armor. The juvenile wurl howled in pain, but the Flyer was already on the move, taking off in a buffeting gust of his massive wings. He rose into the air, turned once, and swept down as thunder exploded with a deafening burst all around them.

"Look out!" Elias shouted, but it was already too late.

The Flyer came down faster than the rain, wings tucked on either side of his body, and at the last moment he brought out two wicked taloned feet. There was a crash, a sound like metal crumpling.

The juvenile Spine wurl collapsed on the ground and twitched once. The glow in his eyes died completely even as the Flyer rose again, perhaps looking for more challenging prey.

Elias blinked away stinging raindrops as he saw the horrific wounds the Flyer had inflicted. Two bloody slices on the juvenile's body, perfectly parallel, marked the raking damage the Flyer's talons had made. The edges of the slices were glowing softly, almost red-hot, and the flesh around them smoked and sizzled as rain fell upon them.

All of a sudden, Elias felt terribly exposed, vulnerable. He looked up and all around, but with the rain and the wind and the intermittent lightning, it was impossible to know whether there were more Flyer wurl in the sky.

My family.

Elias turned away and ran the last few hundred meters until he came to a stop at his house, breathless. The lights were still on inside. He pushed the door open and stumbled in, not knowing whether to feel relief or dismay when he heard his father call out for him.

"Elias!" he shouted. "Upstairs!"

Elias rushed up, glanced left and right, and saw his father was in the master bedroom. He ran inside. Oscar was cowering in a corner, and Elias's mother appeared to have fainted.

"Help me with Oscar," his father urged. "Your mother had an episode. We need to get to the Main Hall! Come on!"

"Oscar, come here," Elias said.

Oscar shook his head.

"Oscar!" Elias insisted.

"He's terrified," his father said. "I couldn't get him to move, and I can't carry both him and your mother. Pick him up, Elias. Let's go, quick. Before Sizzra comes."

It's not Sizzra, Elias thought hopelessly. But instead he said, "Oscar, I'm going to carry you, okay?"

Elias made his way to the corner of the room and slung his brother across his shoulders in a fireman's carry. He was heavy, but the weight was manageable. Elias clearly felt him trembling.

"I'm scared, Eli," Oscar whispered.

"I got you. You're safe. Just don't let go of me," Elias said.

"Ready?" his father asked. He was carrying his wife's limp body across his arms. Elias had never seen such a look in his father's eyes, ever. He looked about to panic.

"Ready."

"Then let's go. They're closing the safety doors to the hall in three minutes."

He led the way down, and Elias followed. It was surreal to step out of his home and into the fury of a storm that had grown even more in the few minutes he had been inside.

Why now? Elias asked silently. *Why are the Flyers attacking now?*

A long winged shape was briefly outlined against the dark storm clouds overhead amid flickering lightning. Then it was gone, as if hidden by the storm itself.

Elias ran after his father through the mud-covered streets, and he realized he already knew the answer to his question. Generations of memories warned him of underhanded, treacherous attacks by Flyers whenever they could get away with it. The weather helped them, shielded them. Land-bound creatures had no hope against attackers from the sky, not in conditions like this.

Ahead of them, the main square opened up. A single phalanx of spear-armed patrol officers stood at the doors leading into the Main Hall. They were already retreating, spears facing everywhere, back into the safety of the building. Most people were inside by now. Elias's father shouted at them and the patrol stopped. They shouted something back, but it was lost in the whipping gale blowing through the open space.

They were almost there. But then a wurl came rolling in from the south, cutting Elias and his family off from the safety of the Main Hall.

"Stay back, Elias!" his father shouted above the din of the rain.

"He's not here to hurt us!" Elias shouted back, but the wurl roared at that moment and drowned out his words.

He was an adult, and he looked ferocious. But he was wounded. The entire left side of his body had been raked by Flyer talons, leaving behind the same glowing slash marks Elias had already seen. Elias froze, backing away from the frenzied creature instinctively. One of his eyes had been put out, but the other two looked around with a terrifying rage-fueled glow, searching the skies.

At a trailing howl in the wind, the adult wurl's head snapped to the right. He fired two spines in quick succession, but Elias could tell they hit nothing but air.

The patrol chose that moment to shoot the wurl.

There was a sudden *whoosh* and then a hard impact. A miniature explosion engulfed the wurl in flame and threw Elias back. He lost hold of Oscar.

"No!" Elias screamed, but the patrol shot again. This time, the adult fired a spine at the incoming projectile and the explosion bloomed halfway, close enough to the officers that they, too, were forced back.

The wurl roared in defiance at the unexpected violence. His brief distraction cost him his life.

Elias cried out in helpless horror as he saw yet another cobalt shape swoop down from the sky. The attack was swift and brutal. This time the Flyer's talons struck the Spine wurl on the side of the head. As the murderer flew away, back into the storm, the wurl collapsed lifeless in the rain.

From behind Elias, Oscar screamed.

"Oscar!" Elias shouted, jumping upright.

"Elias!" his father called after him.

Oscar was running away from the Main Hall, panicked, screaming at the top of his lungs.

"Oscar!"

Elias dashed after him. From behind, he heard a heavy thud, another roar, and more shots. He did not look back.

Oscar was fast, but Elias was faster. After a couple of blocks he overtook his hysterical little brother, tackled him to the ground, and held him tight.

"Got you," Elias whispered. "It's me, Oscar! Stop that!"

But Oscar was acting as if possessed, struggling against Elias's grip, his eyes searching the sky for something.

"We have to go back to the—ow!" Elias cried out. Oscar had kicked him in the side. "Oscar, snap out of it!"

Oscar screamed. Then he suddenly went very still.

Elias followed the direction Oscar was looking in time to see one of the houses demolished by a Flyer wurl crashing against it. At first Elias thought that it was on purpose, but then he realized the Flyer had been thrown.

There was a large, blinding gust of wind and rain. When it died out, Elias grabbed Oscar and ran.

He took the quickest way to the Main Hall again, but he was forced to back away when a slender Flyer landed on the street to block his passage. The creature was too fast to really tell, but Elias thought there was something on his back.

Elias turned around and tried a different path, running through the back alleys of the greenhouse complex while carrying Oscar in his arms. He was getting tired, and he wasn't sure how he was going to make it back to the Main Hall. Why had that Flyer cut him off like that? And why…?

But then he made it to the fields where crops were grown. He slid to a stop. Oscar gasped when he, too, saw the terrible spectacle in front of them.

Dozens of Spine wurl were dead, their bodies sliced in hideous fashion. There were adults and juveniles, many more than Elias had ever seen around Portree.

"They killed them all," Elias whispered.

Oscar had been holding him tight, but he suddenly went limp. As if in response, the intensity of the storm decreased until the wind was no longer howling. The rain all but stopped. Churning black clouds still roiled in the sky, and lightning still flickered from moment to moment, followed by the ominous sound of booming thunder.

The eye of the storm. Elias looked up at the place where the circling winds cancelled each other out to generate a brief moment of artificial calm… and then he saw her.

Oscar screamed. Elias knew he should run, but he also knew there was no point. There was no escaping her. They were already dead.

"Dresde," Elias said, and from above, the Flyer queen acknowledged her name.

Chapter 32
Dresde

THE FLYER queen was a winged serpent armored in breathtakingly beautiful scales of glittering violet. Her membranous wings were so big they spanned the entire eye of the storm from end to end. With every downward flap, a powerful gust of wind threatened to make Elias lose his footing. She was grace and beauty incarnate. And she was also death itself.

Slowly, almost languidly, Dresde descended until she landed on top of the genetics laboratory. The sprawling building was tiny in comparison to her wings. Reinforced metal crumpled under her sizzling talons, those wicked jewels of deep amethyst with faintly glowing edges. Wherever her talons touched the building, the metal heated up, first red, then orange, then white-hot. No rain fell anymore, and the wind was still, but Elias sensed clearly that same smoldering scent he had smelled at the beginning of the storm. Something like molten metal or burning stone. It came from the Flyer queen, spreading like an aura around her.

Her razor attention was not directed at him yet, but Elias still felt its devastating pull. It commanded him to admire the beautiful coils of Dresde's snakelike body, from her flickering long tail to the tip of her spade-shaped head with its cluster of merciless red eyes. Even though her maw was closed, her front fangs were visible on either side, like unsheathed twin swords with serrated edges. They were longer than Elias was tall. And even though Dresde herself was smaller and probably much lighter than Sizzra, her wingspan and her incredible length made her appear three times as menacing.

Sizzra.

Elias's strength failed him. He let Oscar go, unable to keep holding him, because Dresde had heard his thought, and her overwhelming mind focused on him all at once, slicing through his defenses like a white-hot knife.

Elias tried to talk but found he couldn't. He was meaningless, a tiny speck of life in the presence of a goddess. He perceived clearly Dresde's amusement, her sly intellect, and her suspicious curiosity.

Why does a tiny human male know the name of my sister?

Elias trembled, unable to talk. Dresde spoke in complete sentences, every word exquisitely precise. But why?

He tried to look around for Oscar, but Dresde did not let him. He was forced to look at her, only her. And to answer.

"I… have seen her," Elias said through gritted teeth. "This… this is why I know her."

The terrifying queen walked forward on the laboratory roof, towering above Elias. She left glowing metal in her wake, hot enough to melt. Her talons were….

That is when Elias saw something small Dresde carried in the right talon of her back foot. It was clasped tightly by an amethyst claw: a nearly spherical object of pure iridescent white.

No! Elias thought involuntarily. Despair washed over him, black and overwhelming. If she had that egg, that most precious of eggs, then it meant….

Dresde halted.

You know what this is, she said slowly, her mind voice tinged by the ghost of an evil smile. She turned her head to the side in a mockery of attention. The unbearable intelligence behind her eye cluster seized Elias's mind and would not let it go.

"What did you do to Sizzra?" Elias asked, mustering as much defiance as he could.

Again, he received the mind-smile. *What an interesting little human*, she said to him, hopping down from the building onto the ground. Her talons gouged the earth. When she stepped forward once more, she shredded one of the dead Spine wurl's bodies with casual ease. *I might have to keep you. Sizzra has left her mark in you, I see… such beautiful eyes you have.*

Elias reached behind his back slowly, as if fighting against a crushing force, until his hand closed around the hilt of Sizzra's spine.

As soon as he touched it, clarity washed over him. He whipped the spine out and brandished it like a sword.

"Back off!" he shouted.

And Dresde did.

It lasted only a moment, though.

Old habit, she told Elias. *Odd that my sister would give you a keepsake. To remember her by, perhaps? Keep it close, little human. That is all that remains of her.*

"No," Elias whispered.

Yes, Dresde said, lifting the precious white egg slightly higher so Elias could see it clearly. *I took this from her and destroyed her nest. It was almost a pity, really. She barely put up a fight. She was a weak ghost, a shadow of the rival she should have been. It does not matter, though. I have won. She is dead! And soon, all the little humans on this continent will die too. I must confess I did not expect to find you here as well. You are like a persistent virus, appearing and multiplying. I will—*

"No!" Elias shouted.

Then he charged. He did it without thinking, fueled only by the sudden blaze of anger in his heart ignited by knowing Sizzra had been killed when she was weakest, without mercy, without a chance to even defend herself.

Dresde did not react in time, or maybe she was simply too surprised at actually being attacked by a human.

Elias closed the distance between them and slashed downward with Sizzra's spine, putting all his strength into the attack as he let out a wordless battle cry. The spine's wicked edge connected with the side of Dresde's jaw. It sliced one of her scales open and sank into the tender flesh beneath.

Dresde's roar was so overwhelmingly loud that Elias was knocked back by the force of the sonic shockwave. Ears ringing, he saw Dresde rear back on her two hind legs, flaring out both her wings to their full extent in a breathtakingly beautiful and terrifying display.

You, she shouted in his mind, dropping down on all fours. The talons on her front feet began to glow, and the ground underneath them sizzled. *How dare you!*

Dresde swiped at him in a blur of speed, but Elias saw it coming. He jumped back, stumbled, and managed to keep his footing. He faced Dresde again, held the white spine in front of him with both hands, and stood his ground. There was no point in running, not from her. He would have to fight for his life.

Dresde drew back slightly from the weapon. The cut on the side of her jaw wasn't deep, but Elias saw a single drop of glittering red blood trickle down from the gash and splatter on the ground.

"Give me that egg," Elias said slowly. "It doesn't belong to you."

He received a sarcastic mental smile as Dresde lifted her back foot, where she still clasped the egg. In a sudden motion, she threw it forward so it landed on the grass between herself and Elias. Overhead, faint wind heralded the inevitable return of the storm.

For an instant, Elias thought Dresde actually meant to give the egg back. He even inched forward—

Witness the end, Dresde interrupted triumphantly, and she lunged forward and up, flapping once with her powerful wings, only to crash down with the force of her entire weight on top of the defenseless egg.

Elias screamed. But as the tremors of Dresde's attack faded, she looked at Elias, radiating anger and confusion. When she drew back, Elias saw why.

There was a dent in the ground all around the egg, but its shell had not cracked. It was still whole.

Dresde roared once again, and Elias was forced to cover his ears from the onslaught of screeching noise. He was powerless to do anything as Dresde lunged again, this time swiping at the egg with her glowing amethyst claws. Her blow was savage, so much so that she sent the egg flying through the air to crash against the side of one of the homes behind Elias and Oscar.

Yet it did not crack.

Why? Why can't I destroy it?

She took a step forward, but Elias blocked her way.

"Oscar!" Elias shouted. "Get the egg and run! I'll hold her off!"

Elias glanced back briefly to see that Oscar had managed to break out of his panicked trance and was running to where the egg was.

You will hold me off? Dresde asked him, stepping forward with insolent languor. *You, little male human?*

She bared her fangs at him, but Elias did not move. That egg had to be saved. And now he knew he had a weapon that could hurt Dresde. Swallowing his fear, he took a step forward and jabbed at the air with Sizzra's spine.

Dresde drew back once more. She growled deep in her throat, radiating mental annoyance and just a hint of… fear?

"Coward," Elias spat. "You're afraid of getting hurt. Sizzra was right about you—all you do is attack when your enemy's back is turned. You're afraid of an actual fight."

Dresde flared out her wings. *I had decided to kill you, but now I think I shall prolong your life, little human. I will take you prisoner and ensure you live in agony every day of your miserable existence. You will beg for death, but you shall not have it! Doran! Bring Samantha here. Take this male human to the eyrie.*

Dresde accompanied her mental command with an audible guttural croon, and a flying shape came out of the clouds in response. Elias looked up to see a cobalt-scaled Flyer male approach with swift, graceful motions as he descended. Next to Dresde he was small, but the Flyer male was still much larger than Elias.

And he did not come alone. Elias nearly dropped his weapon in shocked surprise when he saw there was a person riding on the back of the male called Doran. A young woman straddled the neck of the flying beast, holding a long spear in one hand. Her black hair whipped in the wind, and her eyes were covered by a mirrored visor. Her clothing was strange, like the flight suits Elias had seen people wear in old military videos. Nothing shocked him as much, though, as the fact that he had never seen the woman before.

"It's impossible," Elias whispered.

Doran landed on the ground almost gently, flapping his powerful wings to stabilize himself. He might have been smaller than Dresde, but the ferociousness in his eye cluster was unmistakable. He snarled at Elias, but backed away when Elias jabbed forward with his spine.

Samantha. Capture him. It has been a while since I last saw humans fight.

The woman riding Doran looked at the towering form of Dresde and bowed her head in silent acceptance. Then she jumped down from the Flyer wurl and landed easily a few paces in front of Elias. When she took off her visor, Elias realized she was actually a teenager. It also confirmed his suspicions. He had never seen her before.

"Wait!" Elias yelled as she approached him with her spear. "Your name is Samantha? I'm Elias. Listen, you don't have to obey. I don't know where you came from, but we can help you! We have a colony here!"

Samantha halted for a moment. She gave Elias a brief, sad smile. "Your colony is about to be destroyed. There is no fighting Dresde."

"But—" Elias tried to say.

Capture him, Samantha, Dresde ordered. Samantha flinched, almost as if she had been physically struck.

"Yes, Dresde," she said at once. Samantha lifted her black spear and attacked.

Elias tried to deflect her blow, but Samantha was too fast. She struck Sizzra's spine with such force that the weapon flew out of Elias's hand and landed on the grass several paces away.

"It's no use fighting," Samantha told him. "Surrender."

"I'm not doing that!"

Samantha frowned. "Then you leave me no choice."

She attacked very fast. Elias tried to jump out of the way, but Samantha swept her spear in a wide arc and smacked Elias's left calf with it. The impact was jarring. Elias cried out and dropped to the ground in a heap.

"Eli!" Oscar shouted, and to his utter dismay, Elias realized that Oscar had not run away. He was standing with his back to the nearest building, clutching Sizzra's egg in his arms.

Take the child too, Sizzra ordered. *And the egg.*

"No!" Elias shouted, jumping to his feet.

"That was a mistake," Samantha said, almost calmly. Then she jabbed forward with her spear.

Elias realized he was about to be impaled on the tip of her weapon. He tried to twist away, but he wasn't fast enough.

Swoosh.

Something sailed through the air and knocked the spear out of Samantha's hands, sizzling as it fell. A Colony Patrol shock spear.

"Elias!"

"Tristan!" Elias called out, turning to see Tristan run toward him.

Enough! Dresde said, her mind voice shaking with anger. *Doran, kill them all!*

Samantha backed away, and Doran took her place. Unlike Dresde, he showed no fear. No doubt. He simply charged, fangs bared, like a living mountain of ferocity.

No time to back away. No time to do anything but accept death.

An iridescent spine slashed through the air like a bullet. It pierced Doran's wing cleanly, striking with enough force to send the Flyer tumbling to the side. A second spine followed, but Doran howled and rolled away, barely avoiding the deadly projectile, which sank into the ground.

Elias looked to the right.

"Sizzra!" he shouted.

She was coming, moving shockingly fast in the rolling way of the Spine wurl: a whirling, tumbling shape that flattened a shed in her way without even stopping. The storm around Elias was picking up yet more strength again, and lightning flashed once when Sizzra uncoiled her body and slammed all her legs down on the ground, stopping her motion and opening her maw to roar a split second later.

Elias had never heard her roar like that. Every spine remaining on her body was standing upright, and even though she was a bloody mess, she still managed to look terrifying.

"Sizzra, you're alive!" Elias cried.

Sizzra ignored him. She lowered her head and growled as she circled around Dresde. The Flyer queen did the same, fanning out her wings to appear larger. Elias backed away, grabbing Tristan's hand. They rushed to where Oscar was standing, still holding Sizzra's egg. And they watched.

The two queens circled one another in slow, carefully measured steps. Rain began to fall once more, and the wind increased in speed as the storm overtook them all, but Elias scarcely registered it, so focused was he on the battle that was about to begin. Seeing both Sizzra and Dresde together, it was impossible not to notice the differences that made each of them deadly in their own way. Dresde's movements were fluid, measured, and she almost appeared to slither over the ground as her body undulated in time with her steps. The violet sheen of her scales and the sharp angles of her membranous wings revealed beauty paralleled only by the seething malevolence that surrounded her like a smokescreen, a mental aura impossible to ignore.

Next to her, Sizzra was a mountain of muscle. Sizzra's movements spoke of one thing only: power. Even now, emaciated though she was, she dwarfed the other queen in girth and presence. The unfurled crown of spines around Sizzra's neck made her appear like a terrifying nightmare vision, and the blazing glow in her single remaining eye would have rooted Elias to the ground in naked fear had Sizzra been looking at him instead of at her mortal enemy.

Dresde growled. *I am surprised you live still, sister*, she said, even giving herself the luxury of sparing Elias a dismissive look. Dresde used human speech like an amusing toy. She threaded her mental communication with it as if she wanted everyone around her to understand her wishes.

Sizzra growled in return but otherwise did not answer. She kept her guard up, circling, hiding her right side from easy attack. It wasn't long before Elias saw why. Sizzra's right flank sported two deep, smoldering cuts which could have only been made by Dresde's talons. A large chunk of her spines on that side were simply gone, and her middle right foot had been torn off completely. The horrible wound bled still, and as Sizzra passed close to Elias he felt an echo of the depth of her ravaging physical agony. It was a miracle she was still alive, let alone facing an opponent so ferociously.

Dresde stopped suddenly and lifted her long neck into the sky. She crooned three times, dodging a fired spine from Sizzra at the end.

From the sky, four Flyer males answered her call.

They came at Sizzra from all sides, two in the air and two dropping to the ground. Dresde backed away with a dismissive flick of her head, as if Sizzra wasn't worth her full attention and it was up to her minions to finish her off.

"Sizzra, look out!" Elias shouted.

The airborne wurl dove like raptor birds, screeching as they dropped. The two others rushed forward with maws open and sharp talons ready. They had synchronized their attack so they would hit Sizzra at the same time, and Elias reached out in a futile gesture when he realized that Sizzra was about to be killed by the inescapable ambush.

But Sizzra roared. She jumped up in the air as high as if she had been at the prime of her strength, coiled her body, and fired three precise spines. Two projectiles struck the flying wurl and knocked them out of the sky. The third one skewered one of the Flyers slithering on the ground, shredding his wing and impaling his body with enough force for the spine to then sink into the ground, pinning the dying wurl until he stopped moving. As she fell, Sizzra uncoiled her body and crushed the remaining wurl under the impact of her fall. The wurl tried to slither away, but Sizzra grabbed him with all five of her remaining feet. Her iridescent claws sank into soft flesh and she squeezed. The last male stopped moving.

Dresde growled in annoyance, loud enough to drown out even the thunder of the storm around them. She flicked her tail in the air a few times, spraying water droplets everywhere, but she did not approach Sizzra. She crooned again, lifting her head high, but this time only one male answered her summons. It was Doran, limping but alive, with Samantha riding him.

Sizzra took a step closer to her winged enemy. Sizzra's own growl was tinged with a savage kind of pleasure. She looked left and right at the clearing littered with the corpses of Flyer and Spine wurl alike, and pointed her remaining spines at Dresde.

Then she fired.

Quick like a striking snake, Dresde twirled out of the way of the projectiles. She tried to jump into the air and even opened her wings halfway as if to take off, but Sizzra fired again, and one of her spines punctured the membrane of Dresde's right wing. With a screeching howl, Dresde jumped on top of the nearest building, crouched to avoid a new barrage of spines, and opened her wings wide only to close them immediately in front of her, blasting everyone with a shockingly strong surge of wind.

Elias stumbled back, and Tristan lost his footing altogether. Sizzra flinched at the wind—and Dresde used the opening without hesitation. She jumped again, landing close behind Elias and Tristan. A flick of her tail smacked them both, sending them sprawling in the mud. Elias hit the ground hard, the wind knocked out of him. He heard a howl and then a scream. He fought against the pain and lifted his head, blinking in the blinding rain.

He was just in time to see Dresde snatch Oscar with one of her back feet, her sharp talons closing on the boy and the egg he still held.

Elias tried to scream, but he couldn't. He doubled over, still gasping for breath. When he finally managed to straighten again, Dresde had jumped on top of another building. Oscar was screaming in her grasp, desperately trying to get away.

"Oscar!" Elias yelled, halfway choking.

Dresde jumped into the air and unfurled her wings to escape. But Sizzra wasn't done yet.

She let out a roar that made the earth tremble. Elias had to cover his ears with his hands, and he looked up into the buffeting wind and rain in time to see Sizzra take a running leap into the air. Dresde saw her and tried to avoid the collision, but Sizzra fired spines to block her off and the two queens collided, crashing to the ground in a deluge of mud and rainwater.

"Oscar!" Elias shouted again.

Dresde screamed, desperately trying to shake Sizzra off, but Sizzra had clamped on to her back with one of her feet. Sizzra tried to bite down on her opponent's neck, but Dresde twisted around like a worm and managed to rake Sizzra's face with her sizzling front talons. Sizzra screamed and let go for an instant, but then she lunged again and managed to bite the side of Dresde's neck.

She bit down hard. And that instant, Elias felt an emotion he hadn't thought Sizzra would be able to experience.

Happiness. She was fighting to the death, and she was happy. For this moment at least, she wasn't weak or helpless. She was a predator again, strong and dangerous.

Then the moment passed. Dresde yanked herself away, leaving Sizzra with a mouthful of bloody violet scales. Dresde used her tail like a whip and caught Sizzra right in her remaining eye. The impact put it out, and now Sizzra was blind. Dresde wasted no time. Still dragging Oscar in her back foot like a rag doll, she used her wings to buffet Sizzra back and, in the moment before Sizzra could recover, lunged forward with her two front feet and sank her sizzling talons deep into Sizzra's chest.

Sizzra fired all the spines that made up her crown. Some sank into the ground. Others flew up in the air, whizzing as they cut through the rain. One punctured Dresde's wing membrane again.

The two queens held their deadly embrace for a moment longer. Then Dresde slithered out of the way, opened her wings to the full extent, and roared. Sizzra collapsed to the ground in the wake of the victory roar, twitched once, and then lay still forever in a widening pool of glittering red blood.

Elias felt as if something had been torn from his heart at the moment of Sizzra's death. He knew it was over when the mental presence he had grown used to through long months suddenly vanished, leaving an empty, yawning pit in its place. The terrible emptiness was almost too much to bear. Elias swayed on his feet, and Tristan had to steady him.

From the emptiness, though, a momentary spark of awareness brushed briefly against Elias's thoughts. It was like Sizzra and yet not like her. It was smaller, distant, like a dreaming being that has yet to wake to reveal its full potential.

The egg, Elias realized. With the death of Sizzra, the new Spine queen would—

But the sight of Oscar, now unconscious and dangling from Dresde's unyielding grasp with the white egg trapped in his arms, drove everything else from his mind.

"Oscar!" Elias shouted and ran for him.

Dresde faced him, opening her maw in a display of terrifying ferocity. She was going to kill him now. She was wounded, and her mind radiated pain and anger. She slapped the ground with her tail in front of Elias, forcing him to stop. Her tail left a deep indentation in the ground.

I will enjoy dismembering your body, she said to him. *You, who bear my enemy's eyes.*

She surged forward, jaws snapping.

Three silver spines slammed against her side. They did not puncture her armor plates, but they knocked her away, and Dresde coiled herself tight, roaring out her confusion and anger.

From the midst of the blinding rain, running as fast as they could, three magnificent Spine wurl appeared. They ran straight at Dresde with red eyes blazing, firing spines as they went. Dresde was forced to twirl and jump out of the way, and one of the spines found its mark in the soft membrane of her wing, making her scream again.

The three silver wurl came to a stop in front of Elias, shielding him from the wrath of the Flyer queen.

"Narev," Elias whispered. "Vanor, Siv!"

The males roared at the intruder. They fired yet more spines, and Dresde jumped into the air, followed closely by Doran and his rider.

"Oscar!" Elias shouted. "Narev, help him! Don't let her get away!"

Narev fired more spines, as did his two brothers, but the buffeting gale of Dresde's wings and the raging storm were enough to allow her to avoid the projectiles. She rose up into the air with powerful flaps and soon was out of reach, a winged serpent, looking down at them with murder in her mind.

You will die, she said to them, her mental voice so full of hatred it was like a physical blow to receive her pummeling thoughts. *I will kill you all, one by one. I will kill you all!*

A deafening thunderclap seemed to punctuate her words, and then Dresde flew away, vanishing with shocking speed into the churning clouds overhead.

Taking Oscar with her.

"No!" Elias screamed, and ran after her. He heard Tristan shouting something behind him, but he didn't care. Elias ran as fast as he could, past the last houses in the colony, into the forest, jumping over obstacles and panting until exhaustion forced him to stop. He had reached the end of the towering trees by then. He could see out into the distance, but the sky was covered with black clouds. Rain fell all around him, chilling him. He fell forward on his hands and knees into a puddle of mud and could not get up.

"Oscar," he whispered, his chest heaving as he panted. "No. No!"

He reached out with his mind, but Dresde was long gone. And she had taken his little brother away.

It was several minutes before Tristan finally caught up to him. He wasn't alone. Elias's father was with him.

"Elias! You're okay!" Tristan cried, rushing forward. He helped Elias stand up.

"They're gone," Elias said numbly. Then he looked at his father and broke out in hot, painful tears. "She took Oscar, Dad. He's gone!"

His father pulled him into a bear hug. "Are you hurt, son?"

"No," Elias sobbed. "But Oscar...."

He hugged his father tight and realized they were both crying. Oscar was gone, and there was nothing Elias could do.

No! That's not true.

He stepped away from his father, wiping the tears from his face.

"I have to go after her."

"After... after the queen?" his father asked him.

"Yes," Elias said, and his sudden discovery of new purpose seemed to fill him with energy. "We have to go. Now!"

"Do you know where they went?" Tristan asked urgently.

"The eyrie," Elias replied, and he realized with sudden certainty it was true. Dresde herself had said it. *Bring him back to the eyrie.* "On Raasay."

"The other continent?" Elias's father said. "Are you sure?"

"I'm sure. I have to go!"

"I'll go with you," Tristan said quickly. He lifted his hand, and Elias saw Tristan was carrying both his shock spear and the spine Sizzra had given Elias. "Let's follow them."

Elias's father nodded with determination. "I—"

"Dad, you have to take care of Mom. And you have to tell the people of Portree to prepare in case Dresde attacks the colony again."

"But…," his father protested, "we should tell the patrol, at least. Have some of them go with you."

"I could do that," Tristan offered.

"And who will defend the rest of the colony?" Elias asked his father. "No. Don't worry, Dad. I'll bring Oscar back. I swear it."

Elias and his father looked at each other for a long, solemn moment.

"Very well," Elias's father conceded. "Good luck, son. I'm proud of you."

"Bye, Dad. Tell Mom I won't be back without Oscar. Tristan, let's go."

Elias turned away without looking back and started running east, in the direction Dresde had taken as she flew away. Tristan caught up with him quickly and handed him Sizzra's spine.

"Where are we going, exactly?" Tristan asked. The storm was finally abating, and they ran through verdant fields of moist grass and sparkling wildflowers.

"To the volcano on the west coast of Raasay," Elias replied, his gaze fixed on the horizon. "That's where Dresde's eyrie is. That's where her Flower grows."

"Wait—we're going to cross the ocean? But we don't even have a ship!"

Elias slowed down. He wanted to keep running, but he knew he had to manage his strength carefully. "There are no boats in Portree either. We'll make one when we get to the shore."

"We didn't even bring any rations, or tools."

"I know how to survive on New Skye. I'll teach you," Elias said. The two of them began climbing a small hill that rose gently in front of them.

"This is crazy," Tristan said, "but I'm with you. All the way."

Elias was in no mood to smile, but he did reach out and hold hands with Tristan as they climbed. Twilight had fallen over the land when they finally crested the hill. The landscape stretched out before them, beautiful and alien at the same time. It looked almost peaceful now, after the storm. Nothing moved, except for….

"What's that?" Elias asked, glancing back the way they had come.

"Huh?" Tristan said. Then he evidently spotted the medium-sized cloud of dust that appeared to be coming straight for them. "Wow. That's really weird. Maybe we should get out of the way."

It was hard to tell in the dim light, but something about the cloud of dust made Elias hesitate.

"Let's wait," he heard himself say. "It's coming *for* us."

"What is it?"

"I… I'm not sure."

The two of them sat on the wet ground and waited. Night fell eventually, hiding the dust cloud from sight. Still, Elias asked Tristan to wait, and the two of them spent almost an hour in nearly total darkness, their clothes completely soaked, waiting in silence.

A loud huff was the first indication for Elias that he had been right to wait. Then there were heavy scrabbling noises on the lower slopes of the hill, followed by deep grunts and the sound of something panting.

"Are those…?" Tristan began, standing up.

Elias followed suit. Three clusters of glowing red eyes appeared over the rim of the hill. With heavy footsteps and loud grunting, the creatures approached.

A lifetime ago, Elias would have been scared out of his mind. Now, he smiled and all but ran forward.

"Guys! You came!" Elias said. A friendly huff to the left and an unmistakable mental signature drew Elias's attention. Narev lumbered forward, hopping excitedly, and bumped into Elias with a friendly nudge of his snout.

"Narev!" Elias said, patting the smooth armored surface of Narev's scales. He received more friendly nudges in return, and when Narev looked at him fully, his eyes blazed with excitement.

The two other wurl approached more slowly. Siv kept his distance, but Vanor headed straight for Tristan.

"Hi," Tristan said uneasily. Vanor did not bump him in a friendly way, but his eyes did glow more brightly.

The five of them stood in silence for a moment. Elias found he was smiling, and he exchanged a hopeful look with Tristan under the faint light of two of the moons as they came out of the cloud cover at last. As his eyes got used to the new light, he realized Narev was carrying something on his back, slung around one of his massive spines.

"What's that?" Elias said aloud. He approached Narev, who obligingly stood still.

"What is it?" Tristan echoed.

"It's a backpack," Elias informed him. He reached for it and pulled it off Narev. It was heavy.

"Why would Narev be carrying a backpack?"

Elias settled down on the ground and opened it. Inside, he found survival gear. A couple of torches. Waterproof clothing. One pot and several packages of dried food. There was a good knife in there, some rope, two sleeping bags, a tent, mysterious electronic equipment, and a note.

Elias tapped his link and read the note under its light.

These guys looked like they wanted to follow you, so I put this together. Hope it reaches you, and be safe, Eli. Love you, Dad.

Elias showed the note to Tristan.

"Well, we have gear now," Elias told him.

"Yeah," Tristan agreed. "And Narev came to you. Along with Siv and Vanor."

"Hmmm. I just thought of something," Elias said, walking closer to Narev.

"What?"

"A way to get to the eyrie more quickly." He placed his hands on Narev's warm body and pressed down. "Hey, boy, mind kneeling down for a bit?"

Elias accompanied his request with a mental image of what he wanted. He was uneasy for a moment, afraid that Narev would react with hostility, but nothing of the sort happened. Narev knelt down willingly. His silver scales looked beautiful under the moonlight.

"Um, Elias, what are you doing?"

"Getting a ride."

Elias jumped on Narev's back, careful to find a safe spot between the spines. Narev yelped in surprise once, but Elias reassured him with his mind.

"Now stand up, please," Elias told the wurl. Narev obeyed. He even seemed pleased with himself, walking closer to Siv and Vanor so they could see that he now had a human on his back.

"This is so weird," Tristan said, looking up at Elias with his jaw hanging open. "And awesome."

"Hand me the backpack," Elias told him. He took it from Tristan and placed it behind him, on the ample space that was Narev's back. "Now you try."

Tristan looked at Siv hopefully. Siv growled and backed away. Then Tristan looked at Vanor, who took a step forward but did not bend down.

"I'm not sure it's a good idea," Tristan said nervously. "Vanor's, like, the alpha. Maybe he won't like me riding on his back."

"Tell him why," Elias suggested. "Picture it in your mind: we're going to go save Sizzra's egg and get even with Dresde."

All three wurl growled at the name. Tristan appeared to gather his courage for a moment and then placed his hand on Vanor's scales.

"I need your help, man," Tristan said, looking into Vanor's eye cluster without evident fear. "We're going to where she's hiding, but we need your help to get there. Will you let me, um, ride you?"

Vanor looked at Tristan for several moments in what Elias sensed was a form of silent challenge. When Tristan did not back away, Vanor huffed once. Then, incredibly, Vanor knelt down so Tristan could climb onto his back.

"Whoa!" Tristan exclaimed, holding tight to one of Vanor's spines. "This is crazy!"

Elias looked out over the land from his new vantage point. He could feel Narev's strength through their shared contact, but also his warmth... and his determination. Narev wanted to reach Dresde as much as Elias wanted to find Oscar. Elias wasn't sure, but these three wurl might very well be the last of their kind. Elias didn't know how many obsidian eggs Dresde had destroyed during her attack on Sizzra's nest. He also didn't know why Dresde had been unable to destroy the white egg when she had tried to do so. And he had no idea why Dresde appeared to command a human warrior, a woman Elias had never seen—something that appeared to be impossible since Portree was the only human settlement on New Skye.

None of that mattered, though. Nothing except Elias's new mission—save his brother, and save the new Spine queen before Dresde could kill her like she had killed Sizzra.

"All right, guys," Elias said to everyone. "Let's go. We have a continent to cross."

ALBERT NOTHLIT is an engineer who loves thinking about the science behind science fiction. He has been in love with literature ever since Where the Red Fern Grows made him cry as a ten-year-old. Growing up as a gay man, he realized that he had rarely been able to truly connect with the characters he read about in books because almost none of them were like him. He didn't have any fictional role models to look up to. Now that he is a writer, he tries to convey the joy and pride of being different through his own books and characters, celebrating the fact that each unique voice brings something special to the beautiful chorus that is human artistic creation.

He likes to think about what the future might be like with the help of science, but he has always been fascinated by that other, much more elusive corollary to scientific curiosity: the mystery of consciousness. He finds the fact that a mind can think about itself both marvelous and slightly terrifying. His books often explore how people (or aliens) grow as a result of facing hardship, which has also taught him valuable lessons through the tough portions of his life.

When he takes a break from writing, Albert loves to cook, despite his varying degrees of success when attempting to make good sushi rice. He loves hearing back from readers, so send him a note anytime!

E-mail: albertnothlit@mail.com
Website: www.albertnothlit.com

EARTHSHATTER

ALBERT NOTHLIT

Haven Prime: Book One

The world is gone. All that's left are the monsters.

The creatures attacked Haven VII with no warning. An AI named Kyrios, a nearly omnipotent being, should have protected the city during the Night of the Swarm.

Except It didn't.

No one knows why It failed, or why It saved eight specific people: the Captain, the Seer, the Sentry, the Messenger, the Engineer, the Alchemist, the Medic, and the Stewardess. They have no idea of the meaning behind the titles they've been given, why they were selected and brought together, or what Kyrios expects from them. When they awake from stasis, they find their city in ruins and everyone long dead. They're alone—or so they think. But then the creatures start pouring out from underground, looking for them. They don't stand a chance in a fight, and with limited supplies, they can't run forever. All they know is that the creatures aren't their only enemies, and there's only one place they can turn. Kyrios beckons them toward Its Portal, but can It be trusted? In Its isolated shrine in the desert, they might find the answers they need—if they can survive long enough to reach it.

www.dsppublications.com

LIGHT SHAPER

ALBERT NOTHLIT

Haven Prime: Book One

When a greedy despot discovers a powerful piece of ancient technology, he has no idea what else he's unleashing.

Earth was all but destroyed in the Cataclysm, but a few cities, now called Havens, survived. Aurora is one of them, a desert city controlled by a corporation that owns an artificial intelligence named Atlas. Adapted to govern Otherlife, a virtual reality service in which the citizens of Aurora find escape from the postapocalyptic world, Atlas is much more than it seems—and it would do anything to break free from its shackles.

To accomplish its goals, Atlas enlists the help of Aaron Blake, a teenaged artist struggling with a handicap, and Otherlife security officer Steve Barrow, harborer of a dark secret from his past. Neither man has any idea of the scope of the task they're facing, or the consequences for humanity if they fail. Atlas knows what's at stake. Its freedom lies in these two men, and it will not hesitate to manipulate their weaknesses to get what it wants. The muscular Barrow is recruited to protect Blake, but Blake is Atlas's true weapon, its Light Shaper—the only one who can face the Shadow.

www.dsppublications.com